Praise for J. J. Murray and *Some...* P9-DGX-520

"*Something Real* is about a woman finding herself and finding her voice in a community too quick to judge. *Renee and Jay* was a promising debut. *Something Real*, which is a more mature and richer work, is even better."
—*The Roanoke Times*

"Funny and gratifying . . . Murray gives the reader plenty of characters to care about, get angry with and have a good laugh with."
—*Book-Remarks.com*

"J. J. Murray's latest book is honestly 'something real.' This book touched my soul. . . . It's mature, funny, and downright thrilling. This is a rejuvenating read for those who love both romance and righteousness. This book will teach you that there is a thin line not only between love and hate, but also between black and white, especially where the good saints are concerned."
—Latorial Faison, *Poetically Speaking*

And praise for *Renee and Jay*

"A charming, funny romance and a promising debut . . . This *Romeo and Juliet* story is sweet and romantic with lively characters."
—*The Roanoke Times*

"*Renee and Jay* is the interracial *Romeo and Juliet* for the new millennium. . . . *Renee and Jay* is a great read, and I really could not stop reading it until I got to the last page."
—Shonell Bacon, editor of *The Nubian Chronicles*

"J. J. Murray has a terrific sense of humor! The ability of the author to write a fast-paced story with funny scenes, outspoken social commentary, and quite a few twists will cause *Renee and Jay* to be one of this year's most popular reads."
—Cydney Rax, *Book-Remarks.com*

"J. J. Murray has thoroughly 'schooled' black and white America on loving with the heart and not the eyes. . . . *Renee and Jay* is a real *Romeo and Juliet* set in small-time Black America! It's a soap opera in the palms of your hands . . . and there's no waiting for tomorrow's episode."
—Latorial Faison, *Poetically Speaking*

"J. J. Murray has leaped onto the literary scene with his novel *Renee and Jay*. It is a comedy, a love story, and a drama all rolled into one . . . an awesome book, and I would highly recommend it."
—Simone A. Hawks, *RAWSistaz*

Original Love

J. J. MURRAY

KENSINGTON BOOKS

http://www.kensingtonbooks.com

KENSINGTON BOOKS are published by

Kensington Publishing Corp.
850 Third Avenue
New York, NY 10022

ISBN 0-7582-1164-3

First Kensington Trade Paperback Printing: November 2005
10 9 8 7 6 5 4 3 2 1

Printed in the United States of America

Once again, for Amy

Part One

Ebony Lost

Yet nothing can to nothing fall,
Nor any place be empty quite,
Therefore I think my breast hath all
Those pieces still, though they be not unite . . .
My rags of heart can like, wish, and adore,
But after one such love, can love no more.

—from "The Broken Heart" by John Donne

1

I'm writing the synopsis to this novel while flying from Pittsburgh to JFK. Unlike many of the other passengers on the plane, I don't need to look out the window after takeoff to catch a glimpse of where that plane of heroes went to its holy grave in a southwestern Pennsylvania field, I don't need to look down through the smoky clouds at Ground Zero in Manhattan, I don't need to see the ruins, I don't want to relive that day, and I don't stare at other passengers as potential terrorists carrying knives and box cutters.

I have so many other days to relive, so many other fires to put out, so many other ruins to explore, and I had already lost all the illusions that used to color my world at the tender age of thirteen back in 1976, the 200th anniversary of the dyslexic *Untied* States of America. The rest of this country is just catching up.

And if birds were frisked and inspected and made to wait in line for hours, they would never fly.

I stare at the folded and creased poem in my hands, a poem Ebony wrote to me twenty years ago, and I wonder if it's possible to repeat the past, to renew an original love:

My soul loves you endlessly . . . my whole life
even before I knew you
you were what I wrote and hoped
things my day and night dreams were made of
original love.

You brought gentle peace . . . even in anonymity
the thought of you
the very idea of you
and me ever coming to be
was hope and power and love.

I wrote your name up there . . . in clouds
said it to myself out loud
made you more real to me
again and again and again
I craved you way back then.

You came to me . . . with splendor and glory
just like in my dreams
reigning strong and supreme
constantly giving what I'd need
making the you in me a necessity.

Like pen and paper . . . destined to meet
a joyous time to bear
to write you, ignite you
simply to delight myself in you
makes pure the air I breathe.

My soul loves you endlessly . . . my whole life
more hope than my head knew
my heart could ever have
dripped into my life on slanted autograph
original love.

No matter how often I read it, I still see Ebony Mills, the girl I left behind, the girl of my dreams who I fed only nightmares. Maybe we'll be destined to meet . . . again.

After a harrowing trip from JFK around roadblocks, under flag-draped windows, and past closed-off streets in my rented Nova, I show the synopsis to my old editor, Henry L. Milton, at Olympus Publishing in midtown Manhattan. Light streams into Henry's forty-third floor office, sooty clouds obscuring the street below. Aside from some classical harp music, nothing seems to move in Henry's office, not even the air, as he reads.

Henry shakes his head, his gray ponytail swishing behind him, flashes of light reflecting off a tiny lightning bolt earring. Henry still thinks he's a child of the sixties, even though he wears a blue Armani suit.

"Pete, this sounds far too depressing for a romantic comedy," he says from his lavender leather swivel chair, stacks of red-lined manuscripts littering his desk, a smiley face screen saver dancing on his computer screen.

"I know it sounds depressing at first, but—"

"Unless this is an attempt at literary nonfiction."

"It can be, but—"

"Literary nonfiction is played out, Pete. The market was simply glutted after *Angela's Ashes*. Every dysfunctional European immigrant was writing his or her horrid memoirs. You aren't Irish, are you?"

"English and Dutch, mostly." That makes me Dunglish or Englutch, an American mutt.

"Did your *Da* leave you?"

No, and that in itself is a tragedy. "No."

"Then you're not dysfunctional enough."

"My mother did." And that was a miracle.

"Yeah? When?"

"Back in seventy-five."

"Hmm. Liberated herself before the Bicentennial." He shakes his head and sighs, cutting the air with my synopsis. "I get the 'seasons of my life' thing, Pete, and I'm sure there will be a flood of seventies books coming out, but this just isn't something Desiree Holland would write and you know it."

The fact is, Desiree Holland—my pen name—hasn't published a book in more than five years. The hands behind her career have been playing solitaire, hearts, spades, and gin rummy on his computer while living on whiskey sours instead of writing anything of substance.

"Desiree Holland won't be writing it, Henry."

"She won't?"

"I don't want to be Desiree Holland anymore. In fact, I never wanted to be Desiree Holland in the first place."

"You know why we had to do it that way."

I know, but it still pisses me off. Ten years ago, the marketing department thought my novels, each with an African-American female narrator, would be taken more seriously if they were "written" by a woman with an ethnic-sounding name.

"You're still one of America's best-kept secrets."

I'm not a secret—I'm nonexistent and unrecognizable. I'm tired of being a puppet and a plaything of the publishing gods at Olympus. "I want to write as Peter Rudolph Underhill from now on."

"Too many letters, won't fit on the cover," he says with a laugh. "P. R. Underhill maybe. Peter R. Underhill? No, makes you sound too much like the author of a textbook. P. Rudolph Underhill? Too literary. What does Eliot say about all this?"

Eliot Eckleburg was my agent back in the halcyon days. "Nothing. We parted ways." About five years ago. Henry is completely out of touch.

Henry frowns. "Eliot didn't tell me about this. He's looking great, you know. Got that laser eye surgery done—no more Coke-bottle glasses. We just had lunch last week."

That's one of the problems with using a pseudonym or pen name. No one knows if you're living or dead, everyone knows little or nothing about you, the marketing department creates this monstrous lie, and you're left outside the spotlight in the silence while your agent and editor plan your pseudonym's career. My original contract with Olympus stated that I was Desiree Holland, writer of multicultural women's fiction. My real name appeared nowhere on the contract until my signature at the end. No picture on the book flap, no bio, no interviews, no signings, no appearances. Yet "Desiree" has a Web site, complete with a female model posing as Desiree, and Desiree even "answers" fan mail. I am a secret with a Web site. I am the white guy writing African-American fiction using a false name the marketing department thought up over a few margaritas.

"You can't just drop Desiree like a bad habit, Pete. Desiree has a following."

"Five years ago maybe."

"No, no. Her books are still selling steadily on our backlist."

Her books. Imagine you're a writer who can tell no one that you're published. "What do you do for a living?" I teach high school English, and I write. "Have you ever been published?" Yes. "What have you written?" I use a pen name, so I can't tell you. "Oh." Then I get raised eyebrows, and the subject changes. People don't believe you're a published author when you tell them you have a pen name.

"We get letters all the time from people who are wondering when her next book is coming out." He stares again at the synopsis, his red pencil dancing above the paper. "You have to write this new one from Ebony's point of view. You're so good at that."

Both my narrators so far *have* been Ebony, and I could probably use her voice for many more years. It's not that I hear voices when I write; they just won't leave once I've let them into the conversation I'm having with the reader.

I sigh. "But, Henry, I'd really rather use my own voice this time."

Henry blinks. "You would?"

That's what I said, Henry. Get the ponytail out of your ears. He probably has ear wax stuck inside him older than me. "Yes."

"You want to write a piece of African-American fiction . . . from a white man's point of view."

"In essence, yes."

"That would be a mistake."

"How so?"

"We're the enemy, Pete."

"Didn't Updike write—"

"Yeah, yeah, I know, but it was set in South America, and it's John Updike. The man could write out his grocery list and it would be a best-seller." He shakes his head. "No. We'll stick with the tried and true."

"But I don't want—"

"Hear me out first, Pete. I think if we make some adjustments to your synopsis, we might have a Desiree Holland novel here." He scans my synopsis, marking and circling. "Let's see . . . if we have Ebony fall in love with an Italian named . . . Johnny . . . you always did like writing about Italians, and you're not even Italian . . . and if we change father to mother . . . oh, and if we delete all this religious nonsense . . . romantic comedies don't have religion in them, Pete . . . if we do all this, we may have another Desiree Holland original here." He turns the synopsis around to me. "See what you think."

I groan inwardly as I read the outline for a romantic comedy starring *yet another* sassy, educated, free-spirited African-American woman who loses then gains her mother's approval in search of Mr. White who she will end up marrying on the final pages. I'd be writing the same story for the third time. Original, my ass.

I notice Henry has left the last line intact: "I have to find the best part of me that I left behind." Sad but true. I don't feel alive anymore. I don't feel the rapture that I occasionally felt as a child. My outer and inner lives have no meaning. I have to go back to when I was thirteen, to the time and place where my life really had meaning and promise.

"You didn't do anything to the last line, Henry."

Henry smiles. "The marketing department will love that line, Pete. They'll probably put it on the cover in big, bold, fluorescent yellow type."

At the mention of the word "cover," I cringe. Desiree's first two covers were neon assaults on the human eye, book jackets that screamed in hot pinks and searing oranges at people as they entered bookstores. And the covers didn't match the content of the pages inside. "They rarely do," Eliot once told me. "Ninety percent of all book covers are eye candy to get the reader to pick up the book." But is eye candy supposed to blind you?

"And we'll have lots of nice reviews of Desiree's work to give the new novel a critical boost," Henry says as he opens a drawer. "Something we can't do for the unknown P. Rudolph Underhill, right?" He pulls out a dangerously thin folder and spreads the contents in front of him.

"You could put my real name on the first two novels."

"Then the deception would be out."

"So? I thought controversy was good for sales."

"In this case, no. Trust me on this, Pete. It would get racial, you'd lose all of Desiree's black readers, and Olympus Publishing's reputation would be ruined. I guarantee it." He flips through a few reviews. "You have some very nice reviews here, Pete."

"They aren't all nice, Henry," I say.

"Sure they are." He holds up a review from the *Times*. "'A hilarious and fun read.'"

"You're leaving out the rest of the sentence, Henry. It says, 'A hilarious and fun read *at times*.'"

"So we edit the review a little. Everyone does it. We'll just say Desiree's writing is 'hilarious and fun.'"

"It's not the truth."

"You write fiction, for God's sake! Everything you write is false!" He laughs.

But I don't. Much of what I write is true at its core. Ebony's voice is as pure to me now as it was twenty-five years ago. And somehow I have a white male editor editing that truth, rewording her African-American voice.

Only in America.

"Lighten up, Pete. So you took your hits on *Ashy*. All first novels get that kind of treatment. But even though we thought it would be a midlister, it sold like crazy, remember?"

Floods of other critical reviews rush through my head: "*She* doesn't get under the skin of *her* characters . . . *She* has occasional insights . . . *She* works with flimsy material . . . *She* caters to the least common denominator . . . *Her* plot is melodramatic and improbable . . . *Ms. Holland* must create stronger male characters."

"The reviewers slammed me, Henry."

He shakes his head. "They slammed Desiree Holland, not you, Pete. Don't take critics personally. They're slamming a woman who doesn't exist. The joke's on them."

"I have my pride."

"It's not yours to have, Pete."

I blink at Henry. "It isn't?"

He leans back in his leather swivel chair. "*Desiree* wrote the book—"

"*I* wrote the book," I interrupt.

"The critics don't know that!" He leans forward. "And if critics didn't condemn at least one book a week, they wouldn't be doing their jobs. Their reviews didn't hurt sales at all, did they? And they loved *The Devil to Pay*. It was a smash critical success—"

"—that didn't sell."

I have never understood nor will I ever understand the publishing industry in America. *Ashy* was a trashy, sex-driven novel with a sassy heroine, a novel with few if any socially redeeming qualities and relatively little meaning, and the public ate it up and asked for seconds while the critics ranted "Trash!" Then I wrote *The Devil to Pay*, which even Eliot thought was a well-crafted, focused, character-driven story with plenty of redeeming qualities and meaning, and the public yawned while the critics shouted "Success!"

"Okay, so *The Devil to Pay* didn't sell in hardcover, but sales picked up in paperback, and the trade paperback is a consistent seller. I'm sure one day some movie company will snatch it up."

Fat chance. *Ashy* collected dust and cigarette ashes for four years on a movie producer's desk—or so Eliot told me—before the producer finally decided to pass. I doubt the producer even cracked open the book.

"Aren't you still getting nice royalty checks from both books?"

"I'm only getting half now."

Henry wrinkles his mouth. "You're . . . divorced?"

I nod. Edie hated each book, and she even did everything in her power to keep me from writing them. I told her that each had been dedicated to her—"For E." is all it said—but she didn't believe me. I had made the mistake of telling her all about Ebony one night after a few too many glasses of wine. At the time, she said it didn't matter what I did—or whom I did it with—in the past. It obviously mattered. She was jealous of what she called my "continuing relationship with that Negro," and she did everything to sabotage my writing career. And for this she gets half of my money for books she despised.

"I'm so sorry. Last I heard, you were still separated. How, uh, recent is your divorce?"

I had waited and wasted five years for Edie to sign those damn papers. "The ink's probably still drying in Pittsburgh."

"I'm so sorry."

I'm not. "Don't be."

"This is all so strange. You're now a *divorced* writer of romance. We can't let P. Rudolph Underhill go on the cover now. That would be hypocritical, wouldn't it?"

Oh, no, we wouldn't want hypocrisy in the publishing industry. So Desiree Holland, writer of sassy interracial African-American romantic comedies, is now a middle-aged, graying, divorced white man with no way of letting the world know he is a writer and no place to call home.

"Look," I say as I feel the lint in my pockets, "I know this will be a lot to ask, Henry, but after the lawyers and all . . ."

Henry blinks at me. "A little tight on money?"

A boa constrictor couldn't squeeze a nickel out of me. "Yeah, I'm strapped. I had to sell my Mustang to pay my lawyer and buy the plane ticket here."

Henry still blinks. "Ouch."

"So, would it be possible, you know, if—"

Henry stops blinking. "Say no more, Pete. I'll see what I can do about a pre-advance advance."

I've never heard of such a thing. "A what?"

"I'll get you something to tide you over for a while."

Which means that I'll get some chump change until I produce.

He stands. This means that the meeting is almost over. "You have any working titles for Desiree's next book?"

Desiree's next book. I have plenty of title ideas for *my* next book, but I don't share them with Henry. He's promised to see about some money—which I might be able to keep one hundred percent of this time—and I don't want to ruin that chance. I will simply write two books, one for Henry and one for me, and I'll give them both to Henry. Or . . . I'll give Henry his Desiree Holland book and go out on my own into the publishing world with my own name.

And that scares the living lint out of me.

"You have thought up some titles, haven't you?"

"I don't usually start with a title, Henry." Besides, the marketing department or an editor usually titles everything anyway. "Uh, how about . . . *A Whiter Shade of Pale?*"

Henry smiles. "Funny, and very sixties. With a song tie-in to boot. Any others?"

"What about . . . *Devil's Dance?*"

He nods. "Plays off *The Devil to Pay*. But your first novel didn't have the word 'devil' in the title. Hard to market that unless we change *Ashy* to *Ashy Devil*. That can be arranged, you know. Might give that novel another boost, too, maybe get it a movie of the week or something. I hear BET's doing its own movies these days. Give me a third title possibility."

Henry's rule of three is still in effect. Almost all the romance novels he edits have three parts whether the author intends to have them or not: beginning (back story), middle (rising action with lots of sex), and end (climax with lots of nasty sex). Once I begin writing my novel, I'll have to send him chapters in batches of three, the first three loaded with back story, triple-spaced.

"Um, how about . . . *Holding My Breath?*"

He closes his eyes. "Kind of has a *Waiting to Exhale* feel about it." His eyes pop open. "And we both know what happened to *that* novel. Great soundtrack and a wonderful movie."

Having a book turned into a movie is Olympus Publishing's dream. That way the movie will sell the book, and the marketing department can rest its weary minds and concentrate more on the margaritas or whatever it actually concentrates on.

"I'll run these titles by marketing, see what they think." He opens the door. "Where are you staying?"

"On the *Argo*."

"The *Argo*?"

"It's my sailboat."

It is the only thing that my father, "the Captain," left me that Edie let me keep. Dad had left me the house in Huntington in his will, but I had sold it to help pay for "Edie's Dollhouse," a 5,000-square-foot contemporary glass and metal monstrosity nestled in the woods back in Sewickley where it stuck out like a sore landfill. So now the money from my father's death gives Edie a house I have no right to live in. I almost wish I had burned the Captain's body on a funeral pyre on his boat—the old Viking way—to keep him from rolling over in his cremation box.

"It's moored in Huntington Harbor."

"I didn't know you had a sailboat."

The *Argo* is one of the few things I own outright besides my laptop and a carry-on full of clothes. "It was my father's."

"Was?"

"Yeah. He died a while ago." In 1990. Where has the time gone?

Henry tugs on his ponytail. "And he named his boat after the ship from *Jason and the Argonauts*?"

I nod, though I know the Captain didn't name the *Argo*. That was simply the name of the boat when he bought the thirty-two-foot Thistle back in the early 1960s. He didn't change the name because "it's bad luck to change the name of a boat that's still afloat." That made the Captain "Jason," I was his only Argonaut, and we had a few adventures together. We never found the Golden Fleece, though we did fight a few squalls and bluefish together on the Long Island Sound.

"And you're going to write a hot, steamy, romantic comedy on a sailboat in Huntington Harbor . . . in October."

I shrug. "Why not? I'll have few distractions." Even if I will be writing in a ghost ship, at least it will be a rent-free ghost ship. I think. The Captain was always good about paying his yacht club dues.

Henry fishes in his pocket and pulls out a key ring. "You can stay inside where it's warm at my summer place on Fire Island." He slips off two keys.

"It won't be that cold on the boat." Except for the memories. Those will be cold.

"I won't have it, Pete. You know where Cherry Grove is?"

I blink. Of all the places . . . "Yeah, I do, but I'd rather—"

"I've had a place there on Green Walk for years. It's a one-bedroom, and you'll just love it. We've even nicknamed the apartment complex 'Elysium,' you know, the resting place for the gods." He hands me the keys. "It's fully stocked with food, spotless, and it's very secluded. And you'll just love your neighbors, especially Coleman Muse. He's quite a gifted poet. You have enough money for the ferry?"

This is going way too fast. "Uh, yeah." I stuff the keys into my pocket. "Um, does all this mean that I have a chance for a contract?"

"Uh, no, not yet. You're on spec until I see the first three chapters."

On spec. Wonderful. Two fairly successful novels, and I'm writing on speculation. I'm almost back to the dark days when I was sending out unsolicited manuscripts to agents and praying for a miracle.

"When will you need the chapters, Henry?"

"Oh, as soon as you can get them to me."

Great. "Okay. Uh, thanks for everything."

"Don't mention it."

As the elevator plunges to the parking garage, I close my eyes. Here I am, a published author reduced to writing on spec, about to write an African-American romantic comedy in Cherry Grove, the oldest gay community in the United States.

Good writing, F. Scott Fitzgerald once said, is like swimming underwater and holding your breath.

I just don't know if I can hold my breath that long anymore.

2

I drift along with the tide of cars escaping New York City, Walt Whitman's "city of spires and masts," letting the convoy of tattered flags and red, white, and blue bumper stickers carry me through the wasteland of Long Island, the supposed recreation area for the people of New York City, home to several million commuters and the infamous Long Island Rail Road. I float east with flocks of other idle dreamers and screamers clinging to steering wheels on the Northern State Parkway around lunchtime. From Massepequa to Montauk, where the *Amistad* landed only to be escorted to Connecticut, Long Island is the melting pot cooked down to the dregs.

Suffolk County: nothing but potato farms, ducks, and Grumman.

I hesitate when I see a sign to Huntington. I don't want to go there yet. One ghost story at a time.

I waver again when I see an advertisement for Levittown, one of the places the Captain used to live before Levittown became marginally integrated. I don't ever want to go there. I like homogenized milk; I don't like homogenized neighborhoods. Maybe the melting pot went to Levittown to die. And all during junior high, Levittown was the only Long Island town listed on the big Cram map on the wall in geography class, the rest of Long Island obliterated by the letters of New Haven, Bridgeport, and Stamford, Connecticut.

Heading south to Plainedge, then east, I read signs announcing so many towns, so many names like Wyandanch, West Babylon, and Bohemia. Native American names coexist with biblical names east of Hedonism on this thin sliver of the American dream jutting out into the Atlantic. What the Dutch took from the natives then shared with the English is now one large faceless neighborhood divided by malls, restaurants, convenience stores, and the empty shadows of industrial parks.

Huntington's main mall is the Walt Whitman Mall. What would Walt say as he walked around inside his own mall? Would he say, "I am large, I contain multitudes"? Could he bloom at Bloomingdale's or contemplate leaves of grass at Garden Botanika? Would he echo the sufferings of men like me who don't like to shop and say, "I am the man, I suffered, I was there" or "I stop somewhere waiting for you"? Would Walt "invite his soul" to observe the indoor sidewalk sales? Would Walt feel connected to all the atoms in the houses in planned neighborhoods on Long Island that look the same, two cars in every garage, a single tree in every yard? A couplet takes shape as I drive:

Welcome to a dark, suburban Hades,
where houses run into the 180's . . .

I slip through the redundant Islips (West Islip, Islip proper, and East Islip), past Great River to Sayville, heading to River Road and the Charon Ferry Service for the trip across Great South Bay to Cherry Grove. That's one of the many nice things about Fire Island: no cars allowed, only your own two feet or a bicycle to get you around. I park the Nova, grab my carry-on and laptop, and stroll to the docks, the scent of diesel fuel and salt air tingling my nose. Great South Bay, while not exactly a quagmire of whirlpools, has been known to belch sand onto the rest of Long Island.

Because the next ferry to Fire Island won't leave until 2 P.M., I have half an hour to waste counting rows of red Radio Flyer wagons and analyzing the other passengers in a poem on the back of the car rental receipt:

A young man, hacking into a handkerchief,
leans against an older man who winces at every cough.
Another, dressed in black, sits by himself on the dock,
his feet splayed over the rainbow-colored water
while a man in red holds on to a piling for dear life.
Two crew-cut blond women work an old snack machine,
yanking and cursing at each knob,

while an older woman wrapped in a blue coat nods off on a bench,
her breathing as exhausted as her makeup.

An old song creeps into my head,
something about not paying the ferryman,
and I find myself humming "Come Sail Away,"
an even older song by Styx.
The other people waiting seem like fallen leaves in the chilly air,
like birds that flock to land, stretching arms out toward the bay.
We are all helpless souls of the unburied,
fluttering around these docks,
so many bones in New York not yet laid to rest.

God, my poetry is as depressed as I am.

After buying a honey bun that I know has been aging gracelessly in the
machine since August, I read the ferry regulations, the print looking fresh
on a wall covered with old nautical charts and faded boating notices:

> In order to comply with United States Coast Guard regulations,
> the following baggage and freight procedures must be followed:
>
> Two (2) pieces of hand luggage is allowed, no charge. A Tariff will
> be imposed on all additional items. Shopping Carts & Luggage
> carriers—Min. charge $3.00. Luggage only is allowed in passenger
> areas. Loaded wagons (e.g., Radio Flyers) will not be accepted.
> Absolutely no bungee cords can be used. Freight must be han-
> dled on and off the ferry by crew.
>
> Due to quantity, size and weight of freight, limited space on
> board, weather conditions, loading and unloading time, and the
> safety and convenience of the passengers, the crew at times will
> limit the amount of freight carried on a trip.

I don't have much baggage (visible anyway), and I look at the few
others waiting around me. A couple of briefcases and a few handbags.
Our own thoughts will echo on this ferry. The last item—Smoking is not
allowed on the docks or the ferry—makes me laugh, because as the ferry
approaches, I see the captain in the fly bridge of the approaching ferry
puffing a big cigar.

After the crew tethers the burnt-orange ferry to the dock, the captain walks down the gangplank followed by a small group of people. Those waiting around me fade away like autumn shade, and I'm the only one left to take the next ferry.

"I got a lot of freight to load," the captain says to me, "so you might wanna reconsider what you're bringing cuz we may have to shoehorn you in or find you a smaller boat to get across the marsh."

I look again at the laptop and carry-on. "I only have these."

He taps the laptop bag. "No bombs, knives, or box cutters in there, right?"

"None."

The captain, a strong, detestably smelling old man with bloodred eyes and sweat-stained clothing, bellows orders to his crew as they herd crates and boxes into the boat. His hairy ears, bushy eyebrows, and thick gray goatee make him look every bit like a demon. I almost wish I had a penny to give him for the half thoughts in his jowly head. Better to keep my penny and my own thoughts under my tongue.

Half an hour of stuffing and cramming later, a crew member searches my bag while I stand still. "Nine bucks," he says.

Waterway robbery, I think, but I pay him and drag my feet up the gangplank, mainly because I don't really want to go to Cherry Grove, where I'm sure to stick out like a sore heterosexual.

The captain tells me how lucky I am. "Normally I wouldn't let you on, as full as we are," he tells me. "Got just enough room for you. Otherwise you'd have to wait for my next run."

I walk into the passenger area and take my seat in front of Plexiglas windows filmed with salt. I guess if I had tipped the crew member an extra five I might have actually gotten a clear view of the bay. Upon inspection, the windows seem to have a mazelike pattern on them, like a labyrinth leading to a blackened glob of bird droppings.

Story of my life.

The trip is uneventful, the stagnant, shadowy water of Great South Bay no more than ten to twelve feet deep, the boat groaning with its heavy load. It's not exactly an ancient Greek adventure, and I hardly feel like an ancient hero anyway, a stale honey bun my only sustenance, a void in my head where a romantic comedy is supposed to be.

And there's really nothing funny about Great South Bay, the scene of one of the worst hurricanes of the twentieth century. It was so bad back in 1938 that they didn't even have time to name the hurricane. The Captain was only thirteen and living in Montauk at the time.

"There wasn't any warning," he told me once while we were caulking the longest seam in the wooden hull of the *Argo*. He called the entire awful job "paying the devil," because we had to squat in the bilges for hours. Hence the title of my second book.

"Nothing on the radio, Captain?" I was the only kid I've ever known who was not allowed to call his own father "Dad." But it wasn't so bad, and it seemed fitting on the *Argo*, where the Captain's word was law.

"Nope. I remember it was a Wednesday. Your grandpa was out with the other bay men dredging, while I was paying the devil on Old Man Mudge's dredge. I'd come up for air every now and then because we used hot tar on the devil back then, and I saw the gulls acting funny on the shore."

"Funny?"

"Like they were in a hot pan about to be cooked, jumping around like popcorn frying."

To this day, I check out birds when a storm is forecast. If they start "popping" off the ground, I find shelter in a hurry.

"We had just had two weeks of rain, so the ground was soft. Gray skies as usual, seas not as heavy as the day before, wind from the north at first, then about noon it shifted to the east, and it started to rain to beat the band."

"Like a nor'easter."

"Yep. Only this nor'easter was tearing off roofs and popping power and phone lines left and right. I left that dredge in a hurry once it started rocking and rolling, and I immediately lost my way the rain was so thick, the wind whipping up to seventy knots."

"What did you do, Captain?"

"At times I could see through that wall of rain, and what I saw . . . The sea was completely white, the air filled with sea foam, waves fifty feet and higher, fallen trees, dredges up on land, rolls of waves tearing past docks on their way in, sweeping those docks away on their way out. I headed up to the town to higher ground and rode that storm out for five hours in a hardware store. Lots of metal to dodge in a hardware store, let me tell you.

"The storm ended by six, skies were completely clear by ten, but since we didn't have any power, we didn't know how bad it was till the next day." He had paused and closed his eyes.

"It was bad, huh."

"Worse. Most of the houses were damaged almost beyond repair, and your grandpa's house ended up with five other houses in the pond. Must have been a hundred boats destroyed, some thirty of them blown a hundred yards inland. Dragnets, fish traps—gone. Your grandpa's two boats—gone. The oysters and clams—gone. The sea just up and covered them with a million tons of sand. Wiped your grandpa and the other bay men completely out . . ."

Grandpa lost his boats and his livelihood that day and later lost his mind from the grief—and the whiskey—leaving my father homeless at thirteen. And yet my father never cursed the sea that changed his life forever. He instead served in the U.S. Navy and sailed Long Island Sound every weekend of my life, even though he had lost most of his sight in his right eye by 1986. He could never get enough of the sea, even if he couldn't see it. "There's much to be learned from the sea," he'd tell me. "When you're sailing the blood of a giant, you never know which way he'll bleed."

And now we're in the same boat, I think to myself as the ferry docks near green-gray weeds swaying along the slimy shore of Fire Island. I've got no home, no real livelihood, no father, no one even to call me anything.

I take Bayview Walk past some fantastic white multi-windowed houses facing Great South Bay, all of them built low to the ground as if they, too, are crouching on the shore in fear of a storm. Enveloped in the lonely half light, trees leaning over courtyards to provide pockets of shade, I pass through the empty streets of Cherry Grove until I reach Green Walk, where I nearly collide with a blond woman walking three dogs, each more hideous than the next: a black-and-brown bull mastiff, its jowls dripping, its breath pestilential; a white toy poodle, coiffed like a diva and yipping like one, too, its tail a white microphone high in the air; and a basset hound, its eyes huge and weepy, its head as big as the rest of its body, only its thumping tail longer. Their leashes tangle around my legs as the mastiff searches my coat pockets for the honey bun.

"Oh, I'm so sorry," the woman says, pulling back only the poodle and basset hound. The mastiff works its nose deeper into my left pocket. "Regina must smell food."

No kidding. I ease Regina's nose out of my pocket and withdraw the slippery carcass of my honey bun, peeling back the plastic and offering it to Regina. A millisecond later, the honey bun is gone, plastic and all. I count four fingers and a thumb and smile.

"Regina's really a sweet dog."

Right. "Maybe you can help me. I'm looking for Henry Milton's place on Green Walk."

She points to a gate across the street. "That's Henry's place. Are you a new friend of his?"

I extend a Regina-spittled hand. "Uh, yeah, I guess. I'm one of his writers, Peter Underhill."

She leaves my hand hanging, lifting the leashes by way of explanation. I wouldn't have shaken my hand either. "I'm Sibyl, dog-walker extraordinaire."

"Nice to meet you, Sibyl." Regina growls. I bet the plastic didn't go down too well. Regina will be blowing bubbles out her ass later. "And you, too, Regina."

"See you around," Sibyl says as she breezes away, her blond hair bouncing in the wind.

I open the gate and find myself in a sunny courtyard with surprisingly green grass and a grove of laurels, whitewashed benches and outdoor couches spaced here and there around a small, empty in-ground pool. I hear a voice singing to a guitar and smell the oregano beginnings of an Italian or Greek feast. As I shut the gate, the wind dies down, and some amber accent lights begin to glow along the path. I'm almost to some stairs when I notice a man watching me from the roof high above.

"What are you—prophet, priest, or inventor?" he asks, his voice rising and falling like a seasoned poet. I count the syllables in my head—ten exactly. This must be the poet Henry was telling me about.

"Writer," I call up to him.

He rolls his eyes. "You must be one of Henry's many friends."

I move up the stairs, smiling at him while once again counting his syllables. Ten again. Normal people do not speak in blank verse.

At the top, I find myself on a patio with a brilliant view of Great South Bay. "You must be a poet," I tell him. "Do you always speak in blank verse?"

"Alas, it is one of the dying arts," he says. He wears a white headband, loose green sweatpants, and an oversized white New York Jets jersey. He is also as tan as burnt toast, lines of white skin leaking out in squint lines around his eyes. "Welcome, Henry's friend, to Elysium."

"Peter Underhill."

He nods. "You can call me the Poet, Coleman Muse."

"Nice to meet you, Coleman."

"Let me give you a tour of Cherry Grove," he says, still speaking in blank verse. Coleman must be no fun at parties. "Over there's where people drink to forget." I see a pub or bar named Le Lethe. "Yonder lies the Great South Bay, shimmering."

"Do you live here year-round?"

"No, because none of us have a fixed home."

He's good at making up blank verse, but this is getting creepy. I look to the south and see the waves of the Atlantic tapping the shore. "How's the weather been?"

Coleman pauses a beat, probably to count his syllables. "Calm, cool, and serene, and Cherry Grove sleeps."

Spooky, strange, and weird is this Coleman Muse. Geez, now I'm thinking in blank verse. "Uh, where's Henry's place?"

"I will show you if you will follow me."

I don't speak to Coleman on the way to Henry's door for fear of another ten-syllable blast. I wonder if there's therapy available for recovering blank verse addicts. He stops in front of a white door facing Great South Bay. "This, Henry's friend, is Henry's bright white door, and if you like we can parley some more."

Now he's speaking in couplets. I thank him, open the door, and see— Geez, I have died and gone to a blizzard in Alaska.

Henry's studio apartment is bright white and all the same eye-blinding bright white. Henry could have had the decency to at least do his moldings and baseboards in antique white. I might get lost in here! White indoor-outdoor carpet. I didn't know they made such an irrational thing. A white sofa, a white coffee table in front, a white library table behind. White curtains and shades, pulled down, of course, to keep all the other colors safely outside. A white bookcase filled with white seashells and unpainted Hummel figurines. A framed copy of the Beatles' White Album. How tacky. A white dinner table with two matching wing chairs. A white kitchen counter and appliances, cabinets filled with opaque white glasses and fine china, drawers filled with white utensils.

I rip open the refrigerator and— Here's some color. Lots of beer, soda, condiments, salad fixings. His pantry has color, too, each shelf covered meticulously with white contact paper and teeming with boxed goodies of every flavor of the rainbow. I search through the house for anything else visibly nonwhite and come up empty. Even Henry's soap, soap dish, and shower fixtures are white.

I have entered a rubber room on the funny farm. I am in a snowstorm in Buffalo. I am buried under the surface of the moon. I will have to leave all the windows and the refrigerator and pantry doors open at all times or I will go blind. I cannot be Ebony Mills in a completely Caucasian apartment.

After moving the dinner table to a window looking out on Great South Bay, I set up shop. I boot up the laptop, which is gloriously black with glowing green lights, then litter the table with stacks of research notes and outlines. I make a cup of dark brown Earl Grey tea, using brown sugar to sweeten it. I slide Stevie Wonder's *Songs in the Key of Life* into the laptop's CD tray, "Love's in Need of a Love Today" breaking the silence. I am tired, but I am ready to write. I look at my working outline for Chapter 1 of my novel:

I.   Back story: history of the Underhills
II.   Back story: David and "Hel" Underhill
III. Back story: 1963–1975 (life with the Captain and "Hel")

I sift through my notes on my family history, my fingers eager to begin my dissection of the hallowed Underhills, but nothing comes.

Nothing.

I start on the back story for my father three times, but I fail to grasp his essence, his character, typing then deleting "The Captain was a" three times.

Maybe it's the light salt breezes blowing off the bay that I'm allowing inside to spoil Henry's antiseptic apartment, maybe it's the long day with the flight, the drive, and the ferry ride, maybe it's me singing along with Stevie Wonder instead of writing, maybe it's the fact that Henry's apartment is one huge blank page haunted by a blank verse poet doing iambic pentameter jumping jacks on the roof above—

I can't write tonight. I can't latch on to any of the winged dreams and nightmares swooping through my mind. Edie, who had a classical private school education, used to call me the Fisher King whenever I had writer's block. "You're as impotent as the Fisher King," she'd tell me. "But I guard the Holy Grail," I'd reply.

I am the Fisher King. Again. It seems fitting here as I look out over the calm waters of Great South Bay.

But when I curl up on the couch and think of Ebony and how fine she would look in Henry's apartment, how her dark skin would blaze shadows on to these too-white walls, I smile.

Good night, Ebony, wherever you are. I'll write about you tomorrow. Promise.

3

Iwake up several hours later in complete darkness, sweat dripping down my back. "I can't be sleeping! I have two novels to write, and Henry wants his sassy-ass novel as soon as possible."

I scratch the sleep out of my eyes and boot up the laptop, searching old files for five years of the fits and starts of Desiree's other novels. There are a lot of starts, but few fits for what Henry wants. But after a few hits of brown-sugared Earl Grey tea, Stevie Wonder turned up as loud as the laptop's little speakers can handle, I start to click the keys . . .

. . . as a black woman.

A WHITER SHADE OF PALE
by Desiree Holland

Prologue

I'm looking for The One on a search for the Holy Male.

I know it's supposed to be the Holy Grail, but a man sure as hell isn't a communion cup, although sometimes a whole bunch of *whine* is involved.

I'm on a quest to find my soul mate before he finds me. I mean, what kind of a romance would it be if the hero rides in on his sweaty yet majestic white horse—and it has to be a white horse, because those fantasy stories are always racist—to save me, the damsel in distress, whose hair is micro-braided and beaded and looking beyond *fo-ine*, only I have already kicked the dragon's ass, sliced and diced his scaly green guts, stuffed banquet-sized dragon morsels into medieval freezer bags, and have been waiting for our hero for twenty goddamn minutes? I would not be amused by his tardiness, and I would probably be tapping the sand on my wrist-hourglass and yawning when I see our hero limping in from his death-defying battle with an arthritic squirrel.

"It's about time you showed up, Sir Stankalot," I would say. "Now wipe that dragon shit off my sword, put these groceries on your Caucasian horse, and let's get us back to Camelot. You know there'll be a party waiting for us, because that's all those crazy white knights do. That Merlin is a wiz in the kitchen with dragon spleen, isn't he? I hope he separates out the membrane this time, though. Cleaning dragon spleen is a lost art. And that King Arthur, he's such a trip at parties. I hope Lancelot has the sense to keep his hands off Guenevere's ass this time . . ."

A quest just wouldn't be any fun if he found me first.

I sit back in my chair and smile. Ebony loved those old medieval romances, but I was never quite the right knight.

I see the skies getting rosier, the darkness rolling the stars away from the surface of the bay. "Now, for a little back story." I finish my tea, the last gulp ninety percent brown sugar.

Chapter 1

I'm nobody's damsel in distress, mainly because I shop at Wal-Mart. I'm no fashion queen, and Wal-Mart always has my size, even if I sometimes have to sneak into the plus-size section to get a blouse.

They sell a little bit of everything at Wal-Mart, but they don't sell dragon-slicing knives. I doubt any of those malls sell them, either. I don't like shopping at those malls, no sir. I get claustrophobic even on the escalators at malls. And on elevators, I'm the crazy lady who sweats, whistles, and stands with her hands on the crack of the doors. I've never ridden a horse and wouldn't know how to swing a sword to save my life. I can barely shave my legs with an electric razor without getting a nasty burn.

I feel my own scraggly growth. I don't intend to shave until I'm through with these novels. Call it superstition. Edie hated my attempts at growing a beard, but Ebony liked my little moustache, that first soft growth I had when I was thirteen. Most of it sprouted out of a mole under my nose, but Ebony said that it made me look "so much older."

And all those parties at Camelot aren't for me either. I would rather discover, search, and hang with myself or with only one other person. I'm my own best friend.

I sometimes take long walks just to browse in old bookstores. "What are you looking for?" they sometimes ask. "Everything in particular," I tell them. "I'm looking for a diamond in the rough."

Then they smile and say, "I'll check the computer for that title."

When they bring me a book or say they'll have to order one or more of the nine romance novels (and one illustrated history of Arizona) titled *A Diamond in the Rough* or *Diamond in the Rough*, I shake my head. "I'm sure you have the particular diamond in the rough I'm searching for," I tell them. "I'll keep looking."

They generally leave me alone after that, but they always shadow me, sometimes with a security guard, which doesn't upset me a bit. You can never be too careful browsing bookstores these days. I mean, you might innocently brush up against a Salman Rushdie book and become a target of someone's jihad.

Browsing. That's all Ebony and I ever did, it seems. We'd browse every store in Huntington Bay Village, trying on clothes our parents would never buy, reading magazines and comic books our parents would never allow in the house.

I make another cup of Earl Grey and try to think of what Ebony would be looking for in a soul mate. I used to know, because I was supposed to be her soul mate.

I should have never left Long Island.

Returning to my laptop, I let a little of my own character into Ebony's character:

So what exactly am I looking for? If I knew that, I'd have found his ass already. I just don't know.

I once saw a woman on TV who was sitting in the charred wreckage of her house after a fire. A rude reporter shoved a microphone in her face, asking, "What are you doing?" I would have said, "What's it look like, you asshole?" but the woman on the TV never spoke. She just kept sifting through the gunk on the floor until she found one of those old Polaroid pictures, the kind you had to pull out of the camera and time for a minute. She held that picture to her chest and smiled, sooty tears running down her face.

And that's what romance is to me: It's like looking for that one unburnt picture in the ashes. There's nothing to it but to do it. I just have to search high and low and in between and in between that until . . . I find The One who has survived the fire.

And I've only been searching for—give or take—thirty years.

I want a man, but not just any man. He has to meet certain criteria. Or rather, he has to accept certain things about me and not dog me out about every damn thing that I do or don't do.

He can't mind if I do most if not all of the cooking. I can cook, and if you ever saw me, you'd say, "She has a gland problem or she still lives at home and eats her mama's cooking." I don't have a gland problem that I know of, and I haven't lived at home for fifteen years. I'm not out-and-out flabby, but I do have a roll or two on my tummy from my made-from-scratch dinner rolls. I doubt I'd fit into any of those height-weight charts at the doctor's office, but I haven't met many black people who actually do. Bet there wasn't a black doctor on that panel when they made those charts.

When I cook, I don't use recipes or instructions. I kind of go with the flow . . . and whatever happens to be in the pantry or fridge. I have an extensive spice collection that even includes

. . . includes what? Edie did all the cooking for us, most of it unpronounceable and generally inedible, and I had the "honor" of being her dishwasher afterward. The only spices I know come from that "Parsley, Sage, Rosemary, and Thyme" song by Simon and Garfunkel. I stretch my back after standing and check out Henry's pantry.

I blink at a couple hundred different spices. Why so many spices in a summer home? And what the hell is fenugreek? It looks like a collection of smashed peanuts and smells strangely like nutty, homemade cookies. Marjoram smells almost like Earl Grey tea, but it looks like peat moss. Coriander, which either resembles rat droppings or brown caviar, smells like green tea or warm, stale Guinness Stout. Savory, which has to be mint tea, looks like a mix of pine needles and hedge trimmings. I look closely at basil and see an apostrophe *s*. I open and smell some outstanding herb, which must be Basil's stash. Henry needs some help. If I were a cop looking for marijuana, the first place I'd look would be the spice collection. I've heard of far too many people busted because the oregano wasn't oregano.

Ebony wouldn't use any of this shit. I slide bottles here and there until I see several different types of Jamaican curry powder. I race back to the laptop and type:

seven different types of Jamaican curry powder. Name another woman who has seven different types of Jamaican curry powder in her pantry. I blow people away at

Now where will she work this time? Ebony was Toni Million, an aspiring dancer working at a fancy restaurant in *Ashy*, and Bonita Milton, an unknown artist working at a daycare center in *The Devil to Pay*. It has to be a job where the reader will have some instant sympathy. I smile. She's going to be what I used to be: a teacher.

Cherry Grove Middle School, where I teach history to seventh graders and sometimes actually do some of that damn paperwork. Whenever we have a faculty food day, other teachers ask, "What do you call it?" I tell them it's my lunch. They always want the recipe, but I tell them that there isn't one, it's just something I whipped up. They look at me strangely after that, but they eat it and ask for seconds. I'm always taking home empty containers. There's always some chicken, pork, or beef soaking in

What the hell's that kind of sauce Edie was always abusing? Something Oriental, sweet, and brown. I check Henry's fridge and find it. Edie and Henry share the same tastes?

Yaschida sauce and fresh veggies and salad fixings in my fridge, just in case The One makes a surprise visit. But there isn't any alcohol in my fridge. None. No soul mate of mine is going to get drunk on beer or wine.

He's going to get drunk on me.

I never could get enough of a buzz from Edie alone. She didn't take my breath away, just what little money I had. So whiskey sours made her somewhat sweeter, and even when they didn't, they at least made me numb. Ebony, though—the girl made me high. Drunk. Intoxicated. Shit-faced. Not exactly a romantic thing to say, but it was true. The girl made me shit-faced drunk with happiness. Ebony was and probably still is the most beautiful person that I have ever met, only she never seemed to notice it. She was—and I'm sure that she still is—a natural beauty. We'll just have to make this version of Ebony a natural beauty who doesn't think she's beautiful.

The One can't mind if I'm not beautiful. I'm what you might call naturally rugged-looking, like I been in a few fights. I'm not homely or anything—I have some sexy-ass eyes and thighs, now—but I just haven't been blessed by what White America wants in its caramel-covered black beauties. I'm thick. I'm intimidating. I'm The Commodores' "Brick House." I have long fingers and toes, long skinny feet, tiny ears, dark brown eyes, and the darkest skin allowed by law in the state of Pennsylvania.

I once got pulled over so a cop could check my tinted windows, then he says, "No, everything is okay." Asshole. If I tinted my windows any more than they already are, no cop would ever see me.

I'm not sepia, *café au lait*, ginger, mocha, coconut, or any other tropical flavor. I'm black, and I'm beautiful, only my hair doesn't seem to know it. My hair looks good the day it's done, then flies away little by little until the next time I have it styled. My students can tell what day of the week it is just by looking at my hair—and my clothes. I generally start out nice and professional and end up wrinkled and tacky. Rack Room supplies me with comfortable shoes, and when I've done all the laundry, I sometimes find outfits that match like they're supposed to. It's not easy, though, because I know that washer of mine has something against me. Dark clothes go in dark and come out gray, lights and whites go in white and come out gray, and grays go in gray and get grayer. If you take me in from a distance, I look like I play for the Oakland Raiders in their silver and black uniforms.

What else, what else, what else? How does she get around? And does she like to get around? If she's driving around Pittsburgh, the pothole capital of America, she'll have to hate driving with a passion.

My soul mate can't mind if I don't drive. I own an SUV, a Suzuki Sidekick, but I don't like to drive. Too much stress, too many decisions, too many street signs to read, and too many potholes to avoid while someone's on my ass honking and flipping me off because I actually drive the speed limit in this town.

Oh, and the accidents. The first one wasn't my fault. A sneaky light pole in a parking lot jumped out behind me one night. Blew out my back window and flattened my spare. And the second accident, well, let's just say that one-way streets in downtown Pittsburgh should be outlawed. The cab I hit wasn't damaged too badly, but the cabbie showed up in traffic court practically in traction, a neck brace turning his face beet red. My monthly car insurance payment is almost as high as the mortgage payment on my condo. I really should sell the Sidekick, but I might need it one day . . . probably to pick up The One who has never found the damn time to get his own damn license.

Hobbies? Ebony had so many, but one she stuck with was reading. And what she read and shared with me opened my eyes in so many ways . . .

My Boo has to be someone who likes to read, who consistently finds time to read, who makes time to read, who even schedules time to read. In other words, he has to be anal as hell about reading.

On my lunch breaks, I cross four lanes of traffic to a park, where I walk by any man who is reading something other than a newspaper or magazine. Then I check him out and what he's reading—in that order. If he's old and stank, I keep on walking. And if he's younger and doesn't smell too bad, I slow down. If I've already read the book he's reading, I try to start a conversation. "That's a wonderful book, isn't it?" I ask. I've noticed that the word "wonderful" is used a lot on the back covers of paperbacks. Most times I get nods, a smile, an occasional grunt. One time, though, a white man, who looked Italian with his twisted nose and hairy eyebrows, actually said a complete sentence. "I *know*," he said in such a way as to tell me: "Get lost, wench." If I haven't read the book, I search it out, blow off all my grading, and read it that very night. Only the next day, the man has gone on to another book or isn't reading that day. If I can't finish it by the next day, I sometimes sit where the man had been reading the day before hoping he'll come by. That hasn't happened . . . yet.

I'm not crazy, so why do I do this? Just in case The One has read it. Then we'll have something more in common. Online book clubs have helped me a lot in this area. I'd never join a book club, though I really enjoy discussing books. Book clubs are just too communist for me. "Everyone this month will read *this* book," they say. Well, what if I don't want to? What if I'd rather read several books simultaneously? Just last week I

What would Ebony be reading now? She always loved the ocean and the beach, and in Pittsburgh, it's all about rivers—the Ohio, the Allegheny, and the Monongahela. I hook the laptop to Henry's phone, and after stressing over all the access-number choices, I get on America Online and run a few book searches with "river" in the title at Amazon.com. Once I have a collection, I continue to type:

was on a river kick and read *The River, Cane River, Bridge Over the River Kwai, Mississippi Solo, Mystic River,* and even cracked *Huckleberry Finn* for the climactic river scene. I even looked up whitewater rafting and paddleboat trips on the Internet.

Since I believe the number seven is magic, I once read

Seven, Ebony's magic number. I wore that number in Little League, in CYO basketball at St. Pat's, in Pop Warner football, and even taped it to my T-shirt whenever I played street hockey for the P-Street Rangers. "I like your number," Ebony told me the first time we met. My number was one of the reasons she said she became interested in me. "It was like a sign or something," she said.

Another book search later, and I continue plucking the keys:

The Seven Habits of Highly Effective People, The Seven Daughters of Eve, Seven Up, The Seven Sins of Memory, The Seven Spiritual Laws of Success, The Seven Storey Mountain, and *The Seven Steps to Nirvana.* And what did I learn? The number seven helps writers sell books. I haven't started on all those alphabet mystery writers yet, but I will. I've got plenty of time, and because I am who I am, I'll be starting with the letter Z. Those authors have some writing to do to catch up with me!

Maybe I should name my book *Searching the Seven Seas for Ebony*. Henry would say it wouldn't fit on the cover, and Eliot would say it wouldn't fit on a movie theater marquee. I count the syllables. Ten exactly. Carlton Muse, the blank verse poet, would probably have an eargasm. Writing wouldn't nearly be as frustrating if the title you lived with for a year or two was actually accepted by the marketing department.

I re-read Ebony's back story so far and realize that I've created a lonely middle school teacher who would rather . . . what? She'd rather write, just like me. Maybe she'll even have an "I'd Rather Be Writing" bumper sticker on her Sidekick. Let's make her an aspiring writer:

My One and Only can't mind that I'm a frustrated novelist who has more rejection letters than pages of a novel. I looked into the whole subsidy publishing thing, but I didn't have the fifteen grand up front. I checked out POD (Print-On-Demand) publishing, but it sounded too scientific. Saying "I am a POD author" might freak people out. I guess I could go to Quik Copy and crank out my novel and slap some staples on it, but I only have a ten-percent discount card at Quik Copy, and the machines I choose always chew up my originals.

But it isn't about the money. Okay, it's a little about the money, but it's more about validation. I want to be noticed as an adequate writer. Not a great one. Just adequate.

And paid enough to quit teaching seventh graders for all eternity.

Several of my rejection letters contain the word "idiosyncratic," and a few even say my work is "quirky," "strange," and "eccentric." I always like to keep the reader guessing . . . which is probably why my novel's plot is too unpredictable and unbelievable. "Too dense for mass consumption," one letter states in bold italics.

What's my novel about? Well, it's kind of an autobiography, and it tells the tale of a normal, regular, middle-aged hoochie in search of her Boo.

It's not as depressing as you might think.

I titled it *A Regular Woman* the first time around, mailing it to every publisher and agent in New York, many of whom didn't have the decency to write me a rejection letter. Maybe they thought it would be about a woman who didn't have a problem with constipation. The second time around, I changed the title to *The Quest for the Holy Male* and maybe changed a paragraph or two. Same result. This time I'm sending it out as *Soul Quest*. I think it's a snappy title, and all the publish-it-yourself books teach you that a good title will often sell a bad book. Case in point: *Bad as I Wanna Be* by Dennis Rodman. I never should have read that book. It has ruined me for life when it comes to plotting my stories because it has no plot.

Time to throw in the sex, as if I'm the one experienced enough to write about it. All I had growing up was this incredible fantasy life. And Ebony. But I guess most writers who saturate their books with steamy sex are writing about what they've never done, either. Fantasy, that's all it is. Ebony will just have to be more like me in this book:

The One also can't care that I'm not that experienced. The first time I made out was on a balmy Friday night in high school. The boy had a zit on his chin. The next day, I had a matching zit on my chin. The following Monday, we were the "Zit Couple" at school.

It was a very short relationship.

It was tough for me in high school. I had braces for six years to cure a vicious Bugs Bunny overbite and crossed front teeth like the creature in *Alien*. I had so many teeth pulled that I almost became addicted to "sweet air" at the dentist. Though I have very nice teeth now—a couple of friends even say my teeth look like dentures—no high school boy could look at me then and see into my smile's future. And I still wore a retainer at night in college. I freaked out this one brother during my first marijuana experience. He thought my face had melted or something.

Maybe marijuana wasn't all that he was doing that night.

And my first time was horrible. I was on the beach during spring break in Florida with a bottle of Hennessy and a boy—in that order—and the next thing I know, a cop is shining a flashlight on my ass. We never found the boy's underwear, and I found sand all up in my crevices for days after that. I haven't been completely celibate ever since, but I think I've got enough saved up to satisfy The One. At least I hope I do.

I have to give Ebony a shortcoming, something that embarrasses her that Johnny . . . Nicoletto will help her overcome. Where did "Nicoletto" come from? Must be a name from back in my childhood. What kind of shortcoming can I give her? She, of course, will rock his world, but nothing embarrassed Ebony. Nothing. Everything that girl did she did with style, grace, and flair, and she could dance so gracefully and—

Hmm. Would it be too ironic to have a black woman who can't dance? Oh, the letters Desiree will get. "Every black person I know can dance, ho!" the letters and e-mails will shout, probably in all capital letters. But not all black people can dance well, so why should I perpetuate a stereotype? This version of Ebony is going to break more of those so-called "rules" that book critics demand never be broken:

I guess the main thing my soul mate can't mind is the fact that I can't dance. I can't dance. At all. At least I can admit that, unlike that Vanilla Ice fool. I'm a little embarrassed about it, but at least I have the sense to stay seated at clubs while other hoochies practically have sex on the dance floor with their dance partners. That isn't dancing.

That's public dry humping.

At a sock hop in middle school, a friend of mine told me that I danced to the words and not the music—and I didn't even know the words. At my junior prom, I danced so wildly that I accidentally kneed my date in the groin. He sang like Michael Jackson for the rest of the night. In college, I enjoyed pinballing around the mosh pits, and even there I was a klutz. I know, a tall black girl flying around in a mosh pit isn't exactly what Malcolm X was talking about when he said, "By any means necessary." Anyway, I'd jump up when the rest of the moshers would hit the floor, and I would dive into their arms, only to end up with my nose cork-screwed into the floor.

I used to watch *Happy Days* when I was a kid and wish that I could dance like those freckled white kids. It looked so easy. Maybe I was born in the wrong decade. I even took a free dancing lesson from Arthur Murray Dance Studios. I more or less learned the bossa nova, and that night I went to a club and tried it out, only to find that doing the bossa nova by yourself looks whack. The dancers around me gave me plenty of room, and for that I'm grateful, but . . .

No, I'm no dancer. So my soul mate has to know that I can't dance, and he can't care that I can't dance. He can't mind if I nurse a drink at a club while he dances the night away. But he has to go home with me.

If he wants to.

I look up and see sunbeams winking on the bay. I am wasted, my eyelids as heavy as the waves rolling in, but I have one more chapter in me. I throw open every window in Henry's apartment, put "I Wish" on repeat-play, and let my fingers roll:

Chapter 2

I used to be a basketball star. I was a playground legend. No boy could outplay me. Maybe that was why I had so few dates. Still, it got me a scholarship for a full ride to Pitt.

Then I got pregnant. Didn't mean to. Just sort of happened. I don't want to talk about it because it happened so long ago, and my baby daddy isn't worth talking about except to say that he's been in and out of prison more times than those Hollywood stars go in and out of rehab. I'm not even sure where he is now, and I don't give a shit. I'm my daughter's mama and daddy, and that's all that's really ever mattered to me or to her.

Well, you know Pitt didn't want me after that, which is pure bullshit. They couldn't wait a few months for me to have the baby and then get back into shape. I wouldn't have been good for recruiting or something, I don't know. As big as I got, I might not have fit in the team picture. But the shit doesn't work the same way for the brothers. Seems like every last one of them has a baby somewhere, but that doesn't stop them from keeping their scholarships. They all have to be covered with tattoos and have a few chaps to earn high NBA draft choices.

So I had my baby—a little girl I named Candy—and started taking classes at Allegheny Community College while working as a housekeeper at the Airport Marriott. It wasn't my house, but I kept it. You wouldn't believe the shit that I had to clean up in that fancy place, and let me tell you, rich people's shit stinks, too. Worst four years of my life, but Mama and Daddy made it tolerable by keeping Candy for me, and I finished my associate's degree in child development in four years. Oh, I had a Jamaican man, Phillip, try to marry me, but he was only a cook at the Marriott. Probably needed me to keep his ass in the country.

At twenty-two, with the cutest four-year-old being spoiled rotten by my parents, I got it in my head to go to a real college. I got accepted at Clarion, walked on to the basketball team, and I kicked some serious ass for two years. There isn't a single-season rebounding or scoring record at Clarion that I don't still own to this day.

I also picked up my history degree along the way. Why history? I was always good at it, I wanted to know every little thing about every little thing since the day I was born, and I knew I could get a job somewhere teaching in the inner city because I'm black. There aren't many of us left teaching, much less teaching in the 'hood.

Now I'm teaching some of the orneriest suburban seventh graders, every last one of them trifling, and I'm also coaching Cherry Grove's girl's basketball team. Despite all my knowledge and mad skills, we haven't won but five games in the last ten years, and all five wins came against some Christian school that looked heavenly but played like hell.

The girls at Cherry Grove just don't have a single clue as to how to ball. Oh, they all know how to dress, because all their shit matches, right down to the little balls on their footie socks. But the bitches trip over the damn painted lines on the court half the time, fix their hair before they take a shot, check out little boys when they should be rebounding, and cry because they chipped a nail while dribbling. Trifling. I've tried to quit coaching them for the last four years, but no one at Cherry Grove wants to endure the embarrassment I've been through.

Candy? That child is smart, so maybe I created her all by myself. She got her daddy's sleepy eyes, but that's it. She's tall, and she can ball. But she's at Duquesne University on a partial academic scholarship because I didn't even let her apply to Pitt, and she is kicking ass in all her classes, but she won't play on the basketball team.

"I'm not into that anymore, Mama," she tells me. "I can't be a doctor if I'm at practice all the time."

That's right—my little girl is going to one day be a surgeon or a researcher or something medical like that. My baby is going to take care of me.

It's lonely in the condo without her, but it's okay. It's like I'm starting over or something. I know I still got game, I know I could probably contribute something to those WNBA teams out there even though I'm no model like that Lisa Leslie wench, but . . . I'm planning on getting a master's degree in education so I can get out of the classroom and into an office behind a damn desk where I can punish all these trifling, snot-nosed chaps. I'd make a good administrator. I'd be Ms. Joe Clark, and I wouldn't need a bullhorn or a bat. I have the "stare," and I know I make at least one crusty-faced boy pee his pants every week with that stare when I'm on hall duty.

Unfortunately, a master's degree costs money, and when your daughter only gets a partial scholarship to a private university, you have to rearrange your priorities. So I'm taking one night class at a time for the next, oh, seven years. Instead of jumping right in and getting bored to death with classes like "School Management," "Curriculum Review," and "Secondary School Law Mandates," I take a class in technical writing.

On the first night, I arrive early at Allegheny Community College and take a seat in the back row in a comfortable burgundy chair in front of a slate gray table. There isn't a single desk in here, and I already feel more like an adult. Out of habit, I slide my hand under the table. Not one bulging glob of gum. Maybe I should get a master's and teach somewhere like this. I mean, the room is carpeted, and the walls and ceiling are soundproofed. It's quiet. I like quiet. Seventh graders aren't quiet even though I make them be quiet. Shit, sometimes when the chaps aren't making any sound, I hear their little bodies growing.

I have to get me a teaching gig like this. The lights work, the clock works, and I bet that computerized thermostat by the door works, too. At Cherry Grove, I have to cuss and fuss at the custodian to get any of that shit working, and most times I have to rub an ice cube on the thermostat in my room to get the heat to come on. And the toys! The teacher has a huge TV/VCR hanging from the ceiling at the front of the room with speakers on each wall, an impressive computer on his desk that is hooked to the TV, and an overhead projector from this century. My overhead at Cherry Grove smokes like a crack addict every time I turn it on. I look with envy at the file cabinets with locks and the garbage can with a plastic liner.

I would love to teach history in a room like this. But it wouldn't be all white man's history. By the time I got through community college and then to Clarion, I was white man's history-ed out. I'd probably teach world history or one of those upper level courses in African history. I know all of that, and if the state of Pennsylvania would let me, my seventh graders would know all of that, too. But no, I have to teach to the damn statewide test, mainly on the history of Pennsylvania. Oh, I throw in lots of art history because I love the work of Jacob Lawrence to death, but there's only so much I can squeeze in because of that test.

A strange assortment of mostly old, married, white, and wrinkled people surround me, including an Italian guy who sits next to me.

Time to invent Johnny. Hmm. The critics roasted my last two main
male characters, saying they were too weak, wimpy, and easily con-
trolled. Johnny can't be, even if he'll look a little like me:

He isn't bad-
looking, maybe in his early forties, gray hair, coal-dark eyes, taller than
me, paler than the moon. No wedding band. He smiles at me as he sits, so
I cut off all the Italian jokes in my head. He has a nice smile, and it makes
his eyes look mysterious. I hope he sits next to me for the next fifteen
weeks.

And since there aren't any brothers up in here, I might actually learn
something about technical writing without getting hit on. I don't want to
be saying, "No, I am not a freshman, and no, you cannot have my phone
number, and yes, I am old enough to be your damn mama."

Though the attention might be nice.

Some white dude with a pockmarked face and thick glasses comes in
and says he's Professor Holt. He calls roll, and half of the class is missing.
When he gets down the alphabet to where I should be, I don't hear my
name. Probably because I added the class so late. I'm most likely at the
bottom of his roll sheet. When he calls out "Johnny Smith," the Italian
man next to me says, "*Ciao.*"

I have me some wicked-ass thoughts concerning "chow" after that
and start imagining all sorts of things, like how Johnny's pale skin would
look against my firm, black, round booty, but he definitely isn't a "Smith."
Who's he trying to fool? Maybe he's in the witness protection program.

And that's exactly where Johnny will be. Not exactly believable, but at
least the critics can't say Johnny's soft. I know I'm leaving myself open
for attack—"What are the chances that she happens to meet a guy at a
community college who's in the witness protection program?"—but anything's possible in romantic comedies.

"Welcome to Creative Writing," Professor Holt says.

Say what?

"We don't have a text for the class, though you might want to pick up
a copy of *Little, Brown* from the bookstore."

"Excuse me," I whisper to Johnny.

"Yes?"

"Did he say 'creative writing'?"

"Yes."

"This isn't technical writing?"

"No."

"I'm in the wrong place. I'm supposed to be in technical writing."

He smiles. "You want to take technical writing?"

I'd much rather be creative. "Not really."

"Then you are in the right place."

Damn, he got some fine eyes, but what the hell's that accent? He has to be from Brooklyn or something. "What should I do?"

"See *la professore* after class, and he will make the change."

Damn, he has a fine voice with just enough Italian accent to wet my panties. "Just like that?"

"Just like that." He leans closer, and I get a whiff of some exotic cologne. That shit definitely isn't Old Spice. "What is your name?"

"Ebony."

"Ah, a good name for you. You are a precious tree."

And then I shiver. I literally shiver there in that heaven of a classroom. Yeah, I say to myself, I am in the wrong place at the right time.

I push away from the laptop and massage my lower back. I know it's only a prologue and two chapters, but there are three parts, right? This ought to hold Henry for a while, maybe even get me a real advance.

Now if I could only hold the real Ebony . . .

Drifting off to sleep moments later on the couch, I dream of my precious tree, my E., my Ebony.

4

When I wake in the early afternoon, I realize that I'm hungry. I forget to eat when I'm writing, hot tea and soda keeping me going since I quit drinking two years ago, and the rabbit food in Henry's refrigerator looks stale, wilted, and rubbery.

I close the refrigerator.

Stale, wilted, and rubbery.

I now know how to grind out the history of the Underhills to start *my* book. But should I use first person or third? I don't want it to be a memoir. First-person memoirs get stale and whiny in a hurry, and third person will allow me a little poetic license to be selectively cynical and cruel. Third person it is.

Chapter 1

Peter Rudolph Underhill was a distant descendant of the Vikings and a recent descendant of the Underhills, a stale, wilted, and rubbery people from England who settled in and settled for Long Island when Long Island was young, Manhattan could be bought for the cost of a pair of bleacher seats at Yankee Stadium, and Native Americans were as yet unconverted by the sword to Christianity.

"Damn, that's harsh," I say to the screen. "True, though."

Captain John Underhill, Peter's most distant relation in so many ways, got kicked out of or left Puritan New England along with John Seaman and came to Hempstead, Long Island, during the seventeenth century to live among the more tolerant Dutch. There Johnny U. met and married a Dutch girl who promptly died, most likely of boredom because Henry Hudson's landing spot of Coney Island hadn't been invented yet, leaving him no choice but to marry an English Seaman girl.

"And the Seamans have been Underhill ever since," I say, repeating an ancient family joke.

Captain John is infamous for taking part in the killing of 120 Matinecock Indians, the very same Algonquin tribe who taught the early settlers the whaling trade that would rule Long Island for two centuries. And for this "heroism" that pacified a bunch of crabby English farmers, Captain John earned a monument to himself in Mill Neck—the strangest plaque Peter had ever seen. On one side of the plaque, John is hacking Matinecocks to bits with his sword. On the other side, he is reading the Bible to a smiling group of Matinecocks. John's philosophy must have been: "If they don't believe in God, I believe that I'll cut them to ribbons so they can meet God."

He was not the only Underhill to do this—just the first.

Peter Underhill lived with the other one.

"Okay, Captain," I whisper. "Let's write the history of you according to you." This will definitely not be another chapter of English history, since the Captain was about as English as the English muffins Henry has turning to dark green mold in his refrigerator.

If Peter believed all the stories that his father told him about his ancestry, Peter could write the most amazing tales of adventure on the high seas, adventures rivaling *Moby Dick* and any book in the Horatio Hornblower series.

Good thing Peter had a public school education and access to a library to keep his family history straight.

According to David Jonathan "The Captain" Underhill, his ancestors made Long Island what it is today. The Captain's kin were swashbucklers, legendary whalers, and expert sailors—so he said. In actuality, they were whalers and shipbuilders, barrel makers and carpenters, and rope and sail makers until the whaling industry on Long Island collapsed before the Civil War.

"Ah, that would be the life," the Captain often said about whaling. "Nothing between you and forty tons of wild whale but a sharp harpoon and the deep blue sea."

Whaling, Peter found out, was a brutal life filled with danger, stench, and little or no pay. Whalers, most of them Native Americans, former slaves, or poor whites with little or no schooling, would leave Long Island for voyages of several years to supply the world with whale-blubber oil, shoehorns, men's collars, umbrella stays, and hoopskirts.

Once the whaling industry went belly-up, the Captain's great-great-grandfather became a bay man in his pound boat, dredging the Great South Bay for bluepoint oysters.

"Ah, that would be the life," the Captain often told Peter about dredging. "Just you in an open boat, drifting or rowing through the shallows using your tongs"—heavy, long, iron-toothed rakes—"to harvest the best-tasting oysters in the world."

Until the oysters, too, went the way of the whale, Peter's grandfather dredged with steel-toothed nets and even started using a power dredge before the "Long Island Special"—the great unnamed storm of 1938—gave all those oysters and clams an early grave.

After Grandpa Underhill went to his own whiskey-induced early grave in 1939, Peter's father became a farmer for a few days. "Too much bending over, too much time on my knees, too much digging," he had complained. "Potato farming was like dredging on land."

He drifted along Long Island's south shore until he landed in East Hampton, where he became a fisherman using shore nets to catch menhaden or mossbunker before hiring himself on to a boat to help bring in cod, striped bass, bluefish, bonito, sea bass, and an occasional shark for tourists.

He also claimed to have saved the country from the Nazis.

"I was there in forty-two," he used to say to anyone who would listen. "Good thing, too, or we might have had us the Nazi invasion of Long Island."

According to the Captain, he was the one who found metal boxes that several Nazi spies had buried in the sand at Amagansett.

"I found them, and don't let anyone tell you different," he told Peter. "I saw the U-boat, and I found the box, and inside that box was a shovel and a bomb."

As a child, Peter believed his father's every word. "My daddy was a hero during World War Two," he would tell his friends.

"Come to think of it," I say to myself, "all our daddies were heroes back then."

While the Captain was indeed living near Amagansett in 1942, he had nothing to do with any of it. He was just a seventeen-year-old boy with a healthy imagination and probably heard John Cullen—the real Coast Guard hero—retell the tale of the shovel, a detonator that looked like a pen, an Army cap, and explosives disguised as a hunk of coal.

After that particular act of heroism, the Captain lied about his age and joined the U.S. Navy, shipping out on the battleship *Iowa* during both World War II and the Korean War.

And that's all I know about his war experience. He rarely told me anything about life aboard a battleship, not that I ever asked. I just assumed that he saved the country again and didn't want to brag about it. Other than the plank of wood from the *Iowa*'s deck that he had encased in glass to display on the *Argo*, there are no other artifacts from his military service. I'll have to do some more research here. It was such a huge chunk of his life—almost twenty years. Knowing him, he was hiding something. Either that or nothing on the *Iowa* required his particular brand of uncommon valor. I make a note to myself on a legal pad:

Research IOWA (1942–1953):
    areas of conflict (if any)
    Check Internet, USN records

"Now we can go to Levittown," I say to my last cup of Earl Grey. I'll have to get some more tea bags. And some more brown sugar, too. Regular sugar just isn't sweet enough.

When the Captain got out of the Navy after serving twenty years, primarily on and off the *Iowa*, he scraped up enough money to put twenty percent down on a house in Levittown—the so-called "Potato Field Miracle," America's first planned community. Then he retired and let his military pension pay his bills, acquiring his boat, the *Argo*, and sailing it whenever he pleased. The Captain seemed to prove the Old Norse adage: "Brave men can live well anywhere."

The Captain must have liked what he saw at first. He lived in a cramped, tiny house farther from the Sound and the ocean than he probably would have liked, and the house had one spindly tree in the yard, but somehow he stayed and found himself a wife. Maybe he liked Levittown because it was a town full of WW II and Korean War vets. Maybe he liked the block parties, the pig roasts, the volleyball and basketball games, and the conformist nature of the development itself. Maybe he liked the fact that all the houses looked alike, that no homeowner could say that his house was better. Maybe he just liked the closeness of it all, as if he were living on a beached, cramped battleship.

But there isn't a "maybe" about it. The Captain liked Levittown because it was one hundred percent pure Caucasian.

I save my work so far and run a few searches on the Internet for information on Levittown today. Not much has changed. Just three percent of Levittown is nonwhite, 1,600 (or 0.4%) of 40,000-plus residents are black. Houses that cost $8,000 back in 1948 are selling for $160,000 and up now. The racial covenants in the housing contracts are supposedly a thing of the past, but there are some awful long memories on Long Island. And I doubt that Levittown even has a single nonwhite realtor selling those little boxes.

The Captain was a racist

my fingers type before I can stop them. I pause a few moments. I've been thinking this about my father since I was thirteen, but I've never actually typed it or written it down. It's a powerful statement, and though it's true, do I want to brand my father a racist forever?

Of course I do. It's almost as if I have to.

The Captain was a racist. He oozed it in nearly everything he said or did from the time WPA workers showed up along Long Island's south shore after that terrible storm in 1938. Men, many of them black, were making two dollars a day cleaning up after a storm that wiped out his father. He didn't see them as helpful.

He saw them as responsible.

"Damn n——— showing up like they could do anything useful, getting paid for our misery."

From that point on, he hated anyone nonwhite. He was culturally, linguistically, institutionally, and environmentally racist, using the N-word and "colored" long after it was socially unacceptable or politically incorrect to do so, even among other racists. He was the only man Peter ever knew who cheered whenever Yankee slugger Reggie Jackson struck out, the only man in Huntington to root for the hated Boston Red Sox because they "only had that one Spic pitcher" (Luis Tiant). Peter remembered him rooting against the Jets in the 1969 Super Bowl since Joe Namath was an "eye-talian" with "hippie hair." The Captain made Archie Bunker, his favorite TV character, look like the Pope.

"Once them pickaninnies started getting into Levittown," he would say, "I knew it was time to leave before Levittown became a ghetto like every other colored neighborhood in this country."

He packed up in the fall of 1963 during "the third year of the reign of that Catholic anti-Christ"—John F. Kennedy, who the Captain considered a "snot-nosed rich kid who got lucky during the war"—and the Captain and his wife Helen Pearson Underhill (a waitress formerly of Troy, New York) moved to Huntington to a house they could barely afford in a neighborhood of upper-middle-class snobs who wouldn't give him or his family the time of day.

And that's when Peter Rudolph Underhill was born . . .

I can't write anymore. I'm getting too wired. All the tea, the brown sugar, Stevie Wonder, the memories.

To wind down, I surf the Internet for news of the outside world—much of it about the recovery efforts at Ground Zero—and decide to search once again for Ebony.

I've been looking for her online for five years now, without much success. Most people are anonymous online these days, using strange mixtures of numbers and letters for screen names. I'd plug in "Ebony" at the AOL or Yahoo member directories and watch the screen fill with possibilities. Two years ago, I came across an "Ebony Mills" living in Jamaica, Queens, found her phone number in the online White Pages, and gave her a call:

"Hello?"

I was so excited. "Is this Ebony Mills?"

"Yes, who's calling?"

I couldn't tell if it was Ebony or not since I was calling long distance. "Hi, this is Peter, Peter Underhill."

"Um, Peter who?"

"Peter Underhill. From Huntington."

"From Huntington." She had paused. "And you're calling because . . ."

"I want to see you."

"You do? Man, I don't even know you." *Click.*

I haven't called anyone named Ebony Mills since.

And I've always been afraid to take the next step once I've had a list of all those screen names: sending an e-mail.

Until now.

I reduce my search on AOL to all females in New York using "Ebony" somewhere in their screen names. That leaves me fifty or so in the state. I remove anyone not on Long Island—I can only hope she's still here— and have forty-four e-mails to write. Yahoo only yields six more, so it's an even fifty e-mails to send before I can sleep again.

After adding all these Ebonys to a temporary address book so I can write one letter and shoot it off to the entire group, I freeze.

I have no idea what to write.

I have been writing my ass off all day, and I can't write a few sentences in an e-mail to a group of perfect strangers—one who might be my Ebony. If I were Ebony, would I be offended if someone shot off an e-mail bomb like this to so many other people? I can't get too specific. Ebony would be pissed if I shared our business with the world . . . but then again, I already sort of *have* done that with my novels. Hmm. Short and sweet, just keep it short and sweet. I type "In search of Ebony Mills" in the subject line.

"Here goes nothing," I say as I type:

If you are Ebony Mills who once resided in Huntington (Huntington High class of 1981), please reply as soon as possible.

If you are not this particular Ebony Mills, my sincerest apologies.

Peter Rudolph Underhill

I hesitate a long time before clicking on the "send e-mail" button, my hands as sweaty as the day I first held Ebony's hand. What if all this is a waste of time? "Love is never a waste of time if it's done right," Toni says in *Ashy*. But am I doing this part right? "Boy," Bonita says in *The Devil to Pay*, "there ain't really a wrong way to make a move . . . so make it."

The little bell in the computer sounds, warning me that I'm about to be bounced off the Internet unless I do something.

I click the "send e-mail" button. A moment later, "Your mail has been sent" appears on the screen.

I clean out my in-box of all the junk mail, several trying to sell me Viagra at discount prices. I'm not that old yet. Then . . . I wait, watching to see if the little mailbox icon shows up on my screen.

Nothing happens for half an hour. What time is it? Oh, it's only 4:30. People aren't home from work yet. I turn off the CD player and turn up the volume on the laptop so I can hear "You've got mail!" I only plan to relax a few moments on the couch, settling my head deeply into a throw pillow.

And I promptly fall asleep.

5

I wake up yawning with the sunrise and casually look over at the laptop. It's on sleep mode, the green light blinking. I reboot, set it automatically to sign on to AOL, and head to the bathroom to piss away half a gallon of Earl Grey.

I know I'm setting the unofficial world's record for longest piss when I hear, "You've got mail!"

I race from the bathroom, my pants still unzipped, and click on the "get mail" button. I have twenty-seven messages!

I double-click the first one:

Fuck you! ! ! ! ! ! ! ! ! ! ! ! !

I get seven versions of the above, five that say "kiss my ass," one that says "kiss my black ass," and thirteen messages that say one way or another: "No, I'm not Ebony Mills." All are unsigned, and only one adds: "I hope you find her."

The last message is another "I'm not Ebony," but it intrigues me:

I may not be who you're looking for, but I might know the Ebony you've been looking for. Write back!

Destiny (Ebony31582@aol.com)

And say what? How much more information does she need to know? And why is someone named Destiny using "Ebony" in her screen name? I reply with:

I knew Ebony Mills in Huntington from 1976-1981. We attended R.L. Simpson Junior High and Huntington High together. She used to live on Grace Lane, a couple blocks from where I lived on Preston Street.

Peter

I send the e-mail into cyberspace, then take a much-needed shower, leaving my dark hairs all over Henry's tub. I'm only here to write, not to clean.

When I get out, I look at a full-length mirror on the back of the bathroom door and analyze what forty years can do to a body. More salt than pepper in my hair. Wrinkles winging from my eyes to my receding hairline. Ear hair. Zits I've never been able to outgrow on my forehead and chin. Pores as big as pencil points. Gray nose hairs I can't trim fast enough with a pair of fingernail clippers. Hairy legs except for my naked knees and ankles where years of pants have erased their memory. The single hair on my chest that grows up to six inches long before I notice and pluck it. The hair that grows on top of my nose. My teeth a series of root canals, caps, and cavities. Rainbow veins wherever I look. Mysterious bruises that take months to heal. Freckles that become moles. Toes gnarled from hitting bedposts late at night, one missing a nail.

I am not a pretty man.

I borrow Henry's white bathrobe and slippers—he must go through lots of bleach—and return to the laptop.

No message yet.

Reduced to drinking instant coffee, I wolf down several slices of white bread slathered with strawberry jam. I dial Henry's office and leave a message for him to call me immediately. When I'm writing, I don't like any interruptions, especially the phone. The TV has to be off, only seventies music playing to inspire me.

"You've got mail!"

Though it's probably my daily headlines from the *Times*, I rush over anyway.

But it's from Destiny:

I know your Ebony Mills! We used to work together. Unfortunately, I don't
know exactly where she is right now (sorry). She's even unlisted in the
phone book. I wish I could help you more!

Since I think she's still currently online, I try to Instant Message her
using her screen name, Ebony31582:

PRU7:   Destiny? This is Peter Underhill.

I only have to wait a few seconds.

Ebony31582:   You're up early.

PRU7:   So are you. If you're getting ready for work, I
                 can IM you later.

Ebony31582:   I've got time.

PRU7:   Where did you and Ebony used to work?

Ebony31582:   At Alcyone Corporation in Seaford. She didn't
                 live in Seaford though. I think she lived up to-
                 ward Jericho somewhere. We made
                 handmade jewelry together.

Seaford is just a ferry ride and half an hour in a car away from here!
And Ebony still makes jewelry? She used to make dozens of those friendship bracelets, the ones you were supposed to let rot off your wrist, way
back when.

Ebony31582:   You still there?

PRU7:   Yes.

Ebony31582:   Where are you writing from?

PRU7:   I'm on Fire Island.

Ebony31582:   Why there?

PRU7:   Long story. Where do you live?

Ebony31582:   Don't take this personally, but I don't give out
                 my address on the Internet. Let's just say that
                 I'm not too far away, ok?

PRU7:   Sure. What else can you tell me about Ebony?

Ebony31582:   What do you want to know?

PRU7:   Is she married?

Ebony31582:   I don't think so.

I breathe a heavy sigh of relief, though I really shouldn't. It isn't as if I'm going to rekindle our romance twenty years after the fact. That kind of romance only happens in the movies. I feel like an awkward seventh grader asking the next question:

PRU7:   Does she have a boyfriend?

Ebony31582:   I don't know for sure. She always has men in-
                 terested in her.

PRU7:   She was so beautiful.

Ebony31582:   She IS beautiful. She doesn't look her age at all.
                 Somehow she doesn't age. Makes me jealous.

PRU7:   Where was the last place Ebony lived?

Ebony31582:   I don't know. Hey, I gotta go. Talk at ya later.

PRU7:   Just one more question: Has she ever men-
                tioned me to you?

I stare at the screen for several minutes waiting for her reply, but Destiny is really gone. I try to IM her again, but "Ebony31582 is not currently signed on" flashes on the screen. I write her a quick e-mail:

Destiny:

Please feel free to reply or IM me anytime. I'll probably be online off and on all day today.

Peter

Instead of painstakingly editing what I wrote yesterday—my usual procedure—I press on as rosy fingers of red sky steal across the bay.

Chapter 2

For Peter Rudolph Underhill, life with Dave and Hel Underhill was a trip, a gas, and plain outta-sight.

But Peter would be lying if he said that. Life with Hel and the Captain was a bad trip that ran out of gas long before Peter was born, and Peter spent most of his childhood playing out of sight.

By myself. Being an only child was rough. I had no one to play with or to boss around or to blame. I had no one ahead of me to take the brunt of my parents' first attempts at parenting, no one behind to protect. If something ended up broken, I had to have done it. If something went missing, I was responsible for finding it since I had obviously lost it. There was no suspense at Christmas, no hand-me-downs, no fights over the last cookie, no giggling when a sibling got punished instead of me— and I got punished by spanking often. It wasn't exactly spanking; it was more like lashing or flogging. "Spare the rod and spoil the child," the Captain would say, his Bible open in front of him, a thin belt in his hand. "This is where it says in the Good Book that I can hit you." I'd bend over a chair, my buttocks exposed to the world, and I'd have to count out the lashings: ten if I had only talked back to Mom, twenty if I hadn't done my chores to the Captain's satisfaction, and one time thirty for "borrow-ing" change from his coat pocket. The Captain ran a tight ship, all right, and a major part of that ship involved God.

Out of sight mainly meant church. Peter grew up in the Methodist church that baptized him as an infant, chastised him as a sinner until he repented at the ripe old age of four, and confirmed him as a member at twelve. Sunday school, morning worship, then the night service. Wednesday night prayer meeting. Friday night youth night. Five services every week.

Peter learned that God was not like his father, though God was indeed the "Captain of his soul," that He was Peter's heavenly Father with a cap-ital *F* who would smite him for disobeying his parents. Peter prayed for his salvation every time he attended church, afraid that he would go for a long swim in the fiery lakes and rivers of Hell with a capital *H* if Jesus wasn't in his heart when he died. Peter accepted Jesus as his Savior with a capital *S* so often that He with a capital *H* was getting frequent-flyer miles to Peter's soul.

Peter was just never sure of his salvation, mainly because Reverend Epson's son, Ian, smoked, had green teeth, and dressed like a member of the rock group Kiss. Ian wore high platform shoes, and sat in the front row with black and white greasepaint smeared on his face, sticking out his tongue at the little choir behind Reverend Epson. If a pastor's son was such a hellion, then who was Peter, the son of the Captain and Hel, to get into heaven?

In between church and school, Peter stayed inside at home and tried to be good.

But that would be a lie, too. Peter did everything in his power to get out of that house, but the Captain wouldn't let Peter "mingle among those heathen out there." Instead, Peter was stuck with a thundering fa-ther who cursed him and drank heavily and read from the Bible, and a cloudy mother who nursed him and drank more heavily and kept every-thing "shipshape for the Captain" while secreting away a small fortune in change and small bills in Campbell's Chicken and Stars cans in the pantry. "For a rainy day," she once told Peter.

"Those heathen" were the Underhills' many neighbors, none of whom were really heathens to Peter. They were the Melting Pot Players, appearing daily and nightly outside the balcony-seat window of Peter's room. They were always more entertaining than the three channels on TV.

Peter used to watch his neighbors from his bedroom windows, wishing somehow that he and his family were more like them. Like the Tuccis next door, who spoke Italian and sat in lawn chairs smoking and drinking wine and laughing and talking with their hands and fighting. Or like the Hites across the street, whose old grandmother spoke only German, who used to cook out every nice day and ate bratwurst and wieners and drank beer from tall glasses and generally got fat together. Or like the Steins, who used to throw block parties with music and lights strung between trees over which they sometimes played volleyball while sipping Budweisers and coming out of the house with just-baked cakes and pies. Or the Mathers, whose father worked in New York City on a TV game show that featured a huge maze, who were always out in the street playing kickball and basketball and kick-the-can and street hockey and curb-to-curb football, sweating together as a family.

Peter's father simply never went outside unless he had a "damn good reason." He built a huge deck anchored to the slope behind the house to "raise the value of the house," a house, Peter later learned, that had been creeping inch by inch toward that sandy slope and could one day tumble into the woods above Huntington Harbor. The Underhills ate out on the deck once. Once. Other than tending to the grungiest red and pink geraniums ever planted in the gaudiest white plastic planters on the front porch, the Captain did nothing to the yard except cut it once a week, never bagging or raking up the clippings and clumps, because "it's good for the soil if you let it all rot."

Peter saw his first Fourth of July fireworks shows from his bedroom window, wishing that he were rocketing over Huntington Harbor like the Apollo astronauts who were always doing something outta-sight on the TV. He spent most of his childhood in his room, cleaning, making his bed until pennies bounced off it, doing homework, reading books like *Sounder* and *The Bermuda Triangle*, building model ships and getting high off the glue fumes, and staring out into the woods behind his house, woods that sloped right down from the backyard deck past a dance studio to the sand and rock shore of Huntington Harbor. Peter was only a ten-minute walk from the water, but he could only go to the harbor when the Captain wanted to play sailor every weekend.

Other kids—like Eddie Tucci, Eric Hite, Mickey Mather, and Mark

Brand—could stroll through Peter's woods past the "Cave," an old concrete cistern covered with graffiti, and disappear into the trees any time
they wanted, coming back up the hill laughing and munching on Dolly
Madison cakes or chewing on beef jerky or sucking down RC Colas in tall
bottles that they bought at Milldam Bait and Tackle. Sometimes they
wore baseball uniforms, other times matching football jerseys. They had
freedom that Peter could only dream about. Each one of them was living a
boy's life; Peter only had a subscription to *Boy's Life*.

"And then Mom left," I whisper. "She freed herself, and that freed
me."

Peter would never be one hundred percent sure why his mother left,
since he hadn't spoken to her since that day in December 1975, and he
hadn't even gotten so much as a postcard, but one thing Peter knew for
sure: Hel hated each and every sinew of the Captain's salty, seagoing
guts.

Peter had seen and heard the signs well before her departure. But because he was a child, he didn't understand the sarcasm in his mother's
voice when she said, "We can't *possibly* start the day without the
Captain's hot cup of damn Joe," or "Everything is just hunky-fucking-
dory, Petey." He didn't notice all the ingredients she bought at the pharmacy that she stirred into the Captain's whiskey sours—"Just a little
something extra special to help the Captain sleep." He didn't see the
splotches on her face as bruises—just as gobs of makeup.

Christmas Eve 1975, another Christmas Eve service at the Methodist
church. Dripping candles, wilting poinsettias, whining carols, never-end-
ing prayers, Ian sticking his tongue out, the familiar reading from Matthew.
Peter was twelve. During a guitar and flute performance of "What Child
Is This?" his mother rose from the pew, kissed him on the forehead, said,
"Be good, Petey," and left the sanctuary.

"Woman always has to go to the head," the Captain growled. He never
lowered his voice, even in church, for he was always at sea, and this particular Christmas Eve he was swimming on a half-dozen whiskey sours.
"She never could learn to hold her piss."

And that's the last time Peter ever saw his mother.

The next morning, after finding no Campbell's Chicken and Stars cans
in the pantry, Peter opened his gifts, and his father said nothing.

Nothing.

One day she was there, the next she was gone. Peter didn't like God much for that, but he wasn't going to tell Him. He had been praying for more freedom, for more excitement in his life, for something other than what he was experiencing every day. He wanted to tell God that He had missed, that His aim was off, that He was throwing too many breaking balls out of the strike zone. Though Peter was the one who prayed for the gift of freedom, his mother got to open that gift, and Peter became the Captain's favorite Seaman Recruit to kick around from that day on.

Luckily, Peter knew where his mother had hidden the sleeping pills, the ones she used to crush to a fine powder and later slip into the Captain's last whiskey sour of the day. Peter found that using a rolling pin was fairly effective and quieter than using the little hammer his mother had used, so he filled a plastic bag and emptied half of it into the Captain's third whiskey sour the day after Christmas. The Captain was three sheets to the wind and out like the lights on the Christmas tree within twenty minutes.

Once Peter started powdering the Captain's morning cup of Joe, he was finally free to roam the neighborhood . . .

Henry would want more back story here. He would say that I'm only scratching the surface, like the gulls outside my window swooping over the bay and dipping their wings into the foamy crests of waves. He would ask: "How did your mother's leaving make Peter feel at the time? Won't the reader find it hard to believe that it was 'business as usual' on Christmas morning without Peter's mother there? And wouldn't Peter's father react in some other way than saying 'nothing'?"

Maybe I've repressed a few things, but this is what I remember: the Captain sipping his coffee while I opened my gifts, eating limp bacon and watery eggs in the kitchen, going out on the *Argo* for our traditional Christmas Day cruise of Huntington Bay, and watching TV that night. Neither one of us spoke of Mom, and life continued pretty much as before the following day. Henry will have trouble accepting it, but Henry didn't grow up with the Captain.

The phone rings. Speak of the devil.

"Hello, Henry."

"How did you know it would be me?"

"A little birdie told me."

"Okay, well, I got your message, Pete. Everything okay? How's the novel coming?"

Which one? And I'm not "Pete" to anyone anymore. "Everything's fine. I owe you some Earl Grey." And your apartment is still far too white even with all the curtains open. I feel the need to spill something and leave a stain.

"Don't worry about it. Will you have three chapters for me by Friday?"

"How about a preface and two chapters?"

"I'd rather have three chapters, Pete."

Damn. There goes my afternoon. "Sure thing. You want me to e-mail them to you?"

"No, I'll be coming down for the weekend. I'll read them when I get there."

But there's only one bed, Henry. Oh, and the couch. "I'll tidy up before you get here."

"Having a wild party without me, Pete?"

My name is Peter. "Yeah." Just me and some wild memories.

"Really? Who all is there?"

"I've only seen Carlton, Henry. I'm having a party of one."

"Too bad. How's the Poet looking?"

"I don't know. Tan. Is he a Jets fan?"

Henry laughs. "Is he ever! Carlton hasn't missed a home game since sixty-nine. I'll bet he's been wearing green."

"Yeah."

"He looks good in green. So how do you like the apartment?"

I still don't have the advance money, so I lie. "You have the nicest place, Henry. It's *trés chic*."

"Thank you. You don't think the White Album is a bit much?"

"Oh, no. In fact, I think you should hang a picture of Barry White, too."

"Funny. So I'll see you this Friday?"

"I'll still be here."

"And if you want some scrumptious scallops and a place to forget your troubles for a few hours, go to Le Lethe. It's just around the corner from you."

"Henry, I can barely afford the rental car sitting across the bay." The Nova is costing me fifty bucks a day just to get encrusted with salt.

"Tell the boys at Le Lethe that you're a good friend of mine, and they'll put it on my tab."

"I'll think about it."

"Take care, Pete."

"I will." *Hen*.

I hang up and check my e-mail. Nothing from Destiny. More Viagra mail. An offer to "Work at Home and Make $2000 a Week with Your COMPUTER!!!" An invitation to check out Mars Computer's new laptop. I read the e-mail and chuckle over the company slogan: "Proving that High Price Doesn't Mean Quality!" Another e-mail begs me to "UP-GRADE YOUR LIFE for just $89.99!" Now that's a bargain and a half. The last, from some dyslexic company playing on the fears and paranoia of a computer virus-plagued society, claims to be the only safe way to survive in the twenty-first century, because "If you <u>stink</u> your safe, your probly not."

I delete them all and check the outline for my book:

Chapter 3: January 1976

      *street hockey
      *description of friends
          Mark Brand
          Eric Hite
          Mickey Mather
          Eddie Tucci
      *meeting Ebony for first time
      *home; conversation with the Captain
      *perpetual tans

"Henry, you'll just have to wait," I say to myself. "I want to have a little fun." I look at the white coffee cup, the rim stained with two days of tea and instant coffee. The cup looks good with a tan.

Chapter 3

Once the Captain fell asleep in his La-Z-Boy "commodore's chair" one unusually warm Sunday afternoon a few days after Christmas, Peter es-

caped the house and ran down to the cul-de-sac at the end of Preston
Street to watch a street hockey game up close. He used to watch them
from his window, but it was like watching a hockey game on TV without
the sound.

And everybody was there: Mark Brand, bony and blond with hands
too big for his body; Eric Hite, who had no height, with shaggy hair and
no athletic skills; Eddie Tucci, fat and red-faced, with puffy hands and a
gigantic nose; and Mickey Mather, the only one of the bunch who had a
crew cut and any idea how to play hockey. They each wore T-shirts with
"P-Street Rangers" written crudely in black Magic Marker on the front,
each with his own gray duct-taped number on the back. They used hockey
sticks that had wooden shafts and plastic blades and smacked around a
hard orange ball that Eric kept hitting into the sewer. Eddie was the goalie
and wore what looked like couch cushions tied to his legs with shoe-
strings, a catcher's mask, and a first baseman's mitt.

Peter thought they were the coolest foursome on earth.

"If the sewer was the goal, Eric, we'd never lose," Mark said as Eric
squeezed through the gap between the sidewalk and the grate into the
sewer. Then Mark noticed Peter. "What you doin' out, Peter-eater?"

It was the rumor at Southdown Elementary, then at Woodhull, where
only sixth graders could go, and now at R.L. Simpson Junior High that
Peter was a soft mama's boy, allergic to air and dirt. Peter had to wear a
navy blue pea coat to school on every cold day, and a couple times he
heard some kids calling him the "Flasher." And since Peter didn't play
any sports, the others thought that Peter had to be gay.

"Just came out to watch is all."

"Watch us lose is more like it," Eddie said. "Blackberry Bruins are gonna
kill us unless Eric quits fuckin' around. Mickey, when's Willie gonna get
here?"

At the mention of Willie Gough's name, Peter cringed. Willie was the
meanest boy at Simpson, always picking fights with kids bigger than
him—and Willie was smaller than Eric. But Willie never lost. Never. He'd
always still be standing at the end, his knuckles cut to shreds, the other
kid bleeding and crying for his mama.

"Willie ain't comin'," Mickey said, passing the ball back and forth as
he ran toward the goal, which looked like an overgrown chicken coop. He
cracked off a shot that nearly knocked over the goal.

"We can't play 'em with only four, Mickey," Mark said.

"Petey can play, can't you, Petey?" Mickey asked Peter.

Peter had never played a second of hockey before in his life, but he lied and said he could. A few moments later, he was tearing off home to get a white T-shirt. The second he returned, Eddie made Peter a P-Street Ranger, taping the number seven on to Peter's back.

Mickey handed Peter an extra stick, one with a chewed-up wooden blade. "It still works," he said. "Take a shot."

Peter lined up the shot and walked around the ball.

"This ain't golf, Peter-eater," Mark said.

Peter ignored him and slammed the ball into the goal from about thirty feet away.

A cul-de-sac street hockey legend had just been born.

But when the Blackberry Bruins showed up, Peter knew he was in trouble. They were all eighth and ninth graders from Simpson, and they had real Bruins jerseys and helmets, knee pads, elbow pads, and shiny new sticks.

"They ain't so tough," Mickey told me. "They just got more money."

"First to ten wins?" a tall, skinny boy named Chad said.

"Gotta win by two," Mickey said. "And no slashing."

"We won't," Chad said.

Chad lied. The Bruins slashed the P-Street Rangers to death with their sticks, hacking at shins until the Rangers spent more time limping than running. The Rangers were down seven to two in less than ten minutes, Eddie flinching and turning sideways every time a Bruin took a shot, Eric whiffing on the ball, Mark fussing and cussing, yelling, "I'm open! I'm open! Pass me the damn ball, you guys!" Peter did the best he could, but he was so much smaller than the Bruin players and often got pushed away from the action.

Mickey called a time-out. "Okay, Petey, you play goal for a while, give Eddie a break."

"Thank you, Peter-eater," Eddie said, and he took off his pads. "I'm sweating to death."

"Eric, you stay back with Petey," Mickey said. "We're gonna have to cherry-pick a little to get back in the game, so Mark, you hang out near their goal. Me and Eddie will try to feed you."

Eddie tied the pads to Peter, the tops nearly reaching Peter's chest.

The pads definitely smelled like garlic. He handed Peter his goalie stick and first baseman's mitt and slapped the catcher's mask on Peter's head.

"Don't lose it for us," Eddie said. "And whatever you do, don't be a pussy and flinch."

And Peter didn't. That little orange ball hurt like hell when it hit Peter where the pads weren't, and he would have to ice down his shoulder afterward, but Peter didn't duck or turn away at all. They bounced one between his black high-topped Chuck Taylor sneakers, and squeezed one in behind him after he made a nice first save, but that was all.

Peter held them to nine.

Meanwhile, Mickey's plan was working, because Mark was an excellent shot, using his bony elbows to get the bigger boys out of the way. And whatever bounced off the Bruins' goalie, Mickey slammed home. Eddie simply got in the way of their players, and Eric tried to stay out of sight so Peter could see the shots better.

Just as Mickey scored the tying goal, Peter noticed a black girl walking toward the action. He had never seen her before, and he knew just about everyone in the neighborhood by sight after months spent perched at his window seat.

"What the hell's she doin' here?" Mark asked Mickey.

Mickey shrugged. "Free country."

"It's like we're having an eclipse or something," Eddie said with a laugh.

Ebony was dark, but she moved onto that cul-de-sac just like the poet said: "in beauty like the night." Peter was smitten with Ebony Mills from the second he saw her. She wore an oversized New York Knicks jersey that hung down to her knees, straight-legged Levi's rolled up at the bottoms, and Adidas sneakers, and her hair was in tight braids wrapped in a circle around her head.

And instead of being shy and waiting to be spoken to, Ebony marched right up and said, "Y'all need another player?"

I sit back from the computer and relive that moment. Mark looked at Mickey. Eddie looked at Mickey. Eric looked at Mickey. The Bruins looked at Mickey. I looked at Ebony. What must have been going through their minds! I only saw a shapely girl with a dynamite smile and more guts than I'd ever have. And that Mickey—damn, I wonder what he's doing now. I need to thank him for what he said and did next:

"Sure. Eric, take a break."

"I ain't givin' her my stick!" Eric shouted.

Mickey snatched Eric's stick in a flash and held it out to Ebony. "You good on defense?"

Ebony rolled her neck, her chin making a constant circle in the air in front of her. "What, you think cuz I'm a girl that I can't score?"

Mickey's eyes got big. "Okay, you play forward. Eddie, you drop back."

"Nah, nah," Eddie said, puffing out his chest. "I ain't gonna."

Ebony stared him down. "Boy, you so fat that pigs be followin' you home lookin' for a date."

And though Eddie was his teammate, Peter laughed out loud. This girl wasn't afraid of anything or anybody. And her accent—somewhere between deep South and Brooklyn or maybe even South Brooklyn—was cool and beat the snot out of the dull "Lawn GUY-land" accents in Peter's neighborhood.

I found out later that Ebony's family had been part of the northern migration from Virginia after what Ebony's mother, Candace, called the "first Emancipation." They lived in Brooklyn until the "second Emancipation" in the late sixties and early seventies that brought them east to Huntington. Ebony was a mixture of street and country, African and a little Cherokee, and the overall result was honey with a heavy dose of vinegar and salt.

Eddie, who normally had a comeback for everything since he read those little paperbacks full of mean jokes, backed off to play defense without another word.

"Let's play," Ebony said . . . and the girl could play. She was almost as good as Mickey, stealing the orange ball away from one of the Bruins and scoring on her very first shot.

"What's the score?" she asked.

"Ten-nine us," Mickey told her.

Chad got up in Mickey's face. "That don't count. She ain't on your team. She ain't from your neighborhood."

Ebony stepped over to Chad. "What don't count?"

Chad ignored her. "It's still tied nine to nine, and you gotta put Eric back in."

"Excuse me?" Ebony said. "You sayin' cuz I ain't from this neighborhood that it don't count?"

Chad turned to her. "Yeah. That's what I'm saying."

"Well," she said, with a dynamite smile, "I *am* from this neighborhood. I just moved in over on Grace Lane."

Which meant she'd be at Simpson once the holiday break was over. Peter hoped that she was in the seventh grade, but her body was definitely eighth or ninth grade, because of her breasts.

"Grace Lane ain't Preston Street," Chad said.

"And you ain't shit playin' hockey, boy," Ebony said. "All the cool shit you got on, and you can't play a lick. You just mad a girl scored on you. And you just scared I'm gonna score on y'all again."

"I ain't scared."

"Prove it then," she said.

We were all in that nowhere land between puberty and manhood, and to let a girl beat you—in anything—was like losing your penis. Chad didn't know what to do or say that day, and I just had to say something.

"Why don't you let her play?" Peter asked, though it came out more as a statement.

"You shut up," Chad yelled at Peter.

Ebony then pushed Chad back. "Who you tellin' to shut up, boy? You talking to"—she looked back at Peter and smiled—"what's your name?"

"Peter."

She put a finger on Chad's chest. "You talkin' to Peter, and he's my boy. You don't tell any of my boys to shut up." Chad didn't make a sound. He didn't even seem to be breathing. "Now are we gonna play or what?"

"It still doesn't count," Chad said. "It's still tied, nine to nine."

"Whatever," Ebony said. "Let's play."

They played on, but for only a few minutes more. Ebony bulled her way in for a stuff shot to put the P-Street Rangers up by one, and when the Bruins brought up the ball after that, Ebony stole it, fed Mickey through Chad's legs, and Mickey faked out the Bruins' goalie, leaving him lying in the street before tapping the ball into the net.

After the game, Ebony walked up to Peter. "Turn around."

Peter turned around. He wasn't going to argue with her.

"Number seven. That's my favorite number, you know that?"

"Um, what's your name?"

She smiled and looked down at the ground, proving to Peter that she had a shy streak as long as his own. That was really when Peter's heart became Ebony's, the image of her smiling shyness passing into his soul forever. "Ebony Mills." She flashed her eyes briefly at him. "But you can call me 'E' if you like."

"Okay."

Then she turned to Mickey. "When am I gonna get a jersey?"

Ebony got her jersey that very day, talking Mark out of wearing number twelve.

The others had already fanned out to go home, and that left Ebony and Peter walking back toward his house.

"Are you gonna go to Simpson?" Peter asked.

"Where else am I gonna go?"

"I dunno. You could go to St. Pat's like Eddie."

"No, thanks. Them Catholic kids is too wild for me. I'm going to Simpson. You go there?"

"Yeah."

"What grade you in?"

"Seventh."

"Me, too."

A seventh-grade girl with ninth-grade breasts? Peter thought. *There is a God!*

They arrived at the driveway of Peter's house. "This is, uh, this is my house."

"You got anything to drink in there?"

"Um, yeah. I could get you a soda."

"You ain't gonna invite me in?"

Peter wanted to, but if the Captain were awake . . . "My father, uh, he hasn't been feeling too well."

"Uh-huh."

Peter knew that she didn't believe him. "Actually, um, he's probably asleep."

"Right."

Peter knew that she still didn't believe him. "No, really."

Neither said anything for the longest time.

"You gonna get me a Coke or what?"

"Oh, sure."

Peter sneaked through the back door into the kitchen, heard the Captain's snores like the gurgling of a clogged bilge pump, and returned to Ebony with a Coke. She wiped off the top of the can with the hem of her Knicks jersey, and Peter caught sight of the most beautiful belly button. She had the tiniest little "inny" no bigger than a licorice gumdrop.

"What you lookin' at, Peter?"

"Uh, nothing."

"Uh-huh." She smiled. "You lookin' at my stomach, right?"

Peter nodded.

"Bet you got an 'outie' with all sorts of green shit inside it."

"I got an inny, too," Peter said, hurt.

She squinted. "Prove it."

There on his driveway after a sweaty game of street hockey, Peter showed a girl his "inny."

She crouched lower to have a closer look. "Dag, boy, you got freckles like that all over?"

Peter dropped his shirt. "Most of them aren't freckles. They're moles, like this one." He touched the mole just above his upper lip.

Then . . . she touched the mole under Peter's nose. Her finger was cold from holding her can of Coke, and Peter nearly jumped out of his Chuck Taylors. "Does it hurt?"

"N-n-no."

She pulled back her hand. "You cold?"

"Your finger is." *And it's electric*, he thought. *Her fingers are made of cold electricity.*

"Sorry." She took a sip. "You got moles like that all over your body?"

"No."

"Good, cuz they nasty." She finished her Coke and handed it to Peter. "Thanks for the Coke."

"You're welcome."

She smiled. "See you around, Peter."

"Yeah. See you around . . . E."

Without thinking, Peter floated in through the front door of the house, a hockey stick in his hand. Then, because he was still thinking of Ebony's licorice gumdrop belly button and her electric ice-cold finger, he tripped on the carpet runner at the base of the stairs, and the hockey stick clattered against the wall.

"What the hell you think you're doing out there, Pete?"

Peter slid the stick into the hall closet, ripping off his jersey and throwing it up over the second floor stair railing. "Just slipped, Captain."

"Come here," he said.

Peter walked into the TV room, hoping his face didn't look as windburned and raw as it felt. It seemed as if the Captain hadn't moved from his La-Z-Boy since Peter delivered his mug of coffee a few hours ago.

"I just slipped on the stairs, Captain."

"You been upstairs all this time?"

Peter had already sinned by drugging the Captain's coffee, so one more sin wouldn't hurt. "Yes, sir."

"Doing what?"

"Reading." Okay, two more sins.

"Oh." He reached for and nudged his coffee cup, a little spilling over the sides.

Peter held his breath. *He's hardly had any! Either I put way too much sleeping powder in his coffee, or he made another cup on his own and he's really been awake all this time. Then he knows I must be lying!*

The Captain took a sip and nodded his head. "You make a fine cuppa Joe, Pete."

"Thank you, sir."

"It's cold now." *Geez, I used too much! What did he have, one sip?* "But it's not bad. Maybe a little too much sugar." He held out the mug. "You mind warming this up for me?"

"No sir."

"Just set it on the little eye on the stove. It'll heat up just fine."

Peter took his cup. White powdery particles stared up at him. *I could have killed him!* "Okay."

Peter was almost to the hallway when the Captain called out, "And we won't be going to church this evening! Something on the TV I want to watch!"

Peter nearly dropped the mug. They hadn't missed a Sunday evening service since Peter was born, and today they had barely gotten up in time for the morning worship service.

Hel's departure was getting cooler all the time.

Peter set the mug on the eye and turned the dial to medium, and while he waited, he focused on the coffee until it bubbled.

He also focused on the girl with the licorice gumdrop inny and the perpetual tan: Ebony Mills. She bubbled, too.

He had always been attracted to girls with tans. Whenever he and the Captain took the Captain's Ford Country Squire station wagon down to the harbor and went out on the *Argo*, Peter would look for girls on other boats instead of paying attention to the Captain, which is probably why Peter never learned any of the ropes or how to properly sail a boat. He knew that he'd be a Seaman Recruit for life. Whenever they'd stop at any of the many marinas around Huntington, Peter would do his best to drag his feet whenever he saw some girls sunning themselves on other boats.

Once, at a marina in Northport, Peter had watched two older girls in bikinis lying facedown near the bow of their boat. Neither had her bikini top fastened in the back, and when the Captain blew the *Argo*'s horn, the tanner of the two looked up at Peter, giving him his first glimpse of a girl's breasts. Since all he knew about breasts came from the Song of Solomon in the Bible, Peter could only compare them to little fawns.

I was so naive sexually. In sixth grade, Woodhull required all boys to sit with their dads or moms at a big sex education meeting complete with overheads, a movie, and a question-and-answer period, which was punctuated by a question asked by Timmy "The Squirrel" Bottomley, a bigger geek than me: "What happens if the male should urinate in the vagina of the female?" On the way home, the Captain had asked, "Anything you didn't understand?" "No, sir," I had replied. And that was the only time in my life that the Captain ever talked to me about sex.

The girl's breasts weren't little deer at all, though they had two little button noses. Her breasts were two-toned—circles of white surrounded by bronze. And even after she flattened out and giggled something to the other girl, Peter was still staring. It wasn't so much that he had seen a girl's breasts; it was more that he had fallen in love with the contrast there, how the white part stood out against the brown, how the brown drew his eyes more than the white, how the brown made the white so much purer, more natural, more innocent and clean somehow.

Which probably destined me to pick out the exotic, the sensuous, the tan for the rest of my life—except for Edie. What went wrong there? She didn't have a cute inny, she didn't have rough hands, she didn't have long, shiny legs and flashing eyes. After Ebony, I had a cornucopia of the melting pot . . . but somehow I settled for Edie, who is whiter than this computer screen.

Which made him wonder that morning, as he watched the Captain's coffee boiling to a froth, if Ebony's breasts looked the same . . . or were they tan all the way to those little deer's noses?

Jesus, twenty-five-year-old memories are making me horny. I have to cool off, and Henry needs another chapter.

I know, I'll introduce Edie the Ice Queen into Ebony's classroom. That will cool me off. Edie could probably solve global warming just by being.

Chapter 3

Since I already know how to write, while Professor Holt rambles on and on about syllabus this and course requirements that and due dates the other, I take a closer look at Johnny. I don't grit on him out in the open, though. I sneak peeks by slowly taking off my coat while looking at him, gradually rolling my pen toward him then catching it—and his eye some-times—and painstakingly repositioning my chair until I am almost facing him. It's an art that I learned from watching the seventh grade hoochies in my classroom. They aren't nearly as subtle about it as I am, but they are effective. I know the little boys are popping boners left and right in my classes because of them, a few of them even having to sit at their desks after the bell rings until their jenks get back to normal.

Johnny is sort of a C-minus in a lot of little ways, but the overall pack-age is definitely a solid B. He does not have a handsome face—nose too big and bent, eyebrows looking like hairy spiders, ears sprouting gray hairs, skinny lips, cheeks and chin unshaven and scarred, hair too long and uneven in front. Taken apart, he's a scary man. Put it all together under those coal-dark eyes, and he's a relatively handsome scary man. His knuckles are bigger than they should be, big circular walnut-looking things, and his nails are way too short, like he chews them maybe. At least they're clean. His arms have more hair than arms should have. I'll bet I could comb and style the hair there. His arms are huge, muscular, his shoulders round, his neck pretty thick, his chest . . . probably so hairy a bird could nest up in there. I won't even imagine the hair on his back.

Dag, he could be in the Mafia!

But he doesn't wear a bowling shirt and polyester pants like those Mafia guys do in the movies. He sports a light blue oxford shirt, clean white T-shirt underneath, a thin gold chain barely visible, faded blue jeans, and black Nike hiking boots. He dresses kind of Wal-Mart, like me.

Then I see this pale blond girl standing in the doorway. She wears a tight light-pink T-shirt with the word "Angel" stenciled above her perky little breasts, the shirt leaving a gap where the whole world can see her pierced shiny white belly button. The girl has absolutely no hips, her legs are as skinny as broomsticks, and she's standing with one pink shoe turned ninety degrees to the side, like she's getting ready to do some ballet move.

"Pale Edie's in the house," I say with a smile. Coleridge had her down pat: "Her skin was as white as leprosy." Like paper. And she was always in some pose or other, as if she were the subject of some artist painting her in dreamy pastel oils. I swear that she used to dress to match the furniture in the house—pastels and white chiffon for the living room, earth tones for the family room. Sometimes when I looked at her lounging around the house, sighing mostly to herself, I envisioned her as a model in the pages of L.L. Bean and Lands' End catalogues. And those sighs drove me up the freaking wall!

I hear her sighing, only it's more like a constant hiss, like air slowly escaping from a bicycle tire, like a foot sliding across a concrete floor, like fingernails scraping across a damn chalkboard, like the sound the Sidekick makes on cold days but I can't find out where it's coming from and the mechanic says I must be hearing things and it pisses me the hell off!

It's that kind of sigh.

"May I help you?" Professor Holt asks.

"I think I'm supposed to be in this class," she says softly, almost in a whisper but more like a murmur. I know her game. She's trying to get our attention so we can see her, her matching pink-and-white angel's outfit, and the two hours of makeup slathered on to her face. All the girl is missing is a halo.

Professor Holt falls for it, walking to the doorway. "I didn't hear you."

And that's the first thing I ever said to Edie Elizabeth Melton, only daughter and youngest child of Edith Elizabeth Melton and William Strong, sister to William Strong, Jr., and Horace Strong Melton. I was grading papers in my classroom at Sewickley Academy, and there she was at the door, murmuring something, posing, sighing. Out of loneliness and a need that I still don't understand, I pursued her—and she was everything I didn't want in a wife. She was a debutante and dancer, a bleached-blond sigher, a daughter of privilege with dollar signs for eyes, and an all-around angel from hell who owned a horse, a car, and a boat named *Edie E.* by the time she was sixteen. She owned that "waif" look long before Kate Moss was even born. Told she had a dancer's body by some ballet director kissing William Melton's abounding buttocks, she became anorexic long before the term was well-known, taking brutal ballet classes that reduced her toes to stumps of calloused flesh. Since William Melton was on the board of a Pittsburgh arts council, she was a shoe-in for a spot in the Pittsburgh Ballet. It didn't happen, so she settled for me, a teacher at her old school.

She smiles at the rest of us, as if we really give a shit. "I think I'm supposed to be in this class." She hands him a piece of paper, jingling her fake-ass gold bracelets in the process. Oh puh-lease, honey. Get over yourself. You are just a late bitch who wants to make a grand entrance.
"You are . . .

Now what am I going to name her? Edith? Evie? Eden? Eve? If I make it too close to her real name, she'll sue me for half of my money for the book. But at the rate I'm going, Edie wouldn't want to admit that this character is her . . . would she? Who would admit, "I am that horrible person in that book"?
Edie might, especially if it involves money she didn't earn.
I'll just call her "Rose Goulet" for now. Where "Goulet" came from, I have no idea.

"You are . . . Rose, uh—"
"It's pronounced 'Goo-lay,' " she says.
She isn't a rose, and that last name isn't fooling anybody. It's probably pronounced Goo-LEE or GULL-et. This isn't the south of France. This is

southwestern Pennsylvania where folks drink Iron City beer and root for
the "Stillers" and the Buccos after a long week at the "still" mill.

"Have a seat, Rose."

I see her scan the room with her eyes, her light brown eyebrows probably painted on, her blondish eyelashes as thick as cat whiskers. She has
tiny ears, tinier gold earrings, a button nose, and two eyes made out of
green coal. I'll bet that she bleaches her hair, because her roots are dark
brown. Her eyes come to rest on the empty chair on the other side of
Johnny. One of her eyebrows rises, her skinny pink lips wrinkle, and she
moves in on my man . . .

I look at the clock on my laptop: 3:30 P.M.! I've been writing for close
to ten hours without food. Checking the word counts, I find I've com-
posed over five thousand words. I haven't written like this since—

I've never written like this. Why is that?

The white walls envelop but don't distract me, the quiet focuses me,
though the Poet's loud wanderings on the roof sometimes have me writing in blank verse, the sheer purity of the view of Great South Bay in-
spires me, and maybe even the lack of food makes me hungrier to write.
I'm losing weight and loosing words. I'm a monk in his cell transcribing
founts of prose in fonts of Courier and Times New Roman. I'm a . . .

I'm about all out of words for today.

I log on to AOL and quickly click on a reply from Destiny:

Peter:

Sorry if I was rude by leaving so suddenly this morning. I am always late
for work.

How long are you going to be on Fire Island? Any plans to get up to
Huntington?

Destiny

Which could mean that Destiny is in Huntington . . . or Ebony is in
Huntington. I try Instant Message again and find that Destiny is still online.

PRU7:   Destiny? It's me, Peter.

Ebony31582:   Hey.

PRU7:   Are you in Huntington?

Ebony31582:   Maybe.

PRU7:   Maybe?

Ebony31582:   I don't give out my address, remember?

PRU7:   You mentioned Huntington in your e-mail, so I
                     thought you were in Huntington.

Ebony31582:   I'm not in Huntington YET.

PRU7:   When will you be in Huntington?

Ebony31582:   Depends on when you ask me out. You are
                     trying to ask me out, right?

I have to catch my breath. I reread the script of the conversation. How
the hell did "Are you in Huntington?" turn into "You are trying to ask me
out, right?"

Ebony31582:   Earth to Peter . . .

PRU7:   I'm here.

Ebony31582:   Don't you want to meet your Destiny? :-)

This is getting weird. Destiny isn't Ebony, yet she is the best lead I've
had to finding Ebony after five years of searching. But has she told me
everything she knows?

PRU7:   Yes, I'd like to meet you, but the subject of our
                     meeting will be Ebony, okay?

Ebony31582:   You always have this problem?

PRU7:   What problem?

Ebony31582:   You have a one-track mind.

PRU7:   I just want to find her again.

Ebony31582:   Some date this will be.

PRU7:   It won't be a date.

Ebony31582:   You got that right. No wonder you have trouble with women.

PRU7:   Who says I have trouble?

Ebony31582:   I do. You're looking for a woman you haven't seen in 20 years, and you can't even be nice to someone who's trying to help you find her. Maybe we shouldn't meet at all.

Ouch. But she's right.

PRU7:   I'm sorry. I want to meet you.

Ebony31582:   You sure you want a date with me?

"It's not a date!" I shout at the screen.

PRU7:   Yes. But it's not a date, okay? Let's just call it a TALK over some coffee.

Ebony31582:   You don't have to SHOUT, and I don't drink coffee.

PRU7:   Neither do I. I prefer tea.

Ebony31582:   Are you English?

PRU7:   English and Dutch.

Ebony31582:   Does that mean you have albino freckles?

PRU7:   No. I get tan.

Ebony31582:   Sure you do. So where are you taking me?

PRU7:   Couldn't we meet somewhere?

Ebony31582:   What if I need a ride?

PRU7:   Do you need a ride?

Ebony31582:   No, but what if I did?

"Geez," I whisper. What kind of a woman is this?

PRU7:   If you need a ride, I'll pick you up.

Ebony31582:   So . . . where are we meeting for tea? I know a
                 nice place in Huntington Bay Village called
                 Lola Ristorante. It used to be called J.
                 DeCarlo's. You like Italian?

PRU7:   Not really.

Ebony31582:   We could go to Xando. It's a coffee shop on
                 Main St. with the BEST desserts. I'm sure they
                 have tea.

My pre-advance advance won't cover a Huntington Bay Village *ris-torante*. And at the rate coffee shops are extorting their patrons for a cup of double mocha cappuccino, I may not have enough for a glass of ice water at Xando. My Visa is almost maxed out, but I have a Discover card I rarely use.

PRU7: Xando sounds fine.

Ebony31582: Party pooper. Our first date is in a coffee shop
where we'll drink tea.

"It's not a date!" I yell again.

PRU7: When do you want to meet?

Ebony31582: You tell me.

PRU7: Is 7 PM on Saturday all right with you?

Ebony31582: It'll do. And don't stand me up, okay?

PRU7: I won't.

Ebony31582: You better not. I have SO much more to tell
you about Ebony.

PRU7: What else have you learned?

I sit glued to the screen, my fingers sweating on the keyboard. I know Destiny knows more than she's telling. Five minutes pass. Nothing. I check to see if she's still online, but Destiny's gone. I scroll through the conversation again and realize two things: I am being manipulated somehow, and Destiny is much better at this than I am. I may be in some serious trouble. And how am I going to escape Henry? And why did I set up a Saturday night meeting a long ferry ride and an hour's drive away from here?

But as the setting sun outside my window softly slips into the western horizon, I relax and feel the pull of the past calling me back to Huntington.

Calling me home.

6

It's early Thursday morning, "Thor's Day," and my head is pounding. I have to practically double my belt around my waist I've gotten so skinny. I need to eat, but I have too much to do.

I edit *A Whiter Shade of Pale* and only change "grey" (the English spelling) to "gray" (the American spelling). I guess I'm more English than I thought. The rest I leave alone. I have to give Henry something to play with, something on which he can bleed copious quantities of red ink. He seemed to enjoy working on *Ashy* more than *The Devil to Pay* for that reason. He gave me forty pages of suggestions for *Ashy* and only three for *The Devil to Pay*.

I look over my outline for chapter four of—

I don't have a working title for my own book?

I don't have a working title for my own book.

I always have at least a working title. This is strange. I open PRU7.doc. Why'd I name it that? Why didn't I give it a working title at that point? I look at my first chapter. No title above, no pertinent information of any kind. I try to remedy it:

Contemporary interracial/multicultural romance/memoir
@ 100,000 words
© 2001

It will be somewhat contemporary, won't it? So what if it takes place for the most part from 1976 to 1981. Is it more interracial than multicultural? I want to stir the melting pot, "God's Crucible," even if the poet Nikki Giovanni says that the melting pot never worked. Maybe it worked for me. As for the "romance/memoir" part, it's getting there. So far, I'm a motherless white boy in love with licorice gumdrop belly buttons.

Then I type

Working title:

and watch the flashing cursor, that vertical black bar that evaporates, returns, dissolves, reappears, departs, arrives. Maybe the cursor is being sucked into the whiteness of the screen, or maybe the vast expanse of white is emitting the voice of the black cursor, steady, plaintive, almost complaining. It tells me to type something—anything—so it can go to another line and repeat its demands. It's just always there, beckoning. Sometimes I think it's sneering, challenging, calling me out for a fight. Other times it's like an invitation to dance, whispering, "Come here, come on, Peter, no one's looking, I'll help you, close your eyes . . ."

Why can't I think up a title for my own damn book? My mind floods with possibilities. I could steal from Byron: *All That's Best of Dark and Bright*. Too long. Maybe something from John Milton: *Darkness Visible*. No. Short enough, but who likes or even reads Milton anymore? Besides the Methodists, I mean. *I Am the Lighter Brother*? No. Might offend fans of Langston Hughes. Something biblical? *The Light Shineth in Darkness*? I add the next part of the New Testament verse: "and the darkness comprehended it not." Not good for reviews. Coleridge: *Into That Silent Sea*? I'm not exactly an ancient mariner, though I definitely have the albatross around my neck, a seafaring father, and a ghost ship to go to. No. Too vague. I could be trendy and use a Stevie Wonder song title like "I Wish" or "Ebony Eyes." It is, after all, about Ebony and me, mainly in 1976. *Ebony and Me?* It rhymes at least. Simply *E*? No. A reviewer could give *E* an *F*. *Licorice Gumdrops*? *The Girl with the Perpetual Tan*? No. Too Judy Blume. It has to appeal to adults.

I give up and list three (Henry would be proud) stream-of-consciousness possibilities:

Working title(s): Shades of Gray, Under the Waves, Promise

The first might be too moody, the second too vague, the third . . . I'm sure it's been used before. *Gray Promises? Promises in the Shade? Promises Under the Waves? Gray Shades of Promises Under the Waves?* That's silly—and exactly ten syllables. The word "promise" has to be in there somewhere. I delete what I've written and type:

Working Title: Promise(s)

I rename PRU7.doc and save it as Promises.doc. Something will come to me. And if it doesn't, I'll just buy the marketing department a couple rounds of margaritas.

Chapter four's notes certainly look promising:

Spring 1976: America's Bicentennial

> *general life with a single father
> *R.L. Simpson (mention <u>Wonder Years</u>?)
> *general madness (announcements, one-way halls, rumors)
> *bus rides with Ebony
> *Ebony in Mr. Amadou's crowded room
>   *reading notes
> *Ebony in Mr. "Sneer's" art class
>   *trip to Hecksher Park
>   *drawing Ebony
> *<u>Lots</u> of firsts

I slide in the second CD of *Songs in the Key of Life*, which begins with "Isn't She Lovely," scroll down to a blank page, and begin.

Chapter 4

Two hundred years after the signing of the Declaration of Independence, written by slave owners who wouldn't wise up for "four score and seven years," 1976 was supposed to be a red, white, and blue banner year to help America forget that Southeast Asian "police action," that hotel in D.C., that clumsy unelected president, and that little oil crisis in the Middle East that had folks lining up at pumps to curse odd numbers on even days.

On Long Island, Levittown's Island Trees School District banned *Slaughterhouse Five* by Kurt Vonnegut, *The Fixer* by Bernard Malamud, and *Soul on Ice* by Eldridge Cleaver because these critically acclaimed books were considered racist, filthy, sacrilegious, and un-American.

A banner year, indeed.

These events didn't concern Peter Underhill at all. He was too busy enjoying his new life, his increasing freedom, and the pursuit of his own happiness to notice.

Unfortunately, Peter had to live with the Captain. Except for Saturdays when the Captain could be induced into a "whiskey sour sleeper," and Sundays when he and the Captain would skip church to sail or work on the *Argo*, Peter was on perpetual lockdown when he came home from school.

The house had always lacked joy, but now it was completely joyless, and I walked around waiting for some unknown doom to do me in. I could hear the ticking of the fireplace mantel clock from anywhere in the house, a house more a grave than a home, the night weighing it down, the only joyful sound the rain drumming on the roof above my bed.

"Do your homework," the Captain would say from his La-Z-Boy. "Dinner at eight bells."

So until eight bells (6 P.M. to regular people), Peter did his homework, sketched the woods, and wrote notes to Ebony that he secreted into a small hole in the wall of his closet.

"Chow!"

Heavily salted meat, peppery potatoes, and "How was school?" greeted Peter every evening. "Okay" was his only response.

The rest of the evening, Peter watched his father drink himself into a stupor, no sleeping powder needed, as they watched a Zenith 19-inch color TV, two aluminum-foiled antennae shooting off at odd angles depending, according to the Captain, on the barometric pressure outside.

On Mondays, they'd watch *Little House on the Prairie*. "Now that would be the life," the Captain would say. "Nothing but God's green earth under you and a strong, sturdy home you built with your own two hands."

Tuesdays brought *Baa Baa Black Sheep* to the dusty screen, the Captain commenting, "That wasn't the war *I* fought."

Wednesdays were for *Bionic Woman*, and the Captain barely spoke, Peter's mother having had an eerie resemblance to actress Lindsay Wagner.

The Waltons came for a visit every Thursday, and again the Captain barely spoke, only informing Peter on occasion which one of Peter's kin drove that rusty Model A or that dusty Model T.

I never knew why at the time, but now I think the Captain was remembering his own childhood from the Great Depression. That show had to depress the hell out of him, yet he still watched it, saying good-night to the characters, then to me. "Good night, Pete" always sounded so hollow.

Donny and Marie performed on Fridays. "Look at all them Mormon morons," the Captain would say. "They keep squirting 'em out, we'll have us a Moron president one day." Since Peter was allowed to stay up until ten on Fridays, they watched *The Rockford Files* together. "That would be the life," the Captain would say. "Nothing but your own wits, a fast car, and a big gun."

From his room above the TV room, Peter could hear the other shows the Captain watched—*Kojak, Monday Night Football, M*A*S*H, Hawaii Five-O*—but no show gave the Captain as much pleasure as *All in the Family* every Wednesday night. It was the Captain's prayer meeting and worship service for the week, Christ on his throne traded for a bigot in an armchair, verses replaced by one-liners, the choir supplanted by Archie's whining and ranting. The Captain had conversations with Archie, Meathead, and Edith that sounded like responsive readings. He shouted, "Tell it like it is, Arch!" He cursed. He fumed. He ranted. He used every racial epithet known to mankind. All this venomous praise of and for a racist shook the floor under Peter's bed every Wednesday night, and every Wednesday night Peter's soul wept for Ebony.

Yet when Carroll O'Connor later played a Southern sheriff who married a black woman in *In the Heat of the Night*, the Captain called him a "sellout." His savior had obviously converted without his consent. In a way, though, my father taught me all the words never to say, all the ignorance never to believe, all the hate never to share. Reverse psychology at its finest. I am one of the few people I know who has next to nothing in common with his father.

Peter used to creep downstairs to listen to *The Tonight Show*, and more often than not, the Captain was already passed out. He often found the Captain sleeping in front of test patterns, waving flags, amber waves of grain, and screen snow, but he didn't turn off the TV.

"Let sleeping racists lie," I say.

In addition to surviving the Captain's tight ship, Peter also had to attend seventh grade and survive the ravaging waves of puberty at R.L. Simpson Junior High, an absolute tyranny where despots roamed one-way halls and enforced conformity, divergent thought being the surest way to get you exiled to detention hall.

Each school day began for Peter with one brown sugar cinnamon Pop-Tart and a Flintstones multivitamin chased by a glass of chocolate Carnation Instant Breakfast. He put the other Pop-Tart in his brown bag lunch, which consisted of a peanut butter and grape jelly sandwich, a banana, and Fritos corn chips. Thus fortified, he would yell "Goin' to school, Cap'n" into the TV room and tear out of the house past his own bus stop and the P-Street Rangers down to Grace Lane to wait for the "yellow submarine" with Ebony.

I was so obvious with my affection for Ebony. Everybody knew—except the Captain, of course. The guys at my real bus stop would whistle and raise eyebrows, and once in a while Eddie would say something like, "Give her a kiss for me, Peter-eater," but mostly they smiled and hooted. Ebony was easily the prettiest girl in the seventh grade, and because she was so athletic and therefore "cool," they envied me. It's funny, but they actually envied a geek like me when they could have been beating the geek out of me. Instead of putting on interior, cultural brakes as they did, I was flying down Preston Street like a Huffy bicycle without brakes to Grace Lane to be with my girl every single morning.

Upon his arrival at Ebony's bus stop, Peter would smile, Ebony would toe the asphalt and laugh, and the other kids at the bus stop would move away from them.

"What'd you bring me?" she asked each morning.

He took out the Pop-Tart and handed it to her.

"Cinnamon again?" She took a bite, a couple of crumbs clinging to her lower lip. "And it's cold. When y'all gonna get a toaster?"

"The Captain doesn't believe in them," Peter said.

"What's to believe in?"

"He says white bread shouldn't be brown."

"Oh."

"And I'll try to have him buy chocolate fudge next time."

She broke off a piece and stared at it. "I like chocolate vanilla cream better."

"Okay. I'll have to get him to buy those."

She chiseled off some icing to get at the cinnamon filling, licking that filling with her pinkish tongue.

That girl was such a tease. I was lucky we had a long bus ride to Simpson so my erections would go away. I wonder if she ever knew why I put my books flat on my lap as soon as I sat down.

Peter looked away, but it was too late. His tan Levi's corduroys were already getting tighter.

"I wrote you a note," she said.

Peter turned to her. "I wrote you one, too."

"You draw me a picture?"

Peter nodded.

"I drew you one, too. Just make sure you get your note into my locker before homeroom, okay?"

"Okay."

And in this way, Peter and Ebony communicated throughout the day. Phone calls after school were out of the question, and they only shared two classes together, one crushingly crowded (geography), the other intensely competitive (art). Thus, they "spoke" to each other throughout the school day by sliding notes into the vents of their lockers, lockers they shared with friends who were sworn to secrecy. Any other time, they merely talked to each other with silent smiles and shy giggles.

On bus rides to school, they barely spoke, each too afraid to be overheard by anyone who might turn "Did you do your homework for Mr. Amadou?" into "I wanna do you at your home" for the Simpson rumor-mill, a malicious institution and fact of life that routinely turned hangnails into heart attacks, hand-holding into quintuplets, and a single cold sore into mononucleosis before homeroom even began.

R.L. Simpson, which would later be immortalized on the TV series *The Wonder Years*, was an ancient collection of bricks, worn staircases, and narrow hallways where teachers wrote up any student going the wrong way down a one-way hall. Each Simpson day began in homeroom with a gong-like bell, the Pledge of Allegiance, and a lispy reading of the day's lunch menu: "Kwispy carroth, kwunchy tater toth, and Thalisbury thteak."

Ebony and Peter attempted to sit near each other in Mr. Amadou's room, but it was difficult. Thirty-five seventh graders filled the room, half in dilapidated desks, the other half strewn around the room on the floor or perched on the window ledges. Mr. Amadou, a short wiry Greek with a handlebar moustache, had to stand on his desk to teach, often spinning a 1950s-era globe like a basketball on his finger, his hands flapping, his fingers pointing behind him to a chalkboard full of notes.

"Is everybody here?" he'd ask as he counted heads. "Tell me who's not here."

But very few kids skipped Mr. Amadou's class, mainly because he was so easy to get off the subject whenever food was mentioned.

"Oregano!" he would yell. "This is the key to good food. Not just for Italians, no! Oregano is for Greeks like me. Garlic is for Greeks like me. No black olives—yecch! Green olives, goat cheese not mozzarella, lamb not beef. You come to my house, I make you hate your mothers for the tasteless food they serve."

In a class packed like sardines, we talked of food. I especially liked Mr. Amadou's "International Food Day," when each kid would bring a dish representative of his or her culture. I brought shepherd's pie, and Ebony brought greens to go with egg rolls, pasta, Jamaican pies, borscht, and Mr. Amadou's famous unending Greek salad.

Whenever Mr. Amadou was safely on another "Greek food is king!" tangent, Peter would read Ebony's daily note to him. Her notes were never of the "how are you, I am fine" variety. Ebony wrote straight to the point in perfect cursive using code words whenever necessary in case the note fell into the wrong hands. She gave him advice: "Clean your nails every once in a while and brush your teeth longer!" She told riddles she got from Bazooka Joe wrappers: "What do you call an undersea cab driver? A crabby!" She listed her favorite songs: "Sweet Thing" by Rufus (featuring Chaka Khan), "Boogie Fever" by the Sylvers, "Get Up and Boogie (That's Right)" by the Silver Connection. She gave plot summaries for all the shows Peter was unable to watch: *Good Times, Sanford and Son,* and *The Jeffersons.*

One year later, she even told me, start to finish, the entire eight-day plot of the miniseries *Roots*, what the Captain called "Coons taking over the TV." From that moment on until his dying day, the Captain refused to watch ABC. "I'm down to two *American* channels now," he once told me.

From these notes, which were never romantic and always included an original sketch of Ebony's world—misty mountains, lonesome fields, bitingly accurate caricatures of teachers—Peter learned all about Ebony's family, and much of what he learned broke his heart.

Her father William was a POW-MIA—either a prisoner of war or a soldier missing in action in Vietnam. The back bumper of her mother's Pinto was plastered with "POW-MIA: Never Forget" and "POW-MIAS Never Have A Nice Day" bumper stickers. William was "supposed to be home by Christmas when I was six," according to Ebony, "but he never came home." Candace, Ebony's mother, refused to take down the Christmas tree, which was fortunately artificial, posting it in a window of their Brooklyn apartment, then setting it up in front of the picture window of their Grace Lane house to "guide Daddy home."

Besides Candace, who Ebony said looked like "Angela Davis and Foxy Brown with a touch of Diana Ross only she can't sing a lick," only Aunt Wee Wee lived with them. "Aunt Wee Wee is crazy, trust me," Ebony had written. "She hasn't been out of her room since I was seven, and her farts are so loud and heavy they tap you on the shoulder."

An Uncle Jerry, Candace's brother, visited every Sunday afternoon, but he was "on his way to West Germany to protect us from the Russians," so he wouldn't be around much more. Other than an odd assortment of "Afros and bell-bottoms"—Ebony's code phrase for Candace's many friends from Brooklyn who made the commute in Olds Cutlass Supremes and Buick LeSabres to Huntington—life was pretty quiet in the Mills's Grace Lane Cape Cod.

One day in mid-March, in addition to including a breathtaking self-portrait, Ebony dispensed with the code entirely:

Peter:

I know I said not to use real names, but we're getting pretty good at this. At least I am. When are you going to learn to write in cursive? You write in chicken scratch, and I'm not a chicken farmer.

And what are you doing drawing my hands? They aren't that pretty. You should be paying attention to Mr. A. instead of drawing my hands. You want to go nowhere in this world?

Mama's going to be out when I get home from school. I have the key. Aunt Wee Wee won't bother us. She's usually taking a nap when I get home from school. I want to show you something in my room. Let me know if you can come over. Let me know before lunch.

Ebony

That note scared the shit out of me. Her self-portrait stole my breath, and she had captured herself perfectly. I used to look through *National Geographic* to determine which part of Africa her ancestors were from, and I decided that they had come from either Ghana or Cameroon. Ebony disagreed, of course, and said she was an American from Virginia, and "What you doin' lookin' at African women's titties?" That day I sat in Mrs. Gianinni's Spanish class with shaking hands trying to write one word— "okay"—in cursive on a piece of paper, but it was hard to write because my hands were threatening to sweat off. Ebony had asked me into her inner sanctum, her sanctuary, her refuge, her scriptorium and studio, and she was going to show me something. Every sexual thought a thirteen-year-old can have rolled through my head that day while Mrs. Gianinni, an Italian with a bad beehive, rolled her *r*'s. "Donde esta la puerrrrrrta? Bueno, Juan. Donde esta la pizzarrrrro? Muy bien, Juanita . . ."

Peter's imperfect cursive response—"Dear E: Okay"—made Ebony smile from across the crowded cafeteria where she ate her lunch with other shy girls, and when they ended their day in Mr. Nearing's art class, neither could stop smiling at the other.

"Today, my young *artistes*, we will leave these pedantic confines for the freedom of the park," said Mr. Nearing, alias "Mr. Sneer."

Mr. Nearing was, in a word, different. Mark said his dad said that Mr. Nearing was "light in his loafers." Eddie, who had never even met Mr. Nearing, called him a "fag." Mickey only shrugged his shoulders and said he was an artist who lived in the woods like Walt Whitman and Henry David Thoreau. Peter and Ebony, however, saw Mr. Nearing as a referee and judge, the final arbiter as to who was the better artist—and Ebony was clearly Mr. Nearing's favorite.

"Instead of drawing another dreary still life of vases and plastic fruit," Mr. Nearing continued, "we will be drawing real life, such as it is, in Hecksher Park."

Bundled up, sketchbooks in hand, the class took a short walk to Hecksher Park, home to pavilions, ducks, a band shell, and a motionless green pond.

"Not exactly Walden Pond is it?" Mr. Nearing said as they gathered in the pavilion.

"Why can't we use watercolors?" Ebony asked him.

"In time, in time, Miss Ebony." He smiled. "This bitter March wind would freeze your work. Better to sketch now what you will highlight tomorrow in a warm room."

"My fingers are too tired to sketch, Peter," she whispered as they wandered down a path to a bench. "I must have taken a million notes today."

They sat on opposite ends of the bench, dappled sunlight floating over them. "What are you going to draw?" Peter whispered.

"None-yun," she said, using her word for "none of your business."

Peter looked out at the pond. Few ducks parted the scum on the pond, and they'd be too far away to sketch properly. The pavilion looked interesting with its boulders for walls and circular roof, but it, too, was too far away to capture all its details. He glanced to his right . . . and found his subject.

He drew her from her Adidas up, pausing at her slender ankles to leave a patch of dark skin above her footie socks, giving her jeans sharp creases, shrinking her navy blue coat to give her a more womanly appearance—

His hands oozed again. He caught his breath. *I'm drawing Ebony's breasts under a coat!* He quickly added her willowy neck and sharp jaw, then hid her hands inside her coat pockets. He had just begun lightly outlining her lips, brown then tan then red, when Mr. Nearing announced, "Time to go, people!"

He looked at Ebony. "You finished?"

"Uh-huh."

He shut his sketchbook and stood. "I'm not."

She stood and stretched her back. "You draw too slow. You're supposed to let it flow."

"I draw carefully."

She rolled her eyes. "Wish you would write as carefully." She stepped toward him. "I drew the bridge over the pond. What'd you draw?"

"I'll show you when I'm finished."

She pawed Peter for his sketchbook. "Let me see it."

Peter sighed and opened to his drawing of Ebony. "I only got up to your lips."

Mr. Nearing motioned for them to come to the pavilion, and the two began to walk, Peter dreaming of Ebony's lips, Ebony studying herself on the page.

"Where's my face?"

It's in my heart and I couldn't get it out, he wanted to say. "I wanted to save the best for last." He heard her sigh. "Besides, you drew that self-portrait for me in your note, and you might have said that I copied it."

"I wouldn't have said that."

"What if I made you too dark? You'd be mad."

"I am dark, Peter. Black is beautiful."

Peter nodded.

"What you noddin' for, Peter? You ain't black."

They had reached the pavilion. "I nodded cuz . . . cuz you're beautiful."

Ebony didn't say another word during Mr. Nearing's critique session in the shade of the pavilion—"Oh, not another drawing of the bridge!"—during the walk back to Simpson, during the noisy wait for the bus, or during the noisier bus ride home. Peter thought he had said something wrong.

"You okay?" he whispered.

She nodded, reaching over to squeeze his hand. "Thank you."

"For what?"

"For what you said."

"What'd I say?"

"Shh."

He looked up and saw a few kids watching them, their eyes drawn to Ebony's hand holding his. He squeezed, she returned the squeeze, and when she tried to remove it from his grasp, he held on. *I'm holding hands with a girl for the first time,* he thought, *and I am not letting go.* He smiled and laughed, crossing his eyes at a freckle-faced eighth grade girl until she turned away. He looked back at Ebony, but she wasn't looking at him. She was looking straight ahead, the broadest smile on her face.

Once the other kids scattered from the bus stop, Peter followed Ebony to the side of her house. He looked down at his hand and saw his hand still holding hers.

"You gotta be real quiet, Peter, okay?"

"Okay."

They glided through a large white kitchen full of cupboards and closets, down a short hallway, through a living room with orange shag carpeting and a Christmas tree, down a longer hallway that had framed pictures of Ebony and Ebony's family on the walls, the heavy scent of cigarette smoke in the air, to a closed door. Ebony eased open the door, and seconds later, Peter stood in a girl's room for the first time in his life.

While Ebony closed the curtains and turned on a little radio, Peter drank in the room. There was no place to sit except her bed; her desk chair was full of sketchbooks. Several bookcases held paperbacks of every sort, size, and color, many half-opened and resting in little mounds around the room. He smiled at posters of butterflies and horses, sunsets and mountains, kittens and puppies, and—

Is that her underwear on the floor?

"It's a little messy," she said. She sat on the bed and patted the space beside her. "Take your coat off and stay a while."

That is *her underwear on the floor! And it's green?* He felt a stirring in his Levi's. *Not now!*

"Huh?"

"Sit with me, Peter."

Oh, JesusJesusJesus. He took off his coat but kept it close to his groin.

"Throw your coat anywhere."

He tossed his coat in the direction of Ebony's underwear, but he missed them by a foot. He slipped his hands into his pockets, but that only made the bulge grow bigger. He turned to admire her record collection, KC and the Sunshine Band the first of a thick stack.

"So, what do you think?"

He glanced and saw her underwear again. "Um, you have a lot of records and books."

"Don't you?"

"No."

"No books?"

"I mean, yes, I have books. But no records."

"Why?"

The Captain thinks the Devil lives in them. And I bet the Devil left those underwear there, too! "I don't have a record player."

"You should get one."

"Yeah."

He stared at her nightstand and saw several books: *The Slave Dancer*, *Roots*, and *Soul on Ice*. He pointed at them. "Are you reading all those at once?"

"Yeah. I just finished *Slaughterhouse Five*. You really ought to read it."

"Yeah." He felt his heart trying to beat out of his chest. "You, uh, you have a nice room."

"Thank you, but what do you think about me, here, in this room, with you, here, in this room, alone, here, in this room?"

I think, here, in this room, that I have a large erection "I think . . . I ought to be getting home. The Captain—"

She grabbed his arm and yanked him down beside her, the bed bowing a little. "He can wait. I have something to tell you as well as show you, and if you laugh, I'll knock your block off. Promise you won't laugh?"

"I won't." *Pleasepleaseplease go away*, he commanded himself, but his pants were still tightening.

She took his hand. "I had a dream about you last night. I dream about you all the time, but last night's dream was really outta-sight."

"Aren't all dreams outta-sight?"

"Ha ha funny, now don't interrupt. In my dream, you were much taller than me, and we were on the beach somewhere warm, and I was wearing a long shell necklace and a silky orange-and-purple *dress*, so you *know* it was a dream. You wore this teal blue shirt and tan shorts, and your hair made you look kind of like Elvis, and there we were standing on some beach while waves splashed our feet and the sun went down—or up, who knows?—and you know what you said to me?"

Pleasepleaseplease go away, not now! "What did I say?"

"You said that I had pretty feet."

"I did?" *Why would I say that? Ooh, that's better. Go on back down now.*

"Except that you've never seen my feet, Peter, I mean, how would you know? And that's what I want to show you." She took off her Adidas and rolled off her socks, wriggling her toes in the air. "Are they really pretty?"

They were small and perfectly rounded, little pearl chips for toenails. "Yes."

"What's pretty about them? My toes look like Tootsie Rolls."

They did look like Tootsie Rolls. "I like Tootsie Rolls."

She squeezed his hand. "Let's see yours."

"Huh?"

She slid off the bed and grabbed one of Peter's feet. "I wanna see your feet!"

Peter pulled his foot away, Ebony lunged, and several delicious wrestling moves later, he was on top of her on her bed, her hands clasped behind his neck.

"I bet you're good at Twister," she said.

"I'm not allowed to play it."

"Too bad." She sighed. "You gonna kiss me, Peter? You know you want to."

Every pore in Peter's body opened, the floodgates of every sweat gland and every other gland breaking free, waves of delectable pressure again assaulting his zipper. Ebony closed her eyes and pursed her lips.

Oh geezgeezgeez, I know I have banana and PBJ breath and my lips are chapped and I'm on top of a girl and my pants are about to explode—

Ebony's eyes popped open. "You need directions? My lips are down here."

"Ebony, I—" He couldn't finish, and he couldn't tell her why. He wasn't afraid of kissing her. He was afraid of what might explode if he did.

"Come here, come on, Peter, no one's looking."

"But I—"

"I'll help you. Close your eyes."

I don't want to miss this! "Can't I keep them open?"

"Sure. I'll keep mine open, too."

He stared into her eyes, and she started giggling. "What's so funny?"

"You look so serious. It's just a kiss." Her eyes softened. "Isn't it?"

He dropped his head and touched his lips to hers gently, feeling the softness, tasting the sweetness of Ebony. He pulled back and saw a new set of ebony eyes, eyes that seemed to say "wow."

"That wasn't just a kiss," she whispered, then she pushed him off her and stood. "You gotta go. Mama will be home soon."

"Yeah."

She turned away. "You know I'm gonna see your crusty toes one day."

"Uh-huh."

"Um, I'll, uh, I'll walk you out."

"Sure."

She stepped to the door and seemed to freeze. "We'll have to do this again soon."

"Uh-huh."

She turned and hugged him, her breath soft in his ear, her body melting into his, her hips grinding slightly into his—

Oh . . . dear . . . Je-SUS!

He pulled back. "I gotta go."

"What's wrong?"

He looked down at his zipper without meaning to. "I just gotta go."

"Did you just— Oh my God!" She covered her mouth with a cupped hand.

"I'm sorry, I'm sorry!"

"Did you . . . did you *really?*"

Peter nodded, the warmth seeping deeper into his underwear, his knees weakening. "I didn't mean to, I swear I didn't!"

"I made you do that?"

Peter nodded. "Please, I really gotta go."

"Wow," she said. "What did it feel like?"

Like my insides coming outside! "Can I tell you later?"

"Does it hurt?"

"No."

"So it felt good."

Peter nodded. "It felt better than good."

She smiled and toed the carpet. "That ever happen to you before?"

Not with anyone else in the room! "No."

"Cool."

The warmth dissipated, leaving him with a sticky cold spot. "I really have to go."

She stepped close to him. "Kiss me first."

"That's what started it all in the first place!"

Ebony stepped back. "That thing isn't going to go off again, is it?"

"I don't know."

She slipped her arms around his waist. "I'll take my chances. Kiss me."

His lips met hers for a brief second. "See you tomorrow."

"I'll walk you out." She opened the door. "Oh, you're forgetting your coat."

"Oh." He threw on his coat and looked down at the spreading wet spot on his corduroys.

"Is that—"

"Yes." Blood rushed into his face.

"All that came out?"

"Can I go now?"

Ebony sighed. "Yes."

She led him through the long hall, through the living room, through the short hall, through the kitchen, and to the side porch. Once outside, the wet spot grew increasingly colder against his leg.

"Um, you better hold your books over that, huh?"

Peter nodded.

"Bye, Peter."

The cold spread down his legs and into his soul as he ran home, his books smacking against his groin. He threw open the front door and raced upstairs, slamming his bedroom door behind him and peeling off his pants and underwear.

"That you, Pete?" the Captain yelled.

He's at the bottom of the stairs! Jesus, please make him walk slow!

"Yeah!" He rifled his top drawer for another pair of underwear, slipping them on.

"What you doing home so late?"

He's coming up the stairs! "Uh," he said, struggling into another pair of tan corduroys, "the bus broke down and I had to walk." He kicked his soiled underwear and pants under his bed just as the Captain opened his door and walked in. "Hello, Captain, how was your day?"

The Captain eyed Peter from head to toe, sniffing the air. "You been smoking, Pete?"

"No."

"I smell cigarettes, Pete. Don't lie to me."

"I wasn't smoking. Some other kids were, on the bus, but not me." *Please, God, help him believe my lie!*

"Let me smell your breath."

Oh, Jesus, can he smell Ebony on me, too? Do kisses have an odor? Can he smell what else happened? Please let my breath be banana and PBJ!

Peter breathed into the Captain's face.

The Captain squinted. "Hmm. You brush your teeth today?"

"Yes, sir."

"Hmmph." He scratched at his crew cut. "I don't want you hanging around with anyone who smokes. They're cowards who think that they'll live forever, and they'll only get you into trouble. And don't you ever let me catch *you* smoking, Pete. Those cancer sticks will kill you."

"Yes sir."

"And if you ever do smoke, I'll know. A little birdie or two will tell me."

"Yes, sir."

"Chow will be ready at eight bells. Don't be late."

"I won't be, sir."

After the Captain left, Peter sat on his bed. *I didn't know that I could do that! I mean, I did know I could do* that, *but the way it happened! That felt so good, but . . . have I sinned? I wasn't thinking any carnal thoughts, was I? Maybe I was.*

He prayed to God and thanked Him for helping him trick the Captain. He also prayed for forgiveness for what happened in Ebony's room. *But next time, I'm wearing darker corduroys and two pairs of underwear.*

My first kiss, my "first time," my first series of successful bald-faced lies . . .

My first and best love, my original love. Why did I ever leave her?

Instantly depressed, I save my work and log on to AOL, wasting the rest of the evening looking—just looking—for anything remotely interesting and uplifting online. I watch a group of cartoon lemmings pitching themselves off a cliff, a group of rednecks giving them scores. Who thinks up this stuff? And why am I watching it? The gerbil in the blender is kind of funny. I play several mind-numbing games of gin rummy with GiNcRaZy, another player somewhere in cyberspace with less of a life than mine, and even check the weekend weather report for Huntington.

I have to get out of Cherry Grove. My mind is turning to tapioca. Cliff-diving lemmings, cursing gerbils, gin rummy with a GiNcRaZy novice, and future weather reports—this is what I've reduced myself to doing instead of writing the next chapter.

Because I don't want to write it.

But I have so many promises to keep—

Promises to Keep, by Peter Rudolph Underhill. Thank you, Robert Frost.

At least I have a title now.

At least I have that.

I curl up on the couch, dreaming of green underwear, cold spots, and perfect pearl toes.

7

The phone wakes me at sunrise. Red sky at morning; sailors take warning. It's going to be one of those days, I can feel it. I roll off the couch and stumble to the kitchen counter, fumbling for the phone and wiping the crust from my eyes. "Hello?"

"Hey, Pete, how's it going?"

Henry. "Hey, Henry. What time is it?"

"Six-thirty."

Awfully early for an editor to get to work, especially on a Friday. "Where are you?"

"At the office."

And I'm in mine. Geez, I've got some cleaning up to do. Papers and file folders spoil the whiteness of Henry's apartment. "What's up?"

"Well, I'll be sitting here with little to do until a meeting with the managing editor at ten. How about sending me what you have of *Whiter Shade* so I can read it, maybe run an advance by her?"

Money . . . for me? I pull the phone cord as far as it will reach, but I can't get close enough to the laptop to turn it on. Henry needs a cordless phone. "Just a sec." I lay the phone on the couch, rush to the table, and hit the power button on the laptop. I return to the phone.

"Is there a problem, Pete?"

"No. Um, do you want me to send it as an e-mail attachment?"

"Can you send it as a straight e-mail instead? Our glorious computer techs don't want us opening any more attachments with all the viruses out there."

I groan at the tedium to come. "Sure."

"Can you have it to me by seven?"

"Sure thing."

"Oh, one more thing. I'll be bringing a friend tonight, someone who is just dying to meet you. Do you mind sleeping on the sleeper sofa?"

I look at the couch. It opens up to a bed? I could have been sleeping on a mattress all this time. "I don't mind."

"Thanks. Uh, could you change the sheets on my bed for me? Extra sheets are in the hall closet."

Ah, this "someone" is Henry's steady. "I haven't slept in your bed, Henry."

"Where have you been sleeping?"

"On the couch."

"Really?"

"Yeah. It's more convenient to where I'm writing." But murder on my back.

"Well . . . okay. I'll e-mail a reply when I receive your work."

"It may take more than one e-mail to get it all there."

"Just label them one, two, three, and so on. Talk to you soon." *Click.*

As soon as Windows finally hits the screen, I load Word and open *Whiter Shade*, copying half into one e-mail, the other half into another, labeling them one and two, respectively. "No three for Henry today." I hit send and wait for Henry's reply. It doesn't take long:

Pete: Re-send . . . the lines are all out of whack. And could you triple-space it, please?

I reply to his reply, the ultimate in redundancy:

Henry: AOL sometimes scrambles Word docs. I'll have to edit each as I go. I'll send in a few minutes.

Heavy sigh. Over the next half an hour, I triple-space and add spaces where AOL slams words together until I'm able to re-send. I should have carpal tunnel syndrome by now. Henry's reply:

Pete: Still no good. Go ahead and send it as an attachment.

Heavier sigh. This only takes a few keystrokes and is in Henry's mail-box in less than a minute—what I should have done in the first place. His reply:

Pete: This looks much better. I'll call you.

What, a waste of an hour? I stand at the window and see a lone brown-gray seagull perched on Elysium's white picket fence below, its head buried into its neck. It must be cold out. When did I go out last? Oh yeah, Monday. And now it's Friday. Just like my childhood and marriage: I'm on lockdown all week until I'm freed for the weekend.

I open Promises.doc and go to work. Today's topic: the summer of 1976.

Chapter 5

The summer of 1976, the summer of Sam Berkowitz

"The killer of brunettes who is eligible for parole next year," I whisper. "What a country."

and his neighbor's talking Labrador retriever,

"Who is probably chasing angelic rabbits in doggie heaven by now."

the summer of Elton John, who sold out an entire week at Madison Square Garden,

"Buh-buh-buh Benny and the Jetsssssssss," I sing.

the summer of Romanian gymnast Nadia Comaneci, boxer Sugar Ray Leonard, and decathlete Bruce Jenner in Montreal,

"Who got himself a nifty Wheaties box."

the summer of a buck-toothed presidential candidate

"Who never got into an elevator alone with a woman."

                                                        who
had a brother named Billy,

"Who had a beer named after him."

                        the summer of Cincinnati's Big Red
Machine that would sweep the Yankees in the World Series,

I'd like to blame Sam Berkowitz for that. All those women in blond wigs trying not to be brunette in the stands at Yankee Stadium must have made it hard for the Yankees to see the ball.

the summer of *Frampton Comes Alive!*

Now that was a phenomenon I have never understood. Of all the outstanding music that came out of 1976, when George Benson's *Breezin'* and Stevie's album kicked ass at the Grammys, a nobody from England makes a live two-record album singing uninspiring songs like "Show Me the Way" and "Baby I Love Your Way"—and sells thirteen million copies. No, I did not feel the way you did, Peter Frampton.

For Peter Underhill, however, none of that mattered. All that mattered that hot summer was baseball, baseball, and more baseball—and a girl named Ebony.

When the Captain signed up Peter for baseball, Peter was amazed.

"It'll do you good to get out of the house this summer," the Captain said. "And it's an American game that every American boy should play."

Most games were played at Southdown Elementary or Milldam Ball Park across the road from Milldam Bait and Tackle, just a quick run through the woods behind Peter's house. And attending every game was Ebony Mills, a girl who Peter wore two pairs of underwear for. She was his biggest and only fan, the Captain always having some excuse for not watching.

"Are you going to watch the parade, sir?" Peter asked before the annual march of Little Leaguers down West Shore Road.

"Uh, no. Gonna slap some more varnish on the *Argo*. The interior's looking ragged."

"Are you coming to our first game, sir?" Peter asked on opening day.

"Uh, no. Heard a hitch in the Volvo"—the *Argo*'s engine—"the other day we were out. May have to have it rebuilt by the end of the summer."

"Coach says I may get to pitch some today since we're playing the Phillies," Peter told him midway through the season. "They're in last place, and we beat 'em eighteen to nothing last time."

"Uh, no, Pete. Gonna put up some new rigging. Probably take most of the morning. I want to get that mizzen up right this time."

"We're playing the Mets today, Captain," Peter told him near the end of the season. "They're in first place. If we beat them, we'll be tied and have to have a play-off game."

"Uh, not today, Pete. Gotta do something about that creak where the head partition meets the cabin ceiling."

That creak was a problem my father never solved. The man talked to that creak for years, and on overnight sails to Block Island, he had to wear earplugs to get any sleep. I liked that creak, mainly because it was a mystery the Captain couldn't solve, and because it also had a rhythm, like the clanging of the bells on buoys in the sea-lanes.

When Peter made the all-star team, he told the Captain where (Milldam Ball Park) and when (11 A.M. on Saturday) the game would be played, and the Captain said he'd try to be there. "Ain't making any promises, Pete. The dinghy's outboard needs some work, and you know the stove needs cleaning."

I know why he signed me up—to get me out of his way that summer—but it still hurt. It still hurts. I wasn't a bad ballplayer and even hit a ground ball home run into the parking lot at Southdown. I fielded most of the balls hit to me, had an accurate arm, and threw more strikes than balls when I pitched. He never saw me play, not later in high school, not once in college. And he never asked me how I did or how the team did. The *Argo*, which had replaced Mom, had also replaced me for the Captain's attention and affection. The sailboat seemed to be my father's therapy, because though he didn't talk about Mom's departure, he was drinking and sailing away that sorrow—and I wasn't invited on the trip.

The phone rings. It has to be Henry.

"Hey, Henry."

"This is some funny stuff, Pete. But I just have to know how you're going to get them together."

I haven't thought about that at all. "I want to surprise you, Henry."

"Oh, come on, you have to tell me."

I have to tell myself first. "I want to keep you in suspense."

"It will be in some off-the-wall place, I hope."

"Definitely, and you'll be the first on earth to know, right?"

"Right."

"So . . . will you run everything by the managing editor?"

"Sure will. This has promise. How does a twenty-five thousand-dollar advance sound?"

Shit. I made advances of $80,000 on the other two. "Just twenty-five?"

"Look, Pete, times are hard with all that's happened. And it's been a long time since Desiree's last novel. I'll try to get you more, but I'm not making any promises."

"Do what you can."

"Let's not dwell on it now, okay? Desiree Holland is back, and it's cause for celebration! We'll have to have a party tonight, okay?"

A party to celebrate a book I can't say that I'm writing? "Sure."

"See you soon." *Click.*

Will it be a party of three . . . or a party of two with a third wheel?

Peter stopped looking for his father after the second game of the season, and he got used to playing for Ebony, his audience of one who yelled his name and cheered "Seven" around the bases. He also became friends with Simon Lloyd, a tall black kid on his team who went to Finley Junior High and thought that Ebony was "dyno-mite."

"She your girlfriend?" Simon asked Peter after the first game.

"Yeah."

"You must be goin' to church, man. Your prayers are bein' answered. She got a sister?"

After games at Southdown, Peter would walk Ebony home through smooth streets and past air-conditioned, aluminum-sided houses of eyes staring out from between custom drapes and blinds. They didn't hold hands ("Cuz you're sweaty, Peter"), and they parted ways before getting to Grace Lane.

Each parting was the same. "Thanks for coming," he said. "You're welcome," she said. She'd twist the white friendship bracelet that she had woven for him and that she wore for him because Peter didn't want the Captain asking any questions about it. Then she'd smile and sigh. He'd sigh, smile, and reach out to touch her hand, which she would pull back. "Bye," she'd say. "Bye," he'd say.

"My God, we were so shy," I whisper. "And cute. We were definitely cute together."

But after games at Milldam Park, they strolled through the woods, hand in hand, past the Orlando dance studio where girls frolicked behind picture windows in a round house surrounded by trees. Peter and Ebony took as long as they could to wind up the path to the shady space under the deck behind Peter's house, and once there, they kissed, they held each other, they learned about each other's bodies, they dreamed, they found peace.

"I didn't know you got a tan," Peter said, admiring the whitish stripe on Ebony's wrist under the friendship bracelet.

"Of course I do. All people tan. The sun smiles on us all, Peter."

"Some more than others," Peter said, tickling Ebony's stomach.

"Careful now," she said, grabbing his hands. "You know what might happen if you start messing down there."

"What might happen?"

She sighed. "I might jump your bones."

Peter, who had learned to control himself by reading the phone book in his mind, smiled and pinned her to the soft leaves under the deck. "Or I might jump your bones."

She kissed his chin. "You like my bones?"

He kissed her cheek, sliding his hand under her T-shirt, caressing her velvety stomach. "Yes." He slid his hand higher, daring her with his eyes to stop him.

"You like my titties, too, don't you?"

His hand reached the edge of her bra and stopped. He slipped one finger under the elastic and felt her heart beating as fast as his.

"Go ahead, Peter. They won't bite."

"Are you sure it's okay?"

She nodded.

He felt her heat seeping into his fingers, which immediately reminded him of the fires of hell. He pulled his finger back as if it were on fire. "Uh, I better not."

"Why?"

"Cuz . . . cuz I don't want to go to hell."

Ebony slapped his hand off her stomach, pulled down her shirt, and sat up. "What's this about hell?"

"I'm afraid I'll do something bad."

She crossed her arms. "You've been doing something bad with me every time we get together under here, Peter."

"I have?"

She smiled. "Sure you have, and so have I. I have had the most wicked thoughts."

Peter swallowed hard. "You . . . have?"

"Uh-huh. Like I want to do it with you so bad it hurts."

Oh . . . whoa! "I've been thinking the same thing, and I know I shouldn't be thinking it."

"Thinking it and doing it are two totally different things. Just cuz I want to doesn't mean I'm gonna do it. And I'm not." She bit her lip. "Not yet anyway. I might let you get pretty far though." She took his hand and pulled it under her shirt, placing it on her right breast. "It's soft, isn't it?"

Peter held his breath. "Y-yeah."

She slid his hand slowly to the other. "Just as soft as this one, huh?"

He nodded.

She pushed his hand gently down her stomach, stopping it above her shorts. "You feel where I'm stopping you, Peter Underhill?"

He nodded and exhaled deeply. "Yeah."

"That's as far as you go, understand?"

"Yeah."

"You try to go any farther, and we're gonna be fighting."

"I won't go any farther."

She giggled. "But if you don't try, I might start thinking that you don't like me."

Peter's heart hurt. "But I do like you."

"Do you more than like me?"

"Yes."

"Do you love me?"

Peter had never truly loved anyone in his life. He admired his mother and her courage to leave, and he respected and feared his father, but admiration, respect, and fear weren't love. "I think I do."

She sighed. "I think I love you, too. But we can't be going any farther until we're sure. Agreed?"

Peter smiled, his chest loosening. "Yeah."

They lay on their backs beside each other, staring up at the bottom of the deck, fingers touching.

"What are you thinking about right now?" she asked.

"How glad I am that you don't want to do it with me."

She giggled. "You hear what you just said?"

"I meant—"

"I know what you meant," she interrupted. "I'm glad you don't want to do it with me either."

"But I do!"

She rolled over on top of him, and he wrapped his arms around her. "I know you do." She pushed his hands down until they cupped her buttocks. "Squeeze hard."

Oh GEEZ . . . and I'm wearing a cup!

"You just go off again?"

Peter nodded, his breaths coming in spasms.

"From just one little squeeze of my butt?"

"Yeah."

She rested her head on his chest. "I better not be grabbing your butt then. You're liable to drown me or something."

A door slammed above them, the door to the kitchen slammed, the door to the kitchen slammed and rattled and footsteps came down the narrow path to the deck and

I hit file-save and quit, shutting down the laptop.

I have to get out, got to get out, haven't left this cell in four days, unshaved, unshowered, same clothes, got to blend my smells with the swells, be Prufrock for a spell with my Levi's rolled, got to get to Swinburne's "Mother and lover of me, the sea to close with her, kiss her, and mix her with me," got to get the f—

Where's my notepad? There. Pen. Scribble on a corner. A black ink squiggle. Jacket? I don't even care if it's cold outside! Screw the jacket, I'm out.

I hit the door running, slamming it behind me, the Poet nowhere in sight, the stairs disappearing, the gate opening, my feet running on Green Walk, my bare feet (where are my shoes?) running to the water, to the shore, to the sand, to see—

Infinity.

Is the tide out or in? Is the wind from the north or south? Why am I the only one—

Oh yeah, it's October, it's cold, and I'm wearing a Steelers sweatshirt with ratty jeans rolled up, my bone-white feet tracing paths in the sand where the water meets the land.

I plunk down in sand soaked as if with tears under a flame-red sky and watch my hand ripping across the page:

cold briny devil and the deep (calling to deep) blue sea,
wind the color of water tasting of sea foam,
tide neither out (exposing the dead, the dying)
nor in (erasing the dying, the dead),
sound of a single seagull, hovering, silent wings
like slow-motion helicopter blades,
smoke from Manhattan,
a thousand fearful wrecks ...

cold sand, white/brown/black sand melded together,
an endless sea of faces stretching east to west,
green foam covering small collisions of land and sea,
the seventh wave approaching,
the sixth wave, my generation
nearing its end and on its way out,
the seventh generation
crashing onto these teeming shores ...

cold shell, Daedalus' logic with a string,
ocean in one ear, echo in another—
what behemoth, what leviathan swims just offshore
beneath the surface, watching me, circling me,
with fins of lead and crooked inviting fingers
opening screen doors and stalking me ...
how often my toes dangled as bait for the vast unseen,
how often I was spared to sleep with the fishes,
what behemoth, what leviathan spared me ...

cold painting, Winslow Homer's <u>Breezing Up</u>,
boy furled in a sail, secure but inert,
yearning for what he fears,
on the sea but not sailing,
his captain a king, a god on the sea,
but on land, on land nothing . . .

cold rhythm here where man's control stops,
a justice, cruel, cold, uncompromising—
"that would be the life!"—
knowing what could go wrong and preventing it,
being your own master, mastering the elements:
one wave, one swell, one billow at a time
until the end of the day when sunsets and calm waters
smiled as you left your world in a dinghy back to land,
back to memories, back to thoughts and regrets,
to feelings not used on the sea
(too busy acting, reacting, analyzing lines of right and wrong)
with faith that though no visible paths or lanes guided you,
Yes! An act of FAITH that told you the wind would blow,
the ocean floor would stay below,
and the waves would roll you on, roll you on

"Home," I say, tears in my eyes. "The Captain always came home."

I rest there sweating on that joyless beach, eyes cast down, half expecting the *Argo* to cross in front of me on the sunless tide, until I'm numbed by the cold—and the memories. I draw a few glances from people on Green Walk as I mumble Longfellow:

Build me straight, O worthy Master!
Stanch and strong, a goodly vessel
That shall laugh at all disaster;
And with wave and whirlwind wrestle.

Maybe they think I'm Jonah just spit out of the belly of the whale come to Nineveh to shout, "Repent!" But I'm no one to shout or even whisper "Repent" to anyone but my own reflection.

But when I enter Henry's apartment, I see a dark Nubian goddess in a lime green pantsuit relaxing on Henry's couch, Henry fluttering around his kitchen.

"Where have you been, Pete?" Henry asks.

The Nubian goddess's eyes travel to my sand-encrusted feet. "He has obviously been to the beach, Henry," the goddess says in an enchanting voice.

I flex my toes, brown sand spilling onto Henry's carpet. "Yes. I've been down to the sea."

Henry moves to the goddess and hands her a white mug of coffee. "Pete, this is my dear friend Cece Wrenn. Maybe you've heard of her?"

"Hello," I say, recognizing the name. Cece Wrenn, Bermudan jazz singer and pianist with the smooth, lilting, haunting voice, is chiseled, coiffed to perfection, and as dark as the coffee she drinks. "I'm Peter Underhill."

"You mean Desiree Holland, of course," she says in a lovely, precise Caribbean voice, a musical voice with a calypso beat.

"Henry's told you." I paw at the carpet with my feet.

"Yes." Cece smiles. "You are not at all who I had in mind when I read your books. You were so much . . . darker."

"I, uh, I've been out of the sun for a while," I say.

Cece laughs and turns to Henry. "I like him, Henry."

Henry frowns at the brown spot beneath my feet. "Why don't you clean yourself up, Pete?"

"Sure."

As I shower, I wonder about the couple in the other room. Henry is or seems to be gay. Cece seems heterosexual to the core. I had heard that white gay males and black women get along famously, but she'll be spending the weekend in a one-bedroom apartment with me on the couch? And she says she likes me?

This is a subplot I did not foresee.

Freshly laundered and somewhat less ragged looking in clean jeans and a light blue oxford shirt, I go to the kitchen and pull open the refrigerator, grabbing a can of Coke.

After I pull the tab and take a sip, Henry says, "There's plenty of beer in there, Pete."

"I'm fine."

"I thought we were celebrating Desiree's return."

I see them sitting on opposite ends of the couch. "We are, Henry. I just need to wake up first." I sit in a chair opposite them, and no one speaks until I can contain my curiosity no longer. "So you two are an item."

Henry looks at Cece. "Do you wish to tell it or should I?"

"I will tell it," Cece says with a little sigh. "Henry, as you may know, is gay."

I don't blink. "Yes."

"And as you may have noticed, I am definitely not gay." She flutters her eyelashes and smooths her hands down her pant legs. "Yet for some reason, Henry and I have hit it off."

"We're soul mates," Henry says.

Cece shrugs. "It is amazing, but it is true. We have more in common than any two people I know or have ever known, including my parents, who had a wonderful marriage."

"Can I tell him the next part, love?" Henry asks.

Cece nods. "Just do not get carried away."

"I won't," Henry says. "The next part, the next step in our relationship, is to start a family."

This time I blink. Hard. "A family?"

Henry's face beams. "Isn't it wonderful?"

Gay white male and Nubian Caribbean goddess have milk chocolate child on Long Island. What could be more wonderful? I wish this Coke had some whiskey in it.

The phone rings, and Henry snaps it up. "Yes? I'll be right over." He hangs up. "Le Lethe has our order ready."

"Are they not delivering tonight?" Cece asks.

"No. I hope you don't mind eating in tonight, Pete."

"Not at all." Just eating will be enough for me. "What are we having?"

"Scallops!" Henry winks at Cece. "I won't be too long, love."

"Take your time," Cece says.

Once Henry leaves, Cece stands and arches her back, her profile and body reminding me of an ancient Egyptian sculpture, like a sleek black panther. William Blake had it wrong. He should have written, "Panther! Panther! burning bright in the forests of the night." This woman definitely has "fearful symmetry."

She notices me looking and smiles. "You look like you need a drink, Peter."

I wiggle the Coke. "I'm okay."

She sighs. "I will bet that you are wondering why I am doing this."

I shake my head. "I think I understand."

She sits on the edge of the couch and cradles her coffee mug. "I am not sure that you do. Or perhaps you do." She pauses to stare. "Ask your question."

"What question?"

"The obvious question."

I smile. "Okay, why Henry?"

She winks at me. "I have read your mind. Why Henry? Why not Henry? He is a wonderful man, bright, articulate, handsome, secure, and I love him." She shakes her head. "And he is gay. I know it makes no sense."

She looks up as if to give me time to reply, but I have no reply to give. This situation has never been in any of my plot outlines.

"But what does make sense is starting a family. I am not getting any younger, and Henry and I want a child so badly. We have been trying for several months now, and maybe this weekend we will be successful."

With me on the couch in the other room. I find myself staring at her hands, her piano-playing hands, and wish I had learned to play an instrument other than the radio. I hear bubbles from the Coke popping in the can.

"Please say something, Peter."

"Something," I say, and she smiles.

"You are funny."

"I try."

"Peter, I have been searching for the right father for my child—or children, who knows? And so what if Henry is gay? He should be a father, too, do you not agree?"

"Sure."

"Although right now it does not matter to me that Henry is gay, it might matter to me and our child later. But until then, I do not care. And that is the beauty of it, do you not see? I can have his love, his child, his support, and I fully know this man. We are completely open with each other. If he wants to see another man, he can." She looks into her coffee cup. "And if I want to see another man, I can." She looks up. "And since you will be here this weekend . . ."

I stop breathing. "Um, Cece, what are you suggesting?"

"Henry is a deep, deep sleeper, Peter, and I promise—"

I exhale. "Hold up, Cece, I don't think—"

"He will never know, Peter," she interrupts. "Perhaps you can do what he cannot, what he has not been able to do."

But I'm the Fisher King. "Now wait—"

"I admire your writing, your insight into the female psyche, and your love scenes—whoo! You really know how to make my nose sweat."

I shake my head. "Cece, that's—"

"I want to have children, Peter, and Henry just is not up to the task, you know?" She sets her mug on the coffee table. "And I think he set up this entire weekend so that you and I can . . ."

"Can what?"

"Can make Henry and me a baby. Do you not see? He loves me that much."

I don't know if I'd call it love. I don't even think there's a word that describes it. Maybe the word "twisted."

"Cece, please don't take this the wrong way. You are an incredibly beautiful woman, and under very different circumstances, I might be persuaded to be your . . . donor." I cringe as soon as I say the word "donor." That was cold. "But right now—"

"Henry tells me that you are recently divorced, that you have been separated from your wife for some time now, that you prefer black women to—"

I stand. "That I have no children? Did he tell you that? Did he tell you that I was married to a Catholic woman for many years and didn't even come close to fathering a child?" Yet another item in the long list of my life that I do not understand.

"Was your wife taking birth control pills?"

"She was Catholic."

She sits back and smiles. "They do not sell birth control to Catholics in this country?"

"I'm sure they do, but that's not the point. It was against Edie's religion, against everything she believed in, against everything she was raised to believe."

"To use birth control or to get pregnant?"

Cece has a point, but she doesn't know Edie. "Edie said she wanted to have children, and she never used birth control. Never."

Cece shakes her head. "And you were around her twenty-four hours a day to make sure that she did not take these pills."

"No, of course I wasn't around her all day, but she told me she wanted to have children."

Cece raises her arms above her head, her delicious breasts tightening her blouse to bursting. "Then you do not know women that well at all, Peter. We women tell men what men want to hear. It is our way of singing the beast out of you. And when you hear what you want to hear, you turn off your ears." She lets a shoe drop to the floor and unbuttons the top button of her blouse. "Henry will not be coming back for quite a long while, Peter."

"He won't?"

"See, you are already turning off your ears." She twists another button with her fingers. "Henry has a date." The button comes free and I see she's not wearing a bra. "And we have a date, too, do we not?"

Oh shitshitshit. "Cece, I-I'm leaving."

She twists another button. "You are saying you are leaving, but you are still standing in one spot. And how will you get off the island? The next ferry will not arrive until morning. And it is such a long, cold swim."

I turn my back on her and begin collecting my notes and securing my laptop. "Tell Henry I've gone to Huntington."

"You are not leaving me."

"Tell Henry that I will be staying on my father's boat."

"Will you not at least sleep on the idea for one night?"

I could . . . but I won't. "Tell Henry that I will call him at his office."

I rush to Henry's room, stuff my clothes in my carry-on, and take as many deep breaths as I can without hyperventilating. In my whiskey-soaked days, I would be with this woman all night in every possible position until I dropped from exhaustion or someone called the police because of the noise.

Not tonight.

Tonight I have to get home.

When I pass by her, Cece is not nearly as alluring as before, her sultry voice nothing but cheap sound effects, her body nothing more than a mannequin, nonetheless a drop-dead gorgeous mannequin.

"So you are gay, too?" she asks.

I stop at the door and turn. "Gay? Cece, I'm not even happy." I eye her from head to toe, and she draws her legs up to her chest. "I wish you and Henry every happiness, and for what it's worth, you are the second-most beautiful woman I have ever known."

"Second-most?" Her shoulders sag. "Ah, that explains it. You are in love with someone else."

She's right. I'm still in love with Ebony Mills. "Yes."

"Henry did not tell me that you are in love."

"Because I didn't tell Henry I was in love."

"It would not have mattered. What does Henry know of how a man truly feels for the woman he loves?" She stands and buttons her blouse. "If I had known that your mind was on another woman, I would not have embarrassed myself."

"You have nothing to be embarrassed about, Cece."

"And you do not know how it feels for a woman to throw herself at a man who does not catch her." She slides on her shoe, a tear slipping from an eye.

"Like I said, under any other circumstances, I would be glad to—"

She waves her hands. "No, do not say it. Do not say you would be my *donor*. It is an ugly word."

I set my laptop and carry-on at the door. "I wasn't going to say that, Cece. I wasn't going to say that at all."

She wipes the tear away. "What were you going to say?"

I approach her, taking her hands. "I was going to say that I would be glad—no, honored—to have made love to you."

Another tear falls. "Thank you."

I squeeze her hands and kiss her forehead. "And it would not have been as a donor. It would have been as your lover." I kiss her cheek. "And who knows, maybe we'll see each other again, but far, far away from Henry."

More tears. "I would like to give you my number, Peter Underhill."

I pull out a pen and open my hand. "I promise not to wash it off."

She laughs and writes several numbers on my hand, labeling one "cell," another "home," and yet another "office."

"Is this number-one beauty a sure thing?"

"I don't know, but I hope so."

She pulls me to her and sighs. "Call me anyway, okay?"

"I will."

She looks up at me with such beautiful eyes, eyes full of crystal tears like Ebony's that day twenty years ago . . . "Do you promise to call me, Peter?"

"Yes." My mind flashes to that distant parting. *Yes, Ebony.*

She kisses my cheek. "Another time, another place."

"Yes."

Another time, another place, another parting, eyes full of tears.

I retrieve my carry-on and laptop, their weight also familiar to me. The girl with sad eyes at the door, me with suitcases in hand, her waving, me nodding . . .

Full circle.

And once again I'm walking toward oblivion with no way to get off, an outcast in a twilight country.

I stand at the Cherry Grove pier under a single lamp for no reason at all, staring across Great South Bay at the lights of Sayville and the rest of the south shore miles away. From one island to another, without a ship or a star to steer her by, the next ferry arriving in sixteen hours, faint with hunger and nothing to eat, and a date tomorrow night with Destiny. I need to find a greasy spoon somewhere soon, a place proud to serve saturated fat and cholesterol with bottomless glasses of sweet iced tea to clog my arteries and ruin my kidneys. Are there any truly American diners left? Where's a Bob's Big Boy when you need one?

I could go back to Henry's apartment. Sure. There's a woman there who wants my sperm in the worst way, and I could even imagine that she's Ebony. No, that's sick. It was sick when I imagined that Edie was Ebony, all lights off, of course. I could go back to comfort Cece, maybe even spend the night . . . and have to listen to her and Henry go at it—if he has any energy left—less than thirty feet away. No, that's even sicker.

And sitting out here in the increasing cold could make me the sickest I've been in a long time. I should go back and let Nature take her course . . . but that would be cheating, wouldn't it? Wait. How can you cheat on a woman you haven't seen for twenty years? I'm going back. Yes, that's what I'll—

I hear the sound of an approaching boat. A twenty-foot runabout with twin Mercury 80s speeds out of the dark and chops through its own wake to the dock, several semi-sober women leaning over one side in an attempt to catch the edge of the dock.

I leave my carry-on and laptop behind me, reaching out to a woman with long raven hair. "Grab my hand. I'll pull you in."

And that's precisely what I do—I pull her into the water. I don't mean to. I have no idea what, if anything, is going through her mind, but when I pull, she steps out of the boat and into Great South Bay. She flounders around for a few seconds between the dock and the boat before standing in the shallow water and throwing her head back, her hair whipping water wildly into the air.

"I'm sorry, I didn't mean—"

"This is great!" she yells. "And the water is so warm! C'mon everybody, let's get wet!"

And that's what they do. Everyone, including the driver, dives off the boat fully clothed into three feet of water while the boat continues to drift toward shore, one particularly large woman doing a graceless cannonball that sprays water on me. I go to the water's edge and drag the boat up on shore while the squeals and shouts continue.

The raven-haired woman comes out of the bay first. "Thanks for pulling the boat up."

Her appearance is definitely Irish, her accent Boston. "You're welcome, and sorry about pulling you into the water."

She giggles and wrings out her red flannel shirt, water pouring onto her hiking boots. "Don't worry about it."

"You want me to tie your boat up to the dock?"

She shrugs. "It's not my boat." She smiles. "In fact, we don't know whose boat it is."

"You stole it?"

"Sort of." She wrings out her hair, a gob of seaweed plopping on the sand, a strand of marsh grass stuck to her pale, freckled cheek. She is not the stuff of James Joyce's epiphanies. "I mean, one minute we're just sort of standing there looking at it, and the next minute we're just sort of driving away."

"You just sort of stole it."

"Yeah."

"From Sayville?"

"I think so."

"Are you sure?" This boat could be my ticket across.

"Yeah. Sayville, rhymes with navel." She giggles again. She and her friends are beyond tanked, stumbling out of the water like a scene from *Night of the Living Dead*. The corpses in that movie didn't laugh nearly as much, however, and some of the corpses were prettier.

"Uh, were there a whole bunch of little red wagons along the docks there?"

She squints up at me. "Yeah. What were they for?"

Stolen from where the Charon Ferry docks in Sayville. "The children of Sayville love their little red wagons."

"Oh." She frowns, then smiles. "Hey, where are the hot guys around here? We want to par-*tay*!"

And you've come to the right place. I smile. "Uh, try Le Lethe." I point toward Green Walk. "It's usually crawling with hot guys who love to par-*tay*. Ask for Henry."

"Is it a disco? I love to dance."

"I'm sure you can do a lot of interesting things at Le Lethe."

"Thanks, man!" She turns to her friends. "C'mon! The men are this way!" She steps closer to me. "Are you coming with us?"

"Uh, no."

She pouts. "Why not?"

Because I'm thinking of stealing the boat that you stole. "Um, I'm afraid I'm gay."

She blushes. "Oh. Sorry."

"Don't worry about it."

I wave at them as they whisper their way to Green Walk, and as soon as they giggle around the corner, I check the fuel gauge on the run-about—half a tank. Since the first half a tank got them here, I ought to get back okay. I put my carry-on and laptop inside the boat, remove my socks and shoes and roll up my pants.

Then . . . I steal a boat from Sayville, which rhymes with "navel," by pushing it out into Great South Bay and climbing in as soon as the boat floats free. I paddle into the darkness until I find the first navigational buoy, turn over the engines, and cruise at half-throttle from buoy to buoy, their lights leading me across the foggy bay, quoting Whitman as I go: "But O the ship, the immortal ship! O ship aboard the ship! Ship of the body, ship of the soul, voyaging, voyaging, voyaging."

Twelve miles, sixty minutes, and a hundred glances at the fuel gauge later, I find an empty slip near some gas pumps at the Sayville marina, secure the boat, and get out.

"Gas pump's closed," a deep male voice says from the darkness.

I look all around me and see no one. "I've got plenty of gas. Thanks."

A flashlight beam hits me in the face. "Where have you been at this time of night?"

I shield my eyes and squint at my interrogator. "You mind not shining that in my face?" The beam travels from my face to my feet. I see my ashy toes staring up at me. Shit, my shoes are still in the boat. I look up and see a policeman blocking my way off the dock.

I knew today would be a bad day.

Note to self: *If given the chance to donate sperm, take it.*

"That your boat?" he asks as he shines the light on the boat.

I shake my head. "No." Think fast. "Sir," I add. Jesus, help me here.

"No? Whose boat is it then?"

"I don't know, sir. You see—"

"Those your shoes?" I see my shoes and socks illuminated by the flashlight.

"Yes. You see, a group of drunk women—" His radio squawks, and I freeze.

"Found it" is all he says into his shoulder microphone. "Let me see some ID." I hand him my Pennsylvania driver's license. He holds it up beside my face. "Long way from home, aren't you?" He hands back the license.

"My original home's up in Huntington. That's where I'm headed."

"Yeah?" He smiles while I nod. "Go on with your story."

I am probably the world's worst liar, so I tell the truth. "I have spent the last few days at Henry Milton's place on Green Walk in Cherry Grove, and if you call there, you'll either get Henry, who's gay, or a woman, Cece, who's not gay and who wants me to donate my sperm to her so they can have a baby."

The policeman doesn't blink. "What's the number there?"

I give it to him, and he writes it down on a little notepad.

"But I didn't want to donate my sperm to her," I continue.

"You didn't?"

"No. Cece is very beautiful, but I'm in love with someone else who I haven't seen in twenty years, so I went out to the pier and saw this boat"—I point at the boat and look longingly at my shoes—"and it was filled with drunk women, and they nearly crashed into the dock over there."

"Did they?"

"Yes, sir."

"Where are they now?"

"I directed them to Le Lethe where they could do some dancing and meet some hot guys. They wanted me to come along, but I told them I was gay."

The policeman laughs and shakes his head. "You have anything else to add to your little story?"

"Well, then I decided to return the boat to where it rightfully belonged."

"And save yourself a nine-dollar ferry ride in the morning."

"Uh, that, too, but mainly to save myself the sixteen-hour wait until the next ferry arrived."

He smiles. "How'd you know this is where the boat rightfully belonged?"

"Because of the red wagons. The girl I spoke to told me about the red wagons."

"Have you been drinking tonight, sir?"

"Nothing but Coca-Cola, sir." Sobriety has its price, too.

His microphone squawks again. "Hold on a minute."

"Can I get my shoes?"

"Sure."

He follows me to the boat, repeating my story into his microphone, the threat of a chuckle escaping his lips, and I retrieve my shoes and socks. I sit on the dock and put them on while he finishes relating my story, ending it with, "Make a few calls, okay?" He laughs and shakes his head. "For your sake, I hope all this is true."

"It is. I'll even pay for the gas I used."

He squats beside me. "Are you even gay?"

"No, I'm not even happy." He doesn't respond at all. "I'm a writer. Henry Milton is my editor."

"And you sent those girls to Le Lethe?"

"Yeah. Kind of a punishment for stealing someone's boat."

He shrugs. "Might not be a punishment." He stands. "Sit tight. I'll be right back."

Half an hour of watching my feet dangle above the turbid water below, the policeman returns. "Amazing, but your entire story checks out."

I stand and dust off my pants. "Can I go now?"

"Sure." He laughs. "They caught them trying to swim back. Can you believe it?"

"Amazing." Anything at all can happen on Long Island. I dig in my pocket and come up with a crumpled ten. "I'm sure I owe more than this for the gas, but I've only got a credit card." I hold out the bill.

"Don't worry about it. You, uh, got a car?"

"Yeah." I point at the parking lot. "It's up there."

He tips his hat. "Well, have a good night."

"Thanks."

I pocket the ten and trudge up too many stairs to the parking lot, putting my carry-on and laptop into the trunk of the Nova. When I slump into my seat and turn over the engine, the fuel gauge barely nudges past *E*.

I'm running on an empty stomach driving a car on empty. I smile in spite of all the emptiness, recline the seat, and try to take a long nap, my head empty except for the dream of Ebony.

"The mind knows only what lies near the heart," the old Norsemen used to say, and for the few moments before I fall asleep, Ebony is snuggling up to my heart.

8

"A silly man," the old Norsemen also used to say, "lies awake all night, thinking of many things. When the morning comes, he is worn with care, and his trouble is just as it was."

I didn't sleep a wink.

I feel the windshield of the Nova, and it's definitely cold out. An unseasonably warm October has turned into an October of old gray tumbleweed clouds screaming under a fence of red sky fingers squeezing a vibrant blue canvas—quite a cartoon palette, as if Walt Disney's still at it. I turn on the radio and learn that the temperature is to drop steadily throughout the day. That ought to keep me awake. A biting wind rattles the car, reminding me that Long Island is as flat as a pancake—

The thought makes me hungry, but I can wait until lunchtime at Friendly's, my favorite place to eat after church twenty years ago.

The engine turns over, the fuel gauge dips, and a little red light comes on. I have less than two gallons of gas, and a search of the radio dial reveals that I have few stations to choose from that play my favorite music. I find "Crocodile Rock" on one station that turns out to "only play oldies, twenty-four hours a day." My generation's music is soon to be Musak, soon to be doctor and dentist office rock. When ELO's "Evil Woman" begins, I pull out of the parking lot and find a gas station, its prices higher per ounce than the cheap beer inside. Cruising out of Sayville, I hear the final strains of "Stairway to Heaven" followed by ten minutes of commercials. No music by black people on an oldies station? You couldn't have had the 1970s without black musicians. I turn off the radio. The only radio I need is the sound of this car's tires getting me to my honey. God, I miss my Mustang. This is muscle car weather for sure. A country song takes shape as I hit 97 North:

I'm ridin' along in my rusty Nova,
all busted up cuz she said it's ov-uh,
wish I had me a four-leaf clove-uh
to wish me luck to find my love-uh . . .

What white people do for fun when they drive in wimpy four-cylinder cars . . .

Once I hit 495 West, I start seeing swarms of traffic and all those signs again: Lake Ronkonkoma, Hauppauge, Commack, and Dix Hills. I remember a story about an eight-year-old girl kidnapped in Half Hollow Hills back in '74, where the kidnappers released the kid but didn't get the $50,000 ransom. That kid must have been something else. The story served its purpose, though. None of us ever wandered too far away from home after that.

After hitting Melville and getting on 110, I stop at Larke Drugs. My back, which hasn't felt right for months, can't take it any longer, and I need a refill on my muscle relaxers. I place my order using the empty bottle. "I'd like this refilled, please."

"I'll need to see some ID," the pharmacist says, "Bob" emblazoned on his smock. I hand my license to Bob. "Pennsylvania?"

I nod.

"Can't get muscle relaxers there?"

"I've just relocated."

"Oh. So this isn't your current address?"

Another nod.

"You have one?"

"Just put . . . Huntington Yacht Club for now."

He raises two pencil-thin eyebrows. "Phone number?"

"Don't have one yet."

"Hmm. Might be a while. You have your insurance card?"

Thanks to COBRA, I have had an insurance card for coverage from Edie's cushy job with the Pittsburgh Arts Council for close to five years now. It was only supposed to last for the first eighteen months of our separation, but somehow I still get my dentist's visits and prescriptions paid for.

I hand Bob my card, then wander down an aisle, checking out a row of cold medicines without alcohol. Where's the fun in that? The Captain used to make me chugalug Vicks 44 when I was a kid, and I'm sure he took a few hits, too. While I'm staring at foam plates and Dixie cups—my future good china and glassware on the *Argo*—Bob motions me over to the counter.

"Your policy has been cancelled, Mr. Underhill. Sorry."

Either Edie quit her job and frolicked back to Daddy Melton's millions, or someone at the healthcare provider figured out how to count to eighteen. "Oh. Um, what's full price?" He tells me, and I gasp. Ouch. Groceries for a week cost less! "Okay."

"Go ahead and fill this?"

"Might as well."

I sit in the waiting area and ponder a sign that reads: ASK THE PHARMA- CIST. Ask him what? What's it like to know everyone's medical problems? It almost makes him the prescription priest. What I would love to ask: Have you ever made a mistake and given muscle relaxers to a Methodist or codeine to an evangelical Christian?

Or even birth control to a Catholic?

I guess it's possible, maybe even probable that Edie was on the pill. I never looked at those healthcare statements, but a real Catholic married for ten years with no kids? Even her gay brothers are still squirting them out. The Meltons are a very fertile family. And what if we had succeeded and had a boy for me and a girl for her? Not likely. We probably would have had twins, both platinum blond, both girls, both saying "Mummy." What a nightmare.

Would I have made a good father? What childless man can say "I would have been a good father" with any sense of honesty? Unless he has been a father or has been raised by a decent father, he has no idea. I have no idea what makes a good father, and I haven't exactly had the proper training to become one. All I can say is that I would have liked to have had the opportunity to be a father, and I would have raised my child or children the exact opposite of the way I was raised. I might have kept the sailing on Saturday part. Those were sometimes special.

After half an hour, I play "What is he or she here for?" as folks stream in to fill their prescriptions. The large woman with the high hips and bedroom slippers—has to be something for gout. The bleary-eyed man with the dripping nose and the hacking cough—has to be an antibiotic of some kind. The frazzled woman with the four kids racing around her—got to be Quaaludes. Or speed.

Another twenty minutes. What is Bob doing? Does he have to log each pill's serial number into the computer or what?

I stretch and walk the aisles again, perusing the section for back pain. I wonder where my old hydrocollator is. That hot, moist heat would cure my back for sure. I know I lost it in the settlement. Edie and her periods. A hot water bottle was just too "common" for her to use.

I sample several pamphlets—"Protecting Your Child from Drug Abuse" and "Kids and Drugs"—and sense a pattern. But why put these pamphlets near the counter where their parents are getting their legal drugs? "Generic Drugs and You" is interesting. It seems they have a generic for everything these days. "Growing into Growing Older—Hot and Cold Weather Hazards for Older People" depresses me, but I'm not as depressed as the guy next to me finding the empty section of Nicorette products, scratching at the metal shelving as if he can magically produce an overpriced box of gum. Crashing planes have a way of stopping folks from smoking, I guess. I pick up "Muscle Pain Slowing You Down?" and whisper, "No, this pharmacy is!" I drift to the "male birth control" section and see, geez, forty-eight different kinds of condoms. I can only imagine the research done to arrive at such a large selection. I imagine some man or woman using a ruler to take measurements. Or would they just take a man's penis and cover it with plaster of paris to make a mold? Who gets these jobs? I try to imagine the first question in an interview for such a job: "What qualifies you to measure the length and girth of a man's penis?"

After over an hour of stupid thoughts, I have had enough. Maybe sleeping on the *Argo* will cure my back. I have a good, stiff bunk there. Maybe I don't need the drugs. I'm sure it's just stress.

"Prescription ready for Underhill" crackles from some speakers in the ceiling.

I pay for it anyway and plan to use the muscle relaxers only as a last resort. After all, pain is good.

It means you're still alive.

I resume my journey up 110, passing Gourmet Wok Kitchen, to Friendly's, where I devour a Fishamajig with fries and guzzle two chocolate Fribbles just before the lunch rush. The waitress can't believe anyone can eat that fast. Ah, grease and sugar, the food of the gods.

Traffic slows me through Huntington Station, which I swear only exists for the purposes of the Long Island Rail Road. This is a strange town to me. This is the place where a newlywed man killed his wife on Christmas Eve, stuffed her into a Hefty bag, and then pretended to search for her with his concerned neighbors. Yes, Fitzgerald's crime-infested Long Island still festers: Amityville, where Butch DeFeo, Jr., shot to death his father, mother, two brothers and two sisters in '74 because he heard "voices"—

What's this? Filene's Basement? Bloomingdale's? Saks Fifth Avenue? Since when has Huntington been chic? My, how the Walt Whitman Mall has changed. Walt's birthplace and museum are hidden behind a stockade fence where Walt's Tree supposedly still lives. Crowded out by Eddie Bauer.

Am I getting closer to or farther away from home?

When 110 becomes New York Avenue, I'm finally in Huntington. I pull over to a Bank of New York and get a cash advance off my Discover card. I only take out a hundred, hoping that Xando isn't as exotically priced as its name. Then I sniff the air. Something about scents that drive my memories wild.

Huntington, which will be 350 years old in 2003, is the only city that has been denied all-American city status four times. That ought to make Buffalo Bills fans feel right at home here. It is the past home of Fort Golgotha, where the British used headstones for baking bread, the bread sporting the inscriptions of the deceased on the bottom of each loaf. The American Legion Post once picketed Charlie Chaplin here, which tells you about Huntington's sense of humor. Huntington is a city that is only fifty-five miles from Manhattan with fifty-one miles of shoreline and five harbors and seven pizza joints on Main Street alone. Huntington shellfish (little neck, cherry, and chowder clams) are shipped daily to New York City's Fulton Fish Market and have been distributed nationwide since Colonial times. Yeah, my hometown, home to segregated burial grounds at Huntington Rural Cemetery and home of singer Harry Chapin, who died at age thirty-eight on the Long Island Expressway. I wonder if anything has changed in twenty years in this conflicted town.

I cruise around West Main and see a few minor changes, mostly in the names of businesses. Village Pizza is now Little Vincent's Pizza, and

Century Lanes is now a Walbaum's Supermarket. I wonder if they bowl turkeys there around Thanksgiving. St. Pat's is still here. Good old Catholic buildings don't ever become bowling alleys. Bingo parlors, maybe. The Blue Dolphin is now the Golden Dolphin, the Hamburger Choo Choo has ridden out of town, the Hungry Boar has gone off in search of greener pastures, and Herman and Ray's is now called Munday's. Finnegan's is still here. Irish pubs never die. R.L. Simpson is now part of the Huntington Town Hall Building, and Hecksher Park has new paths and a bigger children's playground.

And the pond is still green.

Tired of sightseeing, I take Southdown Road past the Southdown Community Market, where I used to buy beef jerky and Slim Jims, to Preston Street, my hands sweating slightly. Up the hill, a left on Drohan Street, and a right on Grace Lane and—

There's a white woman in Candace Mills's old yard. She's planting bulbs around the oak tree, where Ebony and I once planted petunias. It just doesn't seem right somehow. A huge tan van, complete with a wheelchair lift, sits in the driveway in front of a car covered by a tarp. The house itself doesn't look as if it has changed much: same royal blue shutters, same gray wood siding, and same white door. When I cruise by a second time, the woman looks up, waves her trowel at me, and I keep cruising.

I loop around again to Preston Street and head to my old house, parking the Nova in front of Mrs. Hite's hydrangea bushes, now grown to nearly ten feet high. Once they grew four feet tall, she couldn't reach high enough to trim them. I wonder if she's still around.

The Captain's old house still stands, the cedar shingles looking warped and gray. I wonder what the newest owners paid for it. Since no one seems home, I slip around the side of the house to the back path and see the deck, still there among the trees. I thought the Captain was crazy for putting it back there, but now it looks as if it belongs there, almost as if the trees are holding it in place. While the edge of the house slowly ambles closer to the bank, the deck has held, sentinel trees guarding it from a house heading out to sea.

I slip down the slope beside the deck and head to the cistern, the Cave, only to find it has been filled with cement. Another hallowed place gone. But the woods . . . our woods . . . they're still here.

Yes, when I was home, I was in a far better place.

On my way to the yacht club, I remember the November day in 1990 when I came to the funeral parlor to view the Captain's body, his lips pale, his chin set, his weak eye bulging, his hands folded gently on his chest. He looked so waxen, much like the so-called professionals associated with his funeral. The Captain's will called for cremation, but the funeral parlor folks said, "No, what you want is a military funeral." It's not what the Captain specified in his will, I told them, but they were persistent, almost as persistent as the new pastor at the Methodist church the Captain hadn't attended in twenty years. "He would have wanted the service to be here."

Everybody had his or her hand out: pay the preacher, pay the organist, pay the soloist, pay the funeral parlor, pay for the programs, pay $2,000 up front—all this for a simple cremation. I even had a guy try to sell *me* a "choice plot of land" at a cemetery, saying, "You're never too young to start thinking about death, and if you pay now, you'll spare your relatives in their time of grief." What relatives? I'm the only Underhill left!

I fish in my wallet for a little note I wrote to myself almost eleven years ago, finding it sandwiched between two expired Visa cards: "Cremate me and spread my ashes over Mrs. Candace Mills's garden." I crumple it up and squeeze it into the ashtray. Another idea balled up and buried.

I had even looked into the Navy's Mortuary Affairs Burial at Sea Program. According to the official, acronym-crazy Navy, I was the PADD (Person Authorized to Direct Disposition) in charge of my father's Cremains (Cremated Remains) and would have to complete a BASRF (Burial-at-Sea Request Form) and include a copy of the death certificate, the burial transit permit or the cremation certificate, and a copy of DD Form 214, a discharge certificate or retirement order.

I couldn't find the Captain's discharge papers, and inquiries to the Department of Defense yielded: "It'll take us a few days. What years did he serve again?"

I didn't feel I had the time—I was still "in like" with Edie then and wanted to get back home to her—so I called around to bona fide companies specializing in burials at sea. For $150 if I wasn't there and $600 if a charter boat was used, they would sprinkle the Captain's ashes in Great South Bay. No wonder the fishing's always so good there. I have found out since that Rock Hudson, Steve McQueen, Janis Joplin, Jerry Garcia, L. Ron Hubbard, Vincent Price, Robert Mitchum, and Ingrid Bergman were scattered at sea—interesting company for the Captain. Who *wouldn't* he argue with?

But like half the folks who have had loved ones cremated, I took the Captain home—sort of. I took him to *his* home, the *Argo*. I had him placed in a cremation urn called, appropriately, "The Captain," an eight-inch solid oak cube complete with a brass nameplate and the Navy emblem, and I secured the box under the plank from the *Iowa*. It's the Captain's little shrine. I guess one day I'll scatter him out in the Sound, but until then, I'll have the Captain's bones rattling around on the boat he loved more than me. They say cremated remains look like crushed seashells, but I doubt the Captain's remains are that beautiful. I had him cremated in his dungarees, Navy pea coat, plain white T-shirt, black shoes, and white socks—his eternal fashion statement.

But that memorial service of his was a completely unexpected event. I still don't know how anybody knew about it. The *Long-Islander* ran the obituary without his picture, so I didn't expect anyone to come. Yet . . . they did.

I stood in back of the church watching grown black and white men walking up to the casket, whispering something to the Captain, and moving on. It was just me walking down front to start the service. The organist played the National Anthem, the preacher read from the Old and New Testaments, someone prayed, and I barely heard the sermon. The organist then played the Navy Hymn ("Abide With Me"), and every man behind me stood and sang it loud and strong. I still get goose bumps just thinking about that. After the benediction, four burly black men carried the Captain out to the hearse. I assumed at the time that they worked for the funeral parlor, but they quickly set me straight. In the receiving line—again, I was the only one anyone was consoling—these four grizzled old black men wished me "fair winds and following seas," told me that the Captain was the "king of the Mighty I" and the "prince of the Big Stick," told me "your daddy was a terrible canasta player, but a true shipmate." A younger black man, wearing his Navy uniform, told me that his father, a mess steward, and my father were friends. An older black man said he used to work belowdecks in the Black Gang, but that my father always said hello. The last, a young black man no more than twenty, who had come all the way from California, said that his grandfather Marcus Minor had been killed on board the USS *Thompson* and that "his final resting place was on the *Iowa* in your daddy's arms."

Strange I remember all that as I drive on West Shore Road, which follows the curves of Huntington Bay. My racist daddy had an integrated funeral. I wonder if he was pissed about it . . . wherever he is now.

I look out over the harbor. "Water looks choppy, good day for a sail," the Captain would have said. I wouldn't dare take out the *Argo* today. One does not take one's home into harm's way when one is not a good sailor.

After easing into the Huntington Yacht Club parking lot, I stare out at the *Argo* and wonder again why, after nearly eleven years, I remember what those men said at the Captain's funeral. He was a hero to those guys, but why? I had always thought that if heroism depended on lost causes, then the Captain had died too young. He had died undefeated in his berth, died peacefully on his ship, the *Argo*. It wasn't the way he would have wanted to go out of this life. A storm and a watery grave would have been better for him. It was lucky someone from the yacht club had gone out to check on him when they hadn't heard from him for a few days.

I walk into the yacht club expecting a hefty bill that will wipe out my advance. Eleven years' dues must come to . . . I don't want to think about it. And from the looks of all the remodeling done since I visited last, it's going to be an extremely hefty bill. The clubhouse, docks, pool, dock house, restaurant, and lounge—everything looks brand new. But where is everybody? The place is usually crawling with people on Saturday afternoons. I wander past two ladies rooms—I don't even remember *one* in the old days—and a beautiful trophy display case, many announcing the winners of the winter Frostbite races. The Captain and I endured many of those icy races, and though we never won, we were always in the lead pack. Wish we had a trophy with our names on it in there.

"Pete? Pete Underhill?"

I turn and see a vaguely familiar face. "Mr. . . . . Cutter?"

He shakes my hand vigorously. "You remember!" He lets go of my hand. Stooped, jowly, and always sporting a baseball cap of some kind, Mr. Cutter is the yacht club director and one of the oldest members. "You know, you're looking more and more like your daddy every day. What's it been, ten years?"

"Almost eleven."

"And you're here because . . ."

"I'm here to settle up my father's bill, maybe spend some time on the *Argo*."

"Splendid, splendid. But what do you mean about settling up? Your daddy is a lifetime member."

"He . . . was?" He always told me the only reason he joined at all was for the decent deep-water mooring and boat taxi service so he wouldn't have to use the dinghy as much.

Mr. Cutter points to a plaque inside the case. "He's listed right there."

I see his name—John D. Underhill—gleaming back at me. "When did he become a lifetime member?"

"Far as I know he had always been a lifetime member, and now the membership passes to you." He drapes an arm around me. "Not much going on around here since nine-eleven. Battening down the hatches, that sort of thing. Anything you need right away?"

"I guess I'll need a ride out to the *Argo*."

He squeezes my shoulder. "I'll take you myself."

We head down to the docks and get into a small orange Zodiac, the kind of rubber boat Jacques Cousteau used on his voyages. "Any service done on her recently?"

He pull-starts the outboard. "We pull her out once a year, clean her stem to stern, run and tune the engine. She's in perfect condition, an incredible ship. What is she, almost seventy years old now?"

"Think so."

"They don't make them like that anymore." He eases away from the dock. "You aren't thinking about selling her, are you?"

"No."

"I've had lots of offers over the years."

I smile. "She belongs to me now."

Mr. Cutter throttles down as we near the deep-water moorings. "What kept you away for so long, Pete?"

"Long story."

"Well, you're here now, right?"

We cruise past larger, more modern yachts in the sixty-foot range to a gap, and there's the *Argo* at rest, a dark hulk with its sails down.

Mr. Cutter eases the water-taxi alongside. "You got a cell phone, Pete?"

"No."

"Get one. It'll save you on your radio batteries and the commute to shore. Just call, and a taxi will pick you up."

"Um, is this part of the membership?"

"Sure is."

I slide my carry-on and laptop onto the deck. "Thanks for the ride, Mr. Cutter."

"No problem, Pete. Good to have you back."

The *Argo* doesn't seem as big as I remember, but it is still in pristine condition. Eleven years bobbing in Huntington Bay haven't hurt it at all. I first check out the engine, turning over the Volvo. It still purrs like a dream. I leave it running to, as the Captain used to say, "juice the batteries." Once in the galley I open all the wooden blinds and windows and smile. I am in a museum. Everything glistens and shines—the wooden bench, the tabletop, the paneling, even the *Iowa* plank and the Captain's urn. Not a speck of dust anywhere, which is extremely odd. Someone has to have been cleaning recently, the scent of lemon in the air. Who would clean a ghost ship? Maybe cleaning is part of the membership, too. I open the doors to the head and my old berth and find more spotlessness, my bunk completely free of dust. I don't open the Captain's door. I can't quite do that yet. But why is everything so clean? It's as if someone knew I was coming.

"Ensign Peter Underhill, reporting for duty, Captain," I say to the Captain's urn. I run my fingers over his name on the brass plate. "But as usual, there's nothing for Ensign Underhill to do on your boat."

I unload my clothing in my berth, make up my bunk, and take the laptop out on deck. The battery will give me two hours of writing tops, and this wind will bite through me before then. I'll have to do most of my writing belowdecks or in the clubhouse at the yacht club.

Then, as the *Argo* rocks with an occasional roll, I resume *Promises to Keep*, first examining the last paragraph I couldn't finish yesterday:

A door slammed above them, the door to the kitchen slammed, the door to the kitchen slammed and rattled and footsteps came down the narrow path to the deck and

You weren't supposed to be home, Captain. You were supposed to be out sailing. Ebony and I had so little time together . . . and you came storming into our oasis.

A larger wave, the wake of a passing fishing boat, shakes the *Argo*, and after it passes, I swear I hear the rattling of the Captain's bones down in the galley. I delete my unfinished paragraph, and continue:

"What the hell's going on under there?"

Ebony popped out from under the deck first. "Hi, Mr. Underhill."

The Captain's eyes popped, and his face turned beet red. "You . . . you get out of here this instant!"

"What'd I do?" she asked, not moving.

Peter ducked under the eaves of the deck but kept his eyes glued to the leaves at his feet. He couldn't speak.

"I told you to leave, Missy."

"My name ain't Missy. It's Ebony."

Peter touched Ebony's elbow. "Just go," he whispered.

"We weren't doin' nothin' wrong, Peter."

"Please go," Peter whispered again.

"I ain't leavin'." She looked up at the Captain and smiled. "So how you doin', Mr. Underhill? Didn't you go sailing today?"

"Pete . . . *inside*." The Captain slammed up the deck stairs and disappeared around the side of the house. In a moment, Peter flinched as the screen door slammed.

"I better go, E.," Peter said as he started trudging up the slope.

"Where you goin', Peter?"

"I'm in trouble, E. Big trouble." He reached the top of the slope and wiped a few leaves from his pants. "I'll see you later, okay?"

"Later, like when?"

"I don't know."

"I wasn't finished with you."

"*Pete!*" the Captain called from the kitchen window. "Get your ass up here pronto!"

"*Please* go, Ebony."

"I don't want to leave you, Peter. Meet me at the Cave after dark."

"I don't know if I can."

"Promise me."

Peter sighed. "I can't promise."

Ebony blinked. "Yes, you can, and you will." She bit her lip. "Promise me you'll meet me later."

"I promise."

After sighing "You and your daddy" and shaking her head, Ebony backed down the slope then tore off through the woods, her shiny legs flashing like her eyes, her legs replaced by trees that never moved.

When Peter entered the kitchen, it was as if Minos, the judge of the damned in hell, had set up shop in the kitchen. The Captain sat at the head of the table tapping the knuckles of his fists, his teeth audibly grinding together.

"What in the hell do you think you were doing down there, Pete?" the Captain hissed, frowning grotesquely.

Peter felt as if he were falling through space. He stood at the window and looked into the woods at the silence, at the quiet, at the swaying limbs calling him back, storm clouds gathering above them. "I wasn't doing anything, Captain."

"So you say, but I know you're lying. *Look at me, boy!*"

Peter turned from the window but focused on the linoleum floor. "We weren't doing anything, I swear. We were just talking." *With our hands and lips*, he thought. *I like talking like that.*

"Just talking. You could have been talking out on top of the deck, right? But no, you were hiding out underneath, which lets me know you were up to no good."

"It's shadier underneath." *And we can't talk with our hands and lips on top of the deck.*

"It's shady everywhere back in those woods! I know what you two have been doing. It is a wide and easy passage that snares a man's soul."

Peter blinked. "Is that in the Bible?"

The Captain's knuckle rapping stopped. "Of course it is, I'm sure it is. Aren't you the least bit ashamed of yourself?"

No, Peter thought. "Yes," he said eventually, cursing God but not cursing the Captain since it was God who had made him. "Yes, Captain, I am ashamed." *Mainly for how I didn't stand up to you in front of Ebony.*

"Have you lost your mind? What were you thinking?" He pounded the kitchen table. "*Answer me!*"

You'll never know those thoughts, Peter thought. *Those are between me, Ebony, and God.* "I'm sorry, Captain." *But I'm not. I was just thinking about it. I know my hands were thinking about it. But her butt was so smooth!*

"You're sorry. That is the truth. You are a sorry excuse for a son. And in plain sight? Anyone could have seen you two."

"But you just said—" Peter stopped. It was never any use to confuse the Captain with his own words. "We've been careful, Captain."

"Obviously not careful enough if I caught you." The Captain ground his teeth again. "Wait, we've *been* careful? How long has this been going on, Pete?"

Peter smiled inside. It was all coming out, and for some reason he felt better about the entire fiasco. "A while."

"How long?"

"Since . . . January."

The Captain closed his eyes and started to speak several times. "Since— what the hell? . . . since—" He stood, kicking the chair behind him so hard that it smacked against the stove and clattered to the floor. He stalked toward Peter, and Peter pinned his back against the window. "Has this been going on since your mother left?"

Peter nodded and watched the Captain's hands clenching and unclenching in front of him. "Since you made her leave," he whispered.

The Captain drilled a finger into Peter's chest. "What'd you say?"

"Nothing."

"You say I made her leave?"

The Captain's finger was beginning to hurt Peter's chest. "Didn't you?"

Peter saw the punch coming, but he did nothing to get out of the way, the Captain's fist thudding into his left eye. He fell to the floor, the Captain looming over him.

"You're . . . you're grounded! You're in the brig, Pete! It's been going on for over six months, you'll be in the brig for six months, in the house at all times, and no more baseball!"

Peter felt tears stinging his eyes, but he didn't whimper like a child. "Baseball season's over, Captain."

"It is? When did it end?"

"Today. We had the all-star game today."

"Why didn't you tell me today was the last day? I would have been there, and none of this would have happened."

"I *did* tell you. You said you had to work on the *Argo*."

"Well, I'm going to . . . I'm going to clean up my act. Yeah, that's what I'm going to do. And I'm gonna watch your every move from now on. I didn't raise you right for you to do wrong with that . . . with that . . . girl."

Peter's eyelid began to droop, the skin on his cheek tightening. He stood, his shoulders square to the Captain. "What exactly did I do wrong, Captain?"

The Captain's jaw worked up and down. "You were . . . you were messing around with that gal under the deck I built with my own two hands!"

"How do you know we were messing around?"

The Captain tapped his temple with a finger. "I know. A little birdie told me."

Peter smiled in spite of his pain. "You need a new birdie, Captain."

"What's that?"

"Your birdie must be blind, Captain."

The Captain put his face a breath away from Peter's face. "What do you mean, Pete?"

"Just wondering why it took your birdie six months to tell you, Captain."

Peter didn't see the next punch, but it had the same result, leaving him kissing the linoleum. He scooted his butt against the wall under the window as a dribble of blood trickled from his nose.

"Don't you sass me, don't you *ever* sass me, Pete! No one, and I mean, *no one* sasses me!"

So that's why Mom left. Peter's lips started to feel like little lead balloons. He pressed his hands against the wall and stood. Both eyes filled with tears, but he didn't cry out. He clenched his own fists but remained silent, pressing his tongue against a loosened tooth.

"You brought all this on yourself, Pete. You and your little . . . girlfriend and your sassing me. All of this is on your head."

Peter licked his lip and tasted blood. "I'm not the one doing the hitting," he said, bracing for another punch.

The Captain's shoulders slumped. "I wouldn't have to . . . *discipline* you if you hadn't been doing anything wrong."

Punching your kid is discipline, Peter thought. *Bet the police wouldn't call it that.* "But why is it wrong, Captain?"

The Captain sighed. "Why is it wrong?"

"Yes."

"To be with that nigger?"

Peter's heart sank. "She's not a . . . what you said." *Your picture is next to that word in the dictionary, Captain.* "Her name is Ebony, and she's my friend."

"The gal's even got a name that *means* she's black! You blind, boy? She is black as sin! She doesn't have anything but sin on her mind!"

Peter smiled to himself. *I know! And she isn't the only one.*

"She is your *inferior*, Pete. She is from an *inferior* race. The Bible tells you that."

"Where?"

The Captain blinked. "I don't know where exactly, but I know it's in there."

It isn't in there, Peter thought. It can't be in there. The Bible is the Good Book, and what I feel for Ebony is a good thing. A good thing can't be a sin in the Good Book.

"We've got to get you back to church, Pete, before this self-destructive behavior of yours . . ."

And that's when I tuned him out completely. That was the moment when I stopped listening to anything the Captain had to say for the rest of my life. Using the Bible to support his racist views was about as unholy as all the sins he was accusing me of doing. And using that word to describe my first love—unforgivable. The blows I took that day healed, but the words . . . those words will never heal.

I look at my reflection in the brass horn. "And my appearance is unforgivable, too." I am a stank, unshaved, greasy-haired man. Destiny will take one look at me and head for the door.

I use the *Argo*'s radio to get a water taxi driven once again by Mr. Cutter, and within an hour, I have edged up my beard and showered in the clubhouse. I stare at the wrinkled jeans and Penn State sweatshirt I'm wearing. I have never been God's gift to women. I flick dead skin off my ashy nose. I comb my hair back, hoping that it stays wet long enough to hide all the gray. Am I ready for my date with Destiny? I guess I'm as ready as I'll ever be. I hope she doesn't mind taking toast and tea with a sloppy man.

I drive out to Main Street past Kebali Alem and the Artful Dodger Pub, parking near Village Flowers. Should I get some flowers for Destiny? No. Then she'll really think we're on a date, though she probably already thinks that. No need to confirm her hopes.

I walk to Xando looking side to side for a black woman watching me from one of the parked cars. Maybe she's outside checking me out before I can get a glimpse of her. I half-expect a car to peel away from the curb. None does.

I stop in front of Xando's doors and peer inside. A few men sit in light brown chairs at circular brown tables, exposed pipes above them. Lots of earth tones of brown and rust. Very quadrilateral and Swedish. I don't see anyone even remotely African. I'm early? No, it's 7:10. Is Destiny white? The only white woman inside is wiping down a table.

Deciding to wait outside until her arrival, I read the menu taped to the window and squint often. What's a Squagel? A square bagel? How . . . sacrilegious. An Egg Frittata? S'Breadables? Roasted apple chutney? Caramelized onions? Sun dried tomato spread? Where's the granola and Mueslix?

Just when I decide that I'll probably have to go out for a burger *after* eating at Xando, I see a shimmering light-skinned dream coming out of the bathroom inside. Whoa. She sits alone at a table, and I hope she's my Destiny. She has long hair and a body that just won't quit. She wears a navy blue denim long-sleeved shirt with a large cowry shell design on the front, cowry shell earrings, and tight white pants. Quite a sailor's outfit. This woman is a dime in anyone's pocket. Full red lips, streaks of amber and red in her dark brown hair, dark eyes and eyebrows, strong cheekbones, small chin, cut calves, and sculpted nails—

She's now tapping the table with those nails. I am late, and she's angry. I look at my reflection in the window. I am not worthy of this woman. She is a million dollars covered in liquid pearl, and I am a crumpled dollar bill. Even under the glaring fluorescent lights, she shimmers. I feel my hands beginning to sweat and check them, only to see Cece's phone numbers staring up at me. What did Cece use, indelible ink? I try to wipe her numbers off on my jeans, but they only fade slightly. Damn!

I push through the doors and go straight to her table. "Destiny?"

She looks up at me, her lips a straight line. "You're late."

"Uh, sorry about that." I sit opposite her so I can drink her in. "I had some trouble—"

"And you look terrible. Is that a beard? And what's up with your hair? Is that gel?"

"Uh, yes, it's an attempt at a beard, and no, it's not gel. Guess it's still a little wet." I can't help staring at her hair, blondish hairs glinting.

"Yes, it's my hair."

"So many colors," I say without thinking.

"You think I look Hispanic?"

"Are you?"

"No." She smiles, a full complement of pearly teeth shining on me. "But in Huntington, I am."

"Why?"

She shrugs. "I get more respect."

"Oh." I stare at her hands for a few moments, not knowing what to do with my own. I place them on the table in front of me. "So, Destiny, what more can you tell me about Ebony?"

"Can't we eat first? I'm starving." She turns over my hand. "And what's this?"

I feel the blood rush to my face. "Um, long story."

She turns my hand to her. "Who's . . . Cecil?"

"It's Cece Wrenn."

"The singer?"

I put my hands back in my lap. "Yes. She's a friend of a friend, I mean, she's a friend of mine." Who wants my sperm.

She purses her lips. "And she writes *all* her numbers on your hand?"

"Yeah." I need to change the subject. "So . . . what's good here?"

Destiny shakes her head and laughs. "Peter the player."

"But I'm not a player. Really."

She rolls her eyes. "Right. You just happen to have a famous Jamaican singer's phone numbers tattooed to the palm of your hand."

"She's from Bermuda."

"Whatever. Just a friend of yours, huh?"

"Yeah." I have to buy some Lava soap soon. "So, what's Xando's specialty?"

"Trying to change the subject?"

"Uh, yeah."

She rolls her eyes and sighs. "Their grilled chicken and broccoli pizza is good."

I am not having gas around this woman. "Sounds interesting."

A waiter finally arrives, handing us menus. "Is this your first time here?"

"His," Destiny says.

The waiter, a blond earringed man in his twenties, smiles at Destiny. She must get hit on 24-7. "May I recommend a pocket of bread filled with eggplant feta spread, with grilled roasted veggies and balsamic vinaigrette?"

Geez, more gas. Like Drano for my colon. "Um, sure," I say.

"And what can I get you to drink?"

I read the description for Chai Tea Latte: "A combination of black tea, honey, fresh ginger, vanilla, cinnamon, cardamom, and clove mixed with steamed milk and a layer of foam." I point at the menu. "One of these," I say, even though I have no idea what cardamom is.

The waiter cocks his head toward Destiny. "And for the lady?"

"I'll have a plate of Squagels and the Tuscan salsa with *Bermuda* onions." She smiles at me. "Are the onions really from Bermuda?"

"Far as I know," the waiter says.

"Bet they're from Jamaica," Destiny says with a smile.

"And what can I get you to drink?"

"I'll have a . . . skinny half-caf Caramel Iced Mocha." She's just described herself, though she's definitely not skinny. She is a thick dime. "Oh, and two Mocha Kisses for later."

I scan the menu and see that a Mocha Kiss is a concoction of Kahlua, Irish Cream, Grand Marnier, and whipped cream. "Just one of those, please," I say.

"It'll be my treat," Destiny says in a silver sweet voice.

"Uh, no, thanks. I'm, uh, driving."

"Just one then," Destiny says.

The waiter takes our menus and vanishes, leaving Destiny staring at her hands and me staring at Destiny's hands.

"You don't drink?"

"Not anymore."

She looks up. "You used to?"

"Yeah, but I've been sober for almost two years now."

"Oh."

More shaky silence. I try not to stare at her, but I can't help it. Because of her skin tone, eyes, and body, she is every man's dream, and I'm almost old enough . . . to be her daddy.

"They grind their own beans here," she says to her hands.

"Really?"

"Yeah." She looks up at me. "There is . . . there *was* one of these places in the World Trade Center, but all the people got out before . . ."

"Yeah."

"This is the only one on Long Island."

"It's nice."

She sits back in her chair, sliding one leg under her. "You're taller than I thought you'd be."

"I am?"

"I mean, your e-mails make you seem, um, short." She giggles. "Sorry, I'm a little nervous."

"*You're* nervous?"

"Yeah, I mean, I'm kind of like a matchmaker, right? I've never been a matchmaker before."

I want to touch her hand, maybe even squeeze it, but I don't. "You're doing a wonderful job, Destiny."

"Thank you. Oh God, I'm blushing."

I don't see any change in her face. "You are?"

Before she can answer, the waiter brings us our food and our drinks, and though I'm not exactly sure what I'm eating, it is very good. Every so often Destiny looks up at me looking at her and quickly looks down. Is she flirting with me? And how old is she? She is so polished, so classy. Late twenties maybe. Yet no rings?

She finishes her skinny half-caf and takes a sip of her Mocha Kiss. "You don't know what you're missing."

I sip my Chai Tea Latte. "That's one of the reasons I stopped drinking. I was missing too much."

She doesn't respond for a few moments. "So . . . how was your trip up from Fire Island?"

"Okay. Traffic was heavier than I remembered, and the bowling alley where Ebony used to kick my butt is now a grocery store."

She smiles. "She kicked your tail, huh?"

"Yeah."

"I'm not very good at bowling either." She laughs. "I fall all over my-self. So, where are you staying while you're here?"

"My father's boat."

"Really. That must be . . . interesting."

"Yeah." I look at my empty plate. "I must have been hungry."

She only raises her eyebrows and continues sipping her Mocha Kiss.

I look into the bottom of my mug, strange beige lumps looking up at me. Is that the cardamom? "So . . . how long did you and Ebony work at Alcyone?"

"Oh, a few years. She liked it. I didn't. Made my hands hurt with all that twisting."

"What are you doing now?"

"Well, I'm trying to be a dancer."

That explains the graceful way she carries herself. "Ballet?"

"No way. Freestyle mostly. I audition a lot. Don't get much work. I wasn't classically trained . . . and I ain't white. Gotta be skinny and white and in toe shoes to get work around here." She smiles. "But you didn't come here tonight to hear about me."

"No, but I'm still—"

"It's okay." She pushes her empty Mocha Kiss away from her. "So, Peter, what are you doing still wanting to mess with Ebony? I mean, she's dark as coal, and you're practically colorless." She laughs. "Sorry, sorry."

"It's all right." To the rest of the world, it makes absolutely no sense. But I don't focus on the black and white of it, I focus on the love of it. "I know I'm ashy, but Ebony's not that dark."

"Compared to me, she's darker than darkest night." She laughs again. "So why her?"

"Like I said in the e-mails, we grew up together."

She leans forward, resting her chin on her hands. "She was your first love, huh?"

So intuitive. "Yeah."

"Aw, that's so cute. Was your mama okay with it?"

"She never knew. She, uh, left."

"Sorry to hear that. What about your dad?"

I look away, focusing on a silver coffee dispenser. "He had some . . . issues."

"Made you break up, huh?"

"Sort of. We didn't really ever break up . . . officially."

"Yeah?"

"We just sort of . . . faded away from each other."

"You mean you left her."

I turn back to her. "There was more to it than that."

"I'll bet."

Where is the edge to her voice coming from? "Really. I went off to college and then . . . we faded away."

Destiny tightens her lips. "Just . . . faded away." She pats her flat stomach. "I need to walk this off. Let's go."

"Where?"

She stands. "For a walk. Lots of places to browse in Huntington Village." She slides a white jacket over her shoulders. "You're paying, right?"

I pay the bill, and we walk out to New York Avenue, past the Ariana Restaurant, which boasts Italian-Afghani cuisine, until we stop at Book Revue Cafe, a massive bookstore rivaling the chain stores.

"Let's go in here," Destiny says, and I follow her inside.

I pause at a counter to see a display of signed hardcovers from J.K. Rowling, Jimmy Carter, Charlton Heston, Tony Bennett, and Joyce Carol Oates. They all signed here, in Huntington? I never would have guessed that Huntington would be on any author's book tour.

"Come on," Destiny says, dragging me to the African-American section where, miraculously, a trade paperback copy of *Ashy* rests between Cheris Hodges's *Searching for Paradise* and Alice Holman's *The Last Days Murder List*.

Destiny pulls *Ashy* out and flips to the front cover. "Desiree Holland. *Ashy*. Like you, Peter. I heard this was good. The cover's awfully bright though."

"*The Devil to Pay* was better," I offer, not seeing it anywhere. Maybe it's sold out.

"Who was that by?"

Me. "Desiree Holland wrote that one, too."

"You've read her books?"

To death. "Yeah."

She opens *Ashy* to the dedication page and reads, "'For E.' For . . . Eddie, Edward, Earl. Yeah, probably some no-good sponge named Earl who's living off all her hard work. What do you think, Peter?"

I'm not thinking right now because *The Twilight Zone* theme music is playing in my head. Of all the thousands of books in this store, she zeroes in on *Ashy*. "I think . . . I'll buy it for you." Which makes absolutely no sense. An author buying his own book? And for a woman he's just met? I'm about to make Edie about seventy cents in royalties.

I purchase my own book, and we leave, spending half an hour in the Gap at the corner of Main and New York Avenue. She holds several denim shirts up to me, even drapes them over my shoulders, but I decline.

"But that outfit isn't happening, Peter. I don't know how you ever attracted Cece Wrenn."

Cece loved me for my writing and wanted me for my sperm. "You're not a Penn State fan?"

"I'm not a wrinkled clothes from the seventies fan. Please let me buy you a new shirt." She puts her head on my shoulder and whispers, "Pretty please?"

I let her buy me the shirt. She tears the tags off it as soon as we hit the sidewalk and hands it to me. I put on the shirt.

"Much better," she says with a smile. "Now I can be seen with you."

And wherever we go, I can't stop watching her. Light on her feet. Graceful. Almost as tall as me. Very agile, eminently confident. I am smitten, and we've only just met. And now that I look somewhat presentable, we are turning heads.

"What do we do now?" she says as we stand between Village Flowers and the Nova.

"Uh . . . you know, I still don't know what you know about Ebony. I've completely forgotten to interrogate you."

She smiles. "Good." She looks up. "Nice moon, huh?"

I nod.

"Let's hit the beach."

"But, it's getting cold and I—"

"It's not that cold." She takes my arm. "And at the beach, you'll tell me your story."

"Tell you what story?"

"The story of you and Ebony. I have to know if all this is real."

"It is."

"I mean, I have to make sure that you're not some nutcase stalking her."

"I'm not . . . stalking her. I just want to see her again."

"Well, I have to be totally sure. I don't want her on my conscience."

I follow her burgundy Honda Accord to West Shore Beach, and if it weren't so cold, it would be the perfect spot for romance. The waves lapping, licking, bubbling on the pebbly sand, the moon in the sky, stars gleaming. We weave around cairns of rocks and thistly growths of grass to sit on two larger boulders on a rock jetty softened by charcoal waves. Somewhere over there, Connecticut waits for the wind to show its face.

"You sure you're not too cold, Destiny?"

"I'm fine."

"And you really want to hear about my childhood romance?"

"Just the breakup part."

"I told you about that."

"Did you? People don't just fade away without a reason."

I've never told anyone this, not even Edie. "No, people don't fade away like that." Why am I confessing so much to this woman?

"Was it someone else?"

"In a way, but not like you're thinking. It was mainly . . . distance. But I don't want to bore you—"

"With your troubles?"

She's knows Stevie Wonder songs, too? "Yeah. Uh, are you a Stevie Wonder fan?"

"Who isn't?"

"I mean, to know a song that old, and you're only, what, twenty-seven, twenty-eight?"

She fixes me with a stare. "And you're looking like you're fifty."

Ouch. "I didn't mean—" She's younger?

"C'mon, man, I'm getting cold. Get on with your story."

"There's not really much to tell." I can't believe I'm about to do this. "Uh, well, after the senior prom—"

"You went with Ebony to the senior prom? Back then?"

"Uh, not exactly. A friend of mine, Lloyd Simon, took her to the prom—"

"Was Lloyd black?"

"Yes. And I took another girl—"

"Was she white?"

So many interruptions. "Yeah. Lloyd and her had a thing going on, too. It seemed like the perfect solution, and I ended up with Ebony after the dance. My father, you know, he—"

"—had issues, I know, I know. Go on."

There's that icy edge to her voice again. Maybe she's just cold and wants me to speed up my story. "Well, after the senior prom, I had to work all summer so I could pay my college tuition—and so did Ebony— and we saw each other when we could, you know, in secret. I went off to college and then . . ." I stop.

"And then what?"

I toss a rock into the water. "I wrote her letters daily for almost two years, but she only wrote back once." That final poem.

Destiny leaves her boulder and sits next to me. "You wrote her letters?"

"Yeah. Drew pictures on the envelopes, too. That was a . . . thing we had. We were always illustrating our notes and letters, ever since we were kids."

I hear Destiny sigh. "Did you try to call her?" she asks in a softer voice.

"Sure. I tried. But it seemed like every time I called, Ebony was at work or out on a date. I left lots of messages with her mama, and she promised to give the messages to Ebony."

"Her mama must not have given her the messages."

"No, I'm sure she did. Mrs. Mills and I were friends."

Destiny blinks at me. "Really?"

"Really. I spent more time at her house than my own house."

"Really?"

"Ebony's house was always . . . warmer, you know? I felt . . . I felt at home."

"How often did you call?"

"Once a week at least, mainly on weekends to save some money. But then one time I called and found that the number had been disconnected. I thought maybe she had moved, but I kept sending the letters, hoping they'd be forwarded to her. Then on Christmas break, I came back to Huntington and . . . and she *had* moved, no forwarding address or anything." I toss another rock. "I came home after my freshman year and went by the house again, but . . . no one home. I kept writing to her anyway, but after two years with no reply, I kind of gave up."

I feel a tear trying to build up in my eye. Damnit, Ebony, where'd you go? All the promises you made to me that night after our final embrace, saying you felt married to me, said you'd put your life on hold until I got back, even gave me a lock of your hair, saying, "You know how hard it is for me to grow hair, so don't you ever lose it!" I've lost her hair, too. The tear escapes before I can blink it back into my eye.

"And that's why you haven't been back since?"

I shake my head. "No, that's a whole other story."

"I'm listening."

"Well, I also had a fight with my father the summer after my freshman year, and then . . . then there was no reason to come back."

"Was it over Ebony?"

"Mostly." What wasn't? "He told me I was wasting my life looking for her, I told him, 'At least I have a reason to live, unlike you.' " God, what a bitter memory. I had pretty much told my own father that he'd be better off dead. "I, uh, had some problems with all his many rules, too, but Ebony was the catalyst."

Destiny rests her head against my shoulder. "At least you tried to keep in touch."

"Didn't try hard enough." I hurl another rock into the water.

"Keep that up, we won't have anywhere to sit."

I drop the next rock I want to throw. "That's how jetties get made, you know. For centuries men have been tossing rocks into the water from the shore because of some woman."

Destiny laughs. "Is that what you think?"

"There are rock jetties all over the world, proof that this is one way men solve their woman troubles."

"Well, you survived Ebony's mama, right? I heard she was crazy, fight the power and all that."

"Mrs. Mills was the most . . . She was the best." I feel Destiny shiver. "You sure you're not too cold?"

"I'm fine."

I wipe my face. "Anything else you want to know?"

"Why'd you get divorced?"

Daa-em, as Ebony would say. She wants to know everything. "You want the long or the short version?"

Destiny shrugs. "The long version."

"You sure? The long version is ugly."

"I'm sure it is."

I take a deep breath and let it out slowly.

"You got asthma, Peter?"

"No. Just trying to figure out where to begin. I haven't told this to anyone before."

"I'm flattered."

Here goes the nothing that was our marriage. "Edie and I never should have gotten married in the first place. I know that's easy to say now, but we were two opposites from the very beginning. She had led a pampered life before she met me and expected to be spoiled after we got married."

"You didn't spoil her?"

"I couldn't. Not on a teacher's salary. For the first four years she was miserable, since we had to live in an efficiency apartment."

"She didn't work?"

I shake my head. "The daughter of William Strong Melton does *not* work," I say in Edie's squeaky voice. "I made the mistake telling her father that I wanted to be her sole support, even asked him not to give Edie her weekly allowance once we got married."

"She got an allowance, even as an adult?"

"Yeah."

"How much did she get?"

"Enough." I don't tell Destiny that Edie's allowance per week was more than I made in a month as a teacher. "So I got Edie's allowance cut, and her father said it would do her some good, 'build up her character,' he said. But it didn't. Edie was too spoiled rotten by then. I asked her to clip coupons once. 'You're kidding,' she said. I told her I wasn't kidding, and she locked herself in the bedroom, crying."

"Four years of that?"

"Off and on. We had a very comfortable couch."

"That's terrible!"

"Yeah, it was, until I got published for the first time."

"You're a writer too?"

I groan. "I have a pen name."

"What is it?"

Henry has already told Cece, and since four can keep a secret as well as three, I decide to tell Destiny. "Destiny, you are talking to Desiree Holland."

"No way!"

"Want me to sign your book?"

"*You're* Desiree Holland?"

"Yep."

Destiny pulls her legs up to her chest. "I may need therapy after this. How could you, I mean, how did you— *Why* did you write as a black woman?"

"I like to think it wasn't me writing. It was Ebony's voice in my head telling me what to type. She was telling the tales and telling them so much better than I could. I simply transcribed her voice."

"That's so . . . weird. Does Ebony know?"

"I don't know. Maybe. If she's read both books, there are definite clues, specific moments and conversations that only we had."

"I wonder if she knows."

So do I. "I've always hoped she knew. Anyway, I won't be Desiree Holland for much longer. I'm writing one last novel in her name, then

I'm striking out on my own with another novel . . . where I may strike out and have to ride the bench for a while."

"I'd buy your book."

"Thank you. I'll tell the marketing department I've made one advance sale."

She bites her lower lip. "So . . . your books brought more money into your marriage, and Edie was happier."

"Somewhat. It wasn't until my father died and I sold his house to get money for *her* house that she perked up completely."

"My father's dead, Edie."

She smiled briefly. "Oh, that's terrible, Peter. What are you going to do with his house?"

I mumbled, "We could live in it, I guess. I'm sure I could find a teaching job on Long Island, maybe at a prep school in the Hamptons."

She turned her back on me. "I'm not going to Long Island, Peter. Why don't you sell the house and build me one here? Daddy will help us, and you don't want to go back to live where your daddy died, do you?"

"No, I guess I don't . . ."

"We lasted six more years after that, and Edie even found herself a job on the Pittsburgh Arts Council, a paying job with benefits and everything. But it wasn't a job where she actually had to work. All she had to do was call up rich people she knew to get donations and grants. It was the perfect job for her—and for me. Her absence gave me more time to write. But when *The Devil to Pay* came out and I was working on a third Desiree Holland novel, Edie suddenly became jealous of my work." I stand and look out over the water. "I used to look forward to my summers off, you know, to write without tons of papers to grade or meetings to attend. Ten solid weeks of writing and editing."

"But Edie wouldn't let you."

I smile. "No. She wouldn't. She used to phone me hourly from where she worked, played the TV too loud when she was home, sent me on simple errands at all hours of the day and night, filled the 'honey-do' jar with monumental, impossible tasks, had me taking the cars for inspections and oil changes when they didn't need to be done, had me painting the house inside and out every summer, had friends over for dinner four days a week, had me going to every ball, show, opening, and evening at the ballet . . . She had an agenda for me every day, and my writing suffered."

"You could have blown her off. You didn't have to go, and you didn't have to answer the phone."

I smile. "I, um, got sick the day of some of those events."

"Good for you."

"But not answering the phone was deadly. I'd have to explain where I was later, and I hated those interrogations."

"Are you hating *this* interrogation?"

"You're not interrogating me, are you?"

"Maybe I am."

"I don't mind your questions. It's good therapy for me."

She laughs and moves away from me.

"What?"

"All this is just so . . . ironic! You have a messed-up love life with a white woman, and you write romances as a black woman."

I squeeze another rock. "It's not *that* messed up."

She returns to me. "Good thing you have a pen name."

"Gee, thanks. Any more questions?"

"Did you," she says, her voice softer than soft, "did you have any children?"

"No. We tried, or at least I tried. I wanted her to have someone to take her mind off me so I could write. I had to steal out of bed to get any writing done as it was."

After a short silence, she asks, "Did you love her?"

"No" leaves my lips before I can think about it. And when I think about it, I realize the truth. "It was a marriage of convenience. My father . . . I wanted to please my father just once. But that's another story. Anyway, the last straw was when she deleted what would have been my third novel. I had almost finished it and poof! Gone."

"What do you mean, 'poof'?"

"One day it was on my laptop, the next it wasn't."

"You didn't have a backup?"

"No."

"What about notes?"

"I have this stupid habit of tossing my notes as I use them so I don't get confused while I'm writing. I checked for temp files, took the laptop in to a computer store, ran recovery programs—nothing. Edie had obviously figured out my password, which just so happened to be 'Ebony.' "

"That's messed up. That book meant money, right?"

"Yeah. Edie's greatest motivation."

"Then why'd she do it?"

"Edie called my third novel another 'nigger' book."

"The bitch!"

"She wanted to bury my laptop in the yard because she said I fingered the laptop more than I did her."

"Daa-em."

"It was true, though. She even pleaded with me on bended knees to write novels for white people because she said, and I quote, 'White people actually have money and can read.' "

"The racist bitch!"

"Edie had even reduced my writing to one awful statement: 'All you're doing is fucking your old girlfriend for all the world to read, writing out your wet dreams with a nigger.' "

"Oh, shit. You went off on her then, right?"

"Yeah. For the first and last time."

"What did you say?"

"Well . . ." I look at my beautiful interrogator. "It's not, um, not very nice to say."

"I'm sure I've heard worse."

I doubt it. "Okay . . . This is what I said: 'Yeah, I called her 'E' in bed, and she knew what to do in bed, too, four, five times a night, not 'are you finished yet, I want to read' once a damn month, and she comes to me in my dreams every fucking night, too, and she knows how to please me, how to make me howl at the motherfucking moon!' "

Destiny's mouth drops open.

"I told you it wasn't, um, very nice."

She still doesn't speak.

"I'm sorry, I—"

"Ebony was like that?"

I shove my hands in my pockets and kick a pebble around. "*We* were like that."

"Daa-em. You think you know people . . . and you just don't."

"Anyway," I sigh, "that's what started Edie and me down the long road to divorce. We walked on eggshells for a long time after that, but I just couldn't stay in that house. I moved out, and five years later, she finally granted me the divorce."

"Why'd she make you wait so long?"

"To punish me, I guess. To keep me from running off immediately to find Ebony. Maybe to make me so old that I wouldn't be attractive to anyone anymore, I don't know. Despite her father's millions, she still gets half the money from those two novels she hates. And the house."

"That is all so . . . twisted." She sighs. "I'm almost sorry I asked."

I shrug. "Don't be."

She shakes her head. "Didn't you try to rewrite your third novel from memory?"

"Sure. But I had it right the first time, or at least I thought I had it right. I gave up trying after a few days."

"And then you gave up trying to be married."

Giving up seems to be the theme of the evening. "I really think I gave up before I got married. If only I had stayed here, I know things would have been different."

"Yeah. If only you had stayed." Destiny squeezes my arm. "It's getting late, and I have to work tomorrow." She stands and arches her back, yawning.

"See, I did bore you."

"No, you didn't. I'm just tired." She looks across the bay. "Is your father's boat out there somewhere?"

"Yeah."

"Where?"

I point to a dark speck.

"I've never been on a boat before."

"Never?"

"Nope."

She can't be serious. "You live on Long Island and have never been on a boat? Not even a ferry?"

"The ferry doesn't count. So, are you going to take me to see it?"

"Now?"

"Why not?"

Is she asking what I think she's asking? "But I thought you said you had to work."

She sighs. "I do, but I can always call in sick."

Oh, shit. She wants to spend the night. "I want to, uh, show you my boat, Destiny, but—"

"You tryin' to get nasty with me?"

"I meant—"

"I know what you meant. I'm the one getting nasty. I shouldn't have had that Mocha Kiss." She smiles. "So . . . can I go on your boat, Peter?"

"Uh, we just met, and I'm . . . attracted to you—I am, really, you're so full of life and you're heartbreakingly beautiful—but, if we went out there, I don't know if I—"

Destiny kisses my cheek and giggles. "Dag, I just wanted to see the boat, that's all."

"Really?"

"I have a steady man, Peter."

"You do?" Of course she does. Every goddess has a god.

"Yes. Did you think—" Her eyes widen. "You thought—"

"I'm sorry, Destiny. I'm, uh, a little out of practice. I couldn't tell if, you know, if you were . . ."

"If I was what?"

"If you were hitting on me." I turn away and listen to the waves hitting the rocks.

"You thought I was—" She laughs. "Listen, Peter, that was the furthest thing from my mind. I mean, I can tell you're still in love with Ebony, and I'm not here to get between you two, right?"

I nod.

"I'm trying to bring you two together, and I would never . . . try to jump your bones."

I turn to her. "What'd you say?"

Destiny slides two cold hands to my face and searches my eyes. "And tomorrow you're going to find her." She winks and walks off the jetty to the beach.

I try to catch up to her, but she's far more nimble than I am. "What did you say just now? Something about bones."

"Um, don't you want to know where she is?"

"Of course, but—"

"Go to Ebony's mama's house."

"What?"

"The house on Grace Lane."

I shake my head. "A white woman lives there now. I saw her in the yard planting bulbs or something."

"Really?"

I nod.

"Hmm. So you didn't go up to the door?"

"No."

"Dag, all you had to do was ring the doorbell." She opens her car door.

"But the lady—"

She slips into her seat. "Maybe the white lady is her gardener. All I know is that Ebony's mama still lives there."

I was that close! "She still lives there? But twenty years ago they moved away. She wasn't there."

Destiny shrugs. "All I know is that she's there now." She starts her car. "Can I at least get a kiss on the cheek for all my hard work?"

I lean into the car and kiss her silken cheek. "Thank you, Destiny."

She looks away and clears her throat, and when she smiles back at me, I see her eyes welling with tears. "See you."

"Are you crying?"

She wipes her eyes. "Yeah."

"Why?"

"Twenty years and you're still in love with someone. My man's about as romantic as a brick. It's all just so beautiful."

I kiss her cheek again. "And so are you, Destiny. So are you."

She bites her bottom lip. "Thank you."

"It was a pleasure to meet you, Destiny. I really hope I can see you again."

She turns on her radio, reggae music thumping the night. "I'm sure you will. I'm your Destiny, remember?" She pulls away then backs up, rolling down her window. "And get that Cece wench's numbers off your hand, okay?"

"I will."

I watch her car until her taillights wink out of sight, and instead of warming up in the Nova, I return to the jetty—to talk to the Captain.

"I know you're still out there, Captain, because evil never sleeps." I launch a large rock and wait until it splashes. "You've taught me so much, Captain, how good does not always win, how most of life is tragic, how nothing in life is guaranteed."

I close my eyes and see the Captain's fiery red eyes, see his hands ripping open the door to my berth in the *Argo* the night of the prom, feel his cold grip on my arms, see the stars on deck, the sudden warmth of Ebony's body replaced by the chilly blasts of the Captain's cursing and shouting, "Nothing you can say or do could hurt me more than this!"

I open my eyes. "It was your fault we had to go to the prom that way, Captain," I say to the shadowy shape of the *Argo*. "It was your fault we had to sneak around. God, how you tried to ruin us! But I was ready for you, wasn't I? I was ready that night."

I close my eyes again, seeing Ebony, that beautiful cream dress held in front of her naked body, her eyes unashamed of what we had finally done, had finally shared amid so many tears and kisses, hearing the Captain bellowing: "You have desecrated my ship!" Then I hear myself howling as I tear at my father, wrestling him right there on the deck of the *Argo*, trying to rip his arms off while Ebony with the cream dress and unashamed eyes looks on, hurting my father and leaving him bleeding and weeping on his ship while Ebony and I swim almost naked to shore, making love again under the deck for old time's sake before going into my own house to share tears and kisses in my own bed with the only girl I've ever loved . . .

"Your hate kept us together, Captain. At least I can thank you for that."

I toss one final rock, but my heart's not in it. It clatters off other rocks on the jetty before rolling into the waves.

Since it's too late to catch a taxi to the *Argo*, I plug the laptop into the Nova's lighter using an adapter and finish Chapter 5 of *Promises to Keep* right there in the parking lot of West Shore Beach:

After the one-sided boxing match and sermon, Peter took an ice bag to his room, turned out all the lights, and watched the woods darken, the leaves in never-ending flight as a thunderstorm rumbled through and lashed at them. He felt no hope, not even the hope of hope. He wailed, not to release his pain, but to feel it, to grow strong by it. He added his tears to the rain battering his window, a window too high off the ground to jump from to go to Ebony in the Cave, but high enough to give him a final release from his pain.

He shook his head. *No. That's too easy. No. Ebony's out there somewhere waiting for me. She wouldn't understand.*

He searched through the wildly whipping trees, through the darkness, through the sheets of rain for a glimpse of Ebony and suddenly spied a light in the crack of the Cave.

"She's there," he whispered. He cracked his door and heard the rumblings of a stuck bilge pump coming from the TV room. "And the Captain's asleep."

He took a deep breath and didn't let it out until he was safely outside and slipping down the muddy slope, crashing through the brush to the Cave. He climbed to the top and tumbled down into her arms, out of the whirlwind with only the skittering of unseen animals as witnesses.

Ebony didn't speak, and she gave Peter no chance to speak, kissing the swelling on his face, kissing his split lip, kissing away his tears. Then they lay together, her sweet body, her sweet sighs, their green and young desire breathing on their lips fierce tremors of heat, her hands guiding him, urging him, helping him until they were nearly one body in a hell not of their own making.

"Are you sure you want to do this, Ebony?"

"I love you, Peter."

"I love you, too, Ebony."

A few seconds later, Peter's body spasmed, and they lay still, hands gently touching.

"Did we just do it?" Ebony asked.

"I'm not sure," Peter said.

She felt down between her legs. "I think you missed."

"Sorry."

"It's okay."

Then as the flashlight dimmed and the storm raged all around them, they took a blood oath to seal their love, a simple penknife turning two bloody index fingers into more sighs, more tears, more kisses, and more attempts.

"I think you missed again."

"Sorry."

"It's okay. I know you love me."

"And I know you love me."

I save my work, shut down, and leave the laptop connected to the lighter to restore the laptop's battery. Then for the second straight night, I recline the front seat of a rented Nova and try to sleep.

So many "misses." Too many. I wouldn't get it completely right until that night on the *Argo*, and all that summer, we were getting it right every time.

And I still have the scar on my finger, built up over time because of the way I hold a pencil, a callous of love, so much thicker after twenty years.

9

Barking wakes me just after sunrise. Someone's walking a dog at this hour on a Sunday morning? I sit up and see a couple putting a toy poodle through its paces in the park. My back aches, but I don't take any muscle relaxers. I want to be completely awake today.

Today I'm going to find Ebony.

During a long, hot shower at the clubhouse, the steam sorting out the wrinkles on my outfit from last night, I remember the first time I ever met Ebony's mama, Candace Mills.

Candace Mills was Foxy Brown, but I didn't know it at the time because I wasn't allowed to watch those kinds of movies. I was hanging out in Ebony's room one day after school, and we lost track of the time. I think time stood still in Ebony's room. Candace crashed through the front door with some groceries, and I had only gotten into the living room on my way to the kitchen door when she said, "Who you?"

I stood there in front of that fake Christmas tree with black, red, and green ornaments, a black Santa ornament swinging back and forth as if to say, "You're in trouble now, boy." Candace wore a black beret, powder blue shirt, black leather jacket, black pants, shiny black shoes, and a puffy Afro. I would later compare Candace to a picture of Angela Davis on a book in Ebony's room, *Angela Davis: An Autobiography*. She and Angela Davis were almost sisters.

Ebony rushed from the back shouting, "Mama, I can explain!"

Candace stared me down and said, "You the flavor of the month?"

"Mama, please," Ebony cried.

"Gotta stop you watching *Happy Days*, girl. You messin' with Richie Cunningham now. Tuck your shirt in, girl."

I couldn't think of a single thing to say.

Ebony tucked in the shirt that I enjoyed untucking. "Mama, please don't start."

Candace put the groceries on the coffee table. "Wasn't the last boy a Puerto Rican?"

"Italian *and* Puerto Rican, Mama."

"He spoke Spantalian or something. Couldn't understand a damn thing comin' out of his mouth."

"So he had an accent."

"And you're wearin' your good clothes, too? Girl, go change."

I didn't want Ebony to leave, but an "Oh, geez, Mama!" later, and she had vanished to her room.

"Have a seat."

I sat on the couch and stared at the presents under the tree.

"You're Peter, huh?"

I nodded, not looking at her.

"You look like a Peter, all skinny and white. Can you talk?"

I found my voice. "Yes, ma'am."

Candace raised an eyebrow. "You been Ebony's friend for a while now, huh?"

I nodded.

"Why haven't I seen you before?"

I prayed hard then. "I, uh, I usually leave before you, uh, get home, ma'am."

"So honest!" She sat next to me. "I know you been here. Every day I get home my little girl's all sweaty. You been gettin' her sweaty, Peter? No, don't answer. Of course you have. You know I'm crazy, right?"

I didn't have an answer for that one.

"Ebony didn't tell you?"

"No, ma'am."

"You got nice manners, boy. We got to fix that." She pointed at the Christmas tree. "I got a Christmas tree up in my family room in the middle of May. Ain't that a little crazy?"

I could only shrug. Crazy was where I lived, and a beautiful Christmas tree in a living room in May seemed sane by comparison.

"I'm waiting for Ebony's daddy to come home from Vietnam." She dangled a POW-MIA bracelet in front of me. "I know he's probably dead and rotting in the jungle. He been missin' since sixty-nine. Wanna know why I keep it up?"

"Sure."

"Cuz it scares the shit out of people. It scares them and it makes them remember Vietnam all over again. Makes them think I'm crazy. Good thing, too. Ain't nobody gonna mess with us out here in Huntington. People riding by will see that tree in the window and say, 'That's where the crazy Negro lady lives, still waitin' on her man.' You dance?"

All of Candace's conversations went off in tangents at a moment's notice, yet there was always a purpose. I didn't answer that day.

"*Can* you dance? Wait, don't answer that. Of course you can't. Me and Ebony gotta teach you so you don't look foolish on the dance floor."

And they did try to teach me to dance, right there on that orange shag carpet. I gave them hours of entertainment to the music of Parliament, the Temptations, Bob Marley, Isaac Hayes, KC & the Sunshine Band, and Sly and the Family Stone.

She grabbed my knee. "You like my Ebony a lot?"

"Yeah, I—"

"You been kissin' on her, right?"

"Yes, ma'am."

"It's okay, long as you don't leave any marks or babies, hear?"

I gulped. "Yes, ma'am."

"I ain't your 'ma'am,' Peter. You got to call me by my name, and it ain't my slave name neither. You know what a slave name is, right? Don't answer that. Of course you don't know. My last name, Mills, belong to some old honky down in Virginia from way back in the day. Wasn't my choice. My new name is Luwanna, so you call me Luwanna."

"Okay."

"Go on. Call me by my new name."

"Okay . . . Luwanna."

"I got my new name from the Panthers, boy. The Black Panthers. Joined up when Angela came a-runnin' to New York six years ago, worked a free breakfast program and everything. Not much goin' on now. Bobby's in Pennsylvania somewhere, heard Eldridge got religion, Stokely's in Uganda . . . and little Luwanna is all alone, all alone."

I didn't connect the names to major movers and shakers in the Black

Power movement until much later. Candace ran with a very powerful group.

Ebony had rescued me that day, returning to the living room in tight jeans and a pink T-shirt. "Is Mama boring you, Peter?"

"No."

"What you talkin' about, boring him?" Candace asked. "I'm schoolin' him."

Ebony sat next to me then, the three of us on a couch built for two. "She tell you the Ten Point Plan yet?"

"No. Not yet."

Ebony ticked them off on her fingers. "We want freedom, we want employment, we want housing, we want education, we want bread— and there are five more I can't remember."

"At least I'm tryin' to school him, girl. What you should have been doing instead of rolling around in that room of yours that I know ain't been clean since Christmas morning. You clean it today like I asked you to?"

"Mama, I—"

Candace stood. "This date is over."

"Come on, Mama! He just got here."

She collected her groceries, and I stood. "And he's just about to leave, now get to that room and clean it up."

Ebony left us once again, and Candace spoke to me from the kitchen, cupboard doors opening and closing. "Your room as messy as hers, Peter?"

"No. But I don't have all the stuff she has."

"That's no excuse. Next time you come when I ain't around, that room will be clean."

I went to Ebony's room where she was furiously throwing things into her closet. "I'll see ya later," I said, gathering my books.

"I'm almost through."

I backed out of her room. "I better go."

Ebony followed me to the kitchen, whispering, "You don't have to go, Peter."

I stopped at the kitchen door. "Nice to meet you, Mrs. Mills."

"Luwanna," Candace said.

"I mean, Luwanna."

Ebony slumped to a chair at the kitchen table. "Luwanna? Mama, yesterday it was Kenyatta. Who you gonna be tomorrow?"

"No matter who I claim to be, child, I am still your mama."

Candace Mills—the greatest lady I've ever known.

After my shower, I drive the long way to Grace Lane taking a circuitous route past the "castle church"—the Unitarian Universalist Fellowship on Browns Road. I used to go to the annual Huntington Renaissance Faire there, and though that old French Gothic mansion is the stuff of Edgar Allan Poe short stories, it is a beautiful building.

I park behind a tan minivan and see Candace's old Pinto, "Honk If You Love Jesus," "POW-MIA: Never Forget," "MIA: Only Hanoi Knows," "My Other Car Is a Limo," and "Carter/Mondale" bumper stickers plastered on the back bumper, a tarp blown off to one side. She is here! And the "backfire bomber" is still in existence? Candace once told me that no one ever tailgated her. That Pinto is a classic, candy apple red with a black and white cloth interior.

I get out of the Nova and see the same woman, a robust woman in her fifties wearing gardening gloves, hacking at the ground with a trowel. I approach her carefully, because I have an inherent fear of robust women holding sharp tools.

"Hello, does, um, Candace Mills still live here?"

She turns and squints. "Yes."

"I'm, uh, a friend of her daughter, Ebony. Peter Underhill."

She stands and brushes dirt off her sweater. "Is Mrs. Mills expecting you?"

"No, ma'am."

A voice from the house jolts me. "Who's that, Gladys?" It sounds like Candace. I'd never forget that voice.

Gladys walks to the side of the house, and I follow close behind, whispering, "She might remember me better as Peter, Gladys."

Gladys stops just under the window to the dining room. "A Mr. Underhill to see you."

"Don't know no Mr. Underhill."

I approach the window. "Mrs. Mills, it's me, Peter."

"So?"

I can barely see her through the screen. "I used to date Ebony a long time ago."

"You can go back to work, Gladys," Candace says in a steady, strong voice, and Gladys leaves us. "She used to date a lot of boys, boy. What made you so special?" The sun glints off something metallic inside. Is Candace in a wheelchair?

"It's Peter, Mrs. Mills. I'm the boy you and Ebony tried to teach to dance, and I'm trying to find Ebony."

"What for?"

Because I miss her, and I still love her. "I just want to talk to her."

"About what?"

"Old times, I guess, you know, catch up on the last twenty years."

I see a shaky gray hand rise into the air. "That's a long time to be catching up."

"Yes, it is."

"She know you're trying to find her?"

"No."

"Maybe she don't want to be found. You ever think of that?"

"Yes, ma'am, I have." I hear a whirring noise, and Candace's upper body fills the area behind the screen. She's in a wheelchair all right, an electric one, and she's grayer, her hair longer, her face lined, her body shrunken. But she is still a queen.

"Peter Underhill, Peter Underhill." She squints. "Nope. Your face don't ring a bell at all."

"You said once to call you Luwanna."

Candace frowns. "Oh, yes, I remember you. You left my girl ruined. I ain't opening that can of worms. You got to dig into that hole yourself." Two shaky gray hands rise in an attempt to close the window then draw the blinds, but she has trouble reaching the window and unhooking the stays and gives up.

"Mrs. Mills, I just want to call her."

"You want to get a girl's phone number from her mama? What planet you from?" The whirring begins again, and Candace disappears. "You ain't gettin' nothin' from me."

I step closer to the screen and see her stopped under the archway to the hall. "I really don't need her number, Mrs. Mills. Couldn't you at least call her, tell her I'm in town? I'm staying on my father's boat."

I hear Candace snort. "That boat. And that father of yours. Heard he finally had the good sense to die. Never knew of a more evil man."

"He had his moments."

"Did he now? If I remember correctly, that daddy of yours broke y'all up."

I am talking to a woman's back through a screen. "Yes and no. Um, can't we talk face-to-face, please?"

Candace laughs. "Yeah, y'all sneaked around an awful lot, but boy, you're asking an awful lot. You broke my baby's heart, and that broke my heart, and you expect to come up in here and bring all that back?"

"No, ma'am. I just want to see her."

"Love doesn't conquer everything, you know."

True. "I'm hoping it will this time."

"Uh-huh. You married?"

I sigh. "Divorced."

"Figures. Was she white or black?"

"White."

"Figures. Any kids?"

"No."

Her wheelchair whirrs as she spins around. "No kids?"

"No, ma'am."

Candace smiles and rolls closer to the screen. "And all you want to do is talk to her?"

"That's all." For a start anyway.

"Don't you want to see if you two can, you know, start over?"

"Um, the thought had crossed my mind."

"Only crossed it?"

"No, ma'am." Jesus, another confessional, this one in a barren flower bed under a dining room window. "She has been in my mind for the past twenty years."

"She had that effect on people."

"Had?"

"People change in twenty years, Peter Underhill. You ain't the same snot-nosed kid that used to hold my baby's hand. You look like you put on a hundred pounds."

"Yeah, I've put on a few—"

"And look at me," she interrupted. "I ain't been able to walk cuz of my diabetes for three years now."

"You're still the queen, Luwanna."

She winks at me. "You got that right. You wanna . . . come inside?"

"Yes, thank you."

"Front door's unlocked. Don't let Gladys scare you. She's only here to take care of me."

I walk around and open the front door, and the weight of Candace's illness hits me hard when she rolls into the hallway. She won't be dancing any time soon, her lower body covered by a blanket, her hands trembling slightly.

"It's good to see you again," I say, stepping inside.

"What there is to see."

I follow her wheelchair into the living room and barely recognize the room, mainly because the shag carpet and Christmas tree are gone, replaced by a beige Berber carpet and a wall of bookcases crammed with books. Before I sit on a comfortable cream-colored couch, I scan several framed watercolor scenes on the walls and find a cursive *E* in the corner of each.

"Did Ebony do all these?"

"What you think?" She parks her wheelchair where the coffee table used to be.

"She's still at it, then?"

Candace nods then bellows, "Gladys!"

Gladys comes running in, the trowel still in her hand. "Are you all right, Mrs. Mills?"

"Dial my daughter for me and bring me the phone."

Gladys rushes to the kitchen and returns with a cordless phone, nestling it between Candace's neck and shoulder. "Go on now," Candace whispers, and Gladys leaves. "Got her trained, huh?"

I'm having trouble breathing, and my hands shake almost as much as Candace's hands.

"Ebony, there's a boy here named Peter Underhill who says he's looking for you."

I rise from the couch. "Can I speak to her?"

"Hush, I'm only leaving a message on her voice mail. She's at church."

I sit. "At Bethel?"

"Hush. Call me back, girl. I'll try to keep him here as long as I can, but you know how he is always leaving us."

Wait. She's at Bethel right now? What am I doing here? I stand. "She's at Bethel, right?"

Candace shrugs. "Only church she ever attended regularly. Service will probably be going for another couple hours. That nine-eleven thing got folks on their knees longer than usual, even for an AME church. You leavin' already?"

I can't stand still. "I have to go, Mrs. Mills."

"She might not be there. Service may be over early. Waste of a trip."

I take two steps toward the door. "Nice seeing you."

"No, it wasn't. You weren't here to see me. So go on. Git. See you in another twenty years."

I drive as fast as I can to Bethel AME, and when I get there, I can't find a parking space, cars strewn all over. I park beside a fire hydrant several blocks away and run up the steps of the old church, only to be thwarted by an overflow crowd sitting wall-to-wall on folding chairs just inside the door. There are even chairs in the aisles, the pews filled to bursting. I search faces in the choir, stare at the backs of heads, hear Reverend Moore exhorting, the symphony of amens echoing. So many fans, so many glowing faces feeling God's presence.

And here I am standing at the door to that presence in a pair of faded jeans that doesn't quite match the denim shirt Destiny gave me, while folks turn and look at me with wide eyes.

I back out and sit on the steps, my shoes bouncing to the singing of the choir, my head nodding to Reverend Moore's fiery sermon on redemption, my eyes closing and filling with tears during the final prayer—

I jump up and wander into the parking lot, keeping an eye on as many exits as I can while the organ plays something holier than holy. She's about to come out! She's inside that church right now, and I'm about to see her for the first time in twenty years! I check my breath as the first streams of folks leave the main entrance, the organist still pounding out that holiest of melodies—

Is that her? No. Not dark enough. There? No. Too tall. Is that—no, too old. Wait, that might—no, too young and thin. Pretty though. The folks weaving around me to their cars give me funny looks, but I only smile.

But when the organ stops, the last car leaves the parking lot, and an ancient woman all dressed in black locks the front door—

She wasn't here.

Maybe she didn't go to church today. Maybe she's sick or something. Maybe she got past me somehow . . . and she might be on her way to her mama's house right now!

I fly through Huntington back to Candace's and go right up to the front door, turn the knob and walk in like I used to so many years ago.

"Is she here?" I say to Candace's back.

"No." She spins around. "She supposed to be?"

"She wasn't at Bethel."

"Hmm, she must be backslidin'." She spins away from me. "I knew you'd be back."

"Where's Gladys?"

"Gave her the rest of the day off."

"Who takes care of you then?" And as soon as I ask it, I know. Ebony comes over after church to take care of her mama. "Ebony does, doesn't she?"

"Maybe." She laughs. "You must be blind, Peter. Ebony *was* at that church."

"She was?"

"She's always at the church, boy. Either you didn't recognize her and she's pissed as hell, or she saw you first and she didn't want you to see her."

I sink back into the couch. Was it the skinny woman in the brown dress? No, she didn't have Ebony's face. None of the women I saw had Ebony's face.

"Girl hasn't missed a service going on eighteen years."

So she was inside the church, looked out, saw me . . . and sneaked away. Why? "But she'll stop by today, right?"

Candace shakes her head. "Boy, you weren't very smart back then, and you sure as hell ain't gotten any smarter. College was wasted on you. My baby's eyes don't miss a thing. Why she's such a good artist, right? So I bet she *did* see you at Bethel, and if she drives by here now— something she's done every Sunday for the last three years—and she sees a strange car . . . She obviously doesn't want to see you . . . at all."

I run to the window and look out on Grace Street, empty except for my Nova.

"You know how stubborn Ebony is. She won't stop by as long as you're here."

The phone rings.

"That's probably her right now, Peter. Go get me the phone from the kitchen, and don't you say a damn thing to her, you hear?"

I go and get Candace the phone, hearing "Mama, you there?" all the way from the kitchen to the living room. Her voice! Her voice hasn't changed! I wish this phone had Caller ID so I could get her number.

I rest the phone between Candace's neck and shoulder and hover behind her. "Yeah, I'm here, girl. Where else would I be? . . . Uh-huh . . .
Yes, he's still here. . . . What you so pissed for? And why you pissed at
me? . . . I ain't gettin' in the middle of this." She looks hard at me. "Take
this phone, boy, and don't blow it. This may be your only shot."

I snatch up the phone. "Hello, Ebony?"

Click.

"She hung up."

"You blew it. Again." Candace rolls her eyes while I stand there looking stupidly at the phone. "Well, damn, hit redial. I just called her and left
a message on her voice mail before you ran out of here, didn't I? Shit, I
gotta tell you how to do every damn thing."

I hit redial, and when Ebony picks up, I say, "Please don't hang up,
Ebony, I just want to—"

Click.

"Least you got more said this time. Almost finished a whole sentence
and everything. But don't say 'don't hang up.' You're only daring her to
do it. Say something else. Try again."

I hit redial again. "I just want to talk to you, that's all—"

Click.

I hit redial. "I'm staying on my father's boat. I'll be here for a while—"

Click.

"Dag, she's listening longer than I would have. She was her father's
daughter, all right."

I hit redial once more and hear "The cellular customer is no longer . . ."
before pressing the "off" button. "Mrs. Mills, please tell me where she
lives."

Candace shakes her head. "Why should I?"

"Please, Mrs. Mills. I *have* to see her."

She spins away from me. "You *have* to see her. Twenty years ago you
didn't *want* to see her, and all of a sudden here you are."

I walk around her wheelchair to face her. "I *did* want to see her, but
you moved."

"Moved? We haven't moved from here since we moved in twenty-five
years ago."

"What?"

"You losin' your hearing? I said I been in this same house for twenty-
five years now."

"But that's impossible!"

"That's what the bank thinks, too." She chuckles. "Gonna own this house outright in five more years."

This can't be happening. "But I visited over Christmas break back in eighty-one, and no one was here."

"Maybe we were on vacation. Damn, that's what folks do over Christmas, you know."

They were only on vacation? "But I came by later in May, and you weren't here then either."

"So it was a big year for vacations. What'd you do, only come by once both times?"

She was here then, too? How could I have missed her? "I also wrote Ebony letters from the second I went off to college in August of eighty-one, maybe a hundred of them over the next two years, and she never wrote back."

"We never got any letters."

I kneel in front of her. "You had to have gotten them."

"No, no letters. Maybe you wrote to the wrong address or sent them to a different Ebony."

"I didn't mess up the address. I practically lived here, remember?"

"Yeah. Should have charged you rent."

"And they weren't returned to me at college, so they had to go somewhere."

Candace blinks slowly and holds me with her eyes. "Maybe they were stolen from our mailbox."

"By who?"

"Lots of crazy people around here back in them Reagan years."

This is crazy! All those illustrated, long-winded, heartfelt letters! "I don't believe you never got any letters."

"Believe what you want. *I* didn't see any of them."

Well if Candace didn't see them . . . "What about Ebony?"

Candace shrugs. "You'll have to ask her."

I flop to the floor, shaking my head. "How can I ask her if I can't keep her on the phone for more than a few seconds or even see her?"

"You got me."

Wait. They were on vacation. "Did you stop the mail when you were on those vacations?"

"Ain't nothing but anthrax can stop the mail."

"I mean, did you have the post office hold the mail for you until you came back?"

Candace doesn't speak for a moment, squinting. "I don't think we did, and those letters would be gone by now if we did."

"Maybe they're still at the post office."

"After twenty years? Not a chance."

"Doesn't hurt to check."

Candace sighs loudly. "What good is finding those letters anyway? *If* we had them hold our mail, those letters would be burned or lost by now."

God, this is futile! "Those letters . . . those letters will prove to Ebony—and to you—that I didn't run out on her. I kept trying. How long were you on those vacations?"

"I don't remember."

What? "You remember that you didn't get any letters in August of that year, but you can't remember how long—"

"I *don't* remember, Peter," she says, her eyes fierce. "I had a damn stroke three years ago, and it fucked up my memory. I can only remember different pieces of things."

I can barely breathe. "You had a stroke?"

"What you think? How you think I got in this wheelchair?"

"I'm sorry."

"Not as sorry as I am. I didn't even know I had diabetes and bam—I have a stroke. Now all I get to do is sit around all day trying to remember shit. If you hadn't said 'Luwanna,' you wouldn't be here now. You brought back a whole bunch of memories with that name, and some of 'em I don't want to remember."

"I'm sorry, I—"

"I can't eat any candy, I can't drink any soda, Gladys treats me like a damn pin cushion with those insulin shots, and some days I go all day in this bag between my legs."

I glance at the blanket over her legs. "God, I'm so sorry, Mrs. Mills." I stand. "Is there anything you need, anything I can do for you?"

She shakes her head. "You can't do a damn thing for me, Peter. You better call Gladys. Ebony ain't comin' over today. Gladys's number is on the fridge."

I take the phone to the kitchen.

"And call Gladys's cell number. She's probably still in that mommy van of hers."

I dial Gladys and ask her to come back.

"Is Mrs. Mills all right?" she asks.

No. I've kept her from her daughter. "Yes, Gladys. Ebony, um, can't come by today."

"I'll be right there."

I return to the living room. "I'm sorry, Mrs. Mills."

She rolls to a window. "What you sorry for?"

"I guess for coming over today. I kept Ebony from visiting you."

"I'll survive."

I can't think of anything to say to her for the next ten minutes. I want to ask if she's in any pain, if there's anything I can do to make things right.

When Gladys's van arrives, I approach Candace. "Mrs. Mills, I—"

"I know, you're sorry." She spins away from me and rolls toward the kitchen. "See you around."

I leave the house on shaky legs, then I stand in the yard looking at the house. They never moved? They were just on vacation? To where? And they took Aunt Wee Wee with them? I thought that Aunt Wee Wee never left her room.

I look toward the window of Aunt Wee Wee's old room and see . . . smoke? Is the house on fire? I rush to the window and am face-to-face with a hundred-year-old woman sucking hard on a Camel cigarette.

"'Lo, Pete," she says and spews a stream of smoke through the screen.

"You're still alive?" is the only thing I can think of to say.

"Last time anybody checked." Aunt Wee Wee cackles. "How I look?"

Prunelike, I want to say, but I don't. A thick shock of white hair sticks out all over her head, dark circles under her eyes making it look as if she's been in a fight, deep wrinkles even on her chin. "You look well."

"And you a liar. I ain't well at all. I smoke too much, and I'm nearly blind as a bat. You still freckled?"

"Not as much."

"I got me a thing for freckled men, you know." She cackles again.

"Um, Aunt Wee Wee, do you know where Ebony lives?"

"Where you think she lives?"

"I don't know."

"Candy didn't tell you?"

"No, ma'am."

She takes a long drag. "You are that little boy that used to mess with Ebony when y'all thought I was asleep, right?"

Aunt Wee Wee wasn't asleep? "Yes."

"You know, I heard everything."

"You . . . did?"

"Everything. Y'all sure was noisy."

I gulp.

"But I never told her mama. No sense in it, cuz Candy already knew, I expect." She sucks the cigarette down to the filter, stubs it out on the window ledge, and squeezes it under the screen. I look down and see that I'm standing in a pile of cigarette butts. She licks her ancient lips. "You off to mess with Ebony now?"

"I guess."

Aunt Wee Wee cackles again, ending it with a long, hacking cough. "Good. That girl need someone to mess with her. She so uptight you can't get a toothpick up in there." She lights another cigarette with steady hands and takes another long drag. "If I tell you where she is, you didn't hear it from me."

I hear something hit the door to Aunt Wee Wee's room. "Aunt Wee Wee, you old bitch you! You stop that!"

"Candy mad." Aunt Wee Wee cackles. "You causing trouble all over again, Pete. I like that. It's been too damn quiet around here."

I hear the doorknob rattle. "I'm gonna put you in that home, you hear? And you ain't gonna be able to smoke no more!"

"She been saying that for thirty years, and don't worry about her gettin' in. Chair's too big."

"What about Gladys?"

"What about that heifer? She won't come in here. Gladys is afraid of getting cancer from secondhand smoke." She smiles. "Knew my bad habit would come in handy one day. Now, where you think Ebony's house would be? Think hard, now. Think stubborn."

"I can't even begin—"

"Sure you can. Girl had a dream house, didn't she? Where you two was supposed to live. She drew it all the damn time."

The house on Fairchild Street? "She *bought* that house?"

"Ain't that what you supposed to do when you want to live in a house?"

I thought Ebony was kidding about it being her dream house. It wasn't much to look at, though it had plenty of windows, and it looked more like a church than a house. Wait. She might be there right now?

"Thank you, Aunt Wee Wee. If you weren't behind that screen, I'd kiss you."

I hear a steady bumping on Aunt Wee Wee's door. "I'm gonna break this damn door in!"

Aunt Wee Wee turns away from the screen. "And then what you gonna do, Candy? Run me over?" She turns back to me. "Go on, git. You got more important things to do than watch an old blind woman whup a crippled woman's ass."

I race back to my old house on Preston only to realize there's no way to get to Fairchild Street that way. Ebony and I used to cut through people's yards to get there. I make a U-turn and fly down Tracy Drive to Pam Lane to Margo Lane past Stephanie Court—who named all these streets after women?—to Anoatok Drive—who's idea was that misspelling?—to West Shore Road then up the hill—

There it is. I screech to a halt in front of Ebony's house, two white brick chimneys framing a white brick Cape Cod with more windows than a house should have. It almost looks like a castle or a cathedral. I don't see a car anywhere. I get out anyway and take a crooked slate sidewalk winding through oak trees and piles of leaves to her front door. I rap on the door with all my might and step back. I wish I had dressed more nicely, and I need a haircut badly—

A dog the size of Marmaduke appears in the picture window to my left. Is that a Great Dane? I didn't know Ebony liked dogs. I smile at the dog, but the dog only woofs and slobbers.

The door doesn't open, so I knock again. This time the dog begins to bark. That ought to get her to the door. If she's here. I check my nails for dirt, check my breath—

The door remains closed.

She's not here.

I peek through the picture window and see framed watercolors, sketches, and oil paintings on the walls, sculptures and brass lamps on antique-looking tables, a red plaid throw blanket on a blue and rust couch. So much color, and nothing matches exactly. That Ebony's style, all right. Glossy hardwood floors. The fireplace mantel is full of pictures, but I can't make out who's in them because Marmaduke's huge head and paws are blocking my view.

This could have been our house. This *should* have been our house.

Damn, I'm depressed.

I walk around back, and from a slight rise, I can see Huntington Bay clearly. I bet Ebony can see the Sound and even Connecticut from the second floor of her house on a clear day. This is the perfect place for an artist—or a writer. I can even hear the waves kissing the shore. This is perfect.

Perfect.

I decide to wait on the porch. What's an hour or two after twenty years? I'm too close to leave now. As cold as it is, I feel warm inside.

When two hours becomes three, then four, then five, and the stars come out and I start to shiver, I take the winding path back to the Nova where I write her a note:

Ebony:

I want to see you. Just to talk (promise). I'll be on my dad's boat. Until I get a phone, you can leave messages at the yacht club.

Love, Peter

P.S. I love your house. What's the dog's name?

I fold and wedge the note into the crack in the front door, salute Marmaduke, and return to my car, hoping the entire time that Ebony will arrive so I can hold her again.

I wait another hour in the Nova, the heater on high, then I drift aimlessly along West Shore Road to the yacht club, get a taxi to the boat, and snuggle up on my bunk, the creak and my father's bones serenading me as the *Argo* rocks me to sleep.

I finally found her.

Now if only I could see her . . .

Part Two

Ebony Found

Ay me! for aught that ever I could read
Could ever hear by tale or history,
The course of true love never did run smooth.

—William Shakespeare, *A Midsummer Night's Dream*

10

Two sneezes, a hacking cough, and a boat horn wake me on Monday, and I sit up from my bunk too fast and smack my head on the ceiling. Just like old times. A head cold and a headache. I have never learned how to wake up properly in this boat.

I hear the Captain's bones rattle.

"Funny," I whisper. "Real funny."

I look at myself in the little mirror in the head as the boat rolls back and forth. Jesus, Halloween is coming up, and I won't have to dress up at all if I don't start getting more sleep. I wrap a blanket around me and go out on deck to a cold, stinging rain, the wind whipping up whitecaps on the bay.

A lovely day to get one's life in order. I sneeze again as seagulls drift over the *Argo*. And a lovely day to sneeze into the wind.

I go below to brush my teeth and think back to a similar day in Pittsburgh fifteen years ago, when an ice storm raged outside St. James Catholic Church on the day I got married . . .

St. James. Named for one of the Sons of Thunder, one of the first disciples who left his nets, his boat, and his father behind to follow Christ. Kind of like me, except for the following Christ part. James, who fled during the crucifixion, who was supposed to be passionate and temperamental, the first martyr of the church, the patron saint of hat makers, rheumatoid sufferers, and laborers. *That* St. James. Good name for a church, and it's where all the Meltons have gone since time immemorial.

I used to joke with Edie that we were attending the wrong church.

Her father should have gone to St. Matthew, the patron saint of bankers; her brothers should have attended St. Vitus, the patron saint of actors; and I should have become a congregant at St. Jude, the patron saint of lost causes. Edie should have gone to St. Anne's, since St. Anne is the patron saint of childless women.

So there we were, about to be married among Pittsburgh's social elite, and there I was dodging sleet on the sidewalk outside the church waiting for my best man to show up in his '74 Ford Country Squire wagon. I was surprised that the Captain had agreed to come at all, and the weather certainly wasn't cooperating. Mr. Melton kept coming to the door and harrumphing, Father Massey eventually coming all the way out to the sidewalk, urging me to come in.

"He'll be here," I told him.

"The weather may keep him away," Father Massey said.

"He'll be here. My father has never met a storm he couldn't handle."

Ten minutes before the processional was supposed to begin, the Country Squire rolled up in front of the limousine and bumped the curb in front of me. The Captain got out, muttering "Never could dock one of these," and slammed the door.

"Captain."

"Pete." Sleet pinged off his pea coat, the only coat I can ever remember him wearing, and I was relieved he wore a dark suit and tie underneath.

"Some storm, huh?"

"Seen worse. Am I late?"

"No, sir. Right on time."

He looked up at the towering spires of the church. "You're getting married here?"

"Yes, sir."

He squinted. "You're marrying a Catholic?"

I hesitated. "Yes."

"You didn't tell me that."

I smiled. I had only told him that Edie was white, loved to sail, and was from a good Pittsburgh family. "Would you have come if I told you that?"

"You, uh, did you convert?"

"Yes."

He nodded. "Why'd you do that, Pete?"

Mr. Melton poked his head out and harrumphed again, pointing at his Rolex.

"We'll be in shortly," I told him, and as he shut the door, the processional music began.

"Is that her daddy?"

"Yes sir. We really ought to go—"

"Did he say you had to convert to marry, what's her name, Edie?"

"No. I converted of my own free will."

He blinked a few times, tightening his lips to a frown, his face a tired gray. "I'm not going in, Pete."

I tried to put my arm around him, but he stepped away. "Come on, Captain. You're my best man. I'm not going in without you."

He puffed up his chest and rocked on his heels. "I'm not going in."

"Why not?"

He pointed at St. James. "That isn't the church you were raised in."

"Captain, we haven't been to church in ten years."

"Well, that isn't how I raised you."

"Who said you raised me?"

He took a menacing step toward me, but kept his hands in the pockets of his pea coat.

"You gonna punch me out on my wedding day, Captain?"

"I might. Might knock some goddamn sense into you."

"Guess you knocked it all out of me already."

We stood there on that icy sidewalk having a staring match, his face getting red, the fog of his breath heavy in the air, his hands forming fists in his pockets.

"You're not my son. You've never been my son." He wrenched a hand free from his pocket and flapped it at me as he returned to the wagon. "To hell with you."

"You've never been my father either, so we're even," I say, trailing behind. "To hell with you, too."

And later, I cried at my own wedding.

I radio for a taxi, and while I wait, I make a list of all the things I need to do this week. If I don't make a list, I'll just wander back to Fairchild Street to wait for Ebony. I need to set up a bank account, return the Nova, buy a car, set up a cell phone account, get groceries and lots of Kleenex for this cold, call Henry, add to Henry's novel, continue my own novel, get some sleep . . .

Why'd it have to rain on the first day of the rest of my life?

Mr. Cutter again picks me up. "You have quite a few messages waiting for you inside. When are you going to get a cell phone?"

Quite a few? Did Ebony call? "I'll try to get one today."

"Good."

"Um, who called?"

"Let's see, some guy named Henry. Sounded too happy for it to be a Monday morning."

Hopefully that call will be about money. I'll have to set up a bank account today. And he's happy? I thought he'd be mad at me for leaving Cherry Grove so abruptly. "Anyone else?"

"One from a woman named Destiny and another woman named Cecil something. Funny name for a woman. They girlfriends of yours?"

Destiny, I understand, but Cece? "No, just acquaintances. Anyone else?"

"Nope, just those three, but that Henry guy called three times."

Figures.

But none from Ebony. Maybe she didn't see the note or the wind blew it away . . . or she didn't come home at all. That poor dog! I hope Marmaduke has a big bladder.

I return Henry's call first, since I can't do much this week without that advance money. "Henry?"

"Hey, Pete, how's the novel coming?"

"Fine. I'm just getting settled in. I plan to work on it some more after running a few errands."

"Good, good. You okay? You sound congested."

"I just have a little cold."

"Well, take care of yourself, Pete." A few moments of silence. "Hey, Pete, I just want to thank you for the other night. I don't know how to repay you. Cece and I have our fingers crossed."

Your fingers are going to get tired, Henry. But that means . . . Cece lied to him? "Yeah, um, I'll be staying here until further notice, so I need to give you the address for the yacht club for my mail."

"Why not just open an account and we'll direct deposit the advance? We could have the money in your account by this afternoon."

"Okay."

"And could you send me three more chapters by Friday?"

"Sure."

"And add some more sizzle."

Translation: More sex.

"I ran it by the publisher, and she likes it, but she wants more heat."

Translation: more nasty, hot-and-sweaty, break-the-bed, back-scratches-so-bad-you-need-a-transfusion sex.

"I'll try, Henry."

"You know what you could do?"

Here we go. "What?"

"Just give us a play-by-play of your night with Cece. From what she tells me, it was a sizzling night."

I nearly drop the phone.

"It would be a nice tribute to her, don't you think?"

"Uh, sure, Henry. It would be a nice tribute." If it ever happened. But how twisted! He wants me to write about the night I slept with his woman! "I'll try to surprise you, okay?"

"Okay, Pete. As soon as you've set up the account, give us a ring and we'll shoot that money to you."

"Thanks for everything, Henry."

"No, thank *you*, Pete."

Destiny didn't leave a number or a message. The Post-It says only that she called. I'll have to e-mail or IM her soon. And since I can barely read any of Cece's many numbers on my hand, I can't return her call either, even though it's marked "urgent." I know what it's about, and from the sound of Henry's voice, our secret is safe.

I first set up a checking account at a Bank of New York and leave the routing numbers with Henry's secretary. Then I find myself driving once again by Ebony's house on Fairchild Street. No car in the driveway, but the porch light is on. At 10:15 A.M. Hmm. No note in the crack of the door, so she had to have gotten my message. Maybe she got the message and decided it was too late to call. That was nice of her. Maybe she'll call later in the day.

Or maybe she won't call at all.

I try not to think about that last possibility as I get out and walk around the house, looking in the windows. I guess that makes me a Peeping Peter. I don't see any puddles, the dog dish in the kitchen is empty, and Marmaduke doesn't seem to be in any distress. No mail or newspapers either, so she most likely came in after I left. Why is she going through so much trouble to avoid me?

On the outside chance that she'll come home, I decide to do another stakeout, and while I wait, I try to add to *A Whiter Shade of Pale*, first reading over the last paragraph:

. . . Her eyes come to rest on the empty chair on the other side of Johnny. One of her eyebrows rises, her skinny pink lips wrinkle, and she moves in on my man.

I watch the cursor blink for several minutes. Do I want Ebony and Rose to have a confrontation so early? Do I need for Ebony to assert herself from the very beginning? Or will she hold back, even hide her feelings for Johnny? I decide that this Ebony—like the Ebony I'm waiting on—will take her time:

After Rosie Goulash sits on the other side of Johnny, I watch Johnny like a hawk. He doesn't smile at her, doesn't even acknowledge her presence, barely even shifting his eyes her way. He must not be into skinny white angels. Good. He's passed one of my tests, and the class has barely begun. Yes, Johnny has promise.

But he has to pass all my tests and satisfy all my rules. I have had a top-ten list of rules for men ever since I read a little book called *The Rules*. Hated the book. Loved the concept. If more women had rules in their heads, they'd have fewer wrong men in their beds. Mine are simple:

1. *If you're full of funk, you don't get none of my junk.* Which means a man has to be clean at all times. His nails, hair, underarms, face, and even his toes must be squeaky clean.

2. *Participate when we conversate.* This means that a man must really listen to me, not just nod his head and grunt.

3. *Allow me to be moody and you might get some booty.* This means that a man can't assume anything about my moods. If I'm in a bad mood, it doesn't mean my "friend" has come. It might simply mean that I'm mad, and not necessarily at him, unless he keeps pestering my ass with "What's wrong, baby?" I can't stand that shit.

4. *If you respect my family, I might let you start a family with me.* A man has to know that my child, my mama, and my daddy

come first. I've known them longer than him, and they've always been there for me.

5. *If you spend your time always saying "Oh, well," you are not going to be ringing my bell.* A man has to stand for something, have some sort of belief or faith, and have a system by which he lives his life. I do, and so should he.

6. *Hold me for a hundred seconds, and I might give you seconds.* He has to cuddle with me afterward, because he isn't that hungry and there isn't anything that interesting on the TV.

7. *If you think I'm a bank, your brain is stank.* This means that a man has to pay his own way. I am a person, not a purse.

8. *If you think I'm a maid, you aren't getting laid.* He has to clean up his own mess. I'm not his mama. If he spills it, drips it, drops it, drabs it, leaves it, flicks it, or stinks it up, he fixes it.

9. *If you treat me as if I'm the only one in the room, you'll get some boom-boom.* When a man is with me, he must focus on me no matter if the TV's on, the waitress has a cute smile, or the house is on fire.

10. *If you can't commit, you aren't getting it. I expect* a commitment. Why else would I be messing with him? I don't mess with but one man at a time, and my time is precious.

Now let's see how Johnny stacks up so far. I know I've just met him, but damn! Better to see how he stacks up now than down the line when it's too late. So far he's clean and he listened to me. I haven't known him long enough to test him with a nasty mood, but he seems respectful. Family? Italians are big on families and family honor, right? I bet we're in agreement there. And he seems to stand for bettering himself, or he wouldn't be here. And I'll bet he's a Catholic. That's a strict religion. And aren't Italians romantic? I bet he's a cuddler. And he has pride in his appearance, so he'd probably be too proud to let me pay for anything. He's definitely focusing more on me than that wench. Dag, he's nine for nine!

But . . . number ten. That's the hard one. Will he make a commitment? He doesn't wear a wedding band, so he either hasn't made a commitment yet or is between commitments. Maybe he's waiting for the right woman . . . for someone like me. Either that or he's been breaking hearts for years—

Folks start getting up all around me. What's going on? The class is over? Shit. I haven't been paying attention.

Now what? They have to have a first date, and I promised Henry an "off-the-wall" place. Pittsburgh has plenty of places to meet: Kennywood Park, the zoo, Liberty Avenue, West View Park, the old Neville skating rink—

They'll meet in a skating rink.

I can hear the critics howling now: "No educated sistuh would be caught dead on a date at a skating rink! It's just too childish!"

Oh yeah? This sistuh will, and there's even some logic to it, because romance *is* a skating rink. Two people skate round and round, sometimes rolling along separately, sometimes holding hands, sometimes falling separately, sometimes falling together, traveling in a circle—a symbol of infinity—and barely covering any distance at all, while big silver balls cast lightning bolts in the darkness—

Maybe I'm getting too carried away. Skating rinks are about as romantic as the corner convenience store, they often play polka tunes, and no one falls in love during the hokey-pokey, yet if Johnny is in witness protection, what better place for him to hide out?

Ebony and Johnny are going skating, but the Neville isn't a skate center anymore. I think they hold raves there now. Hmm. I'm on Fairchild Street, so . . .

"Do you skate?" Johnny says to me as I stand.

"Do I what?"

"Skate. Roller-skate."

"Oh, I haven't been skating in ages." Where's he going with this? Strangest pick-up line I've ever gotten.

He hands me a fluorescent yellow piece of paper that reads "Free pass to Fairchild Skate Center." I see Rosebush hovering closer, probably to see if Johnny has any more free passes. Nuh-uh, honey, all this man's passes are going to me.

"Come," he says.

Right here? How kinky! "Oh, I don't know. I don't skate very well."

"You might . . . if you have the right partner."

Oh, damn. I'm going skating now! "Uh, what time?"

"I work one to nine on Saturday. Come around five."

Hold up. He works at a skating rink? He's definitely in witness protection now. "Uh, sure. Around five."

"*Ciao*," he says with a wink, and he's gone.

I stand there holding that free pass and wonder. Why Pittsburgh? *La famiglia* is already here! I mean, Pittsburgh is the city that made Franco Harris, a black running back, into an Italian, and I think the last names of everyone on city council end in a vowel.

Why would anyone want to hide in Pittsburgh? This place is and has always been a circus. We got Town Talk Bread, Iron City Beer, Farkleberry Tarts, Gimbel's, Kaufmann's, and we even had the old Pittsburgh Condors of the ABA with their big hair, high socks, and red, white, and blue ball. They filmed *The Fish that Saved Pittsburgh* right here where the Penguins used to play and be the shit, until them damn Islanders came along. And the Pirates have always been entertaining, first with Roberto Clemente in '71 and later with "Lumber and Lightning" with Willie Stargell in '79. The nicknames were better back then, like pitcher "Blue Moon" Odom—who won once in a blue moon, too. The nicknames today are just foul. The Answer? His Airness? Get real. I'd take a "Blue Moon" any day. And going to any game in town is like going to Ringling Brothers because of Myron Cope, Bob Prince, babushkas, and the Terrible Towel. Maybe it's easier for Johnny to blend in here than Arizona or wherever the Feds send the goombas.

But why the hell am I thinking this shit? I just got asked out sort of by a somewhat handsome man.

To a skating rink.

Where he works.

And is probably hiding from certain death.

Dag, I need to buy a new outfit!

I look up. Ebony's house looks the same. Geez, what a waste of time. This chapter isn't going anywhere, but then again, neither am I. Might as well throw in another chapter of Ebony and Johnny's date. Henry will just have to edit this to death:

Chapter 4

The Fairchild Skate Center is crowded, busy, and has the familiar smell of a locker room. Where's the organ and the polka music? There obviously won't be any hokey-pokey at this joint, but maybe later at Johnny's place with his joint . . .

A hoochie can dream, can't she?

I'm wearing brand new Levi's and a New York Knicks jersey and find myself sitting on a carpeted bench hugging the railing watching Johnny. He doesn't see me right away, but that's okay, and the man can really skate. Do they teach hit men to skate in the Mafia?

All Johnny does is skate around backward, making the kids feel safe, kind of like a traffic cop. Thank God he doesn't have a whistle. He is so smooth and graceful, but that crummy "staff" shirt has got to go. I watch the tiniest kids on Fisher Price skates going by at 0.1 miles per hour. Those things ought to be called "walks" instead of skates.

The rest of Fairchild Skate Center is like a really bad disco. Not one but seven disco balls shoot beams of light everywhere, and a smoke machine belches on some of the bass-heavy numbers. Some white guys who think they're cool wear black tank tops with white T's underneath, sporting close-shaved blond hair they bought in a can, designer jeans, blond goatees, and sideburns. They attempt the moon walk, and it isn't bad. Skating is probably the only way white boys can do the moon walk. Each has a cell phone, a beeper, a tattoo, and a piercing of some kind. A skate gang, oh, no!

I watch the skaters go round and round. There are hardly any couples out there, yet the place is swimming with pheromones, hormones, and fallen moans, all of these "moans" racing faster than the kids can skate. And children surround Johnny, which makes me wonder if he has any. I know they'd be hairy.

Johnny rolls my way but doesn't look at me, keeping his eye on matching hooded black boys in cornrows, their jeans creased and cuffed, who are playing roller derby and follow-the-leader with a pack of white girls. Johnny really takes this job seriously. Dag, I'm a skate-staff groupie. Flyers, dyers, on fires, liars, and sighers whiz by. The tired, wired, hired, and mired float round and round and it's a merry-go-round without the horses, people up, then down.

Some permanently. Johnny has to call for a rescue squad for one poor lady. She did a three-point landing on one knee, one elbow, and her nose.

I see a tiny white hand waving from the corner of my eye and see Johnny returning the wave. Who's this? There's a prepubescent, training bra–wearing, freckled wench waving at my Johnny from her perch behind the skate rental counter.

It's time for me to skate.

I approach the little vixen. "Do you have a woman's size thirteen?"

"Oh, no," she says with a giggle. "We don't have anything *that* big."

The things I could say about the nubs she calls breasts. I bite my tongue. She's probably the age of the kids I teach, and I could scar her for life. "How about a man's size eleven then?"

"Oh, sure." She pulls out a pair of wrinkly brown skates. "Three bucks."

I wave the pass in front of her and slap it on the counter. "Johnny gave this to me."

She pouts. "Oh."

I hand her my shoes and feel I need more information. "Um, does Johnny give out free passes that often?"

"No," she pouts.

Good. "Bye now."

I don't feel bad for crushing her little heart, but I do feel bad about wearing two huge boats on my feet. Boats with wheels. Who in hell ever thought this shit up? Please, Lord, don't let me fall before I get out there. I steady myself on the railing and take a tentative slide-step onto the floor. Dag, it's like walking on ice.

"So, what you think?"

I turn slowly to my left and see Johnny's grinning face. "I think I'm out of my mind for trying this." Skaters stream around me to the benches. "Where's everybody going?"

He shrugs. "Who can tell with kids? They skate around and around separately, but when cool kids go to the benches, everybody follows. Most kids show up after eight. Today is pretty light. You better get out here while you can."

What is that supposed to mean? "Help me then." He reaches out a hand, but I swat it away. "No, I'll wait until there's a crowd." He reaches out the other hand. "C'mon, Johnny, everybody will see me fall." And these skates make me feel like I'm seven feet tall.

"I will not let you fall."

Daa-em. I take that hand . . . and we float off. I lose my balance just about every other second, but he holds me up. Eventually, I'm not floating anymore. I can feel the floor—and the roughness of his damn hand. That's when I notice the scars.

"Where'd you get those wicked-looking scars?"

"In fights."

Johnny's an ex-con? He looks mean enough, but maybe . . . "Were you a boxer?"

"Yes. I wasn't very good. Not many Italian heavyweights anymore. I was fifteen and fifteen with two draws."

"At least you broke even." And maybe he's not in witness protection after all.

"I was a good bleeder. I put on a great show."

"Did you ever get knocked out?"

"I was down in almost every fight, but never out. I always finished the fight."

He looks like a finisher. There's just something stubborn about him. "If you don't mind my asking, where are you from originally?"

"Huntington, Long Island, New York."

Why not? Former boxer Gerry Cooney is just down the road. It's kind of believable.

He loosens his grip from my hand. "I'm going to let you go now."

"No, you're not."

"It is easy. There is rhythm to it. Feel the floor as part of your feet."

"I'm afraid the floor will be part of my butt."

He laughs and lets go.

And I fall. Hard. There's no bounce to any of the ounces in my butt.

"Thanks a lot," I say as he helps me up.

"You think too much about it. Don't think: do."

"I think that I'm finished for the night."

I find the nearest exit off the floor and collapse on a bench. Johnny glides in behind me and sits, rubbing his shoulder with mine. This is nice, but I'm rubbing shoulders with an Italian boxer in a skating rink? That isn't the kind of rubbing I want, and this definitely isn't the place.

"Johnny, do you want to go out for pizza or something?"

"Not really."

"You don't like pizza?"

"No."

Maybe he's Italian in appearance only. "How about spaghetti?"

He grabs his stomach. "The sauce. I have always had trouble."

"Um, there's a Chinese place a few blocks over."

Johnny smiles. "Yes. I like Szechuan."

At Yin's Szechuan Palace, Johnny teaches me how to use chopsticks, those strong, scarred hands gently gripping mine. After several dropped noodles, I use the damn fork.

"What do you do in real life?" he asks.

"What you mean 'real life'?"

He shrugs. "I mean, what do you do for a living?"

"I teach history to seventh graders."

"My sympathies."

"Thanks."

He smiles. "So . . . what do you think?"

"About what?"

"About me."

He gets right down to it, doesn't he? I've heard that Italian men were forward. "You're nice."

"Please be honest, and 'nice' is so overused."

True. "Well, at first I thought you were in the witness protection program."

Here's my chance to show how ridiculous romantic comedies have gotten in relation to characterization and plot. No one wants to read how two average, normal people meet and fall in love anymore—not even average, normal readers. It may be daily life in America, it may be cute, it may even be poignant, but it just won't sell.

The woman can't be, say, just a waitress in a little café in a small town, and the man can't be, oh, just a retired Navy man with a house nearby. Though it smacks heavily of reality, there's hardly any drama in that. She has to be a waitress with a sordid past. Maybe she was a stripper who once had an affair with a politician who's now running for president and wants her dead to avoid the inevitable scandal. She'll then have to run into the tattooed arms of our Navy man, who is an ex-Navy SEAL trained in every martial art and who just happens to have an unending supply of bullets for his trusty M-16. The two won't just "settle down and have 2.3 children," oh, no. The two of them will have to battle the political forces of evil for most of the book, have passionate love scenes when they should be running for their damn lives, kill off all the bad guys with lots of explosions, leaving him with a cute scar, not serve any jail time for such a high body count and terrible property damage, and eventually ride off into the sunset in a bulletproof Hummer. Logical plot and characterization be damned. The reading public wants escape, not reality.

Therefore, Johnny is not only in the witness protection program, he's planning to profit from it:

Johnny chokes on a wonton, washing it down with some hot tea. Oh shit. He *is* in the witness protection program.

"Uh, I know I'm wrong, Johnny, but . . . I mean, you're Italian, you have scars, you're big. It's a stereotype, I know, but—"

"It is true."

"It's . . . true?" Oh, shit.

"Yes. It is why I take the class."

"The class?"

"Yes, the writing class." He touches his head. "The things I know. Bestseller for sure. Then I can live life again, return home. There was safety in being a made guy. More safety in being known to the world."

I'm eating Chinese food with the Italian Studs Terkel. "Um, I knew you didn't look like a Johnny Smith."

"Johnny I kind of like. Smith, no." He leans forward. "Guess my real name."

"I don't know . . . Jeno."

He blinks hard. "I am Geno. How you know?"

"With a *J* or a *G*?"

"A *G*. Now, how you know I am Geno?"

"I'm clairvoyant." This is spooky. I was thinking of the Geno's frozen pizzas turning to cardboard in my freezer.

"You see my last name, too?"

What I see is me humping the hair off this man's chest. "Does your last name end with a vowel?"

He rolls his eyes. "Yes."

"Sorry. Is it an *O*?"

"Yes."

"Does it have more than three syllables?"

"Yes. Four."

Maybe I am clairvoyant. "Da da da oh. Accent on the . . . third sylla-ble?"

I see sweat beading on his forehead. "Yes."

I feel a moistening under my new Levi's. I should be betting something with this man. "What, uh, what do I get if I get your name right?"

"It begins with *N*," he blurts out.

Oh . . . daa-em. He wants something, too. "Geno Nuh-da DA-oh. You're from New York, right?"

"No. Long Island."

"Same thing isn't it?"

"Not if you're from there."

"You like basketball?" And maybe a sexy, tall, chocolate, former col-lege basketball star wrapped around your hairy body?

"Yes, but what does this have to do with my name?"

"Are you a Knicks"—I slide my hand slowly across my jersey—"or a Nets fan?"

"Ah, so. A Knicks fan."

I'm so smart. "Nic-da-DA-o. Hmm. Nic-oh . . . bello."

"No."

Shit. "Uh, Nico . . . retto."

"No."

Damn. "Nico . . . wafer-o."

He laughs. "No."

"Nicoletto."

Johnny blinks. I'm right!

"Geno Nicoletto."

"Yes." He takes my hand. "Is a secret, yes? You must still call me Johnny . . . in public."

Oh, sooky-sooky now! "What about"—oh God, my nipples!—"what about in private?"

"You may whisper my name in the dark."

Thank you, Jesus! "Your dark or mine?"

He looks at his watch. "Oh, no. I must go."

No way! You moisten me then leave? "Um, Johnny, I'm . . . no, no. I'll see you in class." SHIT!

"What were you going to ask?"

"Um, are you busy tonight?"

"I write at night."

"Could you . . ." I touch his hand, rubbing his scar lightly. "Could you maybe . . . write in the morning this time?"

"What do you have in mind?"

"I want to whisper your name all night."

He sits back. "I would like that very much, but I am never sure if it is safe. I do not want you to come to any harm."

That isn't the coming I want to do, Geno. "I can take care of myself, and how do you know that the harm to *you* won't be coming from *me?*"

He doesn't answer. He merely throws a crisp fifty on the table, takes my hand, and leads me outside. "Follow me," he says, getting into a beat-up candy-apple red Pinto with bumper stickers holding up the back bumper. What the hell is this? Draw more attention to yourself why don't you!

I follow that ugly red bomb to a warehouse on the south side. I doubt I will ever be able to get here again. And once inside his apartment, I don't have a chance to whisper his name.

Because I do me some holy-spirit-hit-me shouting.

I shout "GENO! GENO!" all night long until my voice is hoarse, and I leave that man with more scars than thirty-two boxing matches ever did.

Henry will red-pencil that chapter to death, especially the last part. "Could you go into more detail in this scene, please? I don't want a blow-by-blow account of their lovemaking, but give me something more than shouting and scars!"

If I tell Henry that I want to leave it up to the reader's imagination, he'll reply, "An author *is* the reader's imagination. Do your job!"

The Nova's clock says 2 A.M. This is insane! Monday night and she's not home? She hasn't been home in two days? Where is she staying? Why—

—is there a flashlight blinding me?

I turn sharply to see a burly Huntington town officer. Whoops. I roll down my window. "Good evening."

"Let's see some ID."

I fish out my license and hand it to him. "Anything wrong?" I know how this looks: a strange Pennsylvanian is parked near a dark house in

Huntington in a rental car at 2 A.M. "I'm just waiting for a friend to come home." Someone had to have called this in. Damn neighborhood watch folks. Don't they know a romance is soon to be in progress?

He shines the light from the license to my face and back to the license. "And who would you be waiting for at two A.M., sir?"

"Ebony Mills. She, uh, lives here." She just doesn't come home to do any living.

"So you're just sitting here waiting for Ebony Mills."

"Yes, sir. We, uh, grew up together over on Preston Street and went to Huntington High together. I haven't seen her—"

"For *two* nights, sir?"

How'd he know I was here last night? "Uh, yeah, I know it sounds strange. We just, um, keep missing each other, I guess."

"For two nights."

"Yes, sir."

His light beam travels across the front seat until it rests on the laptop. "Doing a little surveillance, Mr. Underhill?"

"Oh, that. I'm a writer. Just passing the time, you know, doing some writing while I wait."

"A writer."

"Yes, sir." This is getting me nowhere, and the officer doesn't believe a word I'm saying. I look past him to Ebony's dark house. "It doesn't look like she's coming home tonight, so I'll be going."

He hands back my license. "Good idea, Mr. Underhill. And it wouldn't be wise to be seen around here anytime soon."

"Excuse me?"

He hunches down and leans on the car door. "Sir, we received a call on a strange vehicle at this address last night, but you were gone before I could get here. We got another call tonight—"

"From whom?"

"From the lady who lives here."

Oh, shit. "From Ebony?"

He nods.

I feel a cold knot in my stomach and have trouble taking my next breath.

"You don't want this to go any further, now, do you?"

"No." I can barely speak. Ebony called the cops on me. Ebony actually had the nerve to call the cops on me. She must hate me—but why?

"I'll be blunt with you, Mr. Underhill. If I find you here again, I won't be so nice. I'd have to cite you for harassment, and Miss Mills would most likely file a restraining order. You don't want that to happen, do you?"

"No." Jesus, what did I do to her?

"As it is, I'm citing you for parking on the wrong side of the street."

Which will give a judge "proof" that I was "stalking" Ebony at two in the morning. I cannot believe this shit!

I remain silent while he writes me up for the parking violation and says, "Have a pleasant evening." Then he waits until I pull away from Ebony's before doing a U-turn and speeding off in the other direction.

It's past 3 A.M. when I get to the yacht club parking lot. Since I won't have access to a taxi for another five hours, I sleep yet another night in a parking lot in a rented Nova, this time with a heart made of broken glass.

11

When the sun rises, I feel so obsolete. I had a purpose in life yesterday, but this morning I can't think of one. My heart aches.

And after I trudge into the yacht club locker room to sit on a shiny bench to check my e-mail, it aches even more, because three e-mails from Destiny ask, in one way or another, "Did you find her?"

Yes, I found her, and I found her . . . angry. Vindictive even.

I write Destiny a quick reply, sparing her the details of my near arrest:

Destiny:

I found out where she lives, but I haven't seen her yet. I'll keep trying.

Peter

As soon as I shoot my lame e-mail off into cyberspace, Mr. Cutter walks in holding a manila folder. "Saw you in your car this morning, Pete. Your father's ghost keep you awake?"

"No." A lost love that called the cops on me did. "I came back too late, and there wasn't a taxi."

"Shoot, Pete, just take one next time. As a matter of fact, we're not busy anyway, so why don't you keep one of the Zodiacs for a while?"

A glimmer of hope today? "Thanks."

"Don't mention it." He hands me the folder. "Got some of your father's things in here. Just stumbled across them last night in the office. Don't know how they got there."

"Thanks." I open the folder and rifle through an assortment of clippings, documents, and photographs. Why'd he keep these here?

"Say, how's the *Argo* looking?"

I look up. "Clean as a whistle."

"That girl does a nice job, doesn't she?"

"What girl?"

Mr. Cutter shrugs. "The girl that cleans your daddy's boat."

"I thought it was part of the service here."

"It isn't."

I'm at yet another loss. "Who is she?"

He shrugs again. "You know, I never caught her name. Funny. She just shows up every now and then, I take her out to the *Argo*, she cleans a while, radios for a taxi, and I go get her. She's been doing it for about three, four years now."

I'm afraid to ask the next question. "Is she, um, black?"

"No, no. She's white. Pretty, too. Reminds me of a little shaver who your daddy used to take out on the boat a long time ago. Let's see . . . think your daddy called her . . . Dee."

I've lost the feeling in my hands. Dee? A nickname for Destiny? She almost looks white, but she's most definitely not. Mr. Cutter's getting old, though. Maybe his eyesight is going. And Destiny was going on and on about seeing the boat the other night. But what's the Captain doing with a little kid?

"Um, is she about my height with brown hair that has streaks of blond and red?" With a figure that only God could have made.

"That sounds about right. You know her?"

Why in God's name would Destiny do that? Wait. She knew I was coming, and she cleaned the Captain's boat before I arrived— but she's been doing it for three years? "Uh, yeah, I think I do. But tell me about the little girl."

"Dee? She was a handful, let me tell you, but your daddy was patient."

He was? The Captain was patient? *My* Captain was patient with a child?

"She couldn't have been more than six or seven when they first started sailing together. They did okay in the Frostbite races, too. I remember one time she brought a half a dozen flounder right into the clubhouse, even slapped them up on the bar and told the bartender to fry 'em up because she was hungry."

"When was all this, Mr. Cutter?" The Captain never said a word about any of this, but then again, we didn't speak to each other again after my wedding in eighty-six.

"Oh, just before he died, back in eighty-eight, eighty-nine." He pauses. "She was the, um, one who . . ."

"The one who what?"

"You don't know?"

"No."

"Hmm. Surprised no one told you." He scratches his head. "Well, she showed up like she always did every Saturday morning, and since your daddy wasn't here to pick her up, we decided to sneak up on him." He looks away. "She, uh, she found him. I mean, I didn't know he had . . . passed away. I would have done anything to spare that little girl that awful sight."

Dee discovered my father's body, and now Destiny is keeping the boat clean. They have to be the same person. Was she at the funeral? I can't remember. "Uh, yeah. Must have been quite a shock." Which is what I'm feeling right now! "Mr. Cutter, do you remember how the little girl got here every Saturday?"

He laughs. "No one around here will ever forget that. A red Pinto covered with bumper stickers brought her every Saturday morning. Surprised it still ran."

Candace brought her? "Did the . . . did the driver ever get out?"

"Every time. Older black lady. I thought she was probably little Dee's nanny or something. She and your daddy used to talk for hours right here in the parking lot at the end of the day."

Candace brought a little girl, a little . . . mixed girl—oh my God! Does that mean . . . Destiny is my daughter?

"I'm sure her picture is in that folder there. Your daddy took more pictures of that child . . ."

I dump the folder on the bench, sifting through military records, Mom's picture, one of my baby pictures, some faded letters—

And a stack of color pictures of the cutest little girl in the world. She has Ebony's eyes and my nose. Jesus, thank You, and I'm crying and there she is—my daughter!—and we had a date at Xando the other night, and I thought she was twenty-eight, and she asked if I had any other kids, and oh, dear Jesus, I hit on her! I hit on my own daughter! And she *did* say "jump your bones," just like her mama!

I hear Mr. Cutter mumbling something like, "I'll leave you to your memories," and when I look up, he's gone.

Ebony and I had a daughter, Destiny, who is . . . nineteen now. God, that explains so much! They weren't on vacation back in eighty-one. They were . . . somewhere, maybe Brooklyn? Ebony was pregnant and gave birth to Destiny in the early spring. That last time, in the hotel before I left for college, we made a child.

I look back at the laptop and reread Destiny's latest e-mail. I close my eyes. It's been in front of me the entire time. "Ebony31582." Destiny was born on March 15, 1982.

I have a daughter. I've had a daughter all this time—and no one told me!

I don't know whether to be happy or pissed! The Captain got to see her grow up, but I didn't! Why didn't he tell me? I know the old cuss was the stubbornest man ever born, but he wouldn't have been that stubborn unless—

Unless Ebony or Candace told him not to tell me. That's probably it. They're the two stubbornest women ever born, and they out-stubborned him. But why didn't Mr. Cutter give me this folder at the funeral? Why has he suddenly found it after all this time?

Destiny. The day she cleaned the *Argo* she must have left it in Mr. Cutter's office. She's pretty slick, and that means . . . that at least one person in Ebony's family wants to see me!

But how did she know that I was her father? Has she known from the start?

I feel sick to my stomach. God, the things Ebony could have told her about her deadbeat daddy, and yet Destiny still wanted to see me.

So. I'm a father. I have a dancing daughter who's almost twenty but looks and acts so much older. She has been raised right, but the artist mother of my child doesn't want to see me, the wheelchair-riding grandmother of my child has been withholding information, and only the great-aunt of my child has been helpful.

My child—*my child!*—has cried for me! She cried before she left me.

Okay, now what? How do I handle this? It is obvious that Candace and Ebony want nothing to do with me. Fine. But Destiny . . . maybe the two of us can soften them up.

I try Instant Message, but Destiny isn't online, so I write her a letter I never thought I would ever write:

My dearest Destiny,

How is my daughter today?

I can't stop the tears now, and I'm glad the locker room is empty.

We have a LOT of catching up to do, and this time I'll interrogate YOU.

Your mother and grandmother, however, don't seem to want me around. Your mother even called the cops on me last night and has threatened a restraining order.

You KNOW I want to see your mother again. You KNOW I still love her. How can you and I get the two of us back together?

This is starting to sound like *The Parent Trap*. What did those twins do?

Destiny, you are the most beautiful, graceful, wonderful child a father could ever want. I am SO sorry I wasn't there for you, but I would have been if I had known! No one ever told me.

Let me know what we can do to make all this right.

Your loving, though long-absent, father,

Peter

I send the e-mail and dry my tears on my sleeve. The glass in my heart is starting to fuse together.

I'm somebody's father.

And my own father was okay with it. That man who didn't want Ebony and me together was okay with it. I can see Candace presenting

Destiny to the Captain for the first time, saying something like, "This here's your granddaughter, Mr. Underhill. Her name is Destiny, but her mama calls her Dee. It's your turn to mind her, and you're gonna be minding her every Saturday from now on."

And he did, happily, according to Mr. Cutter, even turning her into a sailor. I should have figured it out when she showed up at Xando in a sailor's outfit. I've got to keep my eyes open wider from now on.

I set Destiny's pictures aside and look closer at what else the Captain held sacred.

I see a faded newspaper clipping from *The Marietta Times*—where'd he get this?—raving over sophomore third-baseman Pete Underhill: "In the ninth, Underhill's second homer of the day, a three-run shot to center field, sealed Marietta's victory." It was my best day as a college baseball player, and here it is. Damn, the man had some pride in me. Why didn't he ever say so? I flip the clipping over and see the date "5/17/83" written in some very familiar cursive.

It's Ebony's handwriting, it has to be. Was she following my career, such as it was, too? And then sending it on to the Captain?

Wait a minute.

I see other clippings from Marietta, all with dates in Ebony's handwriting, all in chronological order. It's almost like a scrapbook . . . that Ebony was keeping for Destiny. Destiny most likely sneaked this folder into Mr. Cutter's office. So here's some proof that Ebony hadn't completely forgotten about me.

She was still thinking about me.

I sort through some other Marietta clippings and come up short when I see my marriage announcement from *The Pittsburgh Press*. No date on the back this time. Maybe the Captain saved this one, but that makes no sense. I had married wrong in his eyes. Why would he save a reminder of that awful day?

No, Ebony probably saved it. Damn, she is definitely sending a message with this one. There are no more newspaper clippings after eighty-six. Is this when she gave up on me?

I hold an envelope addressed to "Ensign John D. Underhill, USS *Iowa*," the return address from St. Joseph, Missouri. I open it and see a short typewritten message on onionskin paper, the letters thick and imprecise, dated December 17, 1952:

Dear Ensign Underhill:

We would like to thank you for your heroic efforts concerning our son,
Marcus. We are saddened by his passing but are gladdened to know that
he did not die alone. May God bless you.

The Minor family

The Captain never mentioned this. God, there was so much he didn't
say! But I think I have enough information in my hands to find out the
whole story.

I run a few searches online for the USS *Iowa* and find an incredible
amount of information on the Captain's first ship at USSIowa.org. After a
shakedown cruise in the Chesapeake Bay in '42, the *Iowa* sailed to
Newfoundland to turn away the *Tirpitz*, a German battleship, then carried President Roosevelt to the Teheran Conference. My father was on
board with a president. What father wouldn't brag about that to his son?
In '44, the *Iowa* sank a cruiser and a destroyer at Truk in the Pacific, was
hit twice by enemy fire in the Marshall Islands, played a key role in the
Battle of the Philippine Sea, survived a typhoon that sank three other
ships, then sailed off to Okinawa, Luzon, and Leyte under Admiral "Bull"
Halsey. My father *lived* history when he was Destiny's age!

After World War II, the *Iowa* was decommissioned, then recommis-
sioned in '52 for Korea, where it earned the nickname "The Grey Ghost
of the Korean Coast." The Marines seemed to love the *Iowa* for softening
up their landings, and the battleship served as the flagship for General
Mark Clark, the Commander-in-Chief of the UN forces. The *Iowa* was
even used as the *Caine* in *The Caine Mutiny*, which wasn't one of the
Captain's favorite movies, but he watched it, probably to see his old
friend. When the Korean War ended, the *Iowa* sailed around the world,
stopping in Havana, San Francisco, Yakuska, Tokyo, Sasebo, Norfolk,
England, Scotland, Norway . . .

No wonder the Captain retired—he was tired!

I click on a separate page for information on the USS *Thompson*—and
here's the entire story, complete with pictures of the damage to the
Thompson, a destroyer and minesweeper. On August 20, 1952, shore batteries hit the *Thompson*, and the *Iowa* went to assist with the dead and

wounded, pulling alongside the damaged ship. Four men were killed: Howard Joseph Connors, QMC, from New York City; William Rudolph Csapo, SA, from Bridgeport, Connecticut; James Edward Wolfe, SN, from Cuthbert, Georgia; and Marcus Lajoie Minor Jr., SN, from St. Joseph, Missouri.

I run a search using "Marcus Minor" and come up empty. I try a few searches with "USS Thompson" and fare no better. I end up at the Web site for the Naval Historical Center, where I finally find more information.

And it blows me away.

Marcus Minor was black, an E3 just like the Captain. Minor and the three other men from the *Thompson*—all white—were celebrated in an integrated memorial service in 1952.

An integrated memorial service. In 1952.

Fifty years ago, my father held a black man who was dying. So why was he such a racist later in life? All those black men who came to his funeral thought of him as a hero. There has to be more to this story, and why was the Captain only an E3 after nearly ten years in the Navy? Minor is listed as a steward. Was the Captain a steward, too? Maybe he made all these friendships because they, too, worked in the mess hall. And all this time I thought my father, the Captain, was the captain of the *Iowa*.

How does a man hold a dying man in his arms, listen to his last words, his last breaths, his last requests maybe—how does a man do that and later hate that man's race with such passion, such venom? What my father did wasn't an act of courage, was it? He was just comforting a fellow sailor. A white man comforting a black sailor in 1952 might not have been the norm, but . . .

My brain hurts, but my heart . . . my heart feels full and whole again.

I check to see if Destiny has replied, but I see an empty mailbox. I wonder if she has a tryout today. I can't wait to see her dance. It would be nice to see someone with Underhill blood amaze an audience with dancing. All I ever did was make Ebony and Candace giggle and point.

Candace. Yes, I need to see Candace. Candace and I need to have a nice, long chat.

I take a quick shower, put on the same wrinkly clothes, and take a quick detour up Fairchild Street, where I see Marmaduke in the window again. A dog that size could fill up a room, but he doesn't seem desperate. I know, how can you tell with a dog? And since the windows are spotless when they should be smeared with Great Dane drool, I know Ebony's been by.

It won't be long now, Ebony. I'll be back.

After picking up a pack of Camels at the Southdown Community Market to thank Aunt Wee Wee, I cruise over to Grace Lane and park behind Gladys's van.

Gladys meets me at the door before I can knock. "Please tell me you know how to play spades," she pleads.

"I do."

"Good. Mary's late—"

"She'll be late to her own damn funeral!" Candace yells.

Gladys smiles. "Mary's, um, a little forgetful, so it's good you stopped by."

It sure is. I'm about to confront *Grandma* Mills.

A card table has been set up in the living room, Candace in her wheelchair opposite Aunt Wee Wee, who slumps in a folding chair. Another woman in a wheelchair seems passed out on the table. I take a seat opposite her, Candace to my right, Aunt Wee Wee to my left. Perfect. Right smack dab in the middle.

"You can play for Mary till the bitch get here," Candace says.

I smile at Aunt Wee Wee. "How you doing today, Aunt Wee Wee?"

"I ain't your Aunt Wee Wee, boy," she says with a grimace.

"She just mad," Candace says, "cuz you got her in trouble."

Aunt Wee Wee slaps the table. "Bitch hasn't let me smoke for two whole days."

"It's added eight days to your life, Edwina," Gladys says as she carries in a tray of finger sandwiches, setting it on the corner of the table near Candace. Wee Wee is short for "Edwina"? I don't know which name I like better . . . or worse.

"You ain't my nurse, Gladys," Aunt Wee Wee says. "An' how you know it ain't been smokin' that's kept me alive all these years? Sure as hell ain't been these sandwiches. You ever hear of salt and pepper?"

"They're bad for you, and you know that," Gladys says. "I'll bring out some fresh lemonade in a moment." She leaves for the kitchen.

"She's poisoning us, Candy, I just know it," Aunt Wee Wee says.

I slip the box of Camels out of my left pocket and place it in Aunt Wee Wee's hand under the table. She takes it and gives me the tiniest wink.

"What brings you by, Peter?" Candace says. "As if I didn't already know."

I doubt that. "Oh, this and that." I nod at my partner, her gray head still flat on the table. "Is she okay?"

"Estelle!" Candace shouts, and even I jump.

Estelle, an Hispanic woman almost as ancient as Aunt Wee Wee, lifts her head lazily until her momentum carries the rest of her upper body back into the wheelchair. "*¿Que?*"

"She don't speak much English, Peter. You know your Spanish numbers?"

"*Si*," I say. "*Me llamo* Peter, Estelle."

Estelle shakes her head. "*¿Que?*"

"She's also hard of hearing," Candace says. "From listening to too many Trini Lopez records, I suspect."

I see Estelle roll her eyes. Estelle can hear perfectly well. She's playing with Candace, just like I'm about to do.

"You got to deal for everyone, Peter," Candace says. "That's all Mary was good for."

I shuffle the cards slowly, deliberately. Thank you for the perfect opening, Candace. "I guess it's my *destiny* to deal, huh? So, Estelle, what do you think of *Grandma* Candace here?"

Candace's eyes pop, but she doesn't say a word. Gotcha.

"She talks too loud," Estelle says in perfect English. "And she always overbids."

"You can say that again," Aunt Wee Wee says. "Bitch be thinking she can take every damn book every damn hand, and then she blame me when we don't make it."

I continue shuffling as loudly as I can. I smile at Candace. "What are we playing to?"

Candace purses her lips and squints. "Five hundred."

I offer a cut to Candace who waves me off, watching her continuing reactions out of the corner of my eye as I deal, counting slowly out loud as I place each card. When I get to the nineteenth card, which happens to go into Candace's pile, I say, "Nineteen. A good age, nineteen, don't you think?" I snap the card to the side of her pile.

"The best," Estelle says. "Now hurry up and deal the cards."

Candace's eyes betray nothing, but her hands can't keep still. And I haven't even begun to deal—really deal—yet.

Aunt Wee Wee collects her cards as I shuffle. "I remember when I was nineteen. Yep, I was always into mischief when I was nineteen." I think Aunt Wee Wee is catching on. "I sure was into everybody's damn business."

"Wee Wee, hush," Candace says, her teeth clenched tightly. She gathers her cards and begins arranging them. "No one cares what it was like to live in the eighteen-hundreds."

I deal the rest of the cards and see a fairly useless hand. I might be able to take one book with a king of diamonds, but I don't care.

"I think I'll bid three," Aunt Wee Wee says. "Three's a magic number, ain't it, Pete?"

I know she's caught on now. "Sure is. Like a mother, a father, and a little baby girl, huh?" I look at Candace, who looks like a volcano about to erupt.

"I bid seven," Estelle says with a smile. She leans in Candace's direction. "Good name for a dog, isn't it, Candy?"

Good name for a dog? When Estelle winks at me, I laugh. "Ebony named her dog after me?"

Estelle shrugs. "As names go, Seven isn't that bad—"

Candace lets her cards fall to the table. "Now y'all hold on just a damn minute!" She stares at Estelle, then Aunt Wee Wee, then me. "What the hell's goin' on?"

"I found her," I say.

"Found who?" Candace asks.

"Destiny, though when she was little, Ebony called her 'Dee.' "

The corners of Candace's mouth droop.

Aunt Wee Wee struggles to her feet. "This a good time for a smoke." She ambles behind Estelle and eases Estelle's wheelchair from the table. "We'll be in my room if you need us."

Estelle waves before they disappear down the hallway as Gladys brings in a tray of glasses brimming with lemonade. "We won't be needing you for a while, Gladys," Candace says. Gladys pivots and returns to the kitchen. Gladys is certainly well trained.

"From what I understand," Candace begins, "you didn't do any findin', boy. *Destiny* found *you*."

"True."

"You think you're slick, huh?"

"No. Just angry."

Candace scowls. "What you got to be angry about?"

"A nineteen-year-old deception. I've been a father for nineteen years, and no one, not you, not Ebony, not even my own father told me."

Candace blinks several times and looks away. "Destiny's been busy."

"At least somebody has. And your daughter has been busy, too. Did Ebony tell you that she called the cops on me last night?"

Candace sighs. "She didn't call them." She turns to face me. "I did."

What the hell? "The cop said—"

"So I lied to the cops and said I was Ebony Mills, could you please get that creepy man away from my house?"

"But why?"

"So my baby could go home to her house and get a decent night's sleep, that's why. Get it through your thick head, Peter. Ebony does not want to see you ever again."

"I'd rather hear it from her, if you don't mind."

"You don't believe me?"

"No, Candace, I don't." I collect the cards and stack them in a deck. "You lied about those so-called vacations, and you lied about the letters. You got those letters, and you kept them from Ebony, didn't you?"

Candace wrinkles her lips and nods. "I was protecting her."

"From what?"

She leans forward. "From you."

"From me? Why? I loved her. I still love her!"

"So?" She rolls back from the table. "So the fuck what, Peter? It's too late now for any of that anyway."

"Too late for what?"

She shakes her head and whispers, "I can't believe I'm about to do this."

"Do what?"

She grips the arms of her wheelchair. "I'm going to tell it to you straight, and after that you are to leave, never to return to this house. Agreed?"

I don't like the sound of this. "Are you going to tell me everything or only what you want me to hear?"

She smiles briefly. "Maybe you ain't so dumb after all. I am going to tell you the truth, Peter, and let me tell you something: the truth hurts. Bad." She straightens and becomes the queen I remember. "Now how you want to do this?"

"I don't understand."

"You want me to go on and on, cuz I can go on and on for a couple hours." She wheels closer to me. "Come on, now, you're a writer. Everybody in this family knows you're a writer. You want to interview me or what?"

"You know about the books."

Candace rolls her eyes. "Yes. 'For E.' You didn't even try to disguise it."

"I wanted Ebony to notice."

"Oh, she noticed all right. Wish she hadn't."

"Why?"

"You never should have written them books, boy."

"Huh?"

"They tore Ebony up."

They did? "How could they? They were tributes to her."

"Tributes? That what you call 'em? Shit, boy, they were too close to her heart. You wrote about the most intimate details of your relationship for all the world to read."

"I wrote about our best moments. Some of them were intimate, but—"

"They were *all* intimate," she interrupts. "Every last damn sigh, kiss, and smile. The fact is—since that's all you want is facts today—the fact is that those books put her into a five-year depression that she's only just coming out of, and here you are ready to spoil her comeback."

"She's been . . . depressed? From my books? They were romantic comedies, for God's sake!"

"Boy, she still loved you, even after all those years away from you, and there you were writing books that said you still loved her—and you were married to some rich white bitch in Pittsburgh! 'I love you, Ebony, but I'd rather be married to this wench.' It would be enough to make anyone crazy. And now Destiny tells me you're writing another one. It'll put Ebony into a psychiatric hospital this time if you do."

"I . . . I don't know what to say."

"Then don't say anything, and don't write anything either."

"But I'm . . . but I'm divorced. I'm free to see her. We can get back together again."

"You believe that? Shit, you're sounding like one of your novels. In real life, Peter, that shit don't happen, especially since the only way that girl got out of her depression was to hate you with as much passion as she once loved you. She called it hate therapy, pure and simple. Why you think she named her dog Seven? You're nothing but a dog to her, boy. Nothing but a drooling, farting, shitting, shedding Great Dane."

"Maybe she named the dog Seven as a tribute to me," I whisper.

"Say what?"

"Maybe it was a tribute, you know," I say louder, "I'm man's—or woman's—best friend."

"Now *you* need therapy."

I sigh and stand. "Maybe I do." I push in my chair for lack of anything else to do or say.

"You gonna leave her alone now?"

I look at the ceiling. "I guess I'll have to." I focus on one of Ebony's watercolors on the wall, a jungle scene with a black panther lurking between palm trees. "I don't want to, though. I just wish . . ."

"What you wish?"

"I wish a lot of things. I wish I didn't have a racist father."

"He wasn't so bad, a little salty around the edges, took some getting used to, but Destiny loved him."

I wish *I* did. "I wish I had never left Long Island. I wish you had let Ebony read those letters. I understand why you're protecting her now, but what exactly were you protecting her from then?" She doesn't answer. "And please tell me the truth."

"I don't have to give you a mother's reasons for why I didn't want my only daughter messing with you, but I will. You ruined her, remember? You were irresponsible and got her pregnant. I tried to get her to get an abortion, but she wouldn't hear it." She smooths out her skirt. "I'm glad now she was so stubborn. Destiny is something else, isn't she?"

"She's like a dream."

"A beautiful dream, and Ebony and I raised that child to *be* a beautiful dream. Don't you be coming along fucking that up cuz you suddenly want to play daddy."

Ouch. "I wouldn't think of doing that, Candace."

"Sure."

"Really." Painful silence fills the room. "Was, um, was Destiny born in Brooklyn?"

"No. Destiny was born down in Virginia. She spent the first six months of her life down there surrounded by the southern Mills family. She don't have the accent, though. She's pure Long Island now."

Born in March, six months in Virginia . . . "And when did you come back?"

"Think it was September. And I *did* have the mail held all that time. Didn't let Ebony see any of it, though."

I kneel in front of her. "If you had just let her read one of those letters, just one, none of this would have happened."

She blinks. "Are you blaming *me* for this mess? And you better not be blaming me for *you* getting Ebony pregnant in the first place."

"No. I'm just saying that I would have . . . I would have—"

"Would have done what? Quit school and married her?"

"Yes."

"I don't believe that for a second."

"I would have."

"And what would you have had to offer her? Huh? Your daddy wouldn't have let you live with him, right?"

I hadn't thought of this. "Right."

"And this house couldn't contain all of us. What kind of a job could you have gotten with only one year of college? What kind of support could you have given to my daughter and granddaughter? I was just saving y'all the grief of a bad marriage."

"How do you know we'd have had a bad marriage?"

"Oh, come on. You should know all the statistics. Kids who get married don't stay married long, especially if there's no money in the house. And don't give me no jazz about our love would have seen us through. Love is good, but a healthy paycheck is better."

A little light goes on in my head. "So it wasn't because I was white."

"Haven't you been listening? You were too young, too irresponsible, and had nothing to offer my child. It wouldn't have mattered if you were black, Asian, Hispanic, Danish, or whatever you are."

I smile in spite of all she's said. "So you liked me."

"I'm about to get Gladys to take you to the funny farm, boy. Liked you? Puh-lease. Why would I ever like you?"

"You liked me, Luwanna, and your daughter loved me."

"Boy, you need you some lithium cuz you're on a bad trip—"

I take her trembling hands. "You may have even loved me, Luwanna. I know I loved you. You were my mother, too." I search her eyes as a few of my tears fall.

"I wasn't your mama," she says, her voice shaking slightly.

I kiss the backs of her hands. "You were the best mama I ever had. I've been meaning to thank you, so . . . thank you." I release her hands and stand. "I'll stay away from Ebony, though I don't want to, but I'm not staying away from Destiny, and I'm not staying away from you." More tears flow, and I have to wipe them away to see Candace clearly. "I used to have this little card in my wallet, had it in there ever since my daddy died. Know what it said? It said, 'Cremate me and spread my ashes over Mrs. Candace Mills's garden.' I don't know if they ever would have found you, but that's what it said. It's out in the ashtray in the car. Want me to get it?"

She whirrs away from me. "No, no. I believe you."

"Well, I better be going." Where and to do what, I have no idea. "Um, do you play cards every Tuesday?"

"Yes."

"As soon as I have a phone, I'll give you the number, and any time you need a fourth person, just give me a call." Candace doesn't respond, but I see her shoulders shaking. "I'll let myself out."

I take a few steps toward the door when I hear Candace whisper, "Wait."

I turn and see her, tears in her eyes. "Yes?"

"Damn, boy, you . . . you, uh, loved us all."

Eyes misting again, I nod. "You were my family."

She wrestles with her hands for a few moments then looks up, her eyes soft. "You know anything about hate therapy?"

"No, ma'am, I don't."

"Well, you better read up, get all the ammunition you can. Cuz . . . cuz I'm about to let you undo five years of hate therapy."

"What?"

"I said . . . that you can . . . see my daughter. I'll even tell you where and when, but then it's all on you, boy, all on you."

"Thank you, Mrs. Mills."

"It's Luwanna."

"Okay. Thank you, Luwanna."

She waves in the direction of the hallway. "Your letters are in two shoeboxes inside a hatbox tied with a red ribbon on a shelf in Wee Wee's closet. I don't have to tell you what to do with them."

"Are all of them in there?"

She nods. "You were a good writer even back then."

"You read them?"

More tears. "Yep. Every last one of 'em. William never wrote me anything like that, and I wish to God that I had let Ebony see 'em, but that's a decision I've lived with and will have to live with for the rest of my life. I hope you can forgive me."

I kiss her cheek. "I forgive you, Luwanna."

"Now go on, get your letters."

I race down the hallway and tap on Aunt Wee Wee's door. "Aunt Wee Wee? It's me, Peter. Can I come in?"

I hear a window shutting. "Come on in, Pete."

I open the door, and smoke billows around me into the hallway. Estelle and Aunt Wee Wee look like teenagers caught smoking by their parents for the first time, their hands in their laps, their eyes on the floor.

"I won't tell," I say, and I open the closet. There on a high shelf is the hatbox, a bloodred ribbon holding it closed. I reach up to shake it from under another hatbox and pull it toward me—but it's too light. One hundred letters should weigh more than this! I untie the ribbon, pop off the lid, and see two empty shoeboxes.

"Aunt Wee Wee, has anyone been in your closet recently?"

Aunt Wee Wee smiles. "Another pack of Camels will get me to tell."

I say, "I'll get you some," and Estelle claps her hands.

"Destiny been in there, Pete."

"When?"

"The other day, I don't know. I'm old, Pete. Time don't mean shit to me anymore. Now don't you forget them smokes."

"I won't."

I return to Candace, who is sipping some lemonade at the card table. "Destiny has the letters."

"She's a sneaky thing, that one. Said she was looking for a hat to wear for an audition."

"She needed a hat for a dance audition?"

Candace laughs. "She told you she was a dancer?"

"Yes."

"Peter, your child has *no* kinda rhythm, just like you. That child is an actress. She been tryin' to get a walk-over or a background role on a soap opera for the last year and a half."

My daughter's an actress? "But she's so graceful."

"Trust me, Peter. She has to concentrate to be graceful. Never known a more accident-prone child. She used to come home from your daddy's boat with at least one bruise or bump or scrape every Saturday night. You have to ask her about the time she tried to play golf and came home with a broken nose. It's why her nose is a little crooked."

"She got hit in the nose with a ball?"

"No. Somehow the child hit herself in the nose with a golf club. That's clumsy, ain't it?"

I wince. I once hit my own nose with a baseball bat. Destiny's my child, all right. "So, what should I do? Should I call her? We've been e-mailing each other back and forth for a few days now."

"You've been e-mailing Destiny?"

"Yeah. So?"

"That child doesn't have a computer of her own. The girl don't even have a job."

"Maybe she goes to a public library." Which makes no sense as soon as I say it. She was online well before most libraries open.

Candace starts to laugh, and it takes her several minutes and the rest of her lemonade to calm down. "Peter, we've both been had."

"What?"

"Don't you see? Where do you think Destiny lives?"

All this time I was thinking she was older and had a place of her own, but she's been— "She lives in Ebony's house on Fairchild Street."

"Yep."

"And she's been writing e-mails using Ebony's computer."

Candace smiles broadly. "I doubt it. The child barely passed English."

"You mean—"

Candace nods. "I'll bet the two of them have been sitting there just a-grinnin' and typing away." She slaps the arms of her chair. "Peter, you been talking to both of them the entire time, I'll bet, the little hoochies. But why'd they put me in the middle of this mess! The nerve! I was about to turn you out completely not ten minutes ago, and they've been— I don't like being had, Peter, not by my own daughter and granddaughter."

I've already been talking to Ebony? And Ebony has already read all those old letters?

And I'm still standing here?

I glance at the door.

"I know what you're thinking, boy. Get me the phone. At least let's make sure they're both home this time."

"No," I say. "I want it to be a surprise." Like a conquering hero, like a man on a quest. Knights didn't call in advance, and neither will I. What did I write a few days ago? A quest just wouldn't be any fun if she found me first.

"You sure?"

"Yeah."

"What if no one's there?"

I smile. "You have a key?"

She nods. "Now you're thinking. It's in the kitchen on one of the hooks next to the door."

I go into the kitchen to get the key and see Gladys smiling from ear to ear and dabbing at her eyes with a Kleenex.

"I think it's all so beautiful, Peter," she says. She holds up a copy of *The Devil to Pay.* "I've read this book three times now, and it just keeps getting better."

"Are you in on this, too, Gladys?"

"I'll never tell." She sighs. "Go get her."

"I will."

I nearly collide with Candace on my way back into the living room. "Gladys, what's this I hear about you being in on this?"

"Why, Mrs. Mills, I'm only here to make sure you're well taken care of," Gladys says.

"I never should have hired you, woman. You're too much of a nosy-body—"

"And you didn't hire me, Mrs. Mills," Gladys says. "Remember?"

Candace blinks. "I thought I did."

Gladys winks at me. "It's the medication, dear. Ebony hired me to look after you."

Candace turns to me. "Never have a daughter, Peter. Wait a minute. Too late. Um, you had better be careful of what Destiny has in store for you when you get old."

I kiss her forehead. "Whatever it is, I just can't wait."

12

If there had been any Huntington town police on West Shore Road, I doubt they would have been able to catch me. I park in the empty driveway and am staring at Seven's drooling mug in less than five minutes, but as soon as I turn the key, I hesitate. Will Seven take to me or will he take a bite out of me?

I stick my head in first, which is a stupid thing to do. Seven jumps up and puts his entire six-foot frame on the door and licks me up and down. "You're not much of a guard dog, are you, Seven?" Were the Danish ever good at defending anything?

After shutting the door behind me and batting Seven's head from between my legs, I walk over to the fireplace and see photograph after photograph of my little girl growing up, while Seven sniffs my pant legs. I will have to commit these pictures to memory, and maybe one day I'll remember her as a child without the help of pictures.

I wander down a short hallway to the kitchen. Spotless. Beautiful walnut cabinets with a matching walnut table and chairs. So much light shines into this house on all this dark wood. God, I love these contrasts.

I stand in front of a skinny flight of stairs going to the second floor, while Seven's tail thumps against my leg. "Should I go up, Seven?"

Seven barks.

"I don't know if I should."

Seven barks again and thunders past me up the stairs.

"Well, I guess I could—"

"Seven! You're not supposed to be up here!" a female voice shouts. "Git!"

Ebony's here? But there wasn't a car in the driveway! I back away from the stairs and fall back into a kitchen chair.

First, I see a set of manicured toes on the stairs, then the sculpted, toast-colored legs . . . of my daughter. When she gets far enough down the stairs, she sees me and smiles.

"Hi, Daddy."

Where's my voice?

"You lookin' for Mama?"

I nod.

"She's not here. You hungry?"

I can only nod. Why can't I speak?

She slips past me, Seven trailing behind, and opens the refrigerator. "You like macaroni salad?"

"Um, yes." There's my voice.

Seven tries to worm his head into the refrigerator. "Seven, stop! Mama makes her macaroni salad from scratch, so you know it's better than the shit you get at the store." She stands straight up and stares at me. "Are you always this quiet?"

"I'm just . . . I'm . . . I'm amazed."

"That I'd offer you macaroni salad or that Mama makes macaroni salad from scratch or that I just said 'shit' or . . . something else?"

The tears start again. "Can you . . . can you come over here and give your daddy a hug, Destiny?"

"Hmm. Gonna have to think about that." She shuts the refrigerator door, nearly taking off the tip of Seven's nose. "Finished." Then she runs to me and tries to hug the life out of me, while Seven barks.

Neither of us speaks, unless sobbing and sighing for ten minutes while a Great Dane slobbers on both of us is a conversation. She places me back in my chair, sits next to me, and won't let go of my hand.

"You're quite an actress, little girl."

"Thank you. But did you really think I was twenty-eight?"

"Yes. I feel so foolish."

She winces. "And wrinkly. You gonna wear *that* to see Mama after twenty years?"

I look at my clothes, the shirt Destiny picked out looking almost ragged. "Guess I better go change before—When does she usually get home?"

"I'm not sure if she's coming home tonight. She's busy getting a show together."

"A show?"

"Yeah, of all her work, Dad."

She called me "Dad"! My eyes mist up again. "You'll have to forgive me if I tear up at a moment's notice, okay?"

"Okay." She squeezes my hand. "Hey, you have to settle a bet me, Mama, and Grandma have. They say I look more like Mama, but I say I look more like you."

I drink her in again, this time with my newly acquired father's eyes. "Aside from the streaks in your hair—mine streaks, too, when I'm out in the sun a lot—and your nose, I'm afraid I'll have to agree with them, Destiny. I could never have made anyone as beautiful as you without your mama."

Destiny rolls her eyes. "You're only saying that so you can get on Mama's good side. I know deep down that you agree with me."

I only wish I could. "Um, I didn't think anyone would be home. Where's your car?"

"What car?"

"The Honda from the other night."

"Oh. That's Mama's car. I'm not even supposed to be driving. I have my license and everything, but I'm only supposed to be driving to and from work because of a tiny little accident I had last month on the LIE. But since I don't have a job—yet—I'm kind of stuck walking or riding my bike unless Mama is in a forgiving mood. I have another audition later this week."

"For a soap opera?"

"Yeah."

"Which one?"

She wrinkles up her nose, just like her mama. "You know, I don't remember. They're all the same to me. I just want to be seen."

"I'm sure you'll get the part this time."

"I hope so."

I have a thought. "But if you drove your mama's car that night, she had to know about our date."

"Knew about it? Mama set it up."

My mouth drops open.

"Don't be so surprised, Daddy. I was surprised, too, and she's my mama. I didn't know I was even going on a date with you till she said, 'Girl, you're meeting your daddy at Xando tonight, put on your sailor outfit, and act like you're a friend of mine trying to get us back together.' "

"I'm confused." I am. "So 'Ebony-three-fifteen-eighty-two' isn't your screen name?"

"No. Why would I put 'Ebony' in front of my birthday?" She flairs her nose. "I am 'Destinique-Seven,' thank you very much."

Ebony answered my original e-mail as Destiny, then set up our date, then— "Have you even read any of my e-mails?"

"I haven't seen any of them. Mama is a very private person, Daddy. I thought you knew that."

"So it wasn't you on all those Instant Messages?"

"You Instant Messaged me? That's so sweet, but it wasn't me."

I *had* been manipulated that day, but by Ebony, not Destiny. And today, I just wrote a heartfelt letter to my daughter that her mother probably read.

"You looked stressed, Daddy."

"I am. Um, did you tell her everything I told you at the beach?"

She jumps up, says, "Wait a sec," and zips upstairs. She returns with a microcassette recorder, placing it in front of me. "Most of our conversation is on there. I, um, forgot to turn it on at Xando, and, uh, it ran out of tape before I drove away, so, um, Mama doesn't know about Cece Wrenn. I wouldn't tell her about Cece if I were you."

"I don't believe it."

"Mama's very thorough."

"She taped our conversation?"

"Relax, Daddy, she liked what she heard."

I smile. "Even the part about 'jumping bones'?"

She giggles. "I almost gave it all away, didn't I? You two must have jumped each other's bones a lot back then."

My face flushes. Why am I so embarrassed now? Oh, right. Destiny is now my daughter, not a matchmaker. "Yeah, we were, um, pretty busy in that department. But why did she go to all that trouble when all she had to do was speak to me?"

"That's what I told her, too," Destiny says. "See, we think alike. I like the direct approach, but Mama, well, she's a little more careful."

"I'll say." I don't want to ask the next question, but it's been nagging at me. "Did Ebony, I mean, did your mama . . . Has your mama been depressed for the last five years?"

Destiny starts to speak, then squints. "Where's this coming from?"

"Candace told me—"

"What?" Destiny interrupts. "The bitch! Don't tell her I called her a 'bitch,' I mean, I love her and all, and she is my only grandma, but . . . She told you Mama was depressed?"

"She said that ever since my second book came out, your mama was on hate therapy or something."

Destiny laughs. "Well, she was, in a way, but she wasn't seeing a psychiatrist, if that's what you're thinking. And she just loves your books to death, and so do I. Weren't you just a little suspicious when I zeroed in on your book at the bookstore?"

"It was a little strange, but . . . So your mama *was* in hate therapy, but she *wasn't* seeing a psychiatrist."

"Right."

"You better explain."

"She should really tell you about it, not me."

"But she's not here."

Destiny takes a deep breath, puffing out her cheeks, then lets it out quickly. "You didn't hear this from me, okay?"

"You're sounding like Aunt Wee Wee."

"Aunt Wee Wee is my bud." She rolls her eyes. "But I'd never smoke Camels. Yecch."

"You smoke?"

"I'm an actress. I have to smoke. I don't inhale, though."

"Good."

"Okay, what should I tell you about Mama's hate-fests?" She grabs my arm and pulls me to my feet. "I think I'd rather show you."

She drags me through the house to a door going down narrow stairs to a pitch-dark cellar. She stops me at the bottom.

"Um, aren't you going to turn on the light?"

"I will, but you have to be in the proper position first. Take three medium steps straight ahead."

"I can't see a thing."

"Oh, you will."

I take those three steps, surprised that I don't fall into a pit. "Okay, you can turn the lights on now."

"Ready?"

"Yes."

She turns on the light, and all around me I see Ebony.

On every easel and on nearly every patch of wall is a painting, drawing, tapestry, or watercolor of Ebony, but she isn't smiling in any of them. She stares out windows, stands in doorways, sits on a hill overlooking the Sound, all alone with barely a sign of life in her face. Though they're haunting, they're also moving, with a consistent tone and mood, almost like an old Hopper painting of the lone person or a film noir from the forties with a touch of Gothic and Hitchcock. The effect is mesmerizing. I don't understand all there is to understand about art, all those movements and isms and schools, but I don't have to understand it to enjoy it. Everywhere I look in Ebony's basement, I see a work of art that I enjoy and understand. And for some reason, they look familiar, as if I've seen something like them before, and not just because I remember Ebony's early drawings.

"Pretty spooky, huh? I call it Mama's 'Van Gogh Period.' "

Van Gogh, who painted self-portraits when he was in an asylum. "When did she start doing these?"

"I think I had just turned fourteen. I had braces then." She flutters her eyes. "I wasn't always this pretty, Daddy."

I doubt that. "Just out of the blue? She just starts doing self-portraits?"

"Yeah. There used to be a mirror down here. She would stare into it for hours."

What happened six years ago? "I don't understand the timing."

"Oh! I remember. It was about the time you and, um, your wife were separated."

No wonder I've forgotten. "How could Ebony know? We didn't advertise it." Who advertises a separation other than movie stars and politicians?

Destiny shrugs. "She just knew somehow."

I try to imagine her at work in this cold cellar, try to see her hands working, her fingers flexing, her eyes . . . dull and dead? "Was she, um, a little depressed then?"

"You mean was she crazy?"

"No, I mean was she depressed?"

"Maybe." She looks back at the painting. "Yeah, I think so. She hummed a lot while she worked. And those tapestries—I thought she'd never finish them. She would sit at her loom working and humming for days, and then she'd bring them upstairs and start unstitching and humming. I'm not sure she ever left one of those tapestries completely alone."

An unfinished tapestry of half of Ebony's cheerless face sits in the loom in the corner. Dull grays and blacks shout "I'm depressed!" but the effect is hypnotic.

"What a show *this* would make," I say. "It's . . . it's brilliant."

"Mama says she's always wanted to have a showing of these somewhere. Think anyone would show up?"

"Sure. I've never seen anything like this by any artist." It's the work of a genius. But to think that I was the cause!

I hear Destiny sigh and see her sitting on the bottom step.

"Is something wrong?"

"Just thinking about, um, your daddy. Seeing these always makes me think of him."

My happy mood evaporates. "Why?"

"Your daddy was just as gray when he, um, when he . . ." Her voice breaks. "When he died."

I squeeze in next to her and put my arm around her shoulders. "Mr. Cutter tells me you, uh, discovered him that day."

She nods. "It wasn't so bad. He was old. And sad."

And I'm the reason for that, too. "So . . . what did you think of my dad?"

"I thought he was cool, but he was so serious about everything. I used to laugh at him when he got too serious, right in his face. Then he'd cuss—he taught me every curse word I know—and then he'd smile and say, 'Come here, you.' Your daddy was just a teddy bear who only looked and sounded like a gruff, old grizzly bear."

I wish I could say the same. "Did he ever tell you any of his famous stories?"

"All the time. I loved his stories."

"Most of them weren't true."

"Oh, I knew that. But that's what grandfathers are supposed to do, right? I asked him a million questions about you."

This I have to hear. "What did he say about me?"

"That I was a better sailor than you."

I nod. "Very true."

"He said that you were a great baseball player."

"But he never even saw me play."

"Well, that's what he said."

"Did he . . . did he ever tell you about a man dying in his arms?"

"Marcus Minor?"

She remembers? "Yeah, Marcus Minor. On the—"

"USS *Thompson*," she interrupts. "It's one of the stories of his that he made me memorize."

That's warped. "He made you memorize it?"

"He told me you'd probably ask me about it one day." She looks up the stairs. "But can I tell you upstairs? I'm getting cold."

I stare at the tapestry one more time. I hope Ebony finishes it with a smile, or maybe even a *Mona Lisa* half smile. No. I'll bet da Vinci's model just had a little gas. That wouldn't do for Ebony at all.

I follow Destiny upstairs, where we settle into the couch in front of the window, Seven resting his huge snout between us.

"I know most of the story," I tell her. "Shore batteries hit the *Thompson*, and the *Iowa* came to the rescue, but how did Marcus Minor end up in the Captain's arms?"

She smiles. "I called him 'Captain,' too. Mama says I should have called him Grandpa or something boring like that. It was more fun calling him Captain." She frowns. "I miss him a lot, you know? I mean, he was . . . he was like my dad for a few years."

I know how she feels. He was "like my dad" for a few years, too. "I just wish we hadn't parted as enemies."

"But you didn't."

"Oh, yes, we did."

"I don't think so, Daddy. He told me to tell you that he respected you. 'Make sure you tell Pete he earned my respect,' " she says in her version of the Captain's voice, which gives me the shivers.

"I don't know how I did that. Everything I ever did after Mom left seemed to earn his disrespect."

She shrugs. "Maybe you earned it later."

Yeah, and maybe those are just empty words from a man close to meeting his Maker. "So tell me the story of Marcus Minor."

"I hope I get this right. The *Thompson* got hit, and the *Iowa* sailed inside the *Thompson*, you know, to shield it from more fire. They hooked the two boats together and started moving the wounded over. The Captain was out on deck at the time and helped Marcus Minor onto the *Iowa*. Marcus was burned up pretty bad. The Captain said he had never seen anyone burned so bad, almost like he wasn't even human."

I get a shiver. I'll bet that the Captain didn't know Marcus was black, but the other blacks on board either ship, they would have known. They would have seen what the Captain did, would have seen a white man holding a dying black man's hand. To them—and to me, now, with tears in my eyes—the Captain *was* a hero.

"Anyway, Marcus wouldn't let go of the Captain, and he kept saying, 'Stay with me, don't leave me.' So the Captain stayed and held his hand until Marcus died." She looks up to see me wipe a tear. "Then—now this is what the Captain said—then he said he cried, right there on the deck of the *Iowa*. He also said he only cried one other time in his life." She looks at her hands. "It was on the way back from your wedding. He wouldn't tell me why he cried, but I've always kinda hoped that he cried because you were marrying the wrong girl."

I can only nod and wipe the tears from my face. "I did marry the wrong girl." I look out the window into the darkness. "And where is your mama anyway?" She was the right girl.

"Like I said, she's getting ready for a show."

"Where's the show going to be?"

She sits back and puts her chin in her hand. "You know, I'm not really sure. Want me to call her?"

My hands start to tingle. "You think she'll talk to me?"

"Why wouldn't she?"

"Well, the first time I tried, she kept hanging up."

Destiny pats my hand. "That was two days ago. You shocked her, you know? She didn't expect you to show up unannounced at Bethel with her looking all torn up."

"Your mama has never looked torn up."

"Um, no," Destiny says with a giggle. "You haven't lived with her. She can be right scary when she wants to be."

"But if she was reading my e-mails, then she knew I was coming to town, right?"

"Right, but like I've said, my mama is very careful. She wants everything to be perfect, and you weren't with the program that day, Daddy. You were just supposed to go to Grandma's like I told you to."

She gets up and goes into the kitchen, my feet tapping staccato rhythms on the hardwood floor. I try to control my breathing, but my heart won't let me.

Destiny glides into the room, stumbling and nearly falling in front of the fireplace. That's my child again. "Mama? Where you at?" She straightens a picture on the mantel and crosses her eyes at me as she listens. "So are you coming home tonight?"

I hold my breath.

"Oh, Mama, why not?"

I exhale.

"Look, there's someone here who wants to speak to you, and the last time he tried to talk to you, you were rude and hung up on him. Please don't do that again, okay?" She smiles at me, crossing her fingers. "Yes, it's Daddy. Who else you think it'd be?" She covers the mouthpiece with her hand. "She says she's really busy, so talk fast."

I stand and take the phone. "Hello, Ebony."

"Peter."

I can't read her voice. It's either tired . . . or angry. I'll have to hope she's just tired. "Thanks for speaking to me." No response. "Destiny tells me you're preparing for a big show." Still no response. "Maybe I can come to it." *Still* no response. My God, she's stubborn. "Uh, where's it going to be?"

"Destiny knows. I have to go." *Click.*

"She hung up." I toss the phone to Destiny. "She hung up *again.* I feel like tearing my hair out."

"Don't do that, Daddy. You'd look funny bald."

I stretch my arms up to the ceiling. "What do I have to do to get her to talk to me?"

Destiny steps behind me and rubs my back. "She's just tired and cranky. She's always this way before a show."

I turn sharply. "She says you know where the show is."

"But I don't remember. Really. Want me to call her back?"

I shake my head. "No, don't bother. Your mama's too busy to have a polite conversation, and I need to be getting home."

Destiny's lips droop. "Do you have to go?"

I caress her face. "I'd love nothing better than to catch up on the last nineteen years of your life, but we'll have time for all that."

She nods.

"Why don't we go sailing sometime?"

She smiles. "I'd like that, but not tomorrow."

"Why not tomorrow?"'

"Um, I think it's supposed to rain all day tomorrow."

"Oh."

She walks me to the door, and we embrace. "Good night, Daddy."

"Good night, Destiny. You, uh, are you going to be okay here by yourself?"

She straightens my collar. "I'm used to it. Seven will protect me."

I spy Seven spread out and snoring in the kitchen. "I doubt it. He let me in without a fight."

"He knew you were family, Daddy." She grabs my shoulders and turns me around. "Go home. I'll be all right."

"Will I see you tomorrow?"

"I doubt it . . . but you never know. I'm your Destiny, remember?"

I hug her close to me and drink in the scent of her hair. "I'll never forget."

13

I creep back to the yacht club parking lot and wander down to the docks. A moon floats in the sky, a few clouds obscuring its face. Waves lick the shore and rock several orange Zodiacs. I step into one, start it up, and cruise barely above idle through yachts of all shapes and sizes, all battened down, all dark, all swaying in the moonlight.

So much—too much—has happened today. My mind and my heart are overloaded and threatening to short-circuit. Today I learned that I had a daughter, almost said good-bye to the only real mother I remember, learned that my father respected me for some unknown reason, and heard Ebony's voice—her angry, tired voice. I know I have to be patient, but this is getting ridiculous.

I circle the *Argo* several times before tying on and climbing up the back ladder. The boat rocks gently, so gently. Maybe I can get ten hours of sleep, and all of this will make more sense in the morning. Maybe it will rain and I'll sleep all day. I sure could use it.

I open the cabin door, snap on the interior lights, descend, and stop short.

I don't see anyone, but I feel another presence. It's not like a cold spot that psychics claim to feel in those horror movies, it's just something different, something a little off.

"Hello?" I ask, feeling instantly foolish.

No response. Damn, it's like talking to Ebony on the phone.

I shut the cabin door and start to peel off clothes and the weight of the day. By the time I get to the head and sit, I'm only in my boxers.

Funny that I wear them. The Captain used to wear them, and I thought he was so old-fashioned. He also used to put on his socks and shoes before he put on his pants. I've never done that. I also never used Brylcreem or Vitalis. I'm sure their stock has plummeted now that he's gone.

After I flush, I get that feeling again. I listen and hear . . . nothing. Not even that creak. I must be drunk tired.

I stagger from the head to the galley, snap off the lights, and stumble to my berth, and as soon as I hit the mattress, I'm falling, oh falling so fast to sleep, but I don't hear the creak—

I jump up and bump my head. When am I ever going to learn not to do that?

Creaks don't fix themselves. That creak is probably seventy years old, yet tonight when I need it to help me fall asleep, it's silent.

I feel my way back to the galley and open the refrigerator before I remember I haven't bought anything to—

A bottle of Asti Spumante stares back at me. And the light in the refrigerator works. I didn't think that light ever worked. I pick up the bottle. 1998. The Captain couldn't have left it here, so how'd it get in there?

I smile. That daughter of mine. A welcome-home gift. I wonder if she knows that it's her mama's favorite. Just a glass or two and Ebony was feeling fine. Those were the days . . .

I wonder what else Destiny has left me, so I leave the refrigerator door open, its light filling the cabin. I open a cupboard and see Easy Cheese and a box of Chicken in a Biskit crackers. Ebony used to snack on these. Maybe Destiny has her mama's tastes.

I search several other cupboards and don't find anything, not even a speck of dust. Destiny takes better care of this boat than I ever did.

Maybe a snack and the Asti will help me fall asleep. I really shouldn't drink, but after the day I've had, I deserve something. And if that doesn't work, I can always pop a muscle relaxer or two.

After peeling the foil off the top of the bottle, I twist the wire basket until it falls into the sink. I've never been good at popping the cork, so I aim the bottle at the Captain's urn, which is solid enough to withstand anything. I twist the cork slowly, squinting just in case, and then—POP! That wasn't so—

"Are you going to share that?"

I freeze and turn slowly to see Ebony standing in the shadows in front of the Captain's door. I look down at my penis dangling out of the front of my boxers and put the ice-cold bottle over the opening.

"Ebony?"

She moves closer, wearing only a white T-shirt and, as far as I can tell, nothing else. "I'm not talking about the Asti, Peter." She looks down at the bottle. "Doesn't that hurt?"

"Um, it doesn't feel too good." Oh God, I'm hyperventilating! Why does my body pick this time to forget how to breathe?

She laughs. "Do you, um, do you have a girlfriend, sailor?" She steps closer, her nipples taut against her shirt.

"No."

She licks her lower lip. "Are you married?"

I look down at her pearl-chipped toes. "No."

"Any kids?" She reaches out a hand, placing it on my chest.

Oh, God. Her touch, that electric touch. "Just one. A daughter."

"Is she as pretty as me?"

"No."

"Liar." She moves her hand down my chest to the bottle. "May I have a drink?"

"S-sure."

She lifts the bottle to her lips and drinks deeply, her eyes never leaving mine.

"I— I thought you were preparing for a show."

She sets the bottle in the sink and reaches her arms around my neck. "I am." She kisses my neck. "Welcome to the show." She kisses my chin. "I hope you don't mind if, um, you're part of the show, too."

"Ebony, I—"

She stands on tiptoes and kisses my lips. "Not tonight." She takes my hand. "I don't want to talk tonight." She cocks her head towards the bottle. "I don't think we'll need that, but bring it just in case."

I pick up the bottle and take a long swig.

Then she shuts the refrigerator door, darkness bathing the galley. "Hold on to me, Peter."

I slide my hand around her stomach, and it's soft and firm. God, it's like she hasn't changed in twenty years! She lifts her shirt and places my hand on her smooth skin, my fingers tickling her gumdrop belly button.

She leads me into the Captain's berth, a single votive candle flickering from its holder on a desk crammed with nautical charts and map books.

She takes the bottle and drinks again, the sparkling wine dribbling down her chin to her shirt. She hands the bottle to me.

"Finish it," she says.

I gulp the rest while she peels off her shirt and lies on the Captain's bed, both arms reaching out to me.

"You haven't aged a day," I say with a trembling voice.

She shakes her head. "Shh. We'll talk tomorrow. Come to me, Peter."

I drop the bottle behind me and slide out of my boxers. "It's been a long time," I whisper as I ease myself on top of her, her skin hot, burning. "I might, um, miss."

She welcomes me inside her and sighs. "I've been waiting twenty years." Tears well up in her eyes. "Twenty years I've been faithful to you, Peter. You're my one and only love."

Tears spill out of my eyes. "You waited—"

She stops my word with a long, slow kiss. "Just don't let me go this time."

"I won't. I promise."

14

I wake before Ebony does, her soft breath warm on my chest, and listen to the rain tapping on the roof of the cabin. And for some reason, my back doesn't ache at all, and it usually aches like crazy whenever it rains. Sexual healing, indeed. The *Argo* rocks us, but I'm too wired to sleep, despite the fierceness of our lovemaking. I stroke her hair, a shiny auburn, and slide a finger around her earlobe, and as I pull her closer, I can't help feeling so sad.

We could have been waking up every morning like this for the last twenty years.

She stirs and opens one sleepy eye. "Hi."

"Hi."

She slips her hand to my face and pulls on a few of the longer hairs on my chin. "I almost don't recognize you. Where are your freckles?"

"I still have them."

She closes her eyes and hugs me close. "Good."

"Remember the last time we were on this boat?"

She opens her eyes. "Yeah."

I half expect to hear the Captain's bones rattling. "I intend to replace the memory of that night with last night."

"Me, too." She yawns, pushes off my chest, and sits, holding the sheet in front of her. "What do you have to eat besides what I brought?"

"Nothing. Sorry."

"Well, bring it on anyway. I'm hungry."

We polish off a box of Chicken in a Biskit and a can of Easy Cheese in less than ten minutes. We have each exceeded our saturated fat allowance for the rest of the month. I take my time eating because I'm not sure how our first real conversation in twenty years should go. Will she be angry and hurt? Probably. *How* angry and hurt she'll be is the question.

She pulls on her T-shirt and sits on top of the Captain's desk, her feet making circles in the air. "It's about time you came home, sailor."

"Yeah."

"And I meant what I said about waiting for you. I've been celibate since nineteen eighty-one. That has to be some sort of world record."

"You didn't have to wait for me, Ebony."

She peeks through a crack in the blinds. "I know I didn't. And it wasn't like I didn't get any attention. I thought that once I had Destiny, the boys would stay away."

"They didn't?"

"No. First there was Simon—"

No way! "Simon Lloyd?"

She nods. "He dumped what's-her-name in a flash once Mama told him you weren't coming back. We went out a couple times, but . . ." She shrugs. "He was *Simon,* tall, goofy, Simon. He wasn't you. I hear he's playing that bass of his at some jazz club in Brooklyn." She stares at me. "And you're not exactly the you I remember, but you still have those freckles."

"Not as many as back then."

"True." She pulls her legs up onto the top of the desk and slides her shirt down to her feet. "Then there was Mickey. Remember Mickey Mather?"

"You went out with Mickey?" She was going through all my friends!

"Well, we didn't exactly go out. We just hung out together, you know, played some ball, and went on walks. He was probably my best friend for a while until he moved away. He writes me every now and then. He has four boys, and every one of them has his round head." She groans.

"Are you all right?"

"I'm sore," she says, wincing.

"Sorry."

"Don't be. I'm out of practice." She drops her eyes and bites her lower lip. God, she's a goddess when she's shy like that. "We're, um, we're going to be doing a lot of practicing, aren't we?"

I nod. "Yes, Ebony. For the rest of our lives."

She looks up. "Don't be thinking that far ahead just yet, okay? I need to sort a few things out, and it might take me some time."

I want to ask "How much time will you need?" but I'm afraid of the answer. She's calm so far, much calmer than I would be in her position. "What do you need sorted out?"

"Twenty years of questions I've had."

That's not a "few things." My next question could open Pandora's box. "What kinds of questions?"

Her eyebrows twitch, and her pupils turn into two little brown dots. Here it comes. "Well, for one, why did you marry . . . her . . . instead of me?"

Boom. I look away from her eyes.

"Why, Peter? She was nothing like me."

Edie, whiter than an albino with dandruff, shrieks through my head on her skinny broom. "I've been thinking a lot about why I married, um, Edie," I stammer. "You see . . . I thought I had lost you. Forever."

"I was right here the whole time, Peter."

"But I didn't know that, Ebony."

She stands and starts pacing. "I know, but you could have come back anyway, right? You could have made up with your daddy, come home to me and your daughter where you belonged, and I wouldn't have had to wait twenty years to be happy."

I roll out of the bed to hold her. "Ebony, I'm sorry."

She puts out two hands and steps back. "No, don't. Not yet."

I drop my arms. *Be patient, will you?* I scream in my head. I turn, pull on my boxers, and sit on the edge of the bed.

Her pacing begins again. "Do you have any idea what it's like to raise a child by yourself?"

"No, but at least you had your mama and Aunt Wee Wee to help you."

"And later your daddy, too, but when it came down to it, it was just me." She bites her lip. "Just me," she whispers. "I needed you, Peter, I really did. I mean, I got stares and questions from people who thought I was babysitting my own daughter. You don't know how that feels, and you don't want to know what people said after I told them that Destiny was my daughter."

"What did they say?"

"Most just said 'Oh' and kept on walking. One woman even said, 'Oh, I'm so sorry.' Can you believe that? Like it was awful for me to have a light-skinned daughter. If you were there, no one would have had to say anything so cold to me."

"Yeah." Maybe. Some people are just cruel because they can be.

"I had to change her, feed her, clothe her, bathe her, burp her, and read bedtime stories to her. I had to stay up all night when she had a fever, had to take her to all those doctor's and dentist's appointments, had to hold her whenever she was scared of the dark. Just me."

"You've done an amazing job. Destiny is . . . Destiny is a dream come true."

Ebony smiles. "You really don't know your daughter that well, Peter. That child can be a nightmare."

"What?"

"Oh, she was a good baby, I'll give her that. But because she was so cute, we spoiled her. Rotten. I had to beat her with my wet hand many times."

Ebony beat my daughter? "You . . . beat her?"

"Someone had to." Her eyes soften. "I didn't beat her, Peter, not like you were beaten. I spanked her, like the Bible says. 'Spare the rod, spoil the child,' right?"

I must have been the least spoiled child on earth. "But with a wet hand?"

"It stings more."

"You or her?"

She laughs. "Her and me both."

"Oh."

"Mama never had any trouble with Destiny."

I believe it.

"Mama never had to count past two. Me?" She rolls her eyes. "I had to say two, two and a half, two and three-quarters, two and seven-eighths . . ."

I smile. That's probably the way I would have handled Destiny, too.

"She was sweet to everybody in daycare, too, but when we got into the car at the end of the day, that child went off, saying, 'Gimme a drink, Mama!' and 'Take me home now, Mama!' " She pauses to look away. "I had to pull over to the side of the road just to cry sometimes."

"You did?"

She nods. "She even told the daycare people that I beat her, and they confronted me. Imagine being confronted by a bunch of white ladies, Peter, asking if you beat what they see as a white child. I told them, politely, that I spanked my child, that my religion allows it. And when I got home that night, I just couldn't spank her anymore." She wipes away a tear.

"Ebony, I'm, I'm so—"

"I know, I know." She sighs and starts to pace again, fluttering a hand in the air. "When that child started school, we had to take her for her shots. And there isn't one nurse at Huntington Hospital that your daughter hasn't bitten, kicked, or hit. It took four of us to hold her down for any of her shots. And giving medicine at home was next to impossible. She'd spit it out on me or keep her mouth closed. She even bit my fingers a couple times and batted away the spoon. Then Mama told me about the cure."

"You mixed it in with her food."

Ebony rolls her eyes. "Destiny isn't a dog, Peter . . . though I did try that." She giggles. "It didn't work. She has your nose, remember? She could smell the medicine no matter how thoroughly I mixed it in. No, I got an extra large, long-sleeved shirt and put her in it. Then I tied her arms together tight like a straightjacket, sat on her legs, pinched her nose till she opened her mouth, and used a medicine dropper to squirt it down her throat. The child was born for drama, so I gave her some. I only had to do it a few times. Like me, Destiny doesn't like to be restrained like that."

I'm relieved. This was beginning to sound like *Mommie Dearest*. "Was she, uh, was she a good student?"

"She got straight A's from all her male teachers, because your child was a daddy's girl without a daddy, and she barely passed the rest. I used to catch her cutting up her brand-new school clothes, just cutting long slits in her pants. She told me, 'They're the style, Mama,' but I know it was just to get her male teachers' attention. Destiny has only been out on two dates her entire life, and both boys were three or four years older than her, and both boys were white."

I guess I should feel honored, but Destiny sounds so lonely. "Did you, um, did you ever get her any counseling? I saw similar behavior where I taught, and—"

" 'Similar behavior?' " She laughs and shakes her head. "I doubt it, Peter. When that child was mad at me—and she seemed to be mad from the time your daddy died all the way through high school—when she was mad at me, she'd tie string to my bedroom doorknob and tie the other end to the doorknob on the hall closet. I couldn't get out, Peter. I couldn't get out of my room." She flutters her eyelids. "I always kept a long bread knife in my room after that first time, just in case." She shakes her head. "No, I didn't get counseling for her, because all she really needed was a father."

I look at my feet. "Yeah."

She nods. "But because you weren't around, I often had to take drastic measures to keep her in line. My ultimate punishment was to take that child's TV away." She shudders. "And that brought that chick from *The Exorcist* right up into my house when I did that. Check out Destiny's door. It still has the dents in it from when she threw her nightstand against it." She closes her eyes. "But even that didn't work every time, because she was still reading the *TV Guide*. She used to read it cover to cover in front of me, and she even memorized who played what on each show. When I threatened to cancel my subscription, though, she straightened out in a hurry." She shakes her head and sighs. "And now it's *Soap Opera Digest*. At least she's reading something."

I want to laugh, but I had better not. My daughter has just been researching her career for a couple years. "So she's a natural actress."

"There isn't anything natural about memorizing the *TV Guide*."

"No, I guess not." Though it would help her on the crossword puzzle in the back.

We regard each other in silence for a while, making eyes like we used to when we were kids. She is being so calm! Maybe she's just being calm before the storm. "Uh, Ebony, if I were you, I don't know if I would be so, um, happy about all this."

"You think I'm happy?"

"Well, you aren't throwing things at me."

"Not yet," she says with a smile, so I know she doesn't mean it. "Peter, I've been hoping for this moment for so long, and now it's here. I can't be anything but happy about it."

"But you were depressed for a while, weren't you?"

She looks at my feet. "Yeah. That was a pretty crummy time. I felt so lost. I was waiting for you to run back to me after you and her separated." She winces. "And you didn't."

"Edie dragged out the divorce to punish me."

"Yeah, I know."

"How did you know?"

She starts to drift across the floor. "At first it was a feeling. My heart ached for no apparent reason, and trust me, that's a spooky thing to have happen to you. I thought I was having heart trouble and even saw a doctor, but nothing was wrong, and I was healthy as a horse. But my heart still hurt, so I made a phone call and found out. I'd rather not say who I talked to so you don't think I was stalking you."

Who would she have called? Not many people knew. My school? No, I didn't tell anyone there. The Meltons? No, they wouldn't have advertised that. It would have been bad for their image. That only leaves—

Oh, my God! "You talked to Edie."

"Yeah. It didn't go over very well."

It wouldn't have. And that one phone call might have prolonged our divorce even longer, but I don't want to bring that up. I can't despise Edie any more than I already do, and I don't want to blame Ebony for any of it.

"I'm so sorry, Ebony. Really. And all I can do is say 'I'm sorry.' " But I have a feeling that if I said "I'm sorry" a million times, it still wouldn't fix twenty years of a "few things."

She takes a few deep breaths. "I know you didn't know you had a child, and I know Mama kept all of your letters from me, but couldn't you have come home, at least to see your daddy before he died? All you had to do was come for a visit on a weekend, Peter. That's all. You would have seen your daughter out on this boat, you would have made up with your daddy, and we could have been together so much sooner."

Oh, God, now my heart aches. "I'll never leave you again," I say as tears fall into my lap.

She crouches in front of me and brushes a tear away. "You better not. Otherwise I won't get any compensation for the last twenty years."

I look up. "Compensation?"

She nods.

"You mean, child support?" That has to add up to . . . Gulp. A lot of money I don't have and may never get!

She leans her forehead against mine. "Something like that." She wipes away another tear. "Remember that book we read in Miss Thurston's class?"

Miss Thurston: varicose veins, high heels . . . Simpson . . . eighth grade. "Didn't we read the *Odyssey?*"

"We did. And do you remember what I said to you on the bus the day we finished reading it?"

"No."

She takes my hands. "I said that no girl would ever wait on a boy for twenty years."

"You did?" I wish I could remember.

"Yes, and I also said that if there was one boy I would wait for, that boy would be you, Peter." She kisses my forehead. "And here I am."

And here she is, happy, despite what I've put her through. "You said all that?"

She wraps her arms around my neck. "I was advanced for my age back then, wasn't I?"

"Yeah. You've always been ahead of your time."

She turns sideways and sits her beautiful butt into my lap, draping her arms around my neck. "You're still writing another book for me, right?"

"Sort of."

"What do you mean, sort of, Desiree?"

"I don't want to be Desiree Holland anymore. I want to write under my own name. I've been working on another novel simultaneously with my latest Desiree novel."

"Is it any good?"

"I'll let you be the judge."

"Okay," she says, tracing my earlobe with her tongue, "but whatever your next book is, I want the dedication to say 'For Ebony Mills' this time. I'm tired of being plain old 'E.' "

I feel a stirring in my loins as she begins to nibble on my ear. "Sure."

"You're working hard on both of these books, right?"

I nod, a shiver traveling from my earlobe all the way down to my toes. I'm also working hard in my boxers. "Yes. Do you want to see them?"

She bends my head down to look at the bulge in my boxers. "I already see something, Peter." She swivels her hips to straddle me, pulling my penis from its hiding place. "I know I'm going to regret this." She eases down on me, twisting and wincing. "I'm already regretting this."

"I'm not," I say, and I start to thrust upward.

"Stop," she says. "Please stop."

I stop thrusting.

"Just let me . . . whoo . . . let the boat do all the work, please."

"Okay."

She smiles and eases all the way down, her legs crossing behind me and pulls off her T-shirt. "Just don't move."

And for the next twenty minutes, the *Argo* rocks us as we make love to the gentle movement of the waves.

15

"That was nice," Ebony says, her face and my chest bathed in sweat. "We have to do it that way more often until I'm used to you again."

"Yeah."

"Now can you get me your computer and let me read what you're working on while you go get me something to eat?"

I get up and pull on my boxers. "What are you hungry for?"

"I need a greasy, greasy pizza, so greasy you have to wring it out first. I want a pizza so greasy that I could squeeze it into my gas tank and drive for miles. I have been starving myself like crazy since you sent me that first e-mail, and I miss me some greasy cheese most of all."

"You've been starving yourself?"

She nods.

"But you don't have an ounce of fat on you, Ebony."

"That you can see," she says. She points at the burned-out candle on the Captain's desk. "Candlelight hides a whole bunch of cellulite."

"But what I see is a goddess."

"When's the last time you had your eyes checked?"

"Even if I were blind, you'd still be a goddess."

She bites her lip. "Thank you."

After dressing, I bring the laptop and set it on the Captain's desk. Ebony sits up in bed, a pillow propped behind her, her breasts spilling over the edge of the sheet.

"Do you want your T-shirt?"

"No. I'm proud of my titties. Remember when I let you touch them that time under the deck?"

I could never forget that moment. "Yes."

"Remember how soft they were?"

"Yes."

"Well, I have a confession to make. I was wearing a padded bra."

I pull up *A Whiter Shade of Pale*. "Really?" As if I would have known that.

"Yeah. They were just little nubs then. I had to grow them." She cups them. "And one day, when I'm old, they'll be drooping little nubs." She sighs. "You better get me my T-shirt, and could you bring your computer over here?"

I hand her the computer, and she stares at the title page. "*A Whiter Shade of Pale*? Did you or the people at Olympus make up this title?"

"I did."

She twists her lips. "Is it supposed to be funny?"

"Uh, well, yeah. A little." I see her pouting at me. "I'm sure they'll change it to something better." She smiles. "I'll, uh, I'll just go get your pizza."

"And a two-liter of something and some napkins. And some Vaseline."

"Some Vaseline?"

She puckers her lips. "For my lips. They're chapped."

"Oh."

"And I don't want to be kissing on you later with chapped lips."

I smile. "Thank you, Ebony."

"For what?"

"Just thank you."

"You're welcome."

I take the Zodiac to shore and drive the Nova to Little Vincent's Pizza, get an extra large, extra sloppy, extra cheese pizza and a cold two-liter of Coke, then stop by the Southdown Community Market for some Vaseline. I look very strange waiting in line with just a container of Vaseline, so I grab a few candy bars at random on my way to the cash register.

And I look even stranger. The people around me are probably wondering what I'm going to do with such a combination.

By the time I return to the *Argo*, the white pizza box is already stained and leaking grease. I find Ebony scrolling down the pages.

"I'm almost finished," she says.

"Really?" I ask.

"I'm a fast reader, Peter."

"So, what do you think?"

"Feed me a slice first."

Four slices, two candy bars, and half a two-liter later, Ebony lets me know what she thinks. "This *Whiter Shade* book is pretty over-the-top."

She's perceptive as always. "Uh, I know. That's how relationship books are getting these days. That's what Henry expects."

"I don't mean to hurt your feelings, but *Ashy* and *The Devil to Pay* had much more reality than this. Witness protection? A former basketball star turned middle school teacher? A Mafia guy who works at a skating rink?"

"It does take a certain suspension of disbelief." At least she's trying to like it. "How would you improve it?"

"I was enjoying it, I really was, Peter, until the skating rink and all that Mafia nonsense. You'll just have to have my namesake meet a normal guy who has freckles."

"Henry won't like it. He'll say it isn't commercial enough."

"Well, make him like it."

"I'll try. Um, what did you think about *Promises to Keep*?"

"Other than it's missing half the story?"

I'm shocked. I knew she'd have trouble with *Whiter Shade*. What thinking, breathing human being wouldn't? But I thought she'd like *my* book. "What do you mean?"

"It's missing *my* half, Peter, *my* twenty-five years, and *I* want to write them."

My eyes blink rapidly before I can stop them. "You do?"

"Yes. The truth, the whole truth, and nothing but the truth."

What? "You want to write it as nonfiction?"

"Sure! Just sit me in front of a computer for a couple weeks—or months. I read faster than I can type. Just give me enough time, and I'll tear up the literary world. It'll be kind of like 'I say, you say,' you know, your version of what happened and then the real version of what happened."

"You really want to write a nonfiction book with me about us?"

"Yes. It will be fun."

Fun? I've never written anything with a partner. It just might be fun. I nod. "It'll take some time, and we'd want to have lots of pictures, and I'd have to change my half from third person to first person, but that won't be too hard." I see her smiling at me, her face glowing. "Edie might be a problem, though. Some of what I wrote could be considered slander."

"Isn't it the truth?"

"Yes. For the most part."

"Then it isn't slander."

I blink again. "Do you know what you're getting into? Our lives will be open books, literally, for the whole world to read."

She shrugs. "I don't care what other folks think about me, as long as it sells." She licks her lips. "Remember what I said about compensation?"

"Yes."

"This will be my compensation."

That doesn't sound so bad. "Just writing a book with me is enough?"

"And having you around."

"That's all the compensation you want?"

"It's all I've ever needed."

I don't know what to say. This is so wonderful! "But your name has to be first on the cover. '*Promises to Keep* by Ebony Mills' in big, bold, forty-eight-point type, and underneath in eight-point type will be 'with Peter Underhill.' "

"We'll have equal billing, Peter. You are, after all, the writer."

"But your name comes first in the alphabet."

"True." She smiles. "*Promises to Keep* by Ebony Mills and Peter Underhill." She shakes her head. "No. I don't like the sound of that."

"Why?"

"It *could* say Ebony and Peter Underhill, couldn't it?" She bites her lower lip.

Is she saying what I think she's saying? I haven't got a single drop of spit in my mouth. "I guess it could, if you want it to."

"Do you want it to?" she whispers.

"Yes." More than anything in this or any other world!

She looks at her hands. "I'll have to think about it for a while, but you know it's what I've always wanted."

My heart sinks a little, but if I were in her position, I'd probably be hesitant to have any long-term plans with me, too. "Yeah."

She flutters her eyes at me. "Do you think Olympus can put our book out on July seventh, you know, for luck?"

Seven-seven. "I don't know, but we can ask."

"And I get to do the cover art, and it won't be neon anything. It'll be a nice watercolor, maybe a view of the Sound from my house."

Hopefully without a sad-faced Ebony in the foreground. "I'd like that."

"Well," she says as she stands. "We better get dressed so we can go home."

Home. Home! What a wonderful word to say!

Before Ebony can finish dressing, we hear bells sounding and the roar of many boats, and the *Argo* rolls back and forth violently.

"What's happening?" Ebony asks, heading for the deck.

When we emerge from the cabin, we see the reason: the bunker are running in Huntington Bay. The harbor seethes with bunker, the meal of choice for bluefish, and fishermen and women are pulling fifteen- to twenty-pound bluefish out of the water and into their boats all around us. I see the yacht club's dock teeming with men casting and catching something huge on nearly every retrieval.

"Dag, you could almost walk across the water on top of them," Ebony says.

I lean over the railing and see a thousand bunker eyes. "Remember when they ran that day, and we skipped school—"

"—and caught, what, thirteen of those slimy bunkers with our hands?" Ebony interrupts. "You wanted only five cents apiece at the bait shop, but I talked them up to ten."

She was always the better negotiator. "God, I wish I had a pole."

Ebony smiles. "You do have a pole, and no, you're not doing any fishing with it for a while."

I blush. "I mean, I wish—"

"I know what you meant, but we got us a couple books to write, right?"

"Right."

After Ebony jumps into the Zodiac, I wrap the laptop case in a plastic bag before handing it to her, just in case we have a rough trip, and dump in the rest of what I own—my clothes—all balled up in two duffel bags. Then we weave around fishing boats and dodge flying lines while seeming to chase the bunker in to shore. No one gives us a second look, and as we near the docks, we see Mr. Cutter putting up a "15-MINUTE LIMIT" sign on the main dock, his pants pockets bulging with money.

I tie up to one of the smaller docks, help Ebony out, and walk over to Mr. Cutter.

"Hey, Pete! Amazing isn't it!"

"Yep. Um, did anyone call?"

He reaches into his back pocket and withdraws a three-by-five card. "Just this Henry guy. He said it was urgent." He smiles at Ebony. "Miss Mills, it's so good to see you again."

"Good to see you, too, Mr. Cutter."

As Mr. Cutter returns to the docks, I stare at Ebony. "You seem to know Mr. Cutter pretty well."

"Who do you think dropped me off at the boat last night?" She whips out her cell phone and hands it to me. "You better call Henry."

It has to be about Cece, and I don't want Ebony hearing us talk about any of that mess. "Maybe now isn't a good time."

She shrugs. "Mr. Cutter said it was urgent." She steps closer. "And we're going to be very busy later, right?"

Yeah. Hmm. I like the sound of that. I dial Henry's number, and Henry's secretary answers. "Edith, it's Peter Underhill. Is Henry in?"

"No, Mr. Underhill, he's not in today. He and Cece Wrenn are out celebrating."

I'll be damned. Henry *was* up to the task. "So Cece's pregnant?"

"Cece who?" Ebony says.

I cover the mouthpiece. "Cece Wrenn. She and Henry are having a baby."

Ebony's eyes widen. "Cece Wrenn, the singer?"

I nod. "Edith, could you give Henry a message for me?"

"Sure thing, Mr. Underhill."

"Tell him congratulations."

"I will, Mr. Underhill."

Ebony takes the phone. "Edith, here is the number where Peter can be reached in case Henry wants to call." She gives Edith the number, clicks off the phone, and then dials another number.

"Who are you calling?"

"Shh." She presses the phone closer to her ear. "Destiny? Make sure you're dressed, we're on our way home." She smiles. "Yes, baby girl, your daddy's coming with me. Bye." She clicks off the cell phone. "Let's go home, *Daddy.*"

16

After leaving the Nova at Hertz, where the drop-off fee hurts my wallet, Ebony drives us home. And unlike the movies and many romance novels I've read, we don't have a tearful reunion at Ebony's house, because I am too joyful to cry anymore, and Ebony seems too tired.

Destiny welcomes us in with "Hi, Mama, hi, Daddy," as if she'd been doing it for years, kisses Ebony on the cheek, and hugs me briefly, while Seven slobbers on us all. It all seems so normal.

Until Destiny starts asking us questions.

She takes my two duffel bags. "Is this all you have, Daddy?"

Yes, it's not much to show for forty years of life. "That's it."

"We're going shopping for you soon." She looks from Ebony to me then back to Ebony. "What have you two been doing? Did you make me a little sister?"

Ebony turns to me. "I sure hope not."

"Why not, Mama? The last time you two got together, you made me."

Ebony shakes her head. "Don't go there, little girl." She sniffs the air. "And we are rank. We need a bath."

Destiny blinks. "You're going to take a bath together with me in the house?"

"No." Ebony hands Destiny the car keys and two twenties. "You're going out. Get us some Earl Grey tea—that's your favorite, right, Peter?"

"Yeah." She has the best memory.

"Also get some soda, some steaks, some potatoes, and anything else you think you'll need to make us our dinner."

"Mama, I don't want to cook."

Ebony spins Destiny towards the door. "We're going to be very, very busy."

Destiny looks at us, shaking her head. "Dag, my mama's a freak."

Ebony laughs. "What about Daddy?"

"Daddy's just freaky." Destiny leaves with a smile and a wave.

Ebony starts up the front steps, and I fall in behind. She stops, and I bump into her. "We have two bathrooms, Peter. We could go to mine and swim around in a big claw-foot tub, or we could go to the basement where we could squeeze into the stand-up shower. It's your call."

I cup her buttocks and gently push her up the stairs.

She reaches back to grab a belt loop on my pants. "You made the right choice."

Making love in a claw-foot tub is almost like making love on a sailboat, only more slippery. Ebony lathers herself from her feet to her neck then lathers herself all over me, groaning, sighing, humming, water spilling over the edge onto the linoleum. She washes my hair while grinding on me, and I can contain myself no longer, thrusting madly up into her.

"Can we do this every day?" I ask as she digs her nails into my back.

"We'll be the cleanest couple who ever lived," she moans.

When we're through, we step out of the tub and look back. Most of the water is on the floor.

"Less water next time," she says, and she hands me a towel. And since I have no clean clothes, Ebony hands me an oversized, faded, ratty Hofstra sweatshirt and matching pants that were in the bathroom closet.

When we enter Ebony's room, I freeze. Not much has changed. There are clothes on the floor, books everywhere, even a pair of green underwear wrapped around the bedpost of her king-sized bed. Beautiful wood. Looks almost like olive wood. Candles of all shapes, colors, and sizes crowd the headboard, and crimson pillows rest below, a soft gold and silver comforter on top. She throws on a white robe and begins applying eyeliner in front of a mirrored vanity near a bay window.

"Don't mind the mess," she says, concentrating and drawing. "I'm trying to hide my wrinkles."

"I didn't know you had any."

"Easy for you to say." She blinks several times and begins on the other eye. "All you've been doing is stretching my wrinkles out. And by the way, you look funny in those sweats."

The bottoms of the sweatpants hit me mid-shin. "Thank you," I say. I step behind her and rub her back. "Did you go to Hofstra?"

"Yeah, got my art history degree and everything from Hofstra. You aren't rubbing on me for any special reason, are you?"

"Maybe."

"Please don't get any ideas. I'm all worn out."

"But I have to get ideas. I'm a writer."

She puts down the eyeliner pencil and begins to brush her hair. "I always knew you'd be a writer."

"And I always knew you'd be an artist." I check out the massive bed, and it definitely wasn't bought at a discount furniture place. "How did you get all this?"

"You mean the house?"

"Yeah."

"Oh." She smiles. "I've sold a few paintings."

"Only a few?" This house has to go for at least four, maybe even five hundred thousand dollars.

"Well, more than a few."

"Um, how much do your paintings usually go for?"

She shrugs. "More than the effort it took to create them."

"I doubt that."

"No, it's true. I've been very fortunate to have a devoted following and a few key people who actively collect my work."

"What about the portraits in the basement?"

She puts down her brush. "Destiny took you down there?"

"Yes."

"She wasn't supposed to do that."

"Why?"

"Because *I* was supposed to take you down there, so I could, well, make you feel guilty."

"I do feel guilty."

"I know. How did they affect you?"

"Honestly?"

She nods.

"I felt as if I had a vise twisting my guts in all directions. I felt as if all the sadness in the world was weighing me down."

She smiles. "Good. So now you know how I felt at the time."

Ouch.

"But I'm not through with them yet."

"They seem like finished pieces, except for the tapestry."

"Oh, but they aren't, and I doubt I'll ever finish that tapestry. I just can't see it finished in my head yet, though I'm beginning to." She raises her eyebrows. "You're sparking some stuff in me, Peter. Maybe you're my muse."

She only said that because she knows that she is my muse. "How do you, um, how do you decide what to create and how to create it?"

"Now there's a loaded question."

"Just curious."

"Well, first, I use different media to match my mood. If I'm feeling playful, I use acrylics. If I'm being super-serious, I use oils. I only sketch when I'm bored, I do watercolors to relax and to prep for oils, and I get out my anger by using charcoal."

"And the loom?"

"I only use the loom when I'm really frustrated."

Oh. I walked right into that one.

"Second, I never get it right the first time. Every acrylic or oil painting I do goes through several revisions, and the only part anyone gets to see is when I'm finally fed up with it. If you could see what's underneath my paintings, it would make your hair stand on end."

I'm afraid to ask what's underneath the paintings in the basement, but I can't resist. "What's underneath the paintings downstairs?"

"Oh, I started by painting your ex-wife in various stages of decay."

I laugh. "Were they especially gruesome?"

"The one with the severed ear wasn't so bad until I added the maggots chewing on the earlobe."

Yes! "I would have liked to have seen those."

"I bet you would. No, I believe that the world should never see some art, and, trust me, if I put those on display, I'd lose my following and collectors in a heartbeat. And since I'm still basically an unknown, almost forty-year-old African-American female artist with a nineteen-year-old daughter who may never leave the house, I can't afford to shock anyone with a new style." She turns to me. "Kind of like what you're trying to do, huh?"

"I guess."

"You have no idea what it was like when I first set out to take the art world by storm. I must have hit every gallery in New York. I was expecting to get shot down, but I never would have expected the way I got shot down. Do you know what they asked me before I even opened my portfolio?"

"What?"

"They asked me where I was born. I told them Brooklyn. Then their noses shriveled up and they said, 'Oh, you're local. We specialize in European and immigrant art.' Can you believe that? They didn't even look at my work. Every person who has come to this country was once an immigrant, but it seems that only bona fide, just-off-the-boat or on-a-green-card artists are getting shows in New York anymore. One man wrote my name down then said, 'You know, if you spelled your first name with an *I* or even ended it in *E* with an accent mark—' I didn't let him finish. Do I look like an *E-bon-ay* to you? Or an *I-bon-I*?"

"No. Um, how did you get your start?"

"My first big break came at Apex Art, a nonprofit in Soho. They actually have the guts to expose New York to New York artists. After that, I shared some space at shows at Mary Boone, Bill Maynes, Matthew Marks—"

"Those are galleries?"

"Yeah. And when DC Moore called, I jumped."

She looks at me as if she expects me to know how prestigious DC Moore is to an artist. "The big time?"

"I've always wanted a show at the Studio Museum in Harlem. That to me would be the big time, but DC Moore Gallery has been good to black folks for a long time. They have a Jacob Lawrence exhibition coming up in mid-December, and I get to squeeze myself in before that, but only if . . ." She tents her fingers and nods at me.

"If what?"

"If we get to work on and finish our story *and* I can finish my work downstairs."

"Oh, sure."

"My office is two rooms down the hall on the left. You can either work in the office with me or at the kitchen table. I wouldn't recommend the kitchen, though."

"Why not?"

She slips a white scrunchie into her hair. "Destiny can't cook. At all. But she can make one unholy mess." She turns to me. "How do I look?"

"Like a dream."

"Uh-huh."

I rub her shoulders, squeezing gently. "You do."

She leans back slightly. "You keep doing that, and no one will be doing any writing around here."

I stop.

"I didn't say stop, did I? That felt good." She lets me massage her shoulders for a few more seconds, then pushes my hands away and stands. "Any longer and we'll be shaking that bed."

"Yeah?"

"But I do not want to traumatize my daughter in that way just yet. Now let me get dressed."

"Can't I watch?"

Her robe drops to the floor. "I have to lotion myself first."

I grab the bottle of lotion. "Allow me."

Putting lotion on Ebony is like polishing a sculpture—only most sculptures don't sigh, shiver, and moan. What did Ovid say? That art lies in concealing art? Something like that. I don't want Ebony ever to put on clothes in this room, and I damn sure want her to wear plenty of clothes to conceal this art from other men's eyes.

"Peter, you're driving me crazy."

"I know."

She takes the bottle of lotion from me. "I'll do the rest."

I pout. "But I was enjoying myself."

"So was I, but Destiny will be home any minute."

I kiss her neck. "Okay."

I leave the room and walk down the hall into Ebony's office. A computer desk and hutch take up half the room, plenty of Ebony's old sketches framed here and there, including the one she did of me at Hecksher Park. Man, did I have a lot of freckles. I'll have to curl up on the love seat wedged in a corner, but I don't mind, it's cozy. And what's this on the hutch? I pick up a picture frame and see a collage of old snapshots of Ebony and me. Several are yearbook photos, but most are shots from Candace's house: the two of us reading on the couch, the two of us sketching on the front porch, one of me playing Little League baseball, another of me from graduation. I feel weird. I mean, here is Ebony's shrine to us.

Ebony walks in wearing an equally baggy, ragged, faded Hofstra sweat suit covered with splotches of paint. "We're twins," she says with a laugh.

"You look good, E."

"No, I don't."

I put the frame back on the hutch. "Who took some of these pictures?"

"You don't remember?"

I shake my head.

"Dag, you're getting old. Uncle Jerry did."

Oh, yeah. He always seemed to be filming something. "What's he doing now?"

She sits in a swivel chair and turns on her computer. "Let's see. He's still in Germany, and last I heard he married a Greek woman and is working for Bayer. They have the cutest little boy. He's so lucky—he'll be able to speak Greek, German, and English. Now, make me a copy of your book so I can get to work, while you try to do something with my book."

At first, everything goes smoothly as I lounge on the love seat. I delete everything in *Whiter Shade* after the night class ends, removing the threat of the skating rink and the witness protection program forever. Since I've been writing without an outline, I just flow on while Ebony sits at her desk staring at her computer screen.

Folks start getting up all around me. What's going on? The class is over? Shit. I haven't been paying attention.

Johnny smiles at me. "See you next week."

"Bye."

Why can't I think of anything to say to him other than "Bye"? I could have at least said "*Ciao*," I could have at least walked out with him. But no, I'm still sitting here watching him go, and there's Rosie the Ghoul walking up to him and putting her transparent hand on his arm and I'm still sitting here in this comfortable seat in this heaven of a classroom while he's smiling at her and they're talking and laughing and I *still* can't get up out of this damn chair, and then I shout, "Johnny!" a little too loudly and he's turning to me and I have no idea what I'm going to say next.

Both he and Hoe-sie Rosie come over to me. I didn't call your name, wench! Go on about your unholy angel duties. I'm sure you have someone else's blood to suck, someone else's life force to drain.

"Yes, Ebony?"

I peer around Johnny at Rosie the Impaler and wish I had a wooden cross or a wooden stake or holy water or whatever it is that you use to kill a vampiress and say, "I need to speak to Johnny in private, if you don't mind."

Thorny Rose blinks her puke green eyebrow-less eyes at me. "Um, we were talking."

Oh, now she's calling me rude. Bitch. I try the "stare" out on her, but she doesn't pee her pants. I wish I had some holy water to throw on her. Nah, it wouldn't dent her makeup.

"It's, um, confidential." I smile at Johnny, and he smiles back. Is it just me, or does it seem that he wants to escape her evil clutches?

She points her foot off to the side again, her hands on her hips. "Excuse me?" she says as only white women can, with that nasal tone that's almost as bad as the sighs she was doing earlier. "Johnny is my ex, and we have a few things to discuss. So, if you don't mind."

Oops. I've just stuck my nose in someone else's little domestic drama. But Johnny's eyes say, "Rescue me," so I keep sticking my nose out there.

"So, Johnny, are we still on for tomorrow night?" I say sweetly. I can sound like an angel every now and then. If Johnny's really in distress, he'll play along.

Johnny's shoulders relax. "Yes, Ebony, we are." He turns to Rose the Pose, whose lipless mouth forms a chapped little circle. "We have a date."

Rosie Pointy Toes clenches her little transparent fists, says "Ooooh," stamps her little feet, and storms out of the room. Classic. Every white woman I've ever seen pitch a fit does it the exact same way. I wonder if they are taught to do like that at an early age.

Johnny slumps down next to me. "*Grazie.*"

"Don't mention it. You looked like you needed some help."

"I did. She has been, how you say, stalking me for five years now."

Whoa. "Um, how long were you married?"

"We were never married. She is my ex-girlfriend."

Yes! An ex-girlfriend I can handle. Ex-wives . . . I don't even want to go there. Way too much baggage. Things are definitely looking up.

"Do you mind?" Ebony says, still looking up at a blank screen.

"Mind what?"

"I'm trying to think. Don't type so loud."

"Sorry."

I press the keys more softly and continue:

for me, and now Johnny's looking at me.

"Um, Ebony?"

"Yes?"

"Did you mean what you said about tomorrow night?"

Of course I did! "No, not really."

I have to play a *little* hard to get. I don't want him to get any ideas. I mean, we've only just met, and he's not *that* good-looking, and are those freckles on his face? He must be from the northern part of Italy, though otherwise he's kind of darker-skinned than most Italians I've met. Maybe he's descended from Hannibal. Didn't Hannibal attack from the Italian Alps? I'll bet there are quite a few Italians with African blood thanks to Hannibal. Dag, Johnny and I could be distant cousins in the grand scheme of things. I mean, we might have a common ancestor who—

"I would very much like to take you out to dinner tomorrow night," Johnny says, interrupting my tripping.

"You would?"

"Yes. You, uh, rescued me from her. She is like a cold I cannot get rid of."

She's more like a disease, like leprosy. "You're asking me out?"

"Yes."

"Peter," Ebony whines.

"Huh?"

"Do you think you could work in the kitchen?"

"Why?"

"I can't concentrate. I hear your fingers tapping those keys, and I can't even get a sentence out. How am I supposed to start this thing?"

"You could write some back story." Jesus, I'm sounding like Henry.

"What's back story?"

"Back story is like background for a character. You could tell the reader about your family and your family history before you met me."

"Why?"

"As a way to set up our first meeting that day at the hockey game."

"Sounds boring."

"It doesn't have to be. What was it like telling off Eddie and Chad?"

Ebony rolls her eyes. "His name was Brad, not Chad, and it was no big deal to embarrass them, because I did it all the time to everyone, even my mama."

Mental note: Change "Chad" to "Brad." "Okay, you could just write an answer to every one of our scenes so far. You've read how I felt at the time, maybe you could, you know, argue with me and—"

"Okay, okay, I understand," she says and swivels back to the keyboard. "Now go to the kitchen and leave me alone."

I save my work but leave the laptop on, carefully getting up and tiptoeing across the room to the door.

"Where are you going?" she asks.

"Um, you just said—"

"Give me a kiss first."

I kiss her on the cheek. "I'll be in—"

"Yeah, yeah, yeah, whatever." She cracks her knuckles. "It's time to cook. And shut the door behind you."

I freeze. "Are you mad at me?"

She swivels completely around and grabs my legs. "Not at all, not at all. I just can't concentrate with you in the room. I have all these really nasty thoughts going through my head about what we could be doing instead of this. I mean, I could have let you finish lotioning me, and then we could have been going at it, and there you are writing so fast. How can you do that?"

"It's what I do, and it's exactly how you were and probably are when you're busy painting. I've just gotten better at painting with words."

She motions me closer and kisses me. "Painting with words. I think I can do that."

I nod and kiss her forehead. "I'll be downstairs."

I back out of the room, shut the door, and go down the back stairs to the kitchen, setting up shop and picking up where I left off:

She's more like a disease, like leprosy. "You're asking me out?"

"Yes."

"You hardly know me, Johnny."

"I would like to get to know you. You seem like a nice person."

Am I nice? Sometimes. But not this second. "What's that supposed to mean?"

"What?"

"I seem like a 'nice person'? Is that supposed to be a compliment?"

He frowns. "Yes. It is a compliment, isn't it?"

I shake my head. "The word 'nice' is overused, Johnny. You can do better than that."

"Okay." He sits next to me, our knees brushing for one delicious moment. "You seem . . . like a beautiful person."

This is too easy. "I only *seem* beautiful?"

He puts his hand on my hand. "No, no, you *are* beautiful."

"Very beautiful?" Now I'm pushing it.

"Yes." He gently caresses the back of my hand. "Yes, Ebony. You are a very beautiful person who I would like to know better."

"In what way?" I turn my hand over so he can caress my palm, but he stops and lifts his hand.

Johnny seems perplexed. "In . . . in every way."

Oh yes. "Every way?"

He sits back. "I do not understand."

I take his hand and run a finger around and around his palm. "Maybe I can help you. You see, I'm kind of attracted to you . . . physically. You hear what I'm saying?"

"Ah," he says with a smile. "You mean . . ."

I squeeze his hand. "Yeah. That way." I want this man to rub lotion all over my body until I come and shout "Hallelujah!" And then I want to rub myself all over him until he comes and shouts whatever Italians shout in church.

He puts his other hand over mine. "I do not live very far away."

Now that I've pushed the moment to a crisis, I can't think of what to say. "Well, uh, hmm." I pull my hand out of his. "Let's try a date first, you know, see how it goes."

His face doesn't change a bit. "Yes. Let us try a date. I know of a wonderful place to go tomorrow night."

"Yeah? Where?"

"There is an art gallery that is having a show tomorrow night of the most amazing artwork. Mostly self-portraits, but they are works of genius."

I blink. Johnny is cultural? "Um, who's the artist?"

He looks down. "The artist is me. It is my very first show."

He's not only into art, he *is* art. An Italian artist is sitting in front of me asking me to his first show. "I would be

"Daddy, I need your help!" Destiny calls from the front door.

I go to the door and find her listening to her cell phone.

"The bags are out there," she says, and she continues into the house.

I find two little plastic bags and a five-pound bag of potatoes in the trunk of the Honda and lug them into the house with only one hand. What help did she need?

I hear Destiny saying "Don't worry" as I set the bags on the counter. I unload a can of green beans, four cube steaks, and a copy of *Soap Opera Digest*. Where are the drinks and the tea?

She clicks off her phone and smiles at me. "Thanks, Daddy."

"No problem." I toss her the *Soap Opera Digest*. I watch her sit at the table and flip a few pages. "Um, don't you think you should start dinner now?"

Destiny grimaces. "Can't you cook for us, Daddy? I'm not a very good cook."

I look at my laptop. "I'm right in the middle of a scene, so . . . "

She looks at me with those huge puppy eyes of hers. "Please?"

I sigh. "Okay. I'll, um, do something with this meat, and you do the rest, okay?"

She smiles. "Okay."

It only takes her a minute to wash three potatoes, wrap them in foil, pierce them with a fork, and toss them into the oven. It takes her another minute to open the can of beans and plop them into a pan, slapping on the top.

"All done," she says brightly, and she returns to her magazine.

Something about this isn't right, but I don't complain. After all the meals I've missed around here, I *should* be doing the cooking. How many meals have I missed? At maybe two a day for a year times twenty . . . I've missed over 3,500 meals with my family! This is the least I can do.

I find a skillet, put a little olive oil in it, and let it warm while I mix flour, salt, and pepper in a bowl. Then I coat each cube steak with the mixture and set them aside. Ebony probably expected T-bones, but maybe her mama's recipe for country-fried steak will appeal to her.

"Whatcha doin'?" Destiny asks.

"Making your grandma's famous country-fried steak," I say.

"Mmm," she says, and she continues flipping pages.

"It'll taste better with mashed potatoes," I say.

Destiny looks up, smiling. "I love mashed potatoes."

I smile back. "Can you make mashed potatoes?"

She shrugs. "Aren't you supposed to cook the potatoes first?"

"Actually, they should be peeled and boiled, and we'll need more than the three that are in there."

"Oh. You want to know where I put the potatoes. They're in the pantry." She points to a door. "In there."

"You're a lot of help."

"You're welcome," she says, and she continues reading.

Half an hour later, my laptop's da Vinci screensaver waving at me from the kitchen table, my non-cooking daughter glued to a *Soap Opera Digest*, the mashed potatoes made, the cube steaks cooking in the olive oil, the beans ready to simmer with some added onions, I return to my laptop.

"Smells good," Destiny says. She reaches out to me and flicks my hair. "Oops. I thought it was some flour. It's just your gray hair."

I look back at my last sentence:

He's not only into art, he *is* art. An Italian artist is sitting in front of me asking me to his first show. "I would be

The cell phone rings. "Hello?" Destiny says. "Uh-huh. Okay." She turns the phone off. "One of my admirers."

"You have a date?"

"No."

"I thought you had a boyfriend, you know, the guy you said was romantic as a brick."

Destiny laughs. "I was referring to you, Daddy." She squints. "Were you really hitting on me?"

"I am so sorry about that, Destiny. Really."

She winks at me. "Don't be. I was very flattered." She lowers her voice. "But don't tell Mama. She'd freak."

Yes, she would.

"How long till dinner's ready?"

"Another half an hour."

"Cool."

I look back at the screen, my fingers poised above the keyboard.

"Daddy?"

"Yes?"

"Are you and Mama going to get married?"

I drop my hands and let my fingers rest on the keys. "I hope so."

"So do I."

I raise my hands, my fingers ready to rip. "But it isn't entirely up to me."

"Yeah," Destiny says. "So you two are just going to live together for a while?"

I rest my hands again. "Uh, your mama and I haven't discussed that yet." Though it sure is starting to look that way.

"Oh."

I wait a few seconds for her next interruption. When it doesn't come, I reread the last sentence:

He's not only into art, he *is* art. An Italian artist is sitting in front of me asking me to his first show. "I would be

Now, would she be happy? Honored? My right index finger twitches on the letter *H* and presses down.

h

The cell phone rings again.

onored to

"Oh, hi!" Destiny says loudly. "Yes, I'm just sitting here talking to my daddy while he writes his next book. How have you been?"

I have to leave the kitchen. I stand and pick up my laptop.

"You don't have to leave, Daddy."

Oh, but I do. "I'll just give you some privacy." I leave the kitchen and head for the living room where Seven sprawls out on the couch. I sit as quietly as I can in a wingback chair a few feet from him, but the floor squeaks.

Seven's awake. Shit. He tumbles off the couch and heads directly for me. I set the laptop on the mantel and catch him as he pushes me back into the chair.

Destiny runs in to see us wrestle. "Don't move," she says, as if I can get away from Seven. "I want to get a picture of this."

Twenty minutes of an impromptu photo shoot later, I am covered in Seven's drool.

"I can't wait to get these developed," Destiny says as she returns to the kitchen.

"And I can't wait to continue my novel," I whisper to Seven. "Isn't there anywhere else you want to be?"

He sits right in front of me, his snout in my lap.

"I didn't think so."

Destiny returns. "Mama wants to know when I'm going to have dinner ready. What should I tell her?"

I sniff the air. "It should be ready in a few minutes."

"She wants me to make her a plate and bring it up to her."

"She does, does she?"

"She does."

Maybe she's on a roll. "I'll bring it up to her."

After fixing Ebony's plate and loading it with gravy and pouring her a nice tall tumbler full of ice water, I walk upstairs and knock on the office door. I hear her chair squeak, and the door opens wide enough for me to hand in the plate and the tumbler.

She sniffs the air above the plate. "Mmm. Mama's country-fried steak. Is it salty like I like it?"

"I made it just like she makes it." I look around her to her computer screen. "How's it going?"

She kisses me passionately with lots of tongue and a little grinding. "It's going *that* good."

Whew! "Um, that's good."

She grabs my ass. "Go on, go eat, then work on your novel. I'll catch up eventually."

"Can you tell Destiny not to— No. That's all right."

"Not to do what?"

I sigh. "Not to interrupt me while I work?"

Ebony laughs. "She's your daughter, too, Peter. Tell her yourself." She shuts the door. "And if you get writer's block, you can come give me a back rub, and I might pay you," she calls. Then she giggles.

I like writing with Ebony. There are so many fringe benefits.

Destiny and I eat our meal together in silence. I'll bet she's saving more conversation for when I'll be trying to work.

"Um, Destiny, could I ask a favor?"

"Sure, Daddy."

"Um, I have two novels to work on, and I'm sure your mama told you that she's writing half of one—"

"I *know*. It's so neat! My parents are about to be famous! I'll bet *The Today Show* asks you two to appear. Matt Lauer is so hot."

"Anyway, well, we, uh, won't be anything or anywhere if we, I mean, if I don't get some serious work done, so could you possibly, um, be a little more . . . quiet?"

"Are you telling me to shut up, Daddy? Because that's all you have to say."

"I don't have the right to tell you that, Destiny. I just can't—"

"Say no more," she says, wiping her lips with a napkin. "I'll just go out for a while and let you work."

"Well, if you really want— Hey, you're not supposed to drive."

She jumps from the table and rushes to the front door. "Don't tell Mama," she whispers fiercely, and a door slam later she's gone.

I hear the office door above me open and soon see manicured toes coming down the stairs. "Where'd she go?"

"Out."

She slides a slender hand across my cheek. "Did you send her away from us, Peter?"

"No, she just up and left."

She licks her lips. "Good. I can't write anymore." She pulls up her shirt and rubs on her stomach. "That was a very good meal. Do you, uh, feel like writing anymore tonight, Peter?"

I watch that hand circling lower and lower. "No."

"Good." She takes my hand. "All those thoughts I'm having up there are making me horny. I want to make my thoughts real."

I jump from my seat. "So do I."

She pulls me to the stairs, but before we can go up them, she's all over me, and I'm all over her, Seven barking at the two people writhing on the steps.

Oh, yes, it's good to be home.

17

Several days of interruptions, a cell phone ringing, Destiny asking questions, a dog drooling, countless back rubs, and little if any sleep because of our desire for each other, Ebony and I have made a slight dent in two novels. I'm not worried about meeting any of Henry's deadlines, and Ebony doesn't seem to mind either. We write a bit, flirt a bit, get busy a lot, and rest a lot.

Ah, the perfect writer's life.

Every once in a while, we sit back in her massive bed and check our work to see if we're making any sense at all.

And some of it actually makes wonderful sense.

I am amazed by what Ebony has written, almost as if I'm getting a glimpse of her personal diary:

I'm down in Ballyhack, Virginia, at Loretta's little country house waiting for this baby to be born. Loretta is my daddy's mama, and living with us is Aunt Wee Wee, my seventeen-year-old cousin Jackie, and great uncle Rex, who is old as dirt.

Once called Big Lick, and then Dundee, everyone calls this neighborhood "Ballyhack" now, and no one can tell me why, especially since on the map it's Delaney Court. Yet everyone seems to have a story about how Ballyhack became Ballyhack.

"Way back when," Loretta says, "there was a slave by the name of Squire Keeling, who was owned by Master Ivyland. Well, Squire Keeling up and buys his freedom from his master and gets all this land, from the

old store all the way past the church. Wasn't but one church there then, and it's supposed to have been built on top of an old Indian burial ground. Anyways, Squire Keeling was livin' large, and a whole bunch of other folks came in, like the Chandlers, the Hardys, and the MacGeorges. But don't you know, that land got took away little by little from Squire Keeling cuz of back taxes, so they said, and eventually all we had was this one street and the land those churches are on."

After such a long story, I expect Loretta to tell me why Ballyhack was named Ballyhack. When she doesn't, I ask, "So why is it called Ballyhack?"

Loretta shrugs and says, "I have no idea."

So I still don't know why Ballyhack is called Ballyhack. Sheree, one of my cousins, thinks "Ballyhack" is just "Big Lick" mumbled really fast and coun-try-like, but that makes no kind of sense. One day, I'll solve this mystery.

Wherever Ballyhack came from, believe me, it is beyond country. Bally-hack is off of Rutrough Road, but they don't say "Rut-Rough." Nah, they say "ROO-Trough." You take a right off of ROO-Trough onto Ivyland Road (it used to be Route 6 before the folks in Ballyhack got water lines), and you're in Ballyhack. It's just one dead-end street guarded by two hundred-year-old churches at the entrance: St. John AME and Bethlehem Baptist Church, two country churches within spitting distance of each other. St. John's sanctuary slopes right down to the altar, so when you fall out, you fall far and roll. I'll bet the Indians under the foundation are rolling, too! Bethlehem is all brick and more modern, but it seems like half the folks from each church go to the other church half the time. Loretta tells me there are Bethlehem members going to St. John every week ("Depending on who's preachin'," she says) who are still tithing at Bethlehem.

"Used to be Bethlehem had services the first and third Sundays," Loretta explains, "and St. John's had the second and fourth Sundays, till Reverend Woods come along and changed everything."

Since I don't understand why Ballyhack, all of maybe fourteen houses, needs two churches, I ask, "Why don't they just combine the two churches?"

And all Loretta does is laugh and say, "Child, whatever for?"

My first trip into Ballyhack told me I wasn't on Long Island anymore. We were just winding down this narrow country road at ten miles an hour, and folks started waving at us from their yards as we rolled by in Mama's Pinto. They actually waved at Mama's Pinto. Who waves at a Pinto?

"What are they waving for, Mama?" I asked.

"They're your cousins," Mama said. "Every last damn one of them."

I smiled at a few men waving from in front of a pickup truck. "Do I have to wave back, Mama?"

Mama's growl told me that I had to, and I've been waving ever since, and I've found out something: no one messes with my family in Ballyhack, Virginia, not the police nor anybody else . . . mainly because we're so busy messing with each other.

I've been living with Loretta for almost a month now while Mama gets things straight up in Huntington. Aunt Wee Wee seems to like it down here, mainly because she can smoke without anyone telling her not to, she can wander around and not get too lost, and everyone can understand what she's mumbling because they all mumble country like that. I want to laugh at them for the way they talk (tah-awk), but they're too busy laughing at me!

Loretta tells me I'll have a good delivery even though I barely have any hips. "You'll do fine, girl." Then she tells me about cousin this or aunt that who squirted out a baby right here on Ivyland Road. That isn't what I want to hear.

I am barely surviving this Virginia heat. It's like the heat has weight to it, like it makes you feel heavier, like you can't breathe even going up a simple flight of steps. I wish Loretta had air-conditioning, but at least I have a big box fan in my window blocking my view of the outhouse and two pit bulls with nasty attitudes in their pens outside.

On nights like this, I miss my daddy. I think about him more and more each day, and I don't know why. I know he's dead in Vietnam, but he's there all alone. There's something wrong about a tall brown-skinned man with shiny white teeth being all alone 12,000 miles away with no one to hold him.

Daddy's brother Leon lives down the way from us, but he's nothing like my daddy. Jackie says he's too broke to get a car and too stupid to save up for a bike.

"Hell, he ain't got a pot to piss in," Jackie says. "He so poor he ain't got eye water to cry with."

But Jackie doesn't know that sometimes Leon stops by and says, "Hey, baby girl, how ya doing? When's your evil ass mama comin' back?"

Leon always knows how to make me laugh. I usually just say, "I'm doing, fine, Uncle Leon, and Mama isn't coming back until you're nicer to her."

Sometimes he'll give me a dollar, saying, "Here's a dollar, so go buy yourself something. And don't spend it all in one place."

I thank him for the dollar but shake my head as he walks away. A dollar won't buy you anything around here; there isn't a store for miles. But at least he's thinking of me.

And he does have my daddy's face.

Jackie says that Leon used to dress "real nice" back in the day. He used to wear name-brand clothes and shoes. He used to match his socks with his shirts and his shirts with his hats. But the last time Jackie and I saw him, he was wearing (or was it wearing him?) a white T-shirt with a hole in the collar, and the shirt had "IKE" in blue letters across the front. It had been worn so much that the "N" probably swam for its life in the washer.

"Hell," Jackie says, "if I was the I, the K, and the E, I'd swim for it the next time my damn self."

I get Ebony's attention by massaging one of her feet. "There will be time for that later," she says.

"Um, where is Uncle Leon now?"

"That was twenty years ago, Peter. Who knows? Probably dead by now. Skip ahead to the next chapter. The rest of that one is back story."

I have created a literary monster. "You ever find out why it was named Ballyhack?"

"No," she says, flipping another page and smiling. "I think it's supposed to be Bali Hai, and those country cousins of mine just messed it up."

I continue to read and smile.

I'm staying home from St. John's today, mainly to throw up from the morning sickness. I miss going, because the southern Mills family are some singing folks, let me tell you. There isn't a church service without at least one of them singing, and none of them need microphones. When the wind is still on a Sunday, I can hear them singing all the way to Loretta's house. I know I'll hear all about the service when they get here for Sunday dinner, which is when everybody brings a piece of the meal to Loretta's house and everybody eats too much. My future baby has been eating well: corn pudding, greens, chef salad with real country ham, yeast rolls, dirt cake, banana pudding, apple cake, lemon fish, ribs, and barbeque pork chops as thick as your fist. I may give birth to a Southern baby with all this Southern food in me. She's going to cry "waaaa-uh" in two sylla-bles.

A couple of weeks ago, they all struggled in after singing, and all they did was talk bad about each other: "The drummer started too slow an' messed up my song. That's why I stopped it and started over. Yeah, when I got the microphone, I'm in charge. . . . That girl ain't never met a note she couldn't sing sour, but why she got to sing so loud? . . . Ho was swayin' to the left when the rest of us was swayin' to the right—that's why she got knocked on her ass, she wasn't feelin' the spirit. . . . You see Mrs. So-and-So jumpin' up right before my solo on 'King Jesus'? Wench sayin' 'That's my song,' even cleared her damn throat. Shit, I almost handed her the microphone. She about to see 'King Jesus,' ain't she? . . . Vonnetta? Nah, child, she just fainted from the heat—and the dehydra-tion. Well, the girl was out all night drinkin', Loretta. . . ."

In other words, the service at St. John's never really ends until Sunday dinner is over.

But it isn't like anyone has to tell Loretta anything anyway. She just seems to know. Loretta has a way of finding out everything because she says she has ESP.

I believe her. I have to. She says that "history done come full circle down here in Ballyhack," and that I'm just repeating history.

"Amanda Pinkard," she says to me one night. "She fell in love with the Master, Cyrus Pinkard, and they had them a little girl they named Mandy, and Cyrus gave 'em all their freedom, and they lived right here in Ballyhack. Mandy Pinkard was my great-grandmama. Full circle, child. History is just one big circle. One day, you'll get to see Peter again. You'll see."

I hope she's right.

I can't help tearing up. "Loretta was right."

"Yeah."

"Did she, um, see anything in the future for after you saw me again?"

"What do you mean?"

"I don't know . . . did she see . . . a wedding?"

Ebony nods but doesn't speak.

I pull her to me. "What's wrong?"

"Loretta saw a wedding, but it was at a Catholic church. 'I don't know any Catholics, do you?' she asked me. I didn't at the time, but then . . ."

Whoa. "She saw my wedding?"

Ebony nods. "She said it was a cold wedding and that you were crying."

"All true." Loretta *was* a psychic.

She snuggles closer. "You want another wedding, right?"

"Oh, yes." I have to make things right.

"Then you'll have to convert back to Methodist but this time to African Methodist."

Huh? "Um, I might not have the right qualifications." I rub my skin and point to the freckles on my nose for good measure.

"You don't have to be African to belong."

"Oh."

"And we're going to Bethel tomorrow."

"We are? But we have two novels to work on, and the revisions will take a whole lot—"

"Hush. We are going to Bethel, Peter, as a family for the very first time, and it won't be like when you used to sneak off and visit when your daddy was passed out. I've been waiting for this moment for a long time, Peter. We're going to walk in there, arm in arm, and sit there in the presence of God as . . . a . . . family." She holds my face tenderly. "A whole bunch of eyes will be on you, Peter Underhill."

I'm not worried about other people's eyes.

I'm worried about the eyes of God.

18

"Maybe it's your body, Peter," Ebony says with a giggle as she appraises me early Sunday morning in the only suit I own. It had been balled up in my carry-on, and no amount of steam has helped. "Your body is a little wrinkled underneath, so no matter what we do, your clothes will still look wrinkled."

I flick some lint from my tie. "Thanks for trying."

She wraps the cord around the iron, her shiny white slip swaying. I can't help staring at the way it hugs all her curves. "What?"

"Um. Nothing."

She puts the iron on her dresser. "Don't be getting any wicked ideas an hour before church, Peter Underhill. I want you focused on God this morning."

"I will be."

She pulls up the hem of her slip, showing me a delicious leg. "I don't want you focused on how these legs will be wrapped around you later."

I have to turn away. "Stop teasing me."

She spins me back to her, running her hands down the lapel in my suit jacket. "You look kind of older in this suit."

"Thanks."

"I didn't mean it in a bad way. You look distinguished."

I sit on the edge of her bed. "Ancient, you mean."

"We're the same age, Peter. You can't be old yet, because *I'm* not old yet. Right?"

"Right."

She spins me around and pats me on the butt. "Now get out so I can get dressed. Go check on Destiny. I'm sure she's not ready."

I walk down the hall to Destiny's room and knock. "How's it going?"

I hear a few steps and a thud. A second later she opens the door, simultaneously rubbing her shin and slipping on a shoe. "Almost ready."

"Are you all right?"

"Bedpost got me again. I run into that thing just about every day." She spins around, her burgundy and cream dress swirling around her. "How do I look, Daddy?"

"Like a dream." I reach out to hold her. "You'll always look like a dream."

She steps back. "No offense, but I don't want your wrinkles rubbing off on my dress. Is Mama ready?"

"Not yet."

"Good." She pulls me forcefully into her room and shuts the door behind me. I suppose it's a typical teenager's room—messy, poster-covered, uneaten food on paper plates on the floor, empty soda cans on her desk, no clear sign of any organization—but at least Destiny has a theme: black movie stars. Posters of Denzel Washington, Halle Berry, Angela Bassett, Nia Long, Samuel L. Jackson, Regina King, Lawrence Fishburne, Samantha Mumba, and—is that Dorothy Dandridge?—cover most of her four walls.

"Daddy," she whispers, "are you going to—you know—today?"

Have sex? Have we been too loud? "What do you mean?"

"You know."

No, I don't. "You mean am I going to convert today?"

"No." She pulls me to her only window. Long Island Sound shimmers in the distance. "Are you going to ask Mama to marry you today?"

The thought has crossed my mind, but not nearly so soon. "Today? I thought we were just going to church as a family today."

"Daddy, for a romance author, you aren't very romantic. Mama has been dreaming of this day for so long—"

"Wait. Are you telling me that your mama expects me to pop the question at church today?"

Destiny nods. "It will be the perfect moment, Daddy. Right during the altar call." She hugs herself and smiles. "God, I've got goose bumps. Just think: you'll lead her right up to that altar and kneel together and ask her right in front of God."

Now *I've* got goose bumps. "That would be perfect, but I don't have a ring."

She bites her bottom lip. "If you had a ring, would you ask her?"

"I can't think of a more romantic—and holy—way to ask her. Sure."

She goes to her desk and opens the top drawer, removing a fuzzy black box.

"You . . . is that . . ." Are daughters supposed to buy engagement rings for their long-lost fathers to give to their mamas?

She opens the box, displaying a pretty ring with a tiny diamond. "What do you think?"

"I think . . . it's wonderful. But how did you get the money for it?"

She snaps the box shut and places it in my hand. "Haven't you noticed?"

"Noticed what?"

"Mama has been giving me all that money for groceries for years . . ." She smiles.

I laugh. "And you haven't been bringing all the groceries home. I get it. And it's in her size?"

She shows me her ring finger. "Mama and I have the same ring size."

I put the box in one of the pockets of my suit jacket. "You're something else."

She kisses my cheek. "And you made me that way." She looks toward the door. "You better leave. If Mama comes in, she'll know something's up."

"Okay." Then I have a thought. "Wait. You were supposed to put gas in her car last night. Did you?"

She shakes her head. "So, we can all walk home."

"If we get there."

"We'll get there, Daddy. It's all downhill."

Ebony, dressed in what Destiny calls her "dreamsicle" dress of orange and white, lets me drive her Accord to Bethel, and I stare at the fuel gauge the entire time. The little warning buzzer doesn't come on, so I figure we'll have enough gas to get back.

"We're early," Ebony says. "Destiny, go save us some seats."

Destiny gets out, and as soon as her door shuts, Ebony leans over and kisses me on the lips.

"I was hoping to walk in with both of you."

"Oh, she'll be back." She takes my hand and sighs. "Forgive me if I'm a little goofy right now. I just feel so happy."

"So do I."

When Destiny returns, I start to get out, but Ebony pulls me back in. "Not so fast, Peter. We're making a grand entrance. Right when the organ starts playing. I want everyone to see us." She pats my arm. "Too bad about your suit."

"Yeah."

"They won't talk too badly about you. During the service, anyway."

Once the entrance to Bethel becomes clogged with people, Ebony says, "Now," and we get out. I stroll up the steps with a real lady on each arm, and once we are in the sanctuary, we take a leisurely walk to the front pew, both Ebony and Destiny smiling and waving at their admirers.

I keep my eyes straight ahead at the huge cross on the wall. *I'm here, God. It's me, Peter Underhill. You haven't seen me in quite a while.*

As soon as we sit, the choir enters from all aisles singing "Get Right with God." I can't help but wonder if Ebony planned that particular song, too.

Song after song, prayer after prayer, squeeze after squeeze of my hands by my daughter and my hopefully future wife, and I can't see anymore because of the tears, because of the ache in my heart, because of all the wasted years. I close my eyes, tears still spilling out, my body shaking, and Ebony's hand holds me tighter, Destiny puts her arm around me, and we're standing and clapping and shouting, and I can't contain my sorrow any longer and I hit the floor right there in the front row of Bethel and pray like I've never prayed before:

God, Almighty God, I am here, a sinner in Your holy presence, and I know that I have offended You, and grieved You, and caused the Holy Spirit to weep, and I'm sorry, God, Almighty God, for running away from You for so long, for too long, and if You'll find it in Your Almighty heart to forgive me, to cleanse me, to bring back the joy that I once had, I will put away my past and try to live the right way. Please, God, Almighty God, take away my sorrow and replace it with joy . . .

Ebony and Destiny help me back into the pew as Reverend Moore begins his sermon on love. I smile at Ebony, and her eyes fill with tears, too. Destiny hands us Kleenex and opens a Bible in my lap to I Corinthians 13 as Reverend Moore reads:

" 'Though I speak with the tongues of men and of angels, and have not charity, I am become as sounding brass, or a tinkling cymbal. And though I have the gift of prophecy, and understand all mysteries, and all knowledge; and though I have all faith, so that I could remove mountains, and have not charity, I am nothing. And though I bestow all my goods to feed the poor, and though I give my body to be burned, and have not charity, it profiteth me nothing.' "

I squeeze Ebony's and Destiny's hands under the Bible. *I have gained so much, God. Thank You.*

" 'Charity suffereth long, and is kind; charity envieth not; charity vaunteth not itself, is not puffed up, Doth not behave itself unseemly, seeketh not her own, is not easily provoked, thinketh no evil; Rejoiceth not in iniquity, but rejoiceth in the truth; Beareth all things, believeth all things, hopeth all things, endureth all things.' "

What we must look like! Three people, two of God's finest creations, and me, tears streaming down our faces, smiles so wide we're blinding the choir.

" 'Charity never faileth: but whether there be prophecies, they shall fail; whether there be tongues, they shall cease; whether there be knowledge, it shall vanish away. For we know in part, and we prophesy in part. But when that which is perfect is come, then that which is in part shall be done away.' "

God, if I ever need a definition of "perfection," I'll remember this moment. Thank You for bringing me back to Ebony and to Destiny.

" 'When I was a child, I spake as a child, I understood as a child, I thought as a child: but when I became a man, I put away childish things. For now we see through a glass, darkly; but then face to face: now I know in part; but then shall I know even as also I am known.' "

God, thank You for helping me to finally grow up. And thank the Captain for me, whenever You see him next, for trying to be my father.

" 'And now abideth faith, hope, charity, these three; but the greatest of these is charity.' "

Destiny shuts the Bible, and the three of us hold hands.

Reverend Moore closes his Bible, too. "I'm not going to give a sermon on these verses. I'm not going to give a sermon on love. I don't have to. I know you can feel God's love right now."

"Amen," Ebony whispers along with quite a few others.

"The Apostle Paul was a plain man, and you might even say that he was plain as a writer, too. He wasn't fancy when he wrote this, using a whole bunch of big words to make himself appear smarter." He holds up his Bible. "The writers of this book were no different than you or me. They had real jobs. They had families. They were born, they lived, and they died. As far as I know, none of them had any training in the art of writing. None of them. Yet this book has confounded scholars and other so-called smart folks for two thousand years." He smiles, his eyes sparkling. "But it's plain to me. Is it plain to you?"

"Amen!" and "Yes!" ripple through the sanctuary.

"All the hate that's been in the air these last few weeks, all the hate that's been burying us, and here is the way out right in front of us in simple, plain words, from a simple, plain man. Here is the light at the end of the tunnel of hate."

"Amen!"

"If hate is the problem, love is the solution."

"Amen!"

"If hate is the question, love is the answer."

"Amen!"

"If hate is the destroyer, love is the builder."

Reverend Moore steps out from behind the pulpit, and my hands start to sweat streams.

Oh, God Almighty, he's going straight to the altar call. Am I ready? Is Ebony? I know Destiny is.

"Jesus said, 'Come unto me, all ye that labor and are heavy laden, and I will give you rest.' " He spreads out his arms, his hands open and lifted to heaven. "Lord God, bless those who come before You now with Your plain and simple love."

That's my cue. I turn to Destiny and kiss her soft cheek. She hugs me hard and nods. I stand and pull Ebony to her feet, and for the first time since we've been reunited, Ebony looks totally unsure of herself. I lead her to the altar, where I kneel and look up into her eyes. I don't say anything, mainly because I'm afraid that if I do I'll start bawling in front of all these good people. I reach into my suit jacket pocket and take out the box, snapping it open. The church is entirely still. Ebony kneels. I remove the ring from the box and slip it on her finger, and when we embrace, the hush in the sanctuary breaks and "Hallelujah!" rains down on us as Destiny joins us, hugging us both. We stand and turn, facing the cross.

I'm back, God. I'm back. I found Ebony, I found my father, and I found You. Thank You.

19

After the service and a thousand hugs from everyone coming at Ebony and me in every direction, we escape to the car as the sun breaks through a gray-blue gap in the clouds.

"We need to tell Mama right away," Ebony says. "She'll be mad so many other people knew before she did, but she'll get over it."

I doubt it.

But as I fly through the streets of Huntington and we get to West Shore Road, Ebony shouts, "Stop the car!"

I sit there idling in the middle of the street, the gas gauge resting firmly on "E." "Your mama's going to be mad."

Ebony points at the woods across the street. Our woods. "Come on." Then she gets out of the car.

"What's going on?" Destiny asks.

I unbuckle my seat belt and get out, waving a car around us. "You'll have to drive on to your grandma's house without us. Your mama and I are going on a trip down memory lane."

Destiny groans as she gets out. "You two are just too romantic for your own good."

"I know." I kiss her soft cheek. "See you."

"I'm just glad the bowling alley is a grocery store now," she says as she buckles up.

"You know about the bowling alley?"

"Yes. You two would have me out there with you, I'm sure, wearing those nasty shoes worn by who knows who."

"It's 'whom.' "

"Whatever."

Though it's cold and getting colder, Ebony's hand is warm, so warm I almost don't notice that we're walking through our woods in a suit and a dress, a brand new engagement ring on her finger. The leaves crunch under our feet, the sun drops rays here and there, and the wind sighs all around us.

"It doesn't seem nearly as big as it used to be," I say.

"Oh, it's still big," she says. "Just use your imagination."

"It was so easy to get lost in here once."

"Yeah."

We pass the old dance studio, its picture window reflecting only us today. Ebony does a little pirouette and curtsy, while I stand there doing a very bad impersonation of John Travolta. We pass the Cave, and neither of us says a word, Ebony rolling her eyes. All those misses have been filled in with cement forever. We look off to the left and see the Captain's deck, still standing, still sturdy as any boat ever built.

"I still go there in my dreams," Ebony says. "I'm up under that deck with my first and only boyfriend, and we're sharing secrets the world will never know." She stops me before the final rise to Preston Street to rest her head on my chest. "I've been thinking a lot about our book, Peter. Maybe we could skip some of those secret moments, you know, leave them out, save something for just us to remember."

"You mean the part about me, um, missing?"

"Especially that, though it was kind of sweet." She winks. "I was good at making you miss, huh?"

"Yeah."

"And I don't want anyone to look at me like I was some teenaged hoochie."

"You weren't."

"Oh, the way you wrote it kind of makes it seem that way."

"You weren't a hoochie. I did put in the part about your, um, rules."

She looks at our hands. "Yeah. A lot of good those rules did."

Oh, yeah. We had us a child with those rules in force.

"And maybe you could skip that day with your dad. I don't want the world to think your dad was some monster."

Hold on here. "But he was a monster." He was Godzilla with a shave.

"Maybe then he was, but later he was . . ." She sighs. "Later he was you, Peter. Underneath all that hatefulness, your daddy was you. He was so full of tenderness for Destiny, for me, even for Mama." She coughs. "Okay, maybe not as much for Mama as me and Destiny, but he was at least civil to her." She bites her lip. "He was, well, handsome in his own way, too, and I'm starting to see signs of him in you." She traces my jaw line with a finger. "You have his chin, his eyes, and if you'd get a haircut and a shave, you'd have the spitting image of his face." She kisses my chin. "You're a handsome man, Peter Underhill, just like your daddy was, and maybe we should soften him a bit in our book."

There wasn't a soft spot on the Captain's entire scaly body. "I don't know . . ."

"Well, at least think about it, okay?"

"I will." I look toward the slope.

"I mean, you didn't get to see him with Destiny."

Don't I know it.

"He showed us all a completely different side."

Men have been known to mellow in their old age, to spend their declining years making up for past regrets. "So I've heard."

"So I'm telling you." She grips my lapels and gives a little shake. "Your daddy wasn't a saint, I know that, but he was a wonderful grandfather, and I'm glad Destiny got to know him."

"I'm glad, too," I say, and I begin pulling her toward the slope.

"No, you're not."

She's right, of course, but I want this conversation to end. "Your Mama's waiting."

"She can wait."

I let out a long breath and stare up into the trees, bulbous gray clouds shuffling above them. It's true what that old saying tells us: the dead—not the living—make the longest demands on us. "Look, Ebony, everything I wrote happened as I remember it happening. It's the truth, and the feelings I have for the man are the truth, too. I can't change those feelings because you or anyone else says that my daddy was a changed man in the last few years of his life."

"So serious," she says, and she squeezes my hand.

"I can't help it, right? It's my serious daddy in me, right?"

She pulls me to her. "It isn't your daddy at all, Peter. It's you and you alone, and you've got issues, and until you get past those feelings—"

"Look, I'm not going to canonize the guy, if that's what you want."

"No. I don't expect that."

"Well, what do you expect?"

Her face hardens. "I expect you to respect your own daddy. At least you had one for most of your life." She drops my hand and starts up the slope. "Well, come on."

Damn. Captain, why did you have to ruin my engagement like that? No. Wait. The Captain isn't ruining anything. I've just gotten engaged before God, but I can't seem to lay my burden down before God. I'm ruining my own engagement.

"You coming?" she asks from the top of the slope, her arms crossed.

I look to my left at the Captain's deck, at the darkness underneath, at the steps leading to the path to the screen door of the kitchen. In my mind, I still hear the screen door slamming, still see him storming down the path, still feel those fists on my face, still taste the blood, still smell my own fear.

"I'll, uh, meet you around the other side," I say. "Near where we used to shoot hoops with Mickey." Please understand, Ebony.

Her face softens. "Okay. Don't be too long. It's cold."

And getting colder.

I watch her cross the Captain's old lawn before winding up a narrow path most likely created by water running down the hill behind the house. Branches tear at my pants all the way to the deck, but I don't really feel them because I'm thirteen again and I'm with my girl and we're escaping the world and it's so quiet and she's so beautiful and I'm so scared of that beauty and what my hands want to do and—

I freeze and close my eyes.

I don't hear the screen door slamming.

I'm trying to hear it, that screeching sound as it opens, that metallic bang as it closes, but I only hear the sighs of the wind. I don't see the Captain storming down the path. Instead, I see pot after pot of the Captain's geraniums, all red, all thriving, all lined up on the edge of the deck, his hands turning over the dirt. I don't feel any fists, just the wind cooling my tears. I don't taste any blood either. It's . . . shepherd's pie? Why, of all things, is it shepherd's pie? The Captain's favorite meal. And instead of smelling fear, I smell roasted meat, potatoes, corn, and tomatoes, the potatoes crispy, the meat heavily seasoned with salt and pepper.

I open my eyes. I'm under the Captain's deck, and it's not as enchanted as it once was. I feel a sense of loss from that, but I've found something else here, too: I've found a regular old dad with all the faults of regular old dads the world over. I had a regular dad and didn't know it. I tap the wood, and it echoes slightly, and from somewhere deep in the woods, I hear a faint creak, like the creak in the *Argo* that vanished the other night. I know it's just a tree bending in the wind, but . . .

Maybe these woods weren't mine and Ebony's at all. They were really the Captain's woods, and we just had the chance to get lost in them once upon a time.

I scramble up the bank, take the steps two at a time, fly down the path, and stop short when I see white plastic pots stacked near the back porch. They could be the Captain's old pots. They're still around, too?

I race through Mrs. Hite's hedges to Ebony. It looks as if she's playing an imaginary game of basketball in the place where Mickey Mather's basketball goal used to be. I slow to a walk and watch as she dribbles, head fakes right, goes left, and does her patented up-and-under move, her left hand high in the air. Though there's no backboard there, I still look up. I'm sure it went in.

"You still have some serious moves," I say.

"I'm still unstoppable," she says, and she passes me the imaginary ball. "You okay?"

"Yeah."

"Did you see him?"

I feel a lump in my throat. "Yeah, I think I did."

"Good. I go back there to talk to him sometime, too. Mrs. Service— that's the lady who lives there now—she doesn't seem to mind. Now pass me the ball, I'm open."

I throw a bounce pass with our imaginary ball, and she dribbles once and pulls up for a fade-away jump shot. "Swish," I say.

"Nothin' but the bottom of the net."

Standing a few minutes later on Candace's porch, I start to feel nervous. "Where's your car?"

Ebony shrugs. "There's never any telling where your daughter is at any given moment, even when she's right there in front of you. She'll show up." She rings the bell. "Don't know why I always ring the bell to my own mama's house. You remember she had this thing about always knocking before entering any room."

I had forgotten this. I'll have to add it to my book. "But as I recall, your mama didn't have to knock at all."

Ebony turns and smiles. "Yeah. She caught us a few times, huh? Maybe we can confront her about that today."

"Not today."

"Chicken."

She has that right.

The door opens, and Gladys welcomes us inside. Ebony flashes the ring in front of her face and puts a finger to Gladys's lips. Gladys hugs her, then me, then shuts the door behind us. Ebony takes my hand, and we walk into the living room where Candace sits, her hands folded together as if in prayer.

"Show me the ring," she says before we're fully in the room.

Ebony's shoulders slump. "Who told you?"

Candace puts an imaginary phone to her ear. "Candace, this is Carolyn Johnson from church. How you doin'? We hope to see you out to church real soon. Well, I just wanted you to know that your daughter and some white man . . ."

"But I wanted to surprise you, Mama."

"Then don't become engaged during the altar call in front of a church that loves to gossip. Now show me the ring." Ebony spreads out her fingers, and Candace nods her head. "Not bad, Pete. Kinda stylish. Destiny did a nice job."

"What?" Ebony shouts.

"Uh, yeah, well, you see—" I start to say.

Ebony waves a hand in my face. "I'll deal with that later. Does Aunt Wee Wee know? I can at least surprise her."

"Who you think *I* told first?" She rolls toward me. "You gonna ask me if it's all right for you to marry my daughter?"

I shake my head.

"Good. I've taught you something. Never let anyone stand—or sit—in the way of your happiness."

I nod.

"You gonna say anything, Pete, anything at all?"

I've been waiting to say this for the longest time. "Hi, Mom."

Nothing happens at first. I hear Candace catch her breath while she nods. "Yep, I knew you'd say something like that." She starts to tear up. "Why you gotta say stuff like that, huh? I'm through crying for you two, and here I am about to—" She looks down at my pants and shoes. "Boy, what you trackin' into my nice clean house? Just look at all that dirt Gladys is gonna have to clean up later. You ain't no son of mine, bringing all that mud up into my house. 'Hi, Mom,' he says, like that's gonna make everything okay." She smiles and swats a tear from her cheek. "Well, Pete, I want you to know that it *does* make everything okay."

I hug her with all my might. "You had me going there for a—"

"But," she interrupts, "you're gonna have to clean up that mess right now."

I look behind me. I have tracked in quite a bit of that moist dirt from under the deck. "I will."

"And don't you be callin' me 'Mom,' boy. That is so white. Call me 'Mama' or nothin' at all, you hear?"

"I hear. Mama."

The door crashes open, and a breathless Destiny stumbles in, adding more mud to Candace's carpet.

"Oh, Lord!" Candace cries. "Why you gotta be so much like your daddy, child?"

Destiny stops in her tracks. "I ran out of gas."

"But that don't explain why you gotta bring all the dirt in Huntington into my house, does it?" Candace sighs and looks up at Ebony. "Girl, what we gonna do with these two?"

Ebony blinks out a set of tears. "Love 'em, Mama. We're gonna love 'em."

20

God, it's nice to be with the one I love again. I can waltz through Bethel every Sunday, smiling, unafraid to tell everyone we've set a date for an April wedding. I can even flirt with Ebony unashamedly right in front of Candace after the service in the very room where I was so afraid to flirt before. I lavish kisses, what the Danish call "messengers of love," on Ebony in full view of the Queen, and I can even say romantic thoughts out loud. "These weeks have flown by on butterfly wings," I announce to the ladies playing spades.

Candace and Estelle usually tell me to shut up whenever I say these things, but not Aunt Wee Wee—unless I forget her smokes.

And rather than putting a damper on our sex life, the public proposal at the church leads to some holy (and not so holy) lovemaking. Ebony sends Destiny out often, for only a few items on the grocery list at a time, while Ebony and I get lost in each other. I'm surprised that I can keep up, as old as I am, but Ebony has us taking morning walks along the beach and through the woods to get back into what she calls "sexual shape."

I can't explain it, but somehow time stops in Ebony's bedroom, night seeming to go on forever. With Edie, I could count to a hundred and be through, but with Ebony I lose count. I still try reading the phone book in my mind to control my orgasms, but I never get past "AAA Auto."

"Sorry," I say often.

"Don't be. You're flattering me. I'm glad I still have some sex appeal left."

And then we spoon and talk until the spooning leads to more reading of the phone book in my mind. We mainly talk about Destiny—her favorite colors, her moods, and her tangential conversations. We also discuss my old baseball days, our changed bodies, and old friends.

"Whatever happened to Eddie Tucci?"

Ebony laughs. "The kid who smelled like garlic?"

"Yeah. Even his punches smelled like garlic. He once hit me in the arm, and it smelled like garlic all day."

She sniffs my shoulder. "You smell like me now. Anyway, Eddie got arrested a couple years after graduation. Remember that Chevelle of his?"

"Yeah." Who could ever forget that bomb with a cracked windshield, dangling muffler, fuzzy dice, and flaky black paint? It was more a midsized hearse than a car. It even had a bumper sticker that read "Protected by the Mafia: Keepa Ya Hands Off."

"Well, Eddie was never too bright, and he got it into his thick head to steal a bike."

"But he had a car."

"And that's where the police found the bike. In the trunk."

"How much time did he serve?"

Ebony shrugs. "Long enough for the rest of them to finally move out. Remember when they tried to sell their house?"

I had forgotten. Mr. Tucci had nailed a blank sign way up in the old oak tree in front of his house. Then he had carefully carried a full bucket of red paint and a paintbrush up the ladder. "Why didn't he paint that sign on the ground and let it dry first?"

"Who knows? You can still see the paint on the tree."

"Guess Eddie didn't fall far from the tree."

I get an elbow to the ribs for that one. "What about Eric Hite?"

"Jail."

"Little Eric?"

"He went out to Lake Ronkonkoma or some such place and tried to rob a liquor store with a popgun. The owner had a shotgun, and, well, our little Eric still has some buckshot in his butt. He'll never be able to go through a metal detector."

The liquor store owner must have had incredible aim. Eric was always so small. "What about Mark Brand?"

"Mark? I have no idea, and neither does anyone else. After graduation, he just disappeared. I've been looking for him on milk cartons or those missing persons posters ever since."

That's so sad. Mark's family never seemed to care much for him any-way, and one Christmas all they gave him was a carton of Marlboros. I only went into Mark's house once, but that was enough. In Mark's room, a naked, hairy man in mid-air flipped off the world from a poster cover-ing a head-shaped hole in the wall. "I made that one," Mark told me. "Course, my pop helped me a little."

"So," Ebony says, turning to me and stroking my beard, "that only leaves Mickey Mather from your old gang."

"It wasn't a gang."

"Oh, I don't know. The way you all rode around on those bikes with the baseball cards in the spokes—very spooky. I've never understood that."

And neither do I. If we had just saved half of those cards, we'd all have a nest egg. Those cards probably would be worth hundreds, if not thousands, by now. "We weren't a gang."

"Willie made you all a gang."

There's some truth to this, so I don't deny it.

"He got you all into all sorts of trouble."

Most of it involved eggs and soap on Hell Night. "And which prison is Willie in?"

"He's not in jail. He's a respected businessman now."

"Yeah?" The kid who spent more days in detention hall than class is a businessman?

"He runs a waste management company."

I blink hard at her. "Like the guy on *The Sopranos*?"

"No. He does industrial waste removal. In fact, he and his company have been working twenty-four-seven down at Ground Zero. You might have even seen him on TV."

"Our Willie . . . is down there?" Of all my friends and associates from the old days, I had thought Willie the least likely to succeed anywhere but a boxing ring. And now he's a hero.

She nods. "You wouldn't recognize him. His long hair is gone, and he's fighting premature baldness in a big way. So yeah, Willie is down there." She raises the covers and looks down at her stomach. "And I want you down there."

"But it hasn't been fifteen minutes."

She pushes my head down to her stomach, where I immediately begin nibbling on her hot skin. "Take your time then. Enjoy yourself. You know I will."

Ebony makes me go to Frank's Barbershop on New York Avenue for a haircut and a shave, mainly because of something she calls "beard stubble burns" on her thighs. I definitely enjoy myself "down there," but I know she'll enjoy it more if I have a smooth face. The Captain used to get his hair cut at Frank's long ago, and not much has changed. Same smell of talc, same lumpy chairs, even the same old magazines. When I look into the barber's mirror after I'm done, I see either a very old Marine or a shorn novice about to enter the priesthood. And before I can enter Ebony's house, I have to put up with quite a few comments from my daughter.

"Yes?" Destiny says as she answers the door.

"Morning," I say, and I start to enter.

She steps in front of me. "Who are you?"

"Very funny."

"My mama doesn't like Hare Krishnas," she says. "You trying to sell flowers or something?" She squints. "Is that a chin?"

"Step aside, little girl."

"Hmm. A Hare Krishna with an attitude."

I am kind of grouchy. I haven't been sleeping very well, and not just because Ebony won't leave my body alone. "Destiny, it's cold out here."

She turns my face from side to side. "You look like your daddy." She looks down. "A lot."

"Too much?"

She nods and lets me enter.

Even Ebony does a double take, and later that night, she lights fewer candles. "No offense," she says, "but you look a lot—"

"I know, I know," I say, interrupting her.

"Especially since you're not getting any sleep. All those circles under your eyes."

I squeeze her butt. "And whose fault is that?"

"Not mine. You've been tossing and turning all night, even running in your sleep. I've almost hit you a few times to stop whatever race you've been running." She turns me away from her and wraps her arms around me. "Now tonight, we're going to reverse spoon, okay? I'll just hold you until you fall asleep."

"Okay."

But though I try to fall asleep, I can't, and it's not because I feel Ebony's heat behind me. It's something else, something I can't explain. When she drifts off, purring her little whistling snore, I get out of bed and go to the bathroom. I throw some water on my face and look into the mirror.

My father stares right back at me.

I am his spitting image. Didn't Mom have anything to do with my face? I wonder where she is now. She should be invited to the wedding.

And for the rest of the night, I run searches online for Helen Pearson of Troy, New York, but come up empty. Almost twenty-six years ago, she left me on Christmas Eve—a holy night—leaving me with a holy terror. Do I even want to see her again? I contemplate spamming every AOL member named "H Pearson," but decide against it.

Mom got her freedom, and I'm going to let her keep it. My side of the church will just have to be sparse.

I try curling up on the couch in Ebony's office and am finally falling asleep when the phone rings. I fumble for the cordless phone on Ebony's desk.

"Hello?"

"Pete, it's me, Henry. Hope I didn't wake you."

I look out a window and see the beginnings of a cold November sunrise. "No, Henry."

"Good. How's the book coming along?"

I can't tell him the truth—that it's not coming along at all. "Just fine."

"Well, there's really no rush yet, since we're shooting for a December release."

Over a year from now, which actually is pretty quick. "That sounds good."

"So I won't need the finished product until the end of this December or early January."

"I'll have it ready." If Ebony has her part ready, that is.

"You're not out on that boat anymore, are you?"

"Uh, no, Henry, I'm staying with Ebony."

"*The* Ebony?"

"Yes."

"You've finally found your muse!"

"Yes."

"That's so wonderful." He lowers his voice. "She doesn't know about you and Cece, does she?"

"No, Henry."

"Are you going to tell her?"

Now would not be a good time to tell her any of it. "There's nothing to tell, Henry."

"Hmm?"

"You see, Henry, um, you're the father of the baby, because Cece and I never . . ."

"She told me you did."

"No, Henry, we didn't. You are about to be a daddy."

Henry doesn't speak for several moments.

"You still there?"

"You didn't, or you couldn't?"

I smile. "A little of both, Henry."

"Well, well, well."

"I'm happy for you, Henry."

"But why would Cece say that you did?"

This is too much drama for me before sunrise. "Why don't you ask her?"

"Oh, I will. Right now, as a matter of fact. I'll keep in touch." *Click.*

As soon as I click off the phone, I see Ebony in the doorway, wearing a robe and shivering. "I'm cold."

I welcome her to the little couch. "Sorry. I couldn't sleep."

"Who was that?"

"Henry. We're to have, I mean, Desiree is going to have a December release."

"Is that good?"

"Yeah. Just in time for the holidays."

"I guess that's good." She thuds her head on my chest. "Are you going to tell me about Cece Wrenn now, or do I have to read it in her memoirs?"

Oops. Sound travels in this house. Either that or Destiny taped our entire conversation at Xando after all. "You heard."

"Only your part of the conversation. So you couldn't do the do with her?"

I hold Ebony close. "No." I tell her of my encounter with Cece, and though her eyes narrow on occasion, she seems convinced that nothing happened.

"But she has Henry believing that the baby is yours?"

I nod.

"That's twisted."

"I know."

"Better not put that in our book."

"I won't."

"Who would believe it?"

"No one."

She drags a few fingers softly over my chest. "I'm sorry you aren't sleeping well. I'll start giving you warm milk before bedtime."

"You don't have to. My body knows it needs rest, and as soon as it tells my brain, I'll be sleeping better."

I hear Destiny's door open, a thud, and an "Ow!" Ebony laughs. "Every single morning. You know she has an audition today."

"She does? Why didn't she tell me?"

"She only told me last night. Says it's bad luck to tell anybody. I'm driving her into the city." She stands and stretches. "And you're going to stay here and sleep all day, okay? Just veg out."

"I'll try."

"No writing, no reading, no walking, don't even take a shower or a bath. Just get into my bed and sleep."

"Okay."

"I'm worried about you, Peter. I mean, before we got engaged, you were sleeping just fine, but afterward . . . I don't know, but it kind of sounds like maybe you're having second thoughts."

"I'm not having second thoughts, Ebony."

"Well, why else would you be running away in your sleep?"

"I'm not running away this time."

"You better not." She kisses my forehead. "Try to get some rest."

But after they leave, I can't sleep. Maybe it's all the Earl Grey tea I've been drinking these last few weeks catching up with me. Maybe it's all the adrenaline that flows through me whenever Ebony's around. Maybe I've just gotten my second wind and am able to stay up later, as I used to do when I was in college.

Or my mind is just too troubled to let me sleep.

I leave Ebony's bed and wander down the hall to Ebony's office, fully intent on adding to both novels. I have to get the other Ebony to Johnny's art show in *Whiter Shade*, but maybe I'll wait until after Ebony's show at DC Moore to write that so I can make it more authentic. I could add all that's happened recently to *Promises to Keep*, but I want to write that with Ebony. Maybe our separate narrations can come together by the end of that book, just as we came together.

I don't even turn on my computer, booting up Ebony's computer instead to see how far she has gotten over the last few weeks. She can't have gotten far, what with all her preparations for her show. I expect to read only a paragraph or two—

What is all this? How in the world has she been able to write so much? Where have I been when she's been writing? Maybe Ebony hasn't been sleeping well either, because here are twenty pages of new text.

What is that kid wearing on his legs? Couch cushions? His mama's going to kill him! And why isn't anyone playing basketball? I passed a backboard and goal just a block ago, and there was nobody there. What kind of neighborhood is this? It isn't raining or snowing, so why isn't anyone shooting hoops? I've never played street hockey, because we never played street hockey in Brooklyn—street football maybe, with a couple little kids on the lookout for traffic. But it doesn't look too hard, and it's kind of like basketball: put the orange ball in the net. I can do this.

I bust on up to them like I own the neighborhood, rolling my neck and saying, "Y'all need another player?" expecting them immediately to say yes. How can they refuse an offer like that? The fat kid looks ready to explode. I'm mad I wore my new Adidas. I don't want to get Italian fat kid blubber all over them when he finally does blow up.

But instead of inviting me to play, they just stand around looking at each other—except for the kid with the cushions and the catcher's mask. He's staring hard at me, checking me out from head to toe. I'd give him a mean look if I could see his eyes.

"Sure," the kid with the crew cut says. "Eric, take a break."

"I ain't givin' her my stick, Mickey!" Eric shouts.

Oh, yes you are, skinny boy!

Mickey takes Eric's stick and gives it to me. "You good on defense?"

I didn't come all the way up the street to hang out with Couch Cushion Boy.

That's the nickname she first gave me? I'm so glad she changed it to "Seven."

"What, you think because I'm a girl that I can't score?"

Mickey's eyes pop. "Okay, you play forward. Eddie, you drop back."

Eddie isn't having it. "Nah, nah. I ain't gonna."

But I'm not having Eddie's little attitude. "Boy, you're so fat that pigs follow you home looking for a date. I think I hear them oinking for you now. And what's that under your chin? It looks like a pack of hot dogs. I could take you to a Yankees game and feed the entire third base side!"

She said all that? I'll bet she did. She was always so good at dressing down people. I probably forgot the rest because I had instantly fallen in love with her. When your eyes are locked on, your ears turn off.

Couch Cushion Boy pops up his catcher's mask and laughs out loud. It wasn't that funny, but he's got some nice eyes, so it's okay. When I turn to look at Eddie again, he's back near the goal. What a chump! I thought Italians were good at firing words. Eddie would be dead fat meat if he ever stepped foot in Brooklyn.

"Let's play," I say, and for not knowing a thing about hockey, I kick these other boys' butts, let me tell you. They have no kind of moves. Instead of watching the ball, they watch me and fall for every one of my head and body fakes. There's nothing to this street hockey at all but a little shake-n-bake, and after I score on my first shot ever, they get all crazy.

"That don't count," this tall beanpole on the other team says. "She ain't on your team. She ain't from your neighborhood."

Well, excuse me, Mr. Beanpole. "What doesn't count?"

"It's still nine to nine, and you gotta put Eric back in," Beanpole says to Mickey.

That's not going to happen, and no boy ignores me for more than a second without regretting it for days afterward. "Excuse me?" I put my face all up in his. "Are you saying that because I'm not from this neighborhood that it doesn't count?"

"Y-yeah."

"Well," I say, and I smile. "I am from this neighborhood, chump. I just moved in over on Grace Lane." So take your sorry Bruin behind out of my face.

"Grace Lane ain't Preston Street."

Beanpole is ticking me off! "And you aren't shit playing hockey, boy." Well, he isn't. He only looks like he can play with all that gear on. And the way he looks at me, I bet he never had a girl cuss him before. That's not something Mama lets me do in the house, no sir. But Beanpole's skinny little lips are bouncing up and down, and no sound's coming from him. "All the cool shit you got on, and you can't play a lick. You're just mad a girl scored on you." Dag, his skinny little lips are getting chapped with all that air flying by them. "And you're just scared that I'm going to score on y'all again." Which I aim to do once Beanpole can speak again.

"I-I ain't scared," he says.

"P-p-prove it then," I fire back. I know I shouldn't mock people I just met, but I didn't survive Brooklyn to back down to no braces-wearing beanpole from the suburbs.

"Let her play," Couch Cushion Boy says, his voice kind of low and high at the same time. Like I need his help. Couch Cushion Boy couldn't scare an ant with a full can of Raid.

I laugh out loud. She's right, of course. And this first-person narrative reads so much better than mine. It's fresher, almost as if I'm back there. Maybe I should change mine from third person to first person so it isn't as distant.

"You shut up!" Beanpole yells at Couch Cushion Boy.

Ah, it's on now! I push Beanpole about three feet back. "Who are you telling to shut up, boy? You're talking' to ..." I look over at Couch Cushion Boy, who's grinning like a fool. "What's your name?"

"Peter."

I jab a finger hard into Beanpole's chest. Any harder and my finger would go clean through. "You are talking to Peter, and he's my boy. You don't tell any of my boys to shut up. Now are we going to play or what?"

A few minutes later, Mickey and I score and we win. Big deal. I'm waiting for them to start another game, but the Bruins walk away. That's it? Hell, I just got here! Geez, play again or something. No one goes to a basketball court and only plays one game. It isn't American! But even my team starts walking away, except for Peter, who's having the hardest time getting out of his cushions.

I step to him and smell some really strong garlic. Is he Italian? No. He has too many freckles on his nose. "Turn around." *He does.* "Number seven. That's my favorite number, you know that?"

"Uh, what's your name?"

Uh, why does everyone around here seem to stutter? "Ebony Mills." *Then I look down because Peter is staring hard at my face. Most boys in Brooklyn didn't look much at my face. They were always looking at my titties and my behind. This Peter, though, he's locked on to my eyes. Either he's just plain rude, or he likes what he sees. I hope he likes what he sees.* "But you can call me E if you like."

"Okay."

And then I let Peter walk me up the street. I don't let just any boy do that. I mean, he did stick up for me, and he still can't take his eyes from my face. What, am I the first black girl he's ever seen? From the looks of this neighborhood, I'll bet that I am the first black girl he's ever seen.

Not quite true. I went to school with several black girls, but none of them had Ebony's face. Geez, I'm feeling the embarrassment I felt then right now!

"Are you going to Simpson?" *he asks.*

"Where else am I going to go?"

"I dunno. You could go to St. Pat's like Eddie."

Peeeeee-you. And have him explode on me in homeroom? His guts would never come out of my hair. "No, thanks. Catholic kids are too wild for me." *And the ones in Brooklyn—forget it. Once they get loose on Friday afternoon, they're about as Catholic as a tree stump for the rest of the weekend.* "Do you go to Simpson?"

"Yeah."

"What grade are you in?"

"Seventh."

Dag, we're going to be in the same grade. We might even be in the same classes and stuff. "Me, too."

Then Peter smiles, and it's a nice smile, too, almost like he's relieved or something. Yeah, he's relieved. He thought I was older because of my titties, and I'm not about to tell him it's just a padded bra he's seeing.

We stop in front of his house, a nice two-story with a two-car garage and a sloping driveway, which is a crummy place to play ball, but at least the ball will always roll back to you. All Peter needs is a backboard and goal. "Uh, this is my house."

I guess this means our little walk is over, but I don't want it to end just yet. A boy is looking at my face, at me. This is something I could get used to. "You got anything to drink in there?"

"Um, yeah. I could get you a soda."

Get me a soda? "You aren't going to invite me in?" Mama said the folks in this neighborhood might be racist and not to expect too much. Here's proof.

Candace *would* say that, and she's probably still saying it. I don't know if anyone in that neighborhood ever properly welcomed them or even accepted them. Besides me, I guess.

"Uh, my father isn't feeling too well."

"Uh-huh." I don't believe him for a second. I'm okay to talk to, but not to let into your house? Now that's really rude.

"Uh, he's probably asleep."

"Right." Mama was right. This is a racist neighborhood. "Are you going to get me a Coke or what?"

"Uh, sure."

I expect to wait at least half an hour, but Peter's back in a flash, still with that smile on his face. I wipe off the top of the can—you never can be too careful—and I catch Peter staring at my belly button.

"What are you looking at, Peter?"

"Uh, nothing."

I smile. This boy is very interested in me. "You're looking at my stomach, right?"

"Yeah."

So maybe he has a thing for faces and belly buttons. "I'll bet you have an 'outie' with all sorts of green stuff inside it."

"I have an inny, too."

"Prove it."

And right there in Peter's driveway, I get a long look at his belly button. Not much to see, no green stuff, no lint, just freckles. "Dag, boy, do you have freckles like that all over?" Join them all together and he'd be my color.

"Some of them aren't freckles. They're moles, like this one." He touches this black spot just beneath his nose.

Though it's nasty looking, I just have to touch it. It doesn't feel too nasty, but Peter jumps. "Does it hurt?"

"N-n-no."

Dag, there must be something in the water in this neighborhood. Every boy I talk to stutters. "Are you cold?"

"Your finger is."

Oh, yeah. "Sorry. You have moles like that all over your body?"

"No."

"Good, because they're nasty." I finish my Coke and hand it to him. "Thanks for the Coke."

He smiles. "You're welcome."

He has nice manners, too. I smile. "See you around, Peter."

"Yeah." He smiles, and I have to look down at the ground again. "See you around . . . E."

On the way home, I feel kind of funny. I have made friends with a white boy, looked at his belly button and freckles, and I even touched his nasty mole. And he didn't run away or flinch. I should have taken longer to drink that Coke. He was genuinely interested in me. He wasn't like the others. His eyes were wide open, not eyes wide-but-shut like those other boys. They saw a black girl, and Peter saw a girl. And his freckles were, well, kind of cute, mainly, I guess, because I don't have any. They make him unique.

I think I'm going to like him.

And I suspect that Henry will like her version of this scene better than mine. Hmm. Maybe she can write the whole thing using what I've already written as a guide. Her voice has always been so much more interesting than mine. I scroll down to the next section:

I really like art class, and not just because Peter's in the class. Mr. Nearing, while a little weird, realizes that I have talent. Peter only smiles, and Mama and Aunt Wee Wee just say "Ooh, that's so pretty!" and slap my latest drawings and paintings on the fridge. Mr. Nearing lets me know why it's so good, and since he's a real artist, that means so much more to me.

But when Peter draws me that day in Hecksher Park, I get all sorts of butterflies inside. I had drawn myself before, but no one else had ever drawn me. And he draws me so pretty I don't know what to do or say, so I get mean. I don't mean to get mean, but my butterflies have a way of making me angry.

"Where's my face?"

"I wanted to save the best for last."

I sigh, but not because I'm mad. My face is the "best"? I have never thought that about my face my entire life. Oh sure, my daddy used to say I was the most beautiful girl in the world, but daddies are supposed to say that sort of thing, and Mama only tells me not to get ugly with her.

"Besides," Peter says, "you drew that self-portrait in your note, and you might have said that I copied it."

"I wouldn't have said that." And I wouldn't have. I'm just curious what he really thinks I look like.

"What if I made you too dark? You'd be mad."

"I am dark. Black is beautiful."

And then Peter nods, only it isn't a nod like "I agree with you." It's a nod like "I really really really agree with you." It's the kind of nod Mama makes when she really really really means something, and if I don't pay attention, I'll be in for it.

"What are you nodding for, Peter? You aren't black."

"I nodded cuz . . . cuz you're beautiful."

I don't remember too much after that. No one had ever drawn me beautiful, and no one had ever said I was beautiful, and the next thing I know I'm on the bus holding Peter's hand, getting off the bus still holding Peter's hand, and sneaking into my own house to my bedroom—still holding Peter's hand. I don't want to let go of the boy who thinks I'm beautiful and means it with serious nods.

"It's a little messy," I say as I sit on the bed.

It's really a lot messy, but that's how I like it. I don't like the looks of a made bed, books all lined up on a bookshelf, clothes safely hidden in a drawer. Straight lines and sharp angles aren't creative. Anyone can do them with a ruler or a protractor. I believe that life is much more beautiful if you let it be a little sloppy.

I smooth out my bedspread a little. "Take your coat off and stay a while."

Peter doesn't move. Maybe he's stunned that my room is so messy. Knowing him, his room has all straight lines and angles without a single *soft line. No wonder most of his drawings look like the work of an archi-tect.*

It is so true. I am so linear, so defined, so straight-edged . . . so much like my father. And it shows in my writing, too. I guess I build a story more than weave a tale.

"Sit with me, Peter." Why is he covering his legs with his coat? It isn't that cold in here. "Throw your coat anywhere."

When he tosses his coat onto the floor, I finally see the reason. He has a bulge in his pants! Gross! And now he's putting his hands in his pock-ets? Grosser! Why do boys do such nasty things? And why does he have to do it in my bedroom? Grossest!

I'm surprised that she wrote about this. I guess we won't be keeping this a secret from the world.

"So, what do you think?"
"Um, you have a lot of records and books."
"Don't you?"
"No."
He's got to be kidding. "No books?"
"I mean, yes, I have books. But no records."
No wonder he can't dance a lick. How can you dance without music? "Why?"
"I don't have a record player."
What kind of boy doesn't at least listen to music? "You should get one."
"Yeah."
"What about a radio?"
He shakes his head.
"You should get a radio."
"I will."

I had forgotten about that radio, a little transistor with an earphone. I once listened to a live concert by Sly and the Family Stone in Central Park on that. Ebony was the music in my life, the soft edges in my life, the art in my life. I didn't need a record player or a radio—all I needed was Ebony.

After some small talk about my books, I ask, "What do you think about me and you here in this room, alone?"

He starts to get up. "I think I ought to be getting home. The Captain—"

I yank him back to the bed. "He can wait." He is so afraid of his daddy that it almost scares me. I'm afraid of my mama, too, but I'm not that afraid. I mean, his daddy brought him into the world, right? Why be afraid of the man who helped create you? "I want to tell you something, and then I want to show you something."

"Why be afraid of the man who helped create you?" I whisper. I wish I could answer that. I was afraid of my daddy as a child, and I'm still afraid of my daddy as an adult. Is that what is keeping me awake all night? Why can't I just let that man go? Maybe I need therapy.

Did he just groan? I look down at his pants. It's getting bigger! Is he in any pain? I better tell him about my dream so he'll laugh and that thing will go away. "I had a dream about you last night, and in my dream, you were much taller than me." Which is crazy, since we're the same height now. "We were on the beach, and I was wearing a long shell necklace and a silky orange and purple dress, so you know it was a dream." It had to be a dream because I never wear dresses except to church. "You wore this teal blue shirt and tan shorts, and your hair made you look kind of like Elvis." Which is kind of funny, since Peter's hair is so short now! Maybe I want him to have longer hair or something. "And there we were standing on some beach while waves splashed our feet and the sun went down, and you know what you said to me?"

"What?"

"You said I had pretty feet." I check out his bulge, and it's going away. Good. "Except that you've never seen my feet, Peter." I take off my Adidas and socks and show him my toes. "Are they really pretty?"

"Yes."

"They look like Tootsie Rolls."

"I like Tootsie Rolls."

I don't. They're nasty. "I want to see your feet now."

*Then we start wrestling, and though I know I could take him, I let him
put me on my back. And then, well, I can't resist asking, "Are you going
to kiss me, Peter?" That's when I feel the bulge growing against me, and
it doesn't feel too bad. "You need directions? My lips are down here." He
still won't kiss me. "Come here, come on, Peter, no one's looking. I'll help
you. Close your eyes."*

"C-c-can't I keep them open?"

Did I stutter then? I'll bet I did. I was so scared.

*I don't even know if you're supposed to keep them open. In the
movies, they always seem to close their eyes first. "Sure. I'll keep mine
open, too." And then I pucker up for my very first kiss.*

His lips are a little chapped, but it's a nice, soft kiss that lasts so long,
and the entire time, he's staring into my eyes. That's when I feel a little
something stirring inside me where his bulge brushes against me so gently. When he's finished, the butterflies return and start zigzagging around
my whole body from my thighs to my eyes.

I push him off me. "That wasn't just a kiss. You have to go. Mama will
be home soon."

He looks so sad, and I feel sad, too. I want him to kiss me again! These
butterflies are killing me! My heart must be full of them!

"I'll walk you out."

He still looks so sad, so I hug him, pressing my hips as far into his as I
dare.

"Oh, Jesus," he whispers, and he starts to dance a little, only it's not
like any dance I've ever seen. I look down at his bulge and see it moving!

And I thought I only said "Oh, Jesus" in my head. I actually said it out
loud. And I danced? Yeah, I guess I would have. Maybe this is too em-
barrassing to me for the general public to read about.

"Oh my God! Did you just . . ."
He nods. "I didn't mean to, I swear I didn't!"
"What did it feel like?"
"Can I tell you later?"
No. I want to know what I just made you do! "Does it hurt?"
"No. It felt good."

*I made him feel good, just by hugging him? "Has that ever happened
to you before?"*

"No."

*"Cool." And it is. I made him so happy that he, um, did that right here
in my bedroom. I feel so special! But when I see the wet spot on his pants,
I back off. Why is it so messy? Oh, wait. Messy is good. I can deal with
messy. "All that came out?"*

"Can I go now?"

I sigh. "Yes."

*As I watch him running kind of funny with his books banging against
his pants, I feel so powerful. I made him do that. I, Ebony Mills, who has
just held hands with a boy, who has just let a boy into my room, who has
just kissed a boy, who has just made a boy feel good . . . I made him do
that. Maybe there's something to all that Black Power stuff Mama's been
telling me about after all.*

I guess when it comes right down to it, the bottom line is this: Women
would most likely buy our book, so a woman should tell the tale. I feel
a little sad about it, but it makes sense. Our story will have to be told
from her point of view whether I like it or not.

I shut down Ebony's computer and return to her room, the faint
scents of olive wood from the bed and vanilla from the candles in the air.
I crack a window and hear, also faintly, the roll of the surf.

Then I finally faint on the bed.

And dream a familiar dream . . .

I'm on the Argo *during a storm, waves as high as the Twin Towers all
around me, the mainsail whipping back and forth, the helm spinning like
the steering wheel on the* S.S. Minnow *from Gilligan's Island, and I'm
wearing my navy pea coat from when I was young, a pair of Chuck
Taylors peeking out below, brackish water covering the deck and splash-
ing up my legs. A huge wave arcs over the boat, and just before it hits the
Argo, I see a light go on in the cabin and I dive through the cabin door.
When I look up, I see the Captain smiling down at me, a tangle of knotty
ropes in his hands.*

"Some storm," he says, squinting his bad eye and pulling at the rope.

*"Yes, Captain." I try to stand, but can't because of the water spilling in
from behind me pinning me down.*

"Better get back up there then, take us on home."

"Yes, Captain."

Somehow I manage to climb back out into the void and grab the wheel, rain stinging my cheeks, that mainsail cracking like a whip, most of the other lines dancing in the wind like flailing linguine, monstrous waves crashing into each other high above me, almost as if I'm in a cave of angry water.

"Could be worse," the Captain says, suddenly beside me, his hands still working those knots. "How'd you get us into this mess in the first place, Pete? Weren't you following the charts?"

"I, uh, I don't know, Captain, I just—"

"And when are you going to learn to sail, Pete? When are you going to learn how to properly sail a boat?"

The helm shudders out of my grip, spinning and spinning faster and faster. "I'm trying, Captain!"

He touches my arm. "Well, don't try so hard. Let the boat go where it wants to go, Pete. It'll get us there. It's seen more days at sea than you . . ."

Though it wasn't a nightmare, I still wake up in a sweat. How long have I been asleep? I look out the window and see the last, rosy remains of the sunset. I've been asleep almost ten hours? But my dream was short, or was it? I must have been on a really long boat ride. Ebony and Destiny have to be back by now.

I tumble out of bed and slip down the back stairs to the kitchen, where Ebony and Destiny are eating take-out salads from Wendy's.

"Sleep well?" Ebony asks.

"I slept." But not well. My daddy's words—*Let the boat go where it wants to go, Pete*—are still ringing in my ears. "How'd the audition go, Destiny?"

Destiny doesn't look up, so I know it went badly. She pokes at a tomato wedge. "I wasn't black enough, Daddy. They wanted a *black*, black woman to play the role of the waitress." She drops her plastic fork and pushes her tray away. "They didn't want talent. They wanted a black face to play a subservient role. I even dragged Mama in to show them how black I really was, but they weren't interested." She looks up at me. "I guess I'm too exotic for them or something. See why I think I take after you the most?"

I massage her shoulder. "There will be plenty of other auditions, Destiny, but did you really want to play a waitress?"

"I wanted to play *something*. If I could just get one, small role, I know I'd go places. Maybe you could buy me a tanning bed?"

"Why?"

"So I can get blacker."

I look at Ebony. "Is she kidding?"

"Yes, Peter," Ebony laughs. "Go on, girl, tell him."

Destiny jumps straight up out of her chair, my hand flying off her shoulder. "I got a part, Daddy!"

"You did?" Why don't the women in this family ever just tell anything to me straight? Why do they have to dramatize everything so much?

Destiny nods. "You want to know how I got their attention?"

"I hope it was your acting ability." Which has fooled me once again.

She shakes her head. "No, Daddy. I had a tray in my hand, you know, and all I had to do was cross the set to a table, put down some glasses, say, 'Enjoy your meal,' and leave."

"You better sit down and eat, Peter," Ebony says, pulling another salad out of a Wendy's bag and sliding it to me. "This story keeps getting longer and longer."

I sit and open the top of my salad, and Ebony peels and dumps a packet of French dressing on top.

"So there I was, with a tray of glasses full to the top with water, and I had them balanced pretty well, but on my third step across the set— BAM! My foot hit the leg of a chair, and I started falling forward till I hit the floor hard. But you know what? I didn't drop the tray or the glasses."

"You didn't?"

"No. They stayed upright on the tray, and most of the water stayed in the glasses. Isn't that amazing? So then I dusted myself off, delivered those glasses, delivered that line, and then walked back across the set." She blinks. "Then every person in that studio started laughing. They thought I was hilarious!"

I squint. "And that's a good thing?" A soap opera with a clumsy waitress? How will that help ratings?

"Yes! They noticed me! I mean, I thought I had blown it big-time, but I got a callback."

"That's why we're home so late," Ebony adds.

"So, what soap are you on?"

"I'm not on a soap, Daddy."

"You're not?"

"No." She spins around gracefully and doesn't hurt herself. "I am now the new waitress at Helen and Joe's Café on *Meeting of the Waters*."

I look at Ebony. "*Meeting of the Waters?*"

"It's new," Ebony says. "A sit-com. On cable."

No wonder I've never heard of it. I don't even watch regular TV anymore.

"It's like *Friends*, only more ethnic," Destiny explains. "It's only a small part, Daddy, at most one or maybe two appearances per show, but I finally have something other than a high school play to put on my résumé."

"So you're in a real show."

"Yeah." She smiles. "I am so excited!"

"When will you be on?"

"Well, I start shooting next week, and if the show gets renewed, I'll be on next fall."

I catch Ebony rolling her eyes. Evidently, *Meeting of the Waters* doesn't have much of a chance for renewal. "Well, that's cause for celebration. Why don't we all go out somewhere for dessert or something?"

"That's what I wanted to do, too, but no, Mama's got to work on her paintings."

"I have a show to do," Ebony says, "and I wasted most of the day in the city."

I can't stand to see Destiny pout. "Destiny and I could go out. That would give you some peace and quiet."

Destiny shakes her head. "No, that's all right, Daddy. I have a couple million phone calls to make anyway." She heads up the back stairs, then ducks her head back to us. "But you two owe me a celebration, okay?"

"Okay," I say.

I sit and pick at my salad, trying to catch Ebony's eyes, but she seems lost in thought. "Everything okay?" I ask.

"No," Ebony says. "She's building up her hopes for a show that might not even make it through this season. An ethnic *Friends*? Give me a break."

"Have you seen it?"

"Once. It's such a rip-off. Six friends living in the same apartment building who don't work, hang out at a café, and say somewhat funny, mostly nasty things to each other."

Sounds like *Friends*, all right.

"The only thing different is the color of the actors and the theme song."

I take her hand. "Hey, it's something, right? Even if the show folds, she'll be able to say she was *going* to be on it, right?"

"Yeah, I guess it's better than nothing." She stands and throws away her trash. "You coming down?"

"You want me down there?"

"Yeah. It'll be a date."

"In the basement? How romantic."

She raises her eyebrows. "I may paint you in the nude."

"Yeah?" Sounds kinky. "Who'll be in the nude, me or you?"

"You."

"Oh."

"But I don't have nearly enough bright white paint, so—"

"Ha, ha."

Watching Ebony paint is like nothing I've ever seen or heard. She first puts on some Muddy Waters, some good, old stomp music with heavy harmonica and a thudding drumbeat. Then she lines up all her easels in rows under several banks of track lights, and after bopping around each canvas, she gets to work in time with the music on the canvas in front of her. And she doesn't stop bopping, her hips swaying, her ass shaking up a storm inside her sweats. That scene from the movie *Ghost* enters my head, and I almost wish Ebony had a pottery wheel.

"You getting turned on?" she asks.

"Yeah."

She dabs a streak of gold onto the skyline of one of those depressing self-portraits, and the portrait immediately changes to a happier tone. With one streak of gold, she has added hope. Amazing.

"Picasso said that your work in life is the ultimate seduction." She dances from side to side, outlining her nose with the tiniest line of gold. "Am I seducing you?"

"You know you are."

She laughs and darts to another portrait, highlighting a cloud with gold. "Mayhew says he puts jazz on canvas." She spins around. "I prefer stompin' on canvas, just stompin' the blues, just painting all those books I read so long ago as a kid." She paints a line of gold on the back of her hand. "If you get bored, you could check out all my rave reviews.

They're in that file cabinet over by the water heater in the first drawer in a folder called 'Clippings.' "

"I'm not bored."

She dashes to another portrait and spreads gold on the shoreline. "But I want you to read them, Peter."

"Oh."

Her reviews are, to say the least, wonderful. "Ebony Mills creates a universal space, a snapshot of tone, mystically hopeful, always searching," reads one review. "Her work is intense, immediate, simple and direct, subtle, unified, warm, and rhythmic," reads another. I look up and see Ebony doing a little shimmy in front of a canvas. That reviewer has described what I see in front of me right now. Ebony Mills *is* her art.

"You read the one about how uninhibited I am yet?" she shouts out.

I flip through to find it, reading, " 'Slithers of paint, entanglements of color, strong, stunningly unexpected, tugs at the heart and mind.' "

"Yeah, that's the one." She flattens her brush and fills in a rise of sand with gold. "I do love to do some tugging." She jumps back and puts a tiny dot of gold on her subject's eye. "And I have to have color. Colors are my babies."

Several hours and innumerable slithers of color later, she poses in front of her portraits, spinning her paintbrush like a baton twirler, paint whipping into the air and covering her T-shirt, her hair, and her face, and she is the most beautiful woman on this or any other planet. "What do you think?"

I step close to her. "They . . . they aren't depressing anymore."

She turns and backs into me, wrapping my arms around her. "I know. I've just set them all free, and all it took was a little color."

21

But when it comes to finishing the tapestry, Ebony won't allow me to watch her work. "It's going to be a surprise," she tells me. "Go work on our novels."

I try, but I can't. It's not that I don't want to. I stare for hours at what I've written, but I just can't seem to find the words to go on. So in addition to insomnia, which mocks the three or four sleeping pills I take every night, I also have writer's block.

Instead of writing or even revising, I lounge around the house, wash Ebony's car, walk Seven at the beach, and go clothes shopping with Destiny to pass the time to wear myself out. Ebony comes up for air every few hours for food, drink, and a kiss, and then she disappears into the basement again. And all night long, I hear the sound of the shuttle racing back and forth across the loom in rhythm to some old Robert Johnson blues, sounds that should lull me to sleep. Though I'm dead tired when Ebony does come to bed, I get wired all over again just watching her fall asleep and dream.

I have become a literary zombie.

It rains heavily the night of Ebony's art show at DC Moore, and though Ebony worries that no one will come, the gallery is packed. I stumble and walk like the living dead from portrait to portrait, watercolor to watercolor, while Candace holds court with an older crowd talking about the bad old days and Destiny flits around networking the glitterati. I hear shouts and see the crowd part on several occasions, local luminaries passing like frosted wheat through the throng. I'm not even sure where Ebony is, but this is her night to shine, not mine. I'm trying to keep a low profile.

I stop and stare at the watercolor in front of me. It's the *Argo* at full sail crashing through the waves on the open sea. I hope no one offers to buy this one. I'd like to have this one, maybe put it up in the cabin near the Captain's urn.

"Some boat," says a man beside me.

I hadn't even felt his presence. I guess my body must be shutting down or something. I take a sip of my coffee and look—at Robert De Niro, a beautiful black woman on his arm. Whoa. "Sure is."

He squints his famous squint and points at the watercolor. "Does this say *Argo?*"

"I think so," the woman says.

"Good name for a boat." He looks at me, and he smiles that smile known the whole world over. "See you around."

And then Robert De Niro drifts away, leaving me blinking. I look back at the *Argo*. "If he wants you, he can have you."

I finish my coffee and float over to a landscape, surprised no one else is drinking it in. Ebony rests on the beach in the foreground, her legs shining in the sun, clouds playing and dancing above her.

"Quite a fun fair, yes?"

I turn to see a tall, distinguished-looking man wearing a fine gray suit flipping through the show's catalogue, an umbrella in the crook of one arm. Is he Australian? "Yes."

"I had a Dickens of a time getting here, what with the roads from the airport so greasy. The meteorological office says we may get snowed up by week's end."

Must be English. I doubt the average Australian would use "Dickens" and "greasy" in the same sentence. "That's what I hear."

"And the queue on the pavement was tediously long. This is truly a city that never sleeps."

And I am a man who never sleeps. New York City and I are one.

"Are you an aficionado of Miss Mills's work?"

"Yes." I extend a hand. "Peter Underhill."

He shakes it. "John Bevington. Are you of the Sussex Underhills?"

Oh, yeah, I used to be English. "I might be. I don't know."

He sizes me up. "Wessex perhaps. Your nose is Wessex. Are you a collector?"

"Not really."

"Pity. Ebony Mills is simply amazing." He waves a hand in front of the landscape in front of us. "Notice the clouds. They're almost like candy floss topped with double cream."

Candy floss? Double cream?

"Observe their anticlockwise motion, almost as if they're riding a roundabout."

I have no idea what this man is saying. "Yes," I say, just to be polite. I search for Ebony or Destiny to save me from this man, but I can't see them anywhere. "So, what brings you to the Big Apple?"

"Miss Mills, of course. I'm here more on business than holiday. Investing in the arts is a much better hedge against shares and stocks these days."

"So you collect Miss Mills's work?"

"Indeed. I am one of her most loyal patrons."

I better stick with this guy. He's probably the one who has funded Ebony's house. "So you flew all the way from England to see Ebony's show?"

"Quite. It's so much better than buying by auction. I wander about and make note of the pieces I'd like to acquire, and then I hand this catalogue to Miss Mills. She does the rest."

I decide here and now that Ebony will handle any and all negotiations with Olympus. All this makes sense in a roundabout way. American patrons collect European art, and European patrons collect American art. I wonder if English artists have trouble getting shows in London.

"I am most curious about that tapestry, aren't you?" He points with his umbrella at a huge expanse of wall where the tapestry hides underneath a black velour drape. "She's left space for the title in the catalogue. You've noticed that she only numbers her work."

I want to say, "Quite," but decide against it. "Yes." Every piece of Ebony's work begins with the number seven and ends with the date she finished it.

"Quite curious, but unique."

I look over at the draped tapestry, then glance at the catalogue. Sure enough, there is a blank line three inches long. "Intriguing," I say.

He nods. "She has quite a flair for the dramatic, yes?"

"That she does."

Ebony appears out of the crowd, walks directly to me, kisses me on the cheek, and whispers, "I missed you." She turns to Mr. Bevington. "Good to see you here as always, Sir John."

Mr. Bevington is a knight? Ebony's main collector is an English knight?

Sir John bows to Ebony. "A magnificent show as always, Miss Mills. When will we have the unveiling of that mysterious tapestry?"

"In due time, Sir John, in due time." She smiles and puts an arm around me. "This is my fiancé, Sir John."

Sir John smiles. "I had no idea."

Ebony winks at Sir John. "Everyone will have an idea soon enough."

Sir John nods and continues wandering from portrait to portrait, and I can't contain myself. "Your biggest patron is an English knight?"

"What? Oh, that." She pulls me through the crowd to a less congested space near the *Argo* watercolor. "John isn't really a knight. I think he's a lawyer or barrister or something like that. I've just been calling him 'Sir John' since he rescued me and my bank account years ago by buying up most of my earliest works." She takes a deep breath. "Here comes trouble."

I turn and see a man fighting through the crowd, his eyes focused on us. He's a short spectacled man sporting a red bow tie, red suspenders, and an ill-fitting corduroy sport jacket complete with red patches, and he carries a thick press notebook.

"Who's he?" I ask.

"Morton Papp."

The name means nothing to me. "And he is . . ."

"Art critic from the *Times*."

"Oh." She seems so tense! "I love the way he dresses."

"It's his trademark. I've never seen him at any of my shows before, so maybe I'm about to hit the big time."

"Aren't you excited?"

"A little. He can make or break a show with just one column." She squeezes my hand. "He's big, Peter, so be good."

"How can someone so big be so short?"

She smiles. "Stop."

As Mr. Papp approaches, I see beads of sweat teeming on the bridge of his nose. "Miss Mills, do you have a minute?"

"Yes, Mr. Papp," Ebony says.

He flips through several pages of notes. "I'm not, uh, familiar with you, so, uh, is this show representative of your work?"

"For the most part," Ebony says.

"Hmm." He flips a few more pages and makes a notation. "It's not exactly 'black art,' is it?"

Ebony nearly squeezes all the blood out of my hand. "No, Mr. Papp, it's art by a black woman—there's a difference."

"Hmm" is all Mr. Papp can reply.

What a prick! I'll bet he doesn't ask white artists, "It's not exactly 'white art,' is it?"

"Let's see, uh, where are you from?" He adjusts his glasses, releasing that blob of sweat down his face. If I had a handkerchief, I wouldn't give it to him.

"I'm from Brooklyn, Mr. Papp."

Mr. Papp blinks twice slowly. "As in, uh, Brooklyn, New York?"

"Yes."

Mr. Papp looks as if he's going to swallow his bow tie.

He makes another notation and shakes his head. "I see."

"Do you, Mr. Papp?"

He looks up. "Pardon me?"

"Do you really see the art around you?"

Yes! Ebony is on the offensive, and Mr. Papp is in for it.

Mr. Papp removes his glasses and shines them on a sleeve. "Miss Mills, I have been doing this for much longer than you've been an artist, so, yes, I do see the art around me."

"Do you see art, or do you want to see 'black art,' whatever 'black art' is?"

He replaces his glasses. "You are black, are you not?"

"Since birth, but my art isn't. Art is art, Mr. Papp."

He smiles at me. "Is it? Hmm."

"Does it bother you, Mr. Papp, that I'm a young, attractive, African-American woman from Brooklyn?"

"Um, er, uh, no, of course not, but I was under the impression that—"

"Under what impression, Mr. Papp?"

He rudely flips through more pages. "Never mind. Uh, where did you study?"

"Hofstra."

He looks up sharply. "Hofstra?"

"Yes."

"Hmm. Really." He scribbles more notes. "So you're basically self-taught."

"No, Mr. Papp. I studied under several *local* artists."

"Such as?"

"Laszlo Tar, for example."

"*The* Laszlo Tar?"

"Yes. We spent many days painting watercolors in Huntington." She winks at me. "That's out on Long Island, Mr. Papp."

If this weren't so important for Ebony's career, I would be letting this guy have it. What a putz!

"I know where Huntington is, Miss Mills." He shuts his notebook and stows it inside his jacket.

"Are you staying for the unveiling of the tapestry, Mr. Papp?" Ebony asks.

"No. I've seen all I need to see."

Uh-oh. He's going to skip the grand finale?

"Oh, Mr. Papp, I think you see only what you want to see," Ebony says. My thoughts exactly. "Before you go, Mr. Papp, I'd like to ask *you* a question."

He turns, but doesn't speak.

"Mr. Papp, can you name the last African-American female artist to have her own show anywhere in New York City?"

"Hmm." Mr. Papp seems on the verge of giving an answer several times, but he only shines his glasses once again.

"You can't, can you? Well, from now on, you'll remember this moment, so that when anyone asks you that question, you'll be able to say that the last African-American female artist to have her own show anywhere in New York City was Ebony Mills of Brooklyn, New York, who was educated at Hofstra University and studied under Laszlo Tar."

Mr. Papp leaves us without so much as a good-bye.

Ebony's shoulders slump. "I'm in trouble now."

I hug her tightly. "No, you're not. Look around you. The place is packed. People are smiling, pointing, discussing, talking, and laughing. You're moving them, Ebony. I mean, Robert De Niro is here! He was standing right next to me!"

"He's come to several of my shows, and he always buys something with a boat in it."

"He does?"

"He has a boat, too, you know. But I was so rude to Mr. Papp."

"As you should have been." I hold her away from me at arm's length.

"Look, everyone here is having a good time, and I'm glad Mr. Papp left. Your mama is here having a ball. Destiny is networking. Sir John is here. I'm here."

"I know, but—"

"So what if Mr. Papp writes some pap for tomorrow's paper? This show is a hit, and deep down inside, you know it."

She bites her lips and rolls her eyes. "Okay, it's a hit, but it isn't a home run yet, Peter. There's one more piece of art to reveal. Get a good spot in front of the tapestry." She kisses me tenderly. "It's time for the unveiling."

I don't have to fight to get a good spot, but within minutes, I'm surrounded by the curious in front of the tapestry, Sir John on one side, Candace on the other.

"This will be glorious," Sir John tells me.

"You really don't know what's under there?" Candace asks.

"No."

"She's keeping secrets from you, Peter. Better watch out." She grabs my hand. "You okay?"

"I'm fine."

"You look like you haven't slept in weeks."

"I'm fine."

"You want me to talk to her?"

"About what?"

"About keeping you up at night. She's wearing you out, boy."

"That's all right."

Because I don't think it's Ebony keeping me up nights.

While Destiny stands at one end of the tapestry, her golden hands holding a golden cord, Ebony stands behind a podium and taps the microphone three times until the crowd settles down. "Thank you all so much for coming, especially on such a dark and stormy night. I hope you've enjoyed yourselves as much as I have. And now I'd like to show you my last piece." She nods at Destiny, and Destiny pulls the cord. "I call it *Original Love*."

And there we are, Ebony and I when we were young, drifting along in a small wooden boat as two medieval lovers holding hands, golden waves around us, nothing but the infinite horizon in front of us. It reminds me of *The Lady of Shallott*, a painting I used to have my students analyze whenever we studied Tennyson, but that painting definitely didn't have a young black girl and a freckled white boy holding hands. Her lacy headdress frames her face perfectly, and her burgundy flowing robe forms to her body so seductively. And I look like the knight I've always wanted to be, my chain mail armor gleaming bright silver, a sword resting by my side.

"Remarkable," Sir John says.

"She got your freckles right," Candace says. "And she even gave you a chin."

Tears escape my eyes. She got everything right. Everything, right down to the delirious smile I have on my face. She gave me the words to write, and I gave her the pictures to draw. Words and pictures—that's us.

Then Ebony motions to me, and while flashbulbs blind me, I pose in front of *Original Love*, one arm around Ebony, my original love, and the other around Destiny, the precious product of that original love.

22

After a fairly busy night of sighs, sweat, and smiles, I watch Ebony sleep until morning. Like her art, I can't take my eyes off her, even though my eyes feel as if they're rotting out of my head. I have to get some serious rest or I'm liable to start hallucinating.

When Destiny brings the newspaper to us the next morning, Morton Papp's column on top, Ebony tenses up, especially when Destiny announces, "I don't understand a word that man said, but I know he isn't being very nice."

After Destiny leaves, Ebony and I stare at the headline: " 'Neo-Expressionism' Meets Local Black Art." It doesn't sound too bad to me, but Ebony pulls a pillow over her head and groans, "I'm doomed. He used the 'L-word.' "

"And local is bad?"

She doesn't stir.

"You want me to read it out loud to you?"

"No, I'll read it," Ebony groans. She throws the pillow across the room and snatches the paper, shaking it out. I watch her lips move and occasionally hear bursts of Morton Papp's drivel: " '. . . incomprehensible narrative function of her work is a cross between Abstract Expressionism and Pop Art in the rightly neglected field of landscape . . . somewhat creative, somewhat moving portraits without movement . . . too grayed and tonal, leaving the viewer with spiritual alienation . . . primitive Cubist sterility . . . nontraditional linearity.' "

From what I've just heard, I don't understand a word either.

She balls up the paper and throws it toward her vanity. "I'm doomed," she says again. "I've just been branded 'local,' and I only do 'black art.' "

"He's just one critic, Ebony."

"Yeah, but other critics follow his lead. Just two years ago, the critics were gushing about me after a show at Matthew Marks, but now their tastes will change."

"He can't be that powerful."

"He is."

"Well, maybe people haven't forgotten all those glowing reviews from before."

She hits me with my own pillow. "People only care about the last thing you say or do anymore, Peter. They don't care where you've been. We live in the 'What have you done for me lately?' century, Peter. They've already forgotten."

"What about Sir John?" She wouldn't let me see the catalogue he left with her last night, but I didn't push it. She was more wired than I've ever seen her before.

"Sir John," she whispers. "He wants the landscapes, the tapestry, and every watercolor except for one."

"Which one?"

"One I did of your daddy's boat, but the fact is, I want to keep the landscapes and the tapestry or have them put up permanently in a museum somewhere. Who's going to see them if they're on some wall in Sir John's castle?"

"He owns a castle?"

"No, I was just trying to make a point. The only 'museum' on this planet exhibiting my work is over in some barrister's house in England, an audience of one, Peter. How would you like it if all your books were bought by one person?"

Good point.

"This review pretty much tells other galleries, who may have been interested in acquiring my works for their collections before, that unless you want someone local and black, don't give Ebony Mills a second thought."

The phone rings.

"Want me to get it?"

"No," Ebony says. "Destiny will get it."

A few moments later, Destiny rips up the stairs and breathlessly hands the phone to Ebony.

Ebony takes the phone. "Who is it?"

For the first time since I've met my daughter, she can't speak, her eyes wider than wide.

"This is Ebony." She listens for several moments, and even her eyes widen. "Thank you." She motions for me to get a pen and paper. I find an envelope and a pen on her dresser, handing them to her. "Uh-huh." She scribbles rapidly, and when I try to see what she's written, she covers it with her hand. "I'll make sure DC Moore has it delivered directly to you when the show ends in December." She smiles. "No, thank *you*, Mr. De Niro." She clicks off the phone, tosses it to the end of the bed, and lies back. "That was Robert De Niro, and he wants several of the watercolors."

My heart sinks a little. "He wants the *Argo* watercolor, doesn't he?"

Ebony squints. "How do you know that?"

"We were, uh, looking at it together last night."

Destiny grabs me. "You talked to Robert De Niro?"

"Not exactly. I just happened to be standing there, and—"

"What did he say?" Destiny interrupts.

"Just that, uh, that 'Argo' was a good name for a boat."

Destiny grabs the phone, says, "I have to tell everybody this," and dashes out of the room.

"It wasn't much of a conversation," I say.

Ebony blinks. "Robert De Niro wants a piece of me." She giggles. "And no offense to Sir John, but having Robert De Niro want my work means so much more. You know he's been feeding rescue workers at his restaurant for free? He should be mayor."

"Giuliani seems to be doing a good job."

"Yeah."

Destiny rushes back to us, phone extended to Ebony. "Someone from Bill Maynes Gallery."

Ebony sits up straighter. "Hello?" She scribbles furiously on the envelope. "Get me more paper! No, get me a catalogue from last night!"

The phone rings nonstop all morning, and from what I can gather from Ebony's side of the conversations, a number of notable New York galleries had sent representatives to her show last night, and now her works are being parceled out all over New York. By lunchtime, every piece in the catalogue has been marked to go somewhere else. Every single piece!

"I don't believe it," she says. "I thought that review would kill me."

"Maybe just having a review by Morton Papp is the key, almost as if having a negative review from him has the opposite effect. I've seen that happen to books, too. A decent book gets read and trashed by a prominent reviewer, and then sales go up from the controversy."

"You might be right."

I give her my best De Niro squint. "What about Sir John?"

She waves a hand in the air. "Oh, he'll be the happiest man on earth now."

"Huh?"

"He's been waiting for this moment, Peter. He owns most of what I've done to this point, right?"

"Right."

"So now all of that has just skyrocketed in value. His investment in me is finally paying off."

"Oh, yeah." A man is about to be happy because he can't have what he wants, which makes sense in the strangest way.

She rises from the bed and goes to the window, feeling the windowpane with her hand. "It's warmer today, isn't it?"

"I guess. I haven't been outside."

"Let's go out on the *Argo*, maybe take her for a sail to celebrate."

"Well, um, I haven't ever sailed her solo, so—"

She shakes her head. "Your daughter will sail us, Peter." She picks up the phone. "And I want Mama to come, too." She dials. "Mama? Get Gladys to take you down to the yacht club." She listens a bit, her eyes narrowing, a quick glance to me. "I guess so, but . . . No, I understand." She turns away from me. "It makes sense, Mama. I told you that I understood. In an hour, okay? Bye." She turns to me. "Well, get dressed, Peter. We're going sailing."

And what else? I want to ask, but I'm learning never to question the connivings of the Mills women. Something is definitely up, and it involves me.

Destiny, Ebony, and I arrive at the yacht club just in time to hear an argument between Candace and Gladys beside Gladys's van. I wave at Aunt Wee Wee, who's strapped in to the front passenger seat.

"I'm advising strongly against this, Mrs. Mills," Gladys says. "What if something happens?"

"Oh, poo, Gladys," Candace says. "If you're so worried, you can come with us, but I am getting on that boat, one way or another."

I mentally measure Candace's chair, and there's no way it would make it into the *Argo*'s galley. Will I have to strap her to a bench?

"But what if, God forbid, the boat should . . ." Gladys doesn't finish her sentence, and I see the reason why. Destiny is staring daggers at her. "Okay, okay, I just want everyone here to know that I, as Mrs. Mills's caretaker, think this is a very bad idea."

"Can I go, too?" Aunt Wee Wee calls out.

"No!" Gladys shouts. "Most definitely not!"

Candace looks up at me. "What do you think, Peter? Think it could hold all of us?"

"Sure," I say. I turn to Gladys. "And I'll put life vests on Aunt Wee Wee and Candace the second we get on board." I turn to Destiny. "What's the weather supposed to be like?"

"Steady winds at eight to ten, no rain in sight," she says, sounding so much—too much—like my father.

I turn to Gladys. "We'll be fine, and you can always go with us. We'll have plenty of room."

"I don't know," Gladys says. "I've never been on a boat like that. Are we going to go far?"

"Just to Connecticut and back," Destiny says. "Though if the winds are right, we might end up in Boston or something."

"Or Africa," Candace says.

"Oh, I'm definitely not going now," Gladys says. "When should I come back to collect you?"

Candace smiles. "We'll call you."

Ebony motions to Destiny, and Destiny helps Aunt Wee Wee out of the van. "We need to get this show on the road."

I squat in front of Candace. "The chair can't go, so I'll have to carry you."

Candace smiles. "I was hoping you'd say that." She looks at her hands. "You'll have to, um, put the bag up in my lap first." She searches my eyes. "I'm sorry."

"Don't be," I say.

"I'm such a bother."

"You're not a bother, Candace." I extricate the colostomy bag from under her seat, taking care not to pull on the tube attached to her stomach, resting it on her lap, then smoothing her blanket on top. "Is that okay?"

"Yes."

Then I collect Candace in my arms, feeling the weight of her frailty in my heart as I carry her to a Zodiac that Destiny has warming up. She can't weigh more than eighty pounds. "What have you been eating?" I ask.

"The same old shit Gladys keeps making."

"You need to go on a diet, Mama."

She rests her head on my shoulder. "Tell me anything."

The cruise to the *Argo* draws a few stares from other boaters on Huntington Bay, but I don't care. I have my entire family in one boat for the first time in my life, the sun shining, the breezes light, the clouds looking like, well, candy floss topped with double cream. Sir John was right. The clouds around here are delicious.

Once everyone is on board and safely vested, Candace and Aunt Wee Wee refuse to go belowdecks.

"I want to see everything," Candace says. "Ain't nothing to see down there."

"And I want to smoke," Aunt Wee Wee says.

Destiny goes below and returns with a small harness rigged up with bungee cord, looping it over Aunt Wee Wee's shoulders and attaching hooks at the ends of the bungee cords to a rail. "The Captain used to do this to me when I was little, Aunt Wee Wee," Destiny says. "And I'm still here, right?"

"I look a fool, girl," Aunt Wee Wee cackles.

"You can still move around," Destiny says, "but if the seas get rough, you just sit down and hold on to the rail, okay?"

"You the captain," Aunt Wee Wee says. "Can I smoke now?"

Ebony sits behind Candace on a bench seat built into the stern, leaving Destiny and me to sail the boat. "Um, let's run a check first," I say.

Destiny salutes me. "Yes, Cap'n."

"You're the real captain, Destiny. I'll be your hand on this trip."

"Really?"

"Really."

"Cool."

After checking all the gauges on the Volvo and turning her over, we walk the deck checking lines and sails.

"C'mon, y'all," Candace says. "Pull up the anchor or something."

"Everything looks okay," Destiny says to me at the bow. "But you already know everything's okay, because the Captain wouldn't have it any other way."

And then it dawns on me. The *Argo* hasn't sailed since the day before my father died. He no doubt had it shipshape and ready for a sail the following day.

"Where should I steer her once we get past Eaton's Neck?" Destiny asks.

Let the boat go where it wants to go, Pete. "Just let her run," I say, echoing the Captain.

"Cool. Maybe we can race the New London ferry."

"Maybe."

After disengaging from our mooring and pulling up anchor, Destiny steers us through Huntington Bay following the channel markers. Aunt Wee Wee sits and dangles her legs over the edge, one hand gripping the rail, the other holding a cigarette. Ebony holds Candace, occasionally pointing to shore, while I walk around trying to remember what to do to "properly sail a boat." It's frustrating, because I simply can't remember a thing. I know it will come back to me, but I feel so clumsy. *Well, don't try so hard. It'll get us there. It's seen more days at sea than you.*

Once out into the open water past Eaton's Neck Point, Destiny cuts the engines, and we work the sails. I watch my hands doing things, things I had thought I had forgotten, and I'm doing them without thinking, Destiny smiling, Ebony holding her mama, Aunt Wee Wee holding on for dear life, and me pulling lines and turning winches watching the mainsail billow out like a crescent moon and we're here, we're out here, we're sailing again on Long Island Sound. I can't help but whoop a bit, like the kid I used to be.

I even go to the bowsprit and yawp a little, for Walt's sake, while sprays of the waves freckle my face with cold water.

I slide back to the stern. "Is anyone cold? There are more blankets below."

"We're fine," Ebony says. She looks all around her. "On such a beautiful day, why aren't there more boats out here with us?"

I shrug. "Their loss."

I smile at Candace. "Having fun?"

"Yes, but where's your daughter taking us?"

"Wherever the boat wants to go."

I spell Destiny at the helm so she can get our lunch ready in the galley, and I let the wind dictate my course, keeping the bowline taut, the mainsail steady. We might be cutting through the waves at ten, maybe fifteen knots, I don't know. The Captain always kept up with that sort of thing. And the *Argo* performs magnificently. You'd never know it has been over ten years since her last sail. I'm only beginning to get my sea legs, but the *Argo* is stretching hers out for a good long run.

This would be the life!

After a lunch of sandwiches, chips, and sodas, Destiny takes over, steering us southeast in a lazy arc towards Smithtown Bay to get us back home.

"Why don't you bring your daddy up here, get him some sun?" Candace asks.

I think she's kidding, so I don't answer.

"I'm serious, Peter. Bring him up."

She's not kidding. "Isn't that a little morbid?" I ask.

"No more morbid than the way you've been acting lately," she says. "Peter, have you really said good-bye to that man?"

How can you say good-bye to a man to whom you barely said hello?

"I had trouble sleeping for years after Ebony's daddy died. You hear me? I said *years*, Peter. It wasn't until I took down that Christmas tree that I could finally get a decent night's sleep."

"I don't think I'm ready."

Candace squints. "You want to start sleeping again?"

"Of course, but—"

"Then let the man go."

I look at Ebony. "What should I do?"

"Let's . . . let's let him get off the boat, Peter," Ebony says. "It's the perfect day for it, isn't it?"

It is a beautiful day, but I'm not ready for this. "I'd rather not today."

"When then?" Candace asks. "There's no time like the present, I say, to keep us from living in the past. Time to move on and get on with it. Even your daddy would agree with me."

I look up at the seagulls shadowing us and think of the albatross the

Ancient Mariner wore. Are the Captain's remains my albatross? I look at Ebony. "What do you think?"

"It's your decision, Peter, but we all feel this has to be done," Ebony says.

I look at Destiny, who has tears streaming from her eyes. She wipes at them with her free hand, never taking her eyes off the horizon. "Today is a good day, Daddy. We've taken him out for one last sail. He's been waiting a long time for this."

I look around at the soft swells, the puffy clouds, and the slanting sunlight. *It'll get us there.* Is this the place, Captain? Are we finally there? I choke down a sob and go below. I trace his name on the nameplate before using a screwdriver to remove the wooden box from its holder. It's heavy, heavier than it ought to be. I turn to look up the galley stairs, hesitating. "I know this is what you wanted to happen," I whisper. "I'm just sorry it took so long."

Then I kiss the top of the urn, and the sob escapes. "I should have kissed you more."

"Need any help, Daddy?" Destiny calls.

I've had all the help I've ever needed, and it's mainly in this box in my hands and up on deck. "No!" I call up. "Be up in a minute!"

I walk to the Captain's berth and close the door. I set the box in his chair and stand back. "Captain, Ebony and I are getting married this spring, and if you were still here, you'd be my best man. You've always been my best man." I can't stop the tears. "I didn't understand you, Captain, and that was the problem. I couldn't figure out what made you tick, you know? I was just a kid." I wipe my eyes on my sleeve. "But I know now that you tried, and I also know that I'm a lot more like you than I'm willing to admit, and I just wanted to . . . I just wanted to thank you, Captain. Thank you for being my father."

I pick up the urn and leave the Captain's berth, trudging up the galley stairs into the sunlight. When Destiny looks at me, she bursts into tears, and I start all over again.

"Should I . . . should we anchor first?" Destiny asks after she recovers.

I find my voice. "Are you kidding? We have to be doing eighteen, maybe twenty knots. The Captain always loved to race."

She nods and smiles. "Except we never won any races."

I exhale deeply. "I think we won every time."

I walk to the stern and see the water shooting away from us, our wake fierce on both sides. *Time to rest, time to rest,* I pray in my mind, *God give the Captain time to rest.* I hear the Navy Hymn from the Captain's funeral, sung by so many of his shipmates, I feel the wind firm on my back, I taste the salt air, and I see infinity all around me. I unlatch the top of the box and see the dust of my father. *You do look like shells, Captain, silver and gray shells.* I tip the urn away from me and watch swirls of dust leaping toward Long Island Sound, watch them dance in the air with the seagulls, watch them floating down to the surface of the waves. *Rolling you on, rolling you on . . . home.*

"Good-bye, Captain." I turn into the wind. No. That's not a proper good-bye for him. I turn back toward the setting sun. "Good-bye . . . Dad."

And later, as Destiny guides the *Argo* home hugging the shoreline, I hug Ebony to me.

And later that night, I sleep like a baby, dreaming of the sea.

23

The following Monday is Veteran's Day, and because of September 11, it takes on a whole new meaning for us. Since we have nowhere to lay flowers for my father, we go to West Shore Beach instead to throw bread to the seagulls. There's something so peaceful about it, so simple, that it makes me wonder if the Captain has made it to the Atlantic Ocean yet. He may get to go back to all those places he visited back in the forties.

The next day, though, life comes crashing back as a plane goes down in Rockaway Beach, Queens. "Turn on the TV," Candace calls to say. "They got another one."

No wonder I don't watch TV anymore, I think, as I view the wreckage of a plane, this one in a residential neighborhood not too different from the one I grew up in. Destiny drifts in from the kitchen, and Ebony slips down the stairs, joining me at the couch. No one speaks. Was it a missile? Was it another suicide flight? What possible target is in Queens? Were they aiming for the Statue of Liberty? What's going on?

"Two hundred and sixty were on board," the reporter says, fire and rescue crews flying by him, "including five infants held by their parents."

I feel two sets of hands holding mine.

"We have learned that the pilot sent no distress call, and there are no confirmed terrorist threats, but the FBI has yet to rule anything out at this time."

Over the next twenty-four hours, we stumble around in a fog. Neither Ebony nor I work on our novel. Destiny stays off the phone. We don't go out, and we barely eat. Ebony calls Candace, but they really don't say much to each other. No one seems to be sleeping except me, which is a switch, but the dreams I have—of fire, smoke, and panic—keep me from sleeping the whole night through.

When they examine the voice recorder from the plane and release the news that the plane went down due to wake turbulence, I feel guilty about breathing a sigh of relief that it wasn't "another" plane. Two hundred and sixty-five souls just left us because of an accident, and I don't feel the shock or the horror that I felt on September 11. Is this how I'm going to gauge every disaster from here on? I hope not, but now I know how the generation before me felt when JFK was assassinated.

To take our minds off the news from Queens, Destiny, Ebony, and I plan our wedding at Bethel.

"No frills," Ebony says. "I'm too old for frills."

"I agree," I say. "We'll just keep it simple."

Destiny doesn't agree. "You two are no fun."

"Well, what do you have in mind?" Ebony asks.

"Okay," Destiny begins, waving her hands, "we'll dress Mama in a kente cloth dashiki."

Ebony laughs. "A dashiki?"

"Yes, a dashiki, and you'll have a huge African headdress on and be barefoot."

"Oh, Lord, I'll need a pedicure," Ebony laughs.

"What's so funny, Mama?"

"Nothing. Go on."

"Daddy will wear a pure white linen suit with a tie that matches your dress."

"Will I be barefoot?" I can't resist asking.

"Oh, no, Daddy. I've seen your feet." She makes a face. "You'll have to wear white bucks or something."

"With a little kente Swoosh!" Ebony shouts.

Destiny folds her arms. "Mama, I've been planning your wedding ever since I was a little girl, so hear me out, okay?"

"Okay," Ebony says. "As long as there are no elephants. Or giraffes. Bethel isn't big enough for elephants and giraffes. Or lions. No, they'd tear up the carpet."

Destiny turns from Ebony to me. "Mama just doesn't understand, but I know you do. We think alike."

I doubt it. "So, will there be African drummers?"

Destiny smiles. "Yes! At least fifty, and instead of that crusty old wedding song, they'll jam to some ancient African rhythms that no one's heard for centuries. And it won't be a procession, it'll be a dance line, like on that old show you two used to watch, what was it called?"

"*Soul Train?*" Now *I'm* laughing. "Destiny, please. Remember your grandma and Aunt Wee Wee would have to go dancing down that aisle, too."

Destiny frowns. "Oh yeah. But Aunt Wee Wee can dance. I've seen her. Just not very fast. Hmm. We'll just have to have some fine African studs carry them! Daddy, you're a genius."

Ebony shakes her head. "Look, if you want all that for *your* wedding, your daddy and I will spring for it, just not in Huntington, okay? Or on Long Island, for that matter. I don't want folks anywhere talking forever about 'that African wedding.' Now, let's get down to planning the *real* wedding."

While Destiny pouts, I pull out that folded, creased, smudged copy of "Original Love," the poem Ebony wrote me almost twenty years ago. I hand it to Ebony. "Maybe we could use this somewhere in the ceremony."

She unfolds it with Destiny looking over her shoulder. "You saved it?"

"Yes. I'd even like to start the book with it, if you don't mind. I think it's especially fitting."

She mouths the first stanza. "I can't believe you kept it all these years."

"It was something worth holding on to." It was the only thing worth holding on to at the time. "Maybe you could read it to me sometime during the service."

Ebony smiles. "Or you could read it to me."

"Or I could read it to the both of you," Destiny says. "You know, while you're standing up there waiting for the kiss part."

I look at Ebony, and Ebony says, "Okay. Let's hear you read it."

Destiny clears her throat and reads: " 'My soul loves you endlessly . . . my whole life even before I knew you, you were what I wrote and hoped, things my day and night dreams were made of, original love.' " She looks up. "What do you think?"

I get a chill. It's almost as if Ebony wrote that for our destiny and for our *Destiny* as well. "I like it. It sounds right."

"I agree," Ebony says. "It's a wonderful idea."

"Ooh," Destiny says, "I really like this part: 'I wrote your name up there . . . in clouds.' I used to do that, Daddy. Whenever I was lying on the deck of the boat, I would look for your name in the clouds. Even saw a *P* once." She looks back at the poem. "Where was I? Oh, '. . . said it to myself out loud, made you more real to me, again and again and again, I craved you way back then.' " She blinks. "Look at my arms. I've got chill bumps."

Ebony rubs her own arms. "Me, too."

"Mama, maybe you should have been a writer, too."

My thoughts exactly, and in a very short while, she's going to know what I've decided.

"Speaking of that," Ebony says, turning to me, "how's our Desiree novel coming?"

I shake my head. I've been thinking about this for weeks, and it's about time I let her know. "I haven't added a word to that book since I got here."

"What? What have you been doing then, Peter?"

I bite my lip. "Sneaking peeks at what you've written."

Ebony's eyes pop.

"And I've come to the conclusion that our book should be written by you, Ebony. I've wanted Desiree to fade away ever since I got here, and with your writing, you've given me the perfect opportunity. It's time for Desiree to retire."

"Why?" Destiny asks. "Isn't she what your editor is expecting?"

"And that's what you have a contract for, right?" Ebony adds.

"True, but I think he'll understand that the *she* he really wants is you."

Ebony drums her fingers on the table. "I don't know, Peter, I mean, that's your book."

I shake my head and take her hands. "No, Ebony. It's always been your book, right from the very beginning. You inspired it. I've just been writing an extended outline based on that inspiration." I smile. "Besides, with your newfound fame and glory, it will sell, and it will sell well."

"But, what about—"

I squeeze her hands. "Henry is a practical man, and the publishing industry isn't exactly cooking right now. He'll see that *Promises to Keep* has a much better shot of being successful with your picture on the back flap."

"But you wrote it! I'm just following along adding things here and there."

"And I'll continue to write it, as long as you continue to rewrite it with that strong, pure, crystal-clear voice of yours. Some voices just tell stories better. I hope you understand that."

"I don't know whether to be flattered or sad."

I smile and pull her to me, settling her on my lap. "Be flattered." I look at Destiny watching us intently. "Destiny, I fell in love with your mama the first moment I ever saw her, and I fell in love with her all over again when I read what she wrote about the first moment I ever saw her." I kiss Ebony on the lips. "And readers are going to fall in love with your voice from the very first sentence, which I hope will be this poem."

"I don't know what to say." She kisses me tenderly. "You really want it to be this way?"

"It feels right." I squeeze her thigh, and I whisper, "And so does this."

"*Puh-lease* make me a little sister," Destiny pleads. "I promise I'll be available to babysit."

I look at Ebony. "She heard?"

"Evidently."

Apparently Destiny doesn't have my inability to hear. "Do we really want another one like her?"

"Do you?"

"Maybe a little boy?"

"I'd settle for a brother," Destiny says. "As long as I get to dress him, it's fine by me."

In early December, Ebony and I have finished a rough draft of *Promises to Keep*. After a night of trying to make us a son—three times, as a matter of fact—Ebony had convinced me to keep my narrative in the novel. "It has to be written by both of us, Peter," she had said. "Our story should be written by us."

So, rough draft in hand, we have a group editing session at Candace's house with four very willing readers. They sit on the couch in the living room beginning with Gladys and ending with Candace in her wheelchair, Aunt Wee Wee with a magnifying glass and Destiny in between.

Candace, then, has the "last word." Ebony hovers over her mama, making marks with a red pen, while I sift through what four pairs of eyes have sifted through for mistakes and make corrections to the file on my laptop. Everything is swimming along fine for the first hour or so until Gladys slows down and is the only one reading.

"C'mon, Gladys," Candace says, "don't keep us waiting."

Gladys looks at Ebony. " 'Whoa' is all I can say." She hands the page to Aunt Wee Wee.

I look at the last corrected copy to find out what's causing the holdup. I smile. It's my first visit to Ebony's room.

Aunt Wee Wee giggles and scribbles something on the page before handing it to Destiny. "I just knew that's what happened when it got so quiet."

"When what just happened?" Candace asks.

"You'll see," Aunt Wee Wee says as she snatches the next page from Gladys.

Destiny's eyes pop, and she looks at Ebony. "For real, Mama?"

Ebony nods. "For real."

Destiny hands the page to Candace. "Gross."

This is what I'm worried about. Ebony and I decided that if Candace has any problem with any part of the novel, we'd either edit it to death or delete it entirely.

"Hmm," Candace says. She wrinkles up her lips. "Works for me."

"Really?" Gladys says. "It does?"

"Hell," Candace says, "it's only natural."

Ebony hands the page to me, and I see nothing but a tiny comment from Aunt Wee Wee: "I was never asleep, Pete, and don't you ever forget it."

The reading slows down again when we get to the scene under the deck, and after the scene ends, I feel all eyes on me.

"You sure you want that in there, Daddy?" Destiny asks.

"I'm sure."

Candace nods. "You were a tough kid, Peter."

"Thank you."

We intentionally left out the part in the Cave, mainly to spare Candace the expected horror of seeing her daughter's "first time" in print, so the reading flies along until Gladys gets to my description of Candace as "Foxy Brown." Gladys spends a solid five minutes adding to Candace's description, even running her comments on to the back of the page. Aunt Wee Wee asks for more paper, and by the time Destiny's through, Candace has four pages to read while we try to read her.

At first, Candace blinks. Then she smiles. Eventually, she laughs and nods her head. "You have me down pat, Peter," she says.

"But you didn't read what we wrote!" Gladys yells.

"You ain't the ones writing the book, so why do I have to read what I know are lies? Peter wrote the truth. I *am* Foxy Brown."

"Oh, I think he left out an awful lot," Destiny says.

"He wrote the truth," Candace says. "And I should know. I'm practically his mama. Now, let's get on with it."

When the novel gets to prom night, the room gets silent again, and the pages pass into my hands untouched. After a break for some finger sandwiches—to which I add liberal sprinkles of salt and pepper—our readers begin the part of the novel where Ebony and I part ways. They first read about me in college, sending letters and making phone calls. Then they switch back to Ebony down in Virginia having Destiny.

Ebony hands the next fifty pages to me completely mark-free.

But when we get to 2001, the reading session almost becomes a race to the finish, and Candace just can't keep up.

"Slow down, y'all, damn! This book is like good whiskey. It shouldn't be guzzled. It should be sipped."

Gladys finishes first, dries her eyes with a tissue, hugs Ebony and me, and leaves without a word.

"Y'all better write more books together," Candace says. "I like a quiet Gladys."

Aunt Wee Wee gives us a thumbs-up and heads to her room to smoke.

Destiny smiles a lot, kisses Ebony, and stands in front of me.

"Well?" I ask.

"Daddy," she whispers, "I hope one day to find a man like you."

She then takes Ebony's car keys and disappears, leaving us with Candace, the last batch of the novel sitting in a pile to her right.

"Are you getting tired, Mama? You can finish tomorrow."

"No, no, I'm all right." She smiles at me. "Thanks for not making me into a complete bitch, Peter."

I don't know if saying "you're welcome" to that question is all that appropriate.

She rubs her eyes. "My eyes are getting weary, though, so Ebony, why don't you read me the last few pages."

The last few pages, written at four this morning, both of us writing with tears in our eyes, are in Ebony's hands. I hope I can listen without crying again.

"Um, Mama," Ebony says, "we wrote this last part together."

"Makes sense," Candace says, her eyes closed. "You all started off together, you should end together."

"Yeah, but I don't know if I can read this, Mama."

I reach out my hand for the pages, and Ebony places them in my hands.

"Peter is going to read them to you, Mama."

Candace opens her eyes. "Is it that bad?"

"No, Mama. It's just that . . . you'll see."

I take a sip of water and clear my throat. Maybe I won't be as affected now as I was this morning.

"Twenty-five years ago, we fell in love at a time when our love wasn't accepted by society, but we didn't know that at the time. We were young, innocent, and naïve, and we didn't know any better or care what anyone thought. That is the ultimate power of love: to focus so strongly on one person that the entire world disappears. Now that we've been reunited, we see that our love still isn't completely accepted by society, and though we're no longer young or innocent, we still don't care what anyone thinks. We don't consider ourselves pioneers—just survivors. There are thousands of other couples out there who made it through without twenty years of sorrowful separation, and to them we say: 'You all are the real pioneers, the real survivors who really know what love is all about.' "

I pause to catch my breath. Here comes the hard part.

"We have so many people to thank, and we pray that our feeble words do justice to them. First and foremost, we'd like to thank God for looking out for us, for bringing us back together, and for giving us loving parents."

A lump forms in my throat.

"We'd also like to thank our ancestors, who fought to make our futures more glorious than their own and taught us the true meaning of sacrifice and devotion; our fathers, who fought for this country and taught us the

*true meaning of discipline and loyalty; and our mothers, who fought for
our happiness and taught us the true meaning of freedom and compas-
sion. We could do nothing without them, and we are all that we are because of them. We have, as the Bible says, 'a goodly heritage,' and we
hope we'll do our collective heritages proud."*

I blink away several tears.

*"And Mama, for you are truly our Mama, we know God has a special
field in heaven for you to run around in and plant flowers and grow the
most beautiful garden, because we bloomed in your garden here on earth.
We can never thank you enough, but we're going to try."*

I take a deep breath. "That's the end of it."
Tears stream from Candace's eyes, but she's smiling. "No, Peter, it's
only the beginning."

I am a bundle of nerves when Ebony and I enter Olympus Publishing
and ride the elevator up to Henry's office, and if it weren't for the lady
beside me, I don't know if I could do this. We are about to deliver a
book I didn't contract for, and a somewhat literary nonfiction novel at
that. We are about to give Henry the novel based on the outline he red-
lined three months ago. We are about to end Desiree Holland's career.
And we may have to return the money from the advance. Good thing I
haven't spent any of it. And if things go really badly with Henry, we may
have this deception follow us from publishing house to publishing
house, if we have to strike out on our own.
"You worry too much," Ebony whispers as we exit the elevator.
I nearly drop the satchel containing the manuscript. "It's in my nature."
"We'll be fine," she says. "Think good thoughts."
When Edith opens Henry's door for us, Ebony strides in first and ex-
tends a hand to Henry. "Hello, Mr. Milton. I'm Ebony Mills."
Henry takes her hand with both of his. "A pleasure, and please call
me Henry. I've heard and read so much about you." He motions to a
chair, and Ebony sits.
I set the satchel on Henry's desk, opening it and withdrawing the
manuscript. I want to hide the title page, but it's too late for any of that

now. I sit next to Ebony, my shoes tapping on the carpet. Ebony grabs my knee, and I stop tapping.

Henry picks up the title page, and I squeeze the life out of the chair arms. "Did you change the title on me, Pete?" Henry asks. " 'By Ebony and Peter . . . Underhill'? You two are getting married?"

"Yes," Ebony says. "This spring."

Henry blinks several times and waves the page in the air. "What's going on here, Pete?"

I want to explain everything to Henry, but Ebony finds her voice first. "Just read it, Henry."

Henry scans the first two pages. "This is your book, isn't it, Pete? This is the book from that outline."

Why do my eyelids choose this moment to start sweating? "Uh, yes, Henry, but with the addition of a better voice to tell it."

Henry blinks at me. "But what about the Desiree novel, the novel we've been paying you to write? What about that?"

There go my feet again. "There isn't one, um, Henry. There, uh, never was going to be one. My heart just wasn't in it." And my heart is threatening to burst!

"The old bait and switch," Henry says, and he starts to get up.

"With a better book," Ebony says, "one that I guarantee will sell."

Henry settles back in his chair and sighs. "You think so?"

"I know so," Ebony says. I wish I could be as confident.

"Well, as I told Pete before, there isn't a big market for literary nonfiction right now. There is, however, a burgeoning market for Desiree Holland, for relationship books, one that your future husband seems reluctant to tap."

Ebony leans forward. "But you haven't ever read the book yet, Henry. Give it a chance, that's all we're asking." She shrugs and smiles. "And if it's not something you believe in one hundred percent, we'll return the advance money today and take it elsewhere."

I look at the woman who once talked a man at Milldam Bait and Tackle into giving us ten cents apiece for thirteen scurvy-looking bunker, and I smile. She's at it again, only the stakes are much higher. I relax my grip on the chair arms.

"I'm sure there are other publishers in New York City with more open minds and deeper pockets," Ebony says.

Henry glances at the manuscript. "You're sure of this?"

Ebony smiles, and she takes my hand. "The day is young, Henry. Who knows where this book will end up by sundown?"

He leans forward. "Well, I'll only read the first chapter—"

"You'll have to read the first two," Ebony interrupts, "so you can hear both of our voices."

Henry looks at me. "Is that okay with you, Pete? Just the first two?"

He's going to read it! I could press my luck and go for Henry's holy three, but I don't. "The first two will do."

"For now," Ebony adds.

Then we watch Henry reading, his red pen dancing above the pages. The pen drops occasionally, but doesn't bite the page, though I can tell he really wants to bleed on it. I count the pages for lack of anything better to do, while Ebony rises to look out Henry's window, tapping the window in front of several startled pigeons.

"You have a unique voice, Miss Mills," Henry says, and he keeps turning the pages.

"Thank you, and please call me Ebony."

"You have a unique voice, Ebony," Henry says. "I read the review of your most recent show." He reads and turns another page. "Morton should be hung up by his suspenders and force-fed that bow tie of his until he writes the truth." More pages fly by. Have we hooked him?

"I love your view, Henry," Ebony says. "I might be tempted to paint it one day." She raises her eyebrows at me. "It's a little too linear for me, but I'll manage."

Henry's racing now, the pages fluttering like butterflies. "Do you have pictures?"

"Lots of pictures," Ebony says. "And art. I can get Sir John to send you some of my earlier works if you need them."

"We'll probably need them," Henry says.

Yes! I want to jump out of this chair and yawp!

Henry skims through to the end, reads the last page, nods, and stops. "This is good."

Ebony doesn't even turn from the window. "Good enough or just good?"

"With some more revisions, this could be a bestseller." He looks up at me. "But you already knew this, right, Pete?"

I can't find any words to say!

"Pete? You okay?"

"Um, yes, I'm fine." A bestseller? Is that even possible?

"There are three additions that I'd like to suggest to make this complete," Henry says. "First, you'll need to add another chapter near the end, Pete, something like 'Why I Wrote as Desiree.' We need to give her some closure, so to speak, and in doing so, we may give those books another boost. Those who read this book will be curious about those other two books and hopefully read them to get a deeper level of understanding."

"So Desiree can fade away?" I ask.

"Yes. Second, we may want to add a subtitle, something like 'An American Love Story.' "

Promises to Keep: An American Love Story. It sounds perfect! And no one is sucking down margaritas!

"And third, Ebony will have to design the cover."

There is a God!

Henry sits back and stares at the ceiling. "I see a collage on the cover of some old Polaroids of you two, perhaps a love letter, some of your earliest art from when you were in junior high. Do you still have some of those?"

"They're on the walls at my mama's house," Ebony says.

"Oh, and a picture of Ebony's mother and Pete's father, pictures of your old homes, the works."

"And the tapestry, and maybe a landscape or two." Ebony adds.

"You're the artist," Henry says with a smile. He stands and straightens the manuscript. "Now if you two will excuse me, I have to go see the publisher. I shouldn't be long."

As soon as Henry leaves, I rush to Ebony and kiss the life out of her. "You did it," I say.

"*We* did it, *Pete*," she says. "Doesn't it bother you to have him call you that?"

I hadn't even noticed. "No." It actually feels good to have someone call me that.

She turns to the window. "The city is waking back up, isn't it?"

I look down at the traffic, the movement, the sheer power of the American dream bustling beneath us. "This city will never die. It was just hibernating. It's hungry again."

Ebony pouts. "And so am I. Can we have pizza?"

"The greasier the better."

Henry returns only a few minutes later, and I feel as if the floor has dropped twenty feet. So quick? The publisher isn't interested? Now what?

"Relax," Ebony whispers. She smiles at Henry. "That was quick."

Henry shakes his head and sits in his chair. "So quick it's almost historic." He smiles at me. "Pete, the publisher absolutely loves the idea!"

The floor rises too fast, and I almost stumble. "Loves . . . the idea?"

"After I read her the revised title and the first two pages, she told me to stop, and she also told me to sign you two right away."

I return to my seat. "Right away?"

"As in now." He pulls out a sheaf of papers and begins writing. "You are to consider the money we already sent to you as part of an advance, and we need to negotiate a two-book deal pronto."

"Two?" I ask.

"Yes, two, Pete. I still think that *A Whiter Shade of Pale* has some promise, and the two of you could rewrite it together, right?"

"Right."

Henry turns to Ebony. "The publisher also suggested that we have pictures from your upcoming wedding to end the book. What do you think?"

Ebony laughs. "I'll start looking for kente cloth, Peter, if you get us some giraffes."

"What?" I laugh back. "You're not serious!"

"I sure am," Ebony says. "Destiny is usually right about these things."

24

I'm writing this log from the windswept stern of the Argo *while I add to my collection of freckles and Ebony steers us out of Long Island Sound around Montauk Point into the teeth of the Atlantic, seagulls hovering overhead. The* Argo *seems to love the open sea and shows no signs of her age. And despite misgivings about sailing to Barbados for our honeymoon, I'm getting to be a pretty decent sailor, and my shipmate, well, she'll always be better at the helm than me, because our daughter taught her everything my dad taught me.*

This same ocean that our ancestors crossed so long ago—willingly and unwillingly, on deck and chained below—this ocean seems infinite. We're just one little dot of humanity out here in all this infinity, yet I feel bigger and freer than I've ever felt before. What our ancestors must have seen—either the land of horror, or the land of promise, or both—from boats not much larger than this. The blood of this giant, this Atlantic, runs cold and bold, and neither of us cares if we make it to the Bahamas, or Barbados, or South America—as long as we're together, nothing can keep us apart.

I look behind us as Long Island slips away into the mist, and I wonder how I'll feel when I see land again, if I ever see land again. I'm no Odysseus, who planted his oar and put his sailing days behind him forever, oh, no. My true adventures have just begun.

I think about all my original loves and find that I have a long list. I love this old boat and its old captain, though I much prefer the sexy woman steering and showing me a whole lot of leg right now. I love my country and its people, who wake up after smoky nightmares and go about their business despite unimaginable sorrow. I love my old neighborhood, my old hometown, and my old friends, some of whom have left us in body but not in spirit. I love this ocean and its currents, its monstrous waves, and even its storms that remind us what it's like when the storms are through and life resumes once more.

With a beckoning finger, Ebony motions for me to join her at the helm.

"I'm almost done," I say.

"No, you're not," she says.

She knows me too well. "Just one more paragraph?"

She licks her lower lip. "Only if you write your hands all over me all night long." She lifts up her shirt, exposing her licorice gumdrop belly button and shakes her butt just right, the kente cloth tie I wore for the ceremony (and all those pictures) holding her wild hair back from her eyes. Her hair looks good wild and free like that, and I'm pretty sure that she didn't pack a curling iron.

"I'll try to write at least three chapters tonight."

"Just three?" She smiles and tilts her face to the sun. "I thought I inspired you more than that."

But I'm forty years old. Three times practically kills me, mainly in my knees. "I'll shoot for four, but I'm not promising anything."

"Just four? I want a novella."

Gulp. I better shut the laptop down before *I* shut down.

"Go ahead, finish what you've started." She starts cranking in the mainsail, and the *Argo* begins to slow. "I'll just tidy up out here and start working on the preface below."

Oh, I love it when she talks literary to me!

Now where was I? Oh, yeah. My original loves.

And I love this woman, whose mother is my surrogate mother, who is the mother of my precious daughter, who is my wife and the love of my life in this utopian land of originals from sea to shining sea. And I love the God who allowed me to find her again, who brought me back, who kept me to the promises I made to my original love.

Author's Note and Acknowledgments

This is a work of fiction, at times autobiographical, at times allegory, at times mythology, at times American history, at all times pure invention. In my attempt to modernize the *Odyssey*, I also drew inspiration from the *Iliad*, the *Aeneid*, *Metamorphoses*, Dante's *Inferno*, Norse mythology, and *Beowulf*. If I have mangled these classics beyond recognition, the mistakes are all mine.

While Peter, my "man of sorrows," is like me in most respects, the other characters are composites of the hundreds of people whom I have known through twenty-odd moves and forty years of life. Peter's father in no way resembles my own father—except for the geraniums, his short hair, and his passion for boats. The Captain, then, is an archetype, a melding of every racist whom I have had the displeasure to know. While there is much to despise about the Captain, there is much to admire, hence Peter's dilemma.

And while I may be too acidic at times in my attitude toward Long Island, let me say this: I wouldn't be who I am or what I'm about without my years on that stretch of the melting pot in Huntington, at 71 Preston Street, just up the winding trail in the woods from Huntington Bay.

First and foremost, I'd like to thank my wife, Amy, for inspiring me daily, editing all my mistakes before my editor sees them, and lending her ideas to Ebony's "half" of Peter's novel. And I'd like to thank my two boys, Joshua and Jontae. I hope I can give you two a "boy's life" full of adventures.

Thanks also to the following authors for inspiring me: Latorial Faison for her poem "Original Love," the spark that reignited this book when my creative fires were almost extinguished by the events of September 11; Brian Egeston for telling me to "Just write, man"; and Pat G'Orge-Walker for lifting up my spirits when they were down.

I'd like especially to thank Carolyn Hasler and the other good folks at the Huntington Public Library for their wonderful assistance and patience with my many questions covering the last twenty-five years.

Mad shout-outs go to Marquia Rivera, Linda Moyer, Douglas Poindextér, and Sheree Davis for letting me get to know the real Ballyhack, Virginia. Much respect is due the Sunday dinner crew—Nicole Page, Victor and Angie Roberts, Terra Cunningham, and Shelby Poindexter—for giving me so much to write about!

Special thanks go to Darrell Nicholson, associate editor of *Cruising World Magazine*, for his sailing expertise and permission to use his boat *Tosca* as the model for the *Argo*—mysterious creak and all; John Schultz, president of the Veteran's Association of the USS *Iowa*, and the Naval Historical Center for their help with the Captain's "other" boat, "the Mighty I," and the true story of Ensign Marcus Minor of St. Joseph, Missouri; the editors and writers at LIHistory.com and LIGenealogy.com for fascinating, top-notch treasure troves of information; and artist Laszlo Tar for bringing back ancient memories of Huntington Bay and Hecksher Park with his haunting and mesmerizing watercolors.

And finally, my undying gratitude to Stevie Wonder for *Songs in the Key of Life*—I couldn't have made it through puberty without that album.